RECKLESS PASSION

*A*my caught Sebastien's face between her hands and kissed him. He made a harsh sound but took everything she offered, then wound his arms around her and returned fierce, raw energy so erotic that she shuddered and moaned against his mouth. He pulled back. "I said that I wasn't in the mood to be kind to you. There is too much going on inside me tonight. It makes me reckless. This can only hurt you. Now stop—"

"You don't have to worry about hurting me, or make promises about the future, or say a lot of hokey sweet things. You just have to be yourself."

"Most women would be dismayed at that possibility."

"I never look at things the way other people do. I guess you're in luck."

He studied her with a troubled, heartbreaking expression, then shut his eyes for a moment, as if making a decision. "Very much in luck."

He kissed her again, this time sweetly and with obvious restraint. She sagged against him. Bending her backwards, he laid her on the cool, matted grass and undressed her. . . .

Bantam Books by Deborah Smith

THE BELOVED WOMAN
FOLLOW THE SUN
MIRACLE

MIRACLE

DEBORAH SMITH

FANFARE ™

BANTAM BOOKS
NEW YORK · TORONTO · LONDON · SYDNEY · AUCKLAND

MIRACLE

A Bantam Fanfare Book / November 1991

ISBN 0-553-29107-6

Published simultaneously in the United States and Canada

Bantam Books are published by Bantam Books, a division of Bantam Doubleday Dell Publishing Group, Inc. Its trademark, consisting of the words "Bantam Books" and the portrayal of a rooster, is Registered in U.S. Patent and Trademark Office and in other countries. Marca Registrada. Bantam Books, 666 Fifth Avenue, New York, New York 10103.

PRINTED IN THE UNITED STATES OF AMERICA

RAD   0 9 8 7 6 5 4 3 2 1

ACKNOWLEDGMENTS

Many thanks to the following for their help and support: Susan Hall Sheehan, segment producer, NBC; Claude Wegscheider of Alliance Francaise d'Atlanta, Inc.; Charles Andrews, director of Graduate Education, Emory University; Ellen Taber, R.N., B.S.N., surgical nurse; Barbara Croft, M.D.; my helpful and generous California family, Myra and Don Araiza; Laura Taylor, Pat Potter, and Carol Buckland; Andrea Cirillo and Gretchen van Nuys of the Jane Rotrosen Agency; Carolyn Nichols and Nita Taublib of Bantam Books; and Hank Smith, husband extraordinaire. This book is lovingly dedicated to my parents, Jack and Dora Brown.

PROLOGUE

"*Y*'all terrify the hell out of me. Really, truly terrify me." Amy Miracle said, her Georgia drawl putting a slow spin on each word. "Y'all look so . . . so *normal.*"

Most of the members of the well-dressed suburban audience laughed, as they were meant to. Inside the sleek taupe silk of her trousers, bought second hand at a funky Hollywood clothes shop, Amy's knees quivered a little less. The bright stage light felt too hot on her face; the back of her neck was damp under her hair. She wore a loose red jacket over a white blouse because she didn't want anyone to see the blouse clinging to her underarms, where trickles of nervous perspiration were already making their way down her sides.

She wasn't kidding about the fear. She felt as if she were a bat flying in a dark cave emitting nervous vibrations through the packed club to gather feedback so she wouldn't slam into a wall. But she had learned to make the fear work for her.

"It's smart to be afraid of everything," she said. "Only stupid people think it's safe to relax." Beyond the lip of the small stage, somewhere among tables loaded with wine coolers and nachos, a drunk cackled. Amy never missed a beat. "There's one, now."

She waited with practiced timing for the scattering of laughter and applause to fade. God, did she know how to wait. It had taken her years to get here. Pretending to study the small heart tattooed on her wrist, she frowned in thought. "I had a unique childhood, y'all understand. Tough. My Daddy's idea of a home entertainment center was a gun rack and a refrigerator full of beer. But he was mellow, all right? If I forgot to clean up my room he'd say, 'That's okay. I'm just gonna wing ya this time.' "

Settling into the rhythm of her routine, she gave them a practiced look of bewilderment. "Being female makes you afraid, too. Stuff like going to the gynecologist. I always turn into Olive Oyl when I get there." She did her Olive Oyl impression, clasping her throat in befuddled shock and wailing, "Oh, goodness, oh, my, oh, my! If Popeye had shivered his timber, I wouldn't be in this predicament!"

Because her voice was so strange anyway, it fit the impression perfectly. Lots of people in the audience laughed now. Amy leaned toward the microphone as if she and the audience were companions in a conspiracy. A conspiracy against all the ugly, stupid, absurd things in the world. "Women have good reason to be suspicious and scared. Look how everybody lies to us. Like in douche commercials. A sweet little teenage girl asks her mother, 'Mom, are there days when you just don't feel as . . . as *fresh* as you'd like?' I want the truth! I want to hear that girl ask, 'Mom, do you ever feel like . . . like a tuna that's been out of water too long?' "

Women in the audience hooted with glee. Men laughed behind their hands, nodding. The douche bit always struck a chord. It tipped the audience over the line from wary expectation to an affectionate level of camaraderie. The battle was half won. The worst was over. Amy listened to the laughter and sighed with relief. Every night she improved. This was torture, but she loved it. It was worth every painful step. "Well," she added with a thoughtful pause, "I always say that if you can't laugh at yourself, laugh at other people."

She gave them five more minutes, building the momentum, not letting them have a moment's rest, controlling them, *killing* them, and enjoying the sense of power she only found on stage. When the red light began blinking on the back wall of the club, signaling her that her time was up, she gave them one more minute and knew it was the best set she'd ever done.

She left the tiny stage on a crest of enthusiastic applause and calls for more. Floating, she stepped into a narrow hall hung with photos of comics, some famous, many she knew personally, a few she called friends.

The next performer, an acne-scarred young man with a smirking grin, was waiting in the hall. "Not bad. You warmed them up for me, Miracle." He wiggled a lecherous hand puppet at her chest.

"You and Wally the Wonder Hand need all the help you can get. Don't muss the blouse—it's a Kmart original."

"God, it must be nice to have lots of money."

"Right. In my next life I hope bank machines don't self-destruct when I ask for ten bucks."

"Like I really believe that. You write for Elliot Thornton."

Amy grimaced but said nothing. Several other comedians lounged in the hall, waiting their turns to make twenty-five bucks for entertaining the Tuesday-night crowd. They stared at her with a mixture of contempt and awe because they thought she had Elliot's backing, but mostly because she'd been killing the room lately.

She gave them a thumbs-up and moved away. They didn't know how much she'd gone through to reach this place and moment—this ordinary little suburban comedy club thirty miles outside L.A. They didn't know she was jeopardizing a fledgling sense of self-esteem by going up on stage.

She went to the bar and ordered a glass of Château de Savin Fumé Blanc. The manager had begun to stock it after sampling a bottle she'd given him. The de Savin label was expensive but worth it, he'd decided. He had jokingly asked if she were a wine expert. Yes, actually. But the de Savin was a sentimental choice, as well. She pressed the cool lip of the glass against her forehead, remembering. Even after all these years it was always so easy.

Sebastien de Savin was the only person who had ever believed that she was special. She wondered where ten years had taken him and wished that he knew—and cared—how far they had taken her.

ONE

ONE

GEORGIA, 1980

She huddled under the sheet for just one more minute, clinging to the peacefulness of the July dawn and wishing that Pop hadn't ordered her out of bed at two A.M. to scrub the refrigerator. It was hard enough to deal with his tantrums in the daytime. If only she could get things right. If only she didn't screw up so much. If only she could please him.

As she opened her eyes her stomach knotted. The exhaustion and sense of dread were old, familiar companions, honed sharply over the years. Now they were simply a part of her, like the need to daydream and the fear of being ridiculed.

The radio buzzed to life on her cheap pine nightstand. Her skin damp and sticky in the morning heat, she tossed the sheet back and flapped her T-shirt up and down over her stomach. "Wake up, north Georgia," the disc jockey purred. "It's seventy-eight degrees here in Athens and eighty down in Atlanta. Headed for ninety-five. Too late to play hooky. Time to go to work. You could have gone to Lake Lanier today. You could have called in sick and packed the ol' cooler and headed for the water. But *nooooo*."

Amy smiled groggily. She liked it when the D.J. did his John Belushi imitation. She could do a pretty good Belushi herself—and recite most of the classic *Saturday Night Live* routines. Pop said the show was junk, but she had watched it since the very first broadcast, five years before. Pop thought all her TV trivia was junk. There was no tradition to it, he said.

What he really meant, she thought, was that there was no place anymore for *him*, no network variety shows where old circus clowns could get five minutes to do acts that harked all the way back to vaudeville. For Pop's sake she wished Ed Sullivan were still around. She wished for anything that would keep Pop from going on tirades in the middle of the night.

The D.J. babbled about current events as she got out of bed and went to the open window. Dew and misty light covered the neatly mowed backyard. She heard a rooster crowing and the faint sound of tractor trailers roaring along the interstate, a few miles away. A trace of sunlight glinted on the long, narrow chicken coop atop the shallow hill beyond the backyard. Maisie, her stepmother, stout and gray and stoic, was trudging up the path to feed her broilers and fryers.

". . . so who *did* shoot J.R.?" the D.J. finished, laughing. "Ronald Reagan says the Democrats did it. If Ronnie gets elected this November he promises to turn South Fork into a home for old movie stars. Bonzo needs a room."

Amy made a mental note of the joke. *It would have worked better if he'd rearranged the sentences*, she thought, without knowing quite why that would be so. It was instinct, the same instinct that led her to file away every funny story she heard. She paid attention to stuff that nobody else noticed. She was a flake, Pop said.

Amy glanced at her clock and dressed hurriedly. The good thing about being skinny and of medium height was that her clothes fit exactly the way they were supposed to fit. She didn't have to check in a mirror to know that she looked neat and ordinary in baggy denim shorts and a pristine white sports shirt, the breast pocket appliqued with flowers by Maisie.

She slipped her feet into white ankle socks and sparkling clean sneakers. She let Pop corner the market on eccentricity; what she wanted more than anything else was to be normal. Extremely normal. She covered the tattoo on her left wrist with a white sweat band.

Wearing black sunglasses—the same cool brand the Blues Brothers used—she folded a pair of work gloves into her back pocket, tucked her short auburn hair under a big straw sunhat, grabbed her cloth purse, and went to the bedroom door. For a moment she just stood there, gazing distractedly at the high-school football pennants fading on the fake wood. As usual, her heart was racing. Then she took a deep breath and left her room.

After sniffing the air, she sighed with relief. She could smell the sweet, pungent odor of reefer. All was well then, or at least mellow with her father. When she reached the kitchen she found him at the table, his tall body hunched over a bowl of cereal. He had cleaned up and shaved, and he looked presentable in old Bermuda shorts and a T-shirt. His graying red hair was still damp from a shower. He'd slicked it into a long pony tail.

"Your back hurtin'?" she asked, easing toward the refrigerator as casually as she could. He grunted an affirmative. Amy opened the white refrigerator door. Inside, the metal and plastic gleamed with the cleaning she'd given them in the middle of the night. Her fingers were sore from clenching the sponge so tight. The refrigerator hadn't looked much different *before* the scrubbing. It hadn't needed cleaning. That's why she'd let the chore go for a couple of days. Welcome to another episode in Pop's crazy world.

The Midnight Marauder, she had named him years ago. His pet peeves came out after dark, like cockroaches. His first raid had occurred not long after he retired from the circus. "Get your scrawny little butt out of bed," Amy recalled him ordering. He had flicked on the overhead light, making her squint as she watched him in bewilderment and then fear as she saw the revolver dangling in his hand.

"What's the matter, Poppy?"

He waved the gun in drunken circles. "Get up! You worthless little shit, get up!"

So on a frigid February night Amy had tromped back and forth to the garbage pile in her teddy bear pajamas and overcoat, carrying paper bags filled with soot and ash. The mistake that provoked him hadn't even been her own. Maisie had forgotten to clean the fireplace earlier in the day; Pop had discovered the oversight a few hours after bedtime. And so Maisie, her face set in lines of apology, and Amy, frightened and shivering, had done the chore at three A.M. Amy had failed a math test the next day in Mrs. Whitehead's third-grade class, where she was behind the other students in skills, already.

Mrs. Whitehead had never asked if anything was wrong at home. Had she asked, Amy would have been too ashamed to tell the truth. Besides, she wasn't even sure what was wrong, but she suspected that no one else in the third grade had a father like hers. In a world of farmers, tractor salesmen, and factory workers, Zack Miracle was embarrassingly unique. She had failed a lot of tests since that night in February.

The smoke from his joint made her feel a little giddy. She tried not to breathe as she got her lunch box out of the fridge and shut the door. "See ya, Pop. Sorry I upset you last night. Get some rest."

He chewed cereal and eyed her sleepily, but without malice. He slept all day and painted oil portraits of circus life all night, which he sometimes sold at craft shows. He also fiddled with his collection of revolvers and rifles. And he drank.

She was eighteen years old and that was all she'd ever seen him do, aside from hiring out for whatever gigs his chronic back problem would allow. He did his clown shtick for children's birthday parties, business conventions, any other event for which he could get hired. Often he made her go along as his assistant. It was like being forced to pull thorns from a bear's paw. She never knew whether the bear would be grateful or bite her head off.

The joint dangled between his paint-stained fingertips and he blinked at her. "Next time I have to remind you to clean the refrigerator I'll empty the damned refrigerator on your damned bed. Got it?"

"Got it." She backed toward the door. "Have a good day, Daddie Dearest. No more wire coat hangers. I promise."

He dismissed her teasing with a sour look. "Got a date with Charley tonight, smart ass?"

"Yes, sir."

"Huh. Better marry him. Your days of livin' off of me are numbered."

Her stomach churned. He meant it. He really did. He'd always warned that when she turned eighteen he'd give her one year to get out on her own. She'd had her eighteenth birthday in April and graduated from high school in June. With any luck she'd find a job over in Athens before long, maybe as a waitress or sales clerk. The pickings weren't too good with the economy the way it was, and students from the university got most of the jobs, anyhow. But she couldn't think of any other options, aside from marrying Charley.

"Pop, you know what your problem is?" She gave him a cocky smile but felt her hands tremble on her purse and lunch box. Provoking his wrath was not a wise thing, and she wasn't aiming to do it now. "You got no faith in me, Pop."

"Earn your way. Then we'll talk about faith."

"Charley has faith . . ."

"Charley's a religious fanatic. He'd have faith in horse turds if Jesus blessed 'em." Her father grabbed his forehead and frowned. "Get out, quit talkin'. I can't take your squeaky voice this early in the day."

"Love you too, Pop." She slammed the door behind her and strode down the concrete steps. She jammed her straw hat into a carrying case on the back of her battered little motorcycle. Seconds later she was flying down the graveled drive between oak trees and laurel bushes. Once on the pale gray ribbon of two-lane she pushed her face into the wind and let it whip the tears out of her eyes.

Rolling green pastures and small farms flashed by her in the morning sun. Straight, slender pine trees flanked the road. Tacked here and there to the pines were hand-lettered Bible verses, for sale signs for chicken houses, and notices that read Jesus Saves. In these parts hope was built on Jesus and chickens. She and Pop didn't fit in very well.

They had settled here only because Maisie had inherited five acres and a chicken house.

She guided the bike up a side road to a grand brick entranceway flanking a new asphalt drive. A carpet of magnificent, emerald-green lawn made it look like the driveway to an elegant home down in Atlanta. On one side the brick wall held a beautiful scrolled sign. *Maison de Savin Vineyards. Welcome.*

Acres and acres of vineyards stretched under the rising sun, their trellises filled with lush foliage. Rose bushes decorated the ends of each row, and the grass between the rows had a froth of tiny yellow wildflowers. A dozen varieties of grapes grew here in the Georgia soil, just as they did in France, the winery manager said.

The de Savin people had bought land here a few years ago. Everyone had been curious about a French firm purchasing property in the middle of the Georgia hills, until a company representative had explained that the soil and climate were perfect for growing grapes. The local preachers had been a little perturbed by the idea of a winery, but after the place was developed everyone felt awed more than anything else.

On a crest at the center of the fields sat a magnificent château of pink and gray stone, with turrets, a gabled roof, and heavily ornamented casements. Behind it was a low concrete building, where the wine was made. The château was just for show. Right now Mr. Beaucaire, the winery manager, lived there. Someday the château might be turned into a restaurant and wine store. Amy viewed the fairy-tale scene with the reverence of a peasant.

After parking her bike at the back of the winery building, she put her hat on again, then went inside a narrow door to the office. The other grape pickers were there, two dozen or so, black and white, young and old, every kind of person from fresh-faced high-school and college students to grizzled locals, hands gnarled by years of farming. Amy thought it exciting to be part of the vineyard's first harvest; she liked telling people that she was working at a French château. Plus harvest work paid well, though the season was short. It had started a week ago and would end early in September.

Around her people were slipping on gloves and hats for eight hours of hot work. Like most of the younger workers, Amy took a bottle of suntan lotion from her purse and smeared some on her arms and legs, where her fair skin showed freckles along with a deepening tan. The shift started at six-thirty and ended at two-thirty, when the sun was nearly unbearable.

Feeling shy in the crowd, Amy hurried to put her lunch away. In the refrigerator, containers of boiled ham and turnip greens sat next to cups of yogurt. Her lunch box contained candy bars, apples, and crackers, foods that didn't require her to spend much time in the kitchen, where Pop tended to lurk at night, drinking and complaining. It also contained a much-read copy of *The Hobbit*. She liked adventure and fantasy.

Amy clipped a plastic water bottle to her belt. As she deposited her purse in a locker along one wall she smiled at everyone who caught her eye, but avoided talking. She'd spent her whole life fading into the background, the safest place to be.

"*Allons-y*! Let's go!" Mr. Beaucaire gave them all a bored, patronizing look and waved an arm toward the door. Middle-aged with snowy white hair, he had a commanding presence even in brown work pants and a safari shirt. He wasted no time on chitchat and hardly ever spoke directly to one of the temporary workers. Around him Amy was as silent and obedient as a garden tool that could be replaced without a second glance.

She traipsed along with the crowd, enjoying the good, clean morning as best she could, considering how the day had started. She was used to feeling tired and a little depressed; most of her life she'd been isolated from other people by invisible barriers of shame. A few years ago Pop had been busted for driving under the influence. The joint in the Buick's ashtray hadn't helped his case, and he'd served a few months in the county jail.

The gossip at school had made her feel even more alone. Sometimes she had nightmares about someone finding his plants inside the house. Having friends was impossible, because friends asked too many questions and wondered why she never invited them to visit. Only Charley Culpepper was content to accept her excuses, and sometimes she wondered if that was what made Charley so attractive.

Amy entered the vineyards with the other workers. One of the manager's assistants drove a tractor to the end of the rows. On a long, flat trailer behind it sat several wooden crates taller than Amy's head. From the end of the trailer another assistant handed out big white buckets and sharp shears to each grape picker.

Amy took hers and walked down the rows, absently searching for a good spot to start, as if any one spot were different from the next. Her mind was devoted to recreating her daydreams, not deciding which grapevine to attack. She decided to begin where she'd left off yesterday.

She set her bucket down and went to work, vaguely listening to other people chatting to each other while her hands moved carefully among the leafy vines sagging with clusters of purple-green grapes. And she began to fanta-size.

The beautiful red-headed slave is working in the vineyards of a Roman nobleman. He comes along; he notices her and falls in love at first sight. She is obviously brave as well as beautiful. He tries to talk to her. She won't answer. He is fascinated. Finally he carries her away and sets her free. Then they make love. Amy grinned to herself. She could easily spend the whole day thinking up dialogue for this scenario.

A snip here, a snip there. Two hours had passed. The slave was excellent at her work. She trimmed stray leaves and twigs from each handful of rich, bursting grapes and dropped the ripe bundle into her bucket with graceful movements of her hands.

When the bucket was full she carried it without a sign it was painfully heavy to the trailer and dumped the contents into one of the wooden crates. Then she went back to the row and began all over again, kneeling by the vines, her bearing regal. Anyone with the sense to notice would see that she was extraordinary and didn't deserve to be a slave.

Her concentration was so complete that several minutes passed before she realized some workers had moved close to her spot and were whispering loudly among themselves.

"Where'd Beaucaire find *that* guy?"

"He looks like he just came off a three-day drunk."

"Bet he's one of them Cuban fellers from over at Gainesville. Next thing you know, Mr. Beaucaire'll bring in a whole bunch of those sorry shits who'll work for a dollar a hour, and we'll be out of a job."

"Nah. He's not Cuban. They're all swarthy and short. He's kinda swarthy, but I bet he's six-four if he's an inch."

"Look at him! He can barely stand up! Ten to one he falls flat on his grapes any second! And then Beaucaire'll jerk a knot in his tail."

Fascinated by the descriptions, Amy looked up. The others were watching someone far down the row of trellises. She craned her head to see the man.

In the years that followed she would always remember that moment. She would relive it as if watching a movie inside her mind, the colors and sounds extraordinarily vivid, the dramatic impact staggering. He stood perhaps a hundred feet from them, outlined by a nearly tangible solitude, very still, studying a cluster of grapes crushed in one big fist. He was tall, with an elegant kind of brawniness to his body. Amy stared. His mystery excited her imagination.

Grape juice ran down his arm. There was weary anger in the set of his shoulders, and remnants of violence in the way he clenched the pulpy mass of burst fruit. Juice dripped onto his bare, dirty feet. His white T-shirt was stained with sweat down the center and under the arms; his baggy, wrinkled pants were an ugly green color soiled with red clay at the knees. They hung low on his hips as if about to fall off. Only a loosely knotted tie-string kept them from slipping.

He wore no hat, and his thick, charcoal-black hair was disheveled. Dark beard stubble shadowed his cheeks. His eyes were covered by unremarkable black sunglasses, but his face, making a strong, blatantly masculine profile, was anything but unremarkable.

He slung the grapes to the ground, staggering a little as he did. Then, wielding a pair of razor-sharp clippers so swiftly that Amy gasped with fear, he snipped a smaller cluster of grapes and shoved it into his mouth. He stripped it with one ferocious tug of his teeth then slung the empty stem over his shoulder.

"A cocky drunk, ain't he?" someone muttered.

Amy gaped at him. The others chuckled. At any second Beaucaire would come thundering down the aisle of trellises and raise hell. It would be spectacular entertainment.

What would the newcomer do next? For a man who was dirty and apparently soused, he had an aura of graceful arrogance. But then he went to a trellis post and leaned there heavily, resting his head on one arm. He no longer looked imposing. Fatigue seemed to drag at every muscle of his body. Amy clenched her hands, feeling a misfit's sympathy for another misfit but wanting to scold him for making a fool of himself.

She didn't dare. He looked dangerous—his hands were big-knuckled and dirty; ropy muscles flexed in his forearms. He wore his solitude like a shield. He swayed and stared fixedly at the ground, as if searching for a place to fall.

"Here he goes," a man near Amy said gleefully. "Right on his face."

But after a moment he dropped his clippers into a bucket and shoved himself away from the post. Staggering, he headed for a wooden crate that sat at the far end of a row. When he arrived there he disappeared around the corner.

Amy waited breathlessly for him to reappear. He didn't.

"Go get Mr. Beaucaire," someone said. "That guy's behind that crate either taking a nap, puking his guts out, or pissing on a rose bush."

She swung toward the others. "No! I'll go see what he's doing. Don't say anything to Mr. Beaucaire. I mean it!"

Everyone stared at her. It was the first time they'd heard her speak in full sentences. She was shocked by the outburst, herself. "I, uhmmm, I b-bet he's just sick."

"Well, Lord have mercy. We finally heard Olive Oyl make more than a squeak."

Everyone chortled. Amy was mortified. Her voice humiliated her when she forgot to restrain it. People laughed at her behind her back; all through school her classmates had made fun of her. She clamped her lips together and ground her teeth as if she could crush whatever it was that made her sound the way she did. She dreaded getting a job where she had to talk. She stayed awake at night worrying about it.

But now she shoved embarrassment aside and hurried toward the crate, her heart in her throat. Behind her a woman called, "You leave that feller alone! We're gonna go get Mr. Beaucaire!"

Amy kept walking. Maybe she sympathized with all the ne'er-do-wells of the world, or maybe she was an expert on mean drunks. But she felt that there was some good reason for this man's problem.

Uncertainty pooled in her stomach. Slowing down, she crept up to the crate and stopped to listen. She heard only the rustle of grape leaves as the hot wind stroked the vineyard. Tiptoeing in the brittle grass, she sidled up to the crate's back corner and peeked around.

He lay on his back. He had removed the T-shirt and stuffed it under his head as a pillow. His hairy chest held her attention as it rose and fell in a slow rhythm. His hands lay beside his head, palms up, dirty and stained with grape juice but graceful-looking nonetheless.

She stepped forward in silent awe. He slept, but there was nothing vulnerable or relaxed about his face. His mouth remained shut and firm. Above the black sunglasses a frown pulled at his brows. Up close he looked younger than she'd expected, perhaps no more than thirty.

She shifted from one foot to the other, gazing at his sleeping form in consternation. Maybe it would be best just to leave him to his fate. She bent over and sniffed. The scent of his sweat mingled with the sweet aroma of grapes, red clay, and a faint antiseptic smell that puzzled her. She knew the smell of booze and pot; neither was present.

Reassured, she knelt beside him. She removed her sunglasses and tucked them in her shirt pocket. Her hand trembling, she reached out and touched his shoulder. "Hey. Hey, wake up."

A jolt of awareness ran through him. He lifted his head and froze. She jerked her hand back. His eyes were hidden behind the glasses, but she felt as if he were scrutinizing her angrily. She fumbled with the water bottle on her belt. There was nothing else to do except blunder onward and hope he didn't yell at her.

"You gotta get up," she urged, holding the bottle toward him. "You'll get fired if you stay here. Somebody went to tell Mr. Beaucaire. Come on, have a drink of water. You'll be okay. Get up."

When he neither moved nor replied, her nervousness gave way to exasperation. "Don't be a j-jerk! You look like you need this job! Now take a drink of water! Uhmmm, *Habla usted ingles? Si?* No? Comeon, that's all the Spanish I know! Say something!"

"I would rather listen to you say something. You say quite enough for both of us, and I like your voice."

She stared at him, mesmerized. His English was excellent, but accented. The accent was not Spanish, though she couldn't identify it. His voice sank into her senses—rich, deep, beautiful. Fatigue made it hoarse, but the effect was unforgettable.

"Here," she squeaked, thrusting the water bottle close to his mouth. "This'll make you feel better."

He let his head rest on the wadded shirt again. Exhaustion creased the sides of his mouth. "Thank you, but no." He raised a hand and pushed the bottle away. "I need only to rest."

She didn't know why, but she was desperate to keep him out of trouble. He must be too tired and sick to think straight. "You're gonna get fired!"

"No, I assure you—"

"Take a sip." Amy stuck the long plastic tube between his lips and squeezed the bottle hard. He tried to swallow the jet of water and nearly strangled. Shoving the bottle away, he sat up and began coughing.

A stream of melodic non-English purled from his throat,

and she didn't have to understand it to know that he was disgusted. She clutched the water bottle to her chest.

As he finished he whipped his glasses off and turned a stern gaze on her. Dread filled her chest, but she was too stunned to do anything except stare back. No one would call him pretty; in fact, his nose was blunt and crooked, his cheekbones jagged, and his mouth almost too masculine. It was a tough Bogart mouth, and the effect was heightened by a thin white scar that started an inch below his bottom lip and disappeared under his chin.

But all that made him handsome in a way she'd never encountered before. And his eyes, large and darkly lashed in the tough face, seemed to have been inherited from a different, more elegant heritage.

"Are you . . . you're not one of the regular workers," she said in confusion.

"No."

"Are you sick or something?"

"Or something." His expression was pensive for a moment. "I am only tired . . . just tired. . . . It will pass."

"Oh. Okay. Sorry to pester you." She started to rise. He clasped her arm.

"Don't leave. I didn't mean to chase you away. Here. Give me the water. Perhaps you're right. It helps."

While she watched in amazement he drank slowly from the bottle. She spent an awkward moment gazing at the silky movement of muscles in his neck and chest. He lowered the bottle and studied her some more. The skin around his lips was tight and pale. He blinked in groggy thought, then handed the bottle back. "You make me feel remarkably better. *Merci.*" His mouth curved in a private, off-center smile that erased all sternness from his face.

Amy caught her breath. Her shyness returned like a smothering blanket. *Merci.* He was *French.* Maurice Chevalier. The Eiffel Tower. Paris. Tongue kissing. "Don't pass out, okay? Bye." She leapt to her feet.

"A moment, fair rescuer. Do you always conduct yourself this way?"

"W-what way?"

"You leave without accepting the gratitude of your—"

"*Mon dieu!*" Mr. Beaucaire strode around the corner and stopped with his hands on his hips. He glared at Amy and she began to shrivel. "I didn't hire you to flirt, I hired you to pick grapes."

"I'm s-sorry. I was only—"

"You're worthless! You take advantage of good wages and waste my time." He scowled from her to the young man, then back to her. "My vineyard is not a place for you to make a social life. I won't have you sneaking off to play. Do you want to lose your job?"

She gasped. "He wasn't feeling good, but he's okay now. And I just came over to give him some water!"

"I was young not so many decades ago. I know how you girls think up excuses—"

"Pio, *non.*" The man on the ground spoke with a low, authoritative tone. "Enough."

Amy felt desperate. "Please don't fire us."

"Fire *us?*" Mr. Beaucaire asked. "Who do you think is at fault here?" He pointed to her fellow troublemaker. "Him?"

"No!" She nodded toward the man who was now impatiently rising to his feet. "Look at him. He's . . . he's pitiful. And he's *French*, like you. Give him a break. And I was only trying to help."

"Trying to cause trouble, you mean. Trying to ingratiate yourself!"

"Pio, *arrêt.*" The younger man's voice boomed with command. He rose to his full height, towering over both her and Mr. Beaucaire, who looked up at him with surprise.

They held a long, terse conversation in French. Mr. Beaucaire's tone became sheepish. His face reddened. He cut his eyes at her in a shrewd, awkward manner. Amy began to realize the shocking truth, and her legs turned to rubber.

"My apologies, mademoiselle," Mr. Beaucaire said finally. His voice was cold and clipped. "I did not fully understand the situation. Doctor de Savin has explained. You are, of course, in no trouble at all."

Doctor de Savin? She lost all of her adrenaline-provoked bravado and stared at the ground. "Thanks." Then she hurried away without looking back.

She went to her spot by the vines and worked doggedly, her face hot with embarrassment. Dr. de Savin. Of the de Savin winery. He was so young! But he owned this place. She had pestered him, squirted water down his windpipe, and then called him pitiful. She refused to look up or acknowledge the questions of the other workers. The remnants of her pride were all that kept her from leaving and never coming back.

Mr. Beaucaire marched past her. She glanced at him from the corner of her eyes. There was dignity and anger in the ramrod straightness of his back. She had gotten him in trouble, she realized with alarm. Then it began to sink in that Dr. de Savin had defended her—and no one had ever done so before.

A few minutes later Dr. de Savin came around to her side of the trellis. Without a word to her he reached down and took her bucket of grapes, then strode up the row in the direction of the trailer with its dumping crates.

Amy watched him open-mouthed. When he came back he set her empty bucket down and walked on, nodding to her as he passed. Dazed, Amy stared after him. He walked to the edge of the vineyard, retrieved his shirt from a trellis post, then turned and caught her watching him. With an utterly sincere expression on his face, he bowed to her.

He was leaving. Poignant adoration rose in her chest. She wondered if she'd see him again and fought the urge to cry. Something wonderful had happened to her, finally. She lifted one hand in a silent salute to the nobleman who had just made an unforgettable impression on the slave in his vineyard.

TWO

*W*hen Sebastien Duvauchelle Yves de Savin bowed to the girl, he was mocking his own gallantry. But she responded in complete sincerity, raising one hand in a slow, dramatic salute, her palm toward him. He was surprised when goosebumps rose on his flesh. Her gesture was not an affectation; it was as if she were pledging her loyalty to him forever.

The face that peeked out from a floppy straw hat and black sunglasses had a neat little chin and round cheeks. They framed a wide, solemn mouth that looked capable of reaching from one of her small ears to the other, if she ever smiled. At the moment she showed no hint of doing so.

Her legs, sticking out comically from big denim shorts, were well formed but a little too thin. It was easy to see, however, that a few good years and a few good meals would turn those legs into a marvelous asset. The same could be said for the long, slender body above them.

She was obviously no child, but no grown woman, either. He didn't encourage her attention, but when he turned to leave he couldn't stop thinking about her. He hesitated, picked up his clippers again, and worked for a minute longer. His head was fogged by lack of sleep; a mild giddiness obscured his reserve. He entertained himself by recalling how she had come to his rescue and given him orders in her comical, squeaking voice.

When he nearly cut his fingers with the sharp shears he

knew it was time to stop such nonsense. Like most surgeons, he protected his hands at all costs, and was not
above a certain vanity about them. He had a laborer's
hands, big and blunt like those of his mother's people,
hands meant to work a fish net or guide a plow, not perform
delicate maneuvers inside a human heart. Only through
sheer determination had he schooled his hands to move
gracefully, to be as fluid as a dancer's.

He left the vineyard with a distinct feeling of regret,
sensing the girl's gaze tracking him as he departed. He
hadn't expected to find himself receiving gentle bullying
from a primly dressed young woman with an amusing
voice. Nor had he expected Pio Beaucaire to chastise her
so bitterly.

Sebastien knew that his father had instructed Pio to keep
the local females as far from him as possible. And, while Pio
realized he had no control over Sebastien's life, still he tried
faithfully to follow orders. Sebastien shook his head. How
could his father even hope that eleven years of medical
training would fly out the window and his wayward, arrogant
son would come home to fulfill his family obligations?

Had he followed his father's wishes, Sebastien wouldn't
have been in the vineyard to intercede on behalf of a timid
young woman who touched him with her kindness on a
day when he found the world to be particularly ugly. He
would not have been working in an American vineyard that
was no more than an insignificant experiment among his
family's vast business ventures. Perhaps even more important, the vineyard was his father's excuse to keep Pio, a
lifelong de Savin employee, in America to inform on Sebastien. Pio's job was about to end; Sebastien was two weeks
away from completing a fellowship in cardiac surgery at
Gregory University in Atlanta.

His family heritage was, after all, one of nobility and
prestige as old as France itself; of service to kings and
emperors; of fortunes remade in the years following the
revolution; of social pedigrees and political power and
staunch elitism. If he had done what he had been raised to
do, he would, at twenty-nine years of age, have been
working in Paris for Philippe de Savin, his father, and

preparing to take control of a conglomerate that owned or held interests in shipping, vineyards, textiles, and a dozen other businesses.

His younger sister, Annette, with her love for corporate intrigue and her skill with people, was the natural successor to their father's corporate throne. Had she not had the misfortune to be born female, their father might have welcomed her into the business instead of trivializing her commitment to it. She was six years younger than Sebastien, newly graduated from a prestigious *grande ecole*, and anxious to earn their father's respect. She had never understood why Sebastien cared so little for it.

Over the years the family situation had been made even more tense by the fact that Sebastien's younger brother, Jacques, was a lovable but completely irresponsible young man who intended to do little that involved work. Jacques, at twenty, was failing as an art student at the Sorbonne and excelling as a playboy in the trendy Left Bank circles occupied by the offspring of the rich.

Sebastien had never—not even as a teenager—been so carefree as his brother was now. He took his baccalaureate to enter the *grande ecole* at the amazing age of fifteen, knowing he wanted to be a physician, to mend people, to take revenge on death. And, since his father was to blame for what had happened, Sebastien took revenge on him, as well.

He was a very serious and sophisticated man at twenty-nine, and though several years younger than other physicians at the same level of training, he was already gaining a reputation for being mature, brilliant, and demanding. All of which earned him equal shares of respect and dislike among his American colleagues. He was amused by the fact that some of them called him Young Doctor Frankenstein behind his back and that others, citing the scar on his chin, his love for double-breasted suits, and his town house decorated in art deco style, said that he was a gangster at heart.

He did not need anyone's friendship as long as he had their respect, and because virtually all of his waking hours were devoted to his work at the hospital, he did not have time for more than a few social acquaintances. Occasionally he pursued more intimate invitations from the hospital's nurses and female physicians, which he consummated with charm and great skill but with no hint of permanent attachment.

The women who accepted his single-minded dedication to his work settled for his generosity in bed and other ways, including the use of his several cars, his sailboat and cottage on St. Simon Island, and the free run of his town house in Buckhead, Atlanta's most exclusive residential area. Women who wanted more from him were quickly yet graciously ushered out of his life.

On the morning when he drove his white 1936 Cord to the de Savin winery north of Atlanta, he had been at the hospital for three days without sleep. A middle-aged grocer named Alphonso Jones had thrown a clot while undergoing angioplasty, and had to be rushed to the operating room for a bypass.

The bypass had gone perfectly, but two hours later, with the disregard for explanation that often accompanied such things, another clot broke free and went to Jones's brain, causing a massive stroke. Jones, a robust father of five and grandfather of seven, clung to life with the aid of machines.

In the long hours of the second night, Sebastien met Jones's wife, a stern little woman with a graying afro and a no-nonsense attitude. "None of these other goddamn whitecoats will tell me anything," she protested. "And I want to know the truth—if my husband makes it, is he goin' to be an invalid?"

Sebastien studied her for a moment, while he weighed the consequences of answering a question that should go to the patient's cardiologist. But if Mrs. Jones wanted the unadorned truth, she had asked the right man. "Perhaps. We'll have to wait a few days to see how he recovers. And it may take six weeks to determine his long-term problems."

She began to cry. "He'll have to take early retirement, sit in a chair in front of a TV all day, never be able to play baseball with the grandkids again? That sort of thing?"

"I can't predict anything at this point. He could do much better than you think. First things first. Right now, we have to wean him off the ventilator."

"The what?"

"The machine that's helping him breathe."

She gripped Sebastien's arm and looked up at him with a desperate expression. "I want him to die. I want you to tell the others to turn off all those damned machines."

"You know we can't do that."

"What's better—living like a cripple, or dyin' like a man?"

"I won't debate that with you. It's not the issue."

"You coward! 'Course it's the issue! But you're too much of a liar to admit it."

Sebastien looked at her grimly. How her husband lived was not his concern, only that he *did* live. "First things first," he repeated. "Until he can breathe unassisted, he will remain on the ventilator."

She was still crying, but she snorted in contempt. "He's not even a man to you. To you he's just something to fix, like an old truck. Even if it's only got a few miserable miles left, you want to run it into the ground."

She flung herself away and headed down the hall to a waiting room. Sebastien grimaced. He disliked dealing with patients' families. Their mindless sentiment complicated the logic of medicine, the rational, impersonal study of disease and injury. He had more important concerns than their grief. Grief was a useless emotion.

But he was not unaffected by the grocer's death. It tore at him like a personal insult. The man's lungs simply refused to work on their own. Without dramatics, without a fight, he slipped away until the ventilator had more life than he.

Sebastien left the hospital without bothering to change his surgical garb. He kicked off the thick-soled jogging shoes he wore when he worked, seeking freedom in every way that he could, and drove to a garage where he stored his vintage Cord. Then he headed north out of the city, along the interstate. He drove at a speed that would have infuriated lovers of classic cars and would have cost him at least a speeding ticket, more likely a suspended license, if a highway patrolman had spotted him.

He had little control over only one part of his emotions. He had one weakness that he had kept hidden throughout his medical training. The death of a patient enraged him; the helplessness he felt went beyond a rational reaction and gripped him like a phobia. He wanted to keep his patients alive for his own sake more than theirs. He battled that selfishness privately, knowing it was the one weakness that could ruin him as a surgeon and therefore as a person.

He had been in that black, bleak mood when the girl came to him. It astonished him that her fumbling attempt to help him had made his anger vanish. He didn't understand the phenomenon until he realized with disturbing clarity that she was the first person who had ever tried to rescue him from himself.

❦

A few days later Sebastien came back to the winery to sign the paperwork authorizing purchase of more acreage on the estate's southern border. He disliked dabbling in his father's businesses and tried to minimize his involvement. On this trip he drove his black Ferrari, and chided himself when he realized that he had chosen it hoping to impress his rescuer. The vineyard workers were not in the fields when he arrived; he checked the heavy gold Rolex on his wrist and saw that he'd picked lunchtime by mistake. He smiled ruefully at his disappointment. He had never considered himself a preening peacock where women were concerned.

He parked beside the vinting building next to the château, grimacing as he passed the fake turrets and stonework. It was a monument to the tourist trade that would come here someday, and its resemblance to a real château was laughable.

Inside the winery offices Beaucaire's secretary, a matron with an easy smile, looked up from her typing. "Hi. Mr. Beaucaire said to tell you he'd be a few minutes late. He's talkin' to the temps. Here are the papers."

As he signed, Sebastien asked, "Do you know any of the temporary people?"

"Sure. I've lived around here all my life."

"There is a very shy young woman among them who has an unusual voice. She is slender, fair-skinned, and she has a perpetually puzzled expression on her face, as if she were trying to understand some very confusing issue."

"Oh. You're talkin' about Amy Miracle."

"Miracle?"

"Weird, I know. Her stepmother's a member of my church. She says the family comes from circus and carnival people from way back, four or five generations. The name was Merkle to start with. Somewhere along the line somebody changed it to Miracle."

"What else do you know about her?"

"Hmmm, like I said, her folks are circus people. Used to be, anyway. They settled around here maybe ten years ago. Her daddy has a bad back, had to quit the circus. He was a clown. Odd bird. Real odd."

"What do you mean?"

"Oh, he's nice . . . he came over and made balloon animals for my granddaughter's fifth birthday party, but— but"—her voice dropped to a conspiratorial whisper— "*he's a hippie*."

"Hmmm?"

"He's got long hair. A man his age! And he smokes dope. Around here, he's just a weird character, if you know what I mean. His wife's got a chicken house. I think that's all that keeps the family off welfare."

"What do you know about the girl?"

Another shrug. "Shy as she can be. Just graduated from high school this spring. She dates a boy who's going to trade school this fall."

"Trade school?" Sebastien had an excellent grasp of English, but this term eluded him.

"He wants to work on trucks. You know. Big trucks. Be a diesel mechanic."

"Ah." Sebastien impatiently checked his watch. Why indulge his curiosity about the girl? He had to get back to Atlanta. He was working tonight at the hospital, and between now and then he had medical journals to read.

Pio arrived a minute later. Sebastien smiled at his stately manner. He was a very dignified spy who pretended to be insulted each time Sebastien questioned his reasons for following him to America.

Pio slapped him on the back. "*Bonjour. Ca va?*"

"*Comme ci comme ca.* I've taken care of the signings already."

"I could have mailed the papers to you."

Sebastien made a large, distinctly Latin shrug. "I felt like driving out again."

"Hmmm. Come and sample the Merlot your father sent to me."

They went into Pio's darkly paneled office with its stiff, leather-covered furnishings and old photographs of the château de Savin in the Loire valley. The office was spartan but debonair. Pio took a bottle from a wine rack that covered one wall. He opened it with decades of skill, poured small amounts into two tastevins, and presented one of the shallow cups to Sebastien. After a nonchalant examination of the color and clarity, Sebastien sipped the Merlot slowly. "Too sweet."

"No! The best vintage since seventy-two! I will never forget that one!"

Sebastien smiled at the older man's wistful tone. "You should go home, Pio. You miss it."

Sighing, Pio carried the bottle of Merlot to a sideboard and filled two crystal glasses. He and Sebastien raised the glasses to each other. Pio sank onto a couch, wiping sweat from his deeply tanned forehead with a white handkerchief, and gave Sebastien a speculative look. "Did you come back today to admire some more young, pretty grapes?"

"Never fear, Pio, I only choose what is ripe."

"You wouldn't cause an old man trouble with the local fathers, would you?"

Sebastien smiled dryly. "You aren't old. You haven't aged a year since I was a child."

"Oh, but *you* have changed, my boy."

"I have only grown up. I'm not the naive child you put to work each time he came home from school."

"Your papa was proud of that child, no matter how bitter that child became as he grew into manhood."

"He should be proud, now, too. If he's not, that's his business. What do you tell him about me lately?"

"What can I say? I tell him that you are still a doctor. Your son works all the time at the hospital. He lives in a fine home. He makes love to American women. He becomes an American. He forgets his family responsibilities.' "

Sebastien laughed without warmth. "I like your sense of drama. You do me justice."

Beaucaire sighed. "So, tell me why you took such an interest in the girl. Such an odd one . . . she hardly ever talks, but when she does, *c'est comique*, what a voice! You won't cause trouble with her, I hope."

"Perhaps I simply have a gallant streak, eh? You think I'm the kind of hawk who swoops down on birds who have just learned to fly? Like father, like son? No, I'm not like that bastard."

Scowling, Beaucaire slapped the arm of the couch. "Respect!"

Sebastien drained the glass and thumped it down on Beaucaire's desk. "*Honesty*, Pio. *Au revoir*."

He strode from the building, his hands clenched. The one thing he would never do is cause any woman the grief his father had caused his mother. When he saw Amy Miracle crossing a field toward the woods beyond, a lunch box swinging from her hand, he halted and watched her. There was one way to settle this niggling little infatuation of his. He'd simply speak with her, and break the spell.

He trailed her along a path into the woods and debated briefly whether she'd be frightened when she noticed him. Sebastien grimaced at the idea of how this looked—him tracking her into dense forest. He lifted his head and called her name. Her reaction was a startled jump. She swung around on the trail and stared at him, shock evident in her stance, her feet posed as if she might run. Again she wore her hat and sunglasses, baggy shorts, and a plain white blouse. Underneath the hat and glasses her mouth opened in a circle of dismay.

"May I talk to you a minute?" he asked, approaching her slowly.

"Is somethin' wrong? Did I do somethin'?"

"No, nothing."

"Oh." She wavered in place, not looking particularly reassured. Her gaze kept darting over his casual khaki trousers and loosely-woven white cotton pullover as if they were strange. "You look different today."

"Clean, I hope. And wearing shoes." Sebastien stopped several feet from her. "You were going to sit on the rock beside the creek?"

"Oh! You know about it, too!"

"Yes. It's such a pretty spot."

She nodded awkwardly. "But if it's your spot, I'll go back to the winery."

"No, of course not. Would you mind if I sat with you while you eat lunch?"

"Heck, no." She went along the path sideways, crossing one foot over the other while her gaze never left him. Her nervousness and lack of poise was so totally unsophisticated that he felt sorry for her.

"Here, let's walk together, before you hurt yourself," he told her, trying not to smile.

"Oh. Okay." She halted, moved quickly to the edge of the path, and clutched her lunch box in front of her like a shield.

Sebastien stepped to her side and gestured forward with one hand. She looked straight ahead as they walked the remaining short distance to a small creek. The spicy-sweet smell of wildflowers scented the cool, creek-bottom air, and the sunlight was dappled by the greenery of drooping trees. The creek made a pleasant whispering sound. It was an intoxicating place, and he began to regret his decision to follow her there.

She climbed atop a granite outcropping and sat down stiffly, her legs crossed. Sebastien lowered himself to the mottled gray stone a comfortable distance from her and curled one long leg under him. He propped his arm on his updrawn knee.

"Mr. Beaucaire doesn't like me, now," she said, staring rigidly at her lunch box. "I'm real sorry about botherin' you."

"Why do you say that? You were only trying to help."

"I feel sort of responsible for making Mr. Beaucaire mad."

"Hmmm. Do you always feel responsible for so much?"

Her mouth tightened. "Yeah."

"That's too bad. You're a very kind person, very thoughtful."

She fumbled with her sunglasses, removed them, and carefully put them in the pocket of her shirt. Her face was delightful; the eyes nearly hidden behind thick brown lashes, the nose upturned, the large, expressive mouth dimpled on both sides. There was character in it, and intelligence, and a great deal more maturity than he'd expected. "I felt sorry for you," she announced. "You looked sort of rough."

"I appreciate your concern. But perhaps it's not wise to feel sorry for me. Perhaps I'm a terrible person."

"Oh, right," she said without conviction.

"I want you to understand what was going on with me the other morning. I hadn't had any sleep for three days. I'd been at the hospital—there was an emergency. For a moment in the vineyard I felt sick—it was only from needing sleep and food."

"How come you don't sleep or eat?"

He laughed dryly. "I have a tendency to forget everything but my work."

She opened her lunch box and reached inside. "Here. I've got plenty." Between them on the smooth granite she spread candy bars, packages of crackers, and several apples.

"Plenty! Were you expecting guests?"

She blushed. "I just shoved whatever I could find into the box last night. I was in a hurry."

He took some crackers. "Thank you." His attention went to the book she laid aside. "Ah! Do you like Tolkien?"

"A lot. Yeah."

"What do you enjoy about his work?"

"It's easy to tell who's good and who's bad. I like that."

Sebastien nodded in approval. "I agree. The real world has too many shades of gray."

"Yes!"

They traded assessing looks, like two travelers sizing each other up for a long trip along the same road. Then her boldness faded and, again, she stared at her food. Sebastien had never encountered such a mixture of shyness and maturity before. While he opened the package of crackers she fidgeted with the wrapping on a piece of candy. "You're a doctor?"

"A heart surgeon. Yes."

"I always think of doctors as being older."

"I'm finishing my studies. And I'm younger than most. I entered the university in Paris when I was only fifteen."

"How old are you now?"

"Twenty-nine."

"Oh!" She chewed her candy bar rapidly and frowned into the forest.

"Is that too young, or too old?" he inquired coyly.

"A lot older than *me*, but not as old as I thought heart surgeons had to be."

"I assure you, mademoiselle, that I am one of the best."

"Where do you work?"

"At Gregory University Hospital."

"I know where that is. A girl I knew had to have a tumor operation, and her doctor sent her there. A bunch of us went down to Atlanta to visit her. It was the prettiest hospital I'd ever seen."

"I'm glad you were impressed."

She smiled at his droll tone. Her courage apparently growing, she inquired, "How come you work here and not in France?"

He put a hand over his heart dramatically. "I wanted to escape!"

She looked at him askance. "From what?"

"Convention! Tradition! Existential despair! The theories of Descartes!"

Her eyes gleamed with intrigue. He ate the crackers and thought to himself that her eyes were the same shade of green that one found in a fine piece of jade.

"You own this whole place?" She gestured uneasily toward the vineyards.

"My family's company owns it. I have stock in the company, so that makes me a part-owner."

"It's beautiful. I love workin' here."

"You are just graduated from high school, yes?"

"Yes."

"And will you go to a university in the fall?"

Her gaze fell. She busied herself polishing an apple on the leg of her denim shorts. "I'm not goin'."

"You have so much intelligence—in your eyes, in your voice. You can't let that go to waste."

"I'm not a very good student. Average."

"But what work will you do if you don't go to college?"

"Hmmm, I don't know."

"You live at home, with your parents?" She nodded. "So you will live there until you decide?"

She exhaled sharply. "Aw, I don't know what I'll do. I might get married or something."

"You're very young to do that."

For all her shyness, she glared at him. "I'm eighteen."

"Ah, such an elderly woman. I see."

"You're . . . you're really opinionated."

He shook his head. "No, I'm an aggressive, compulsive, arrogant, Type A personality. I've been told that many times. So there."

She burst into laughter, the most attractive laughter he'd ever heard, the sort that makes other people want to laugh too. He listened with bittersweet elation, trying to recall how long it had been since he'd enjoyed talking to anyone this much.

"I guess I can't argue if you already know that you're opinionated," she said finally, peering at him from under the brim of her hat.

"I'm glad to argue with you. That means you're comfortable with me."

She thought for a moment, looking shocked. "That's a new one."

Sebastien noticed wisps of auburn hair feathering her forehead and wished that she'd remove her hat so he could see the rest. Looking at her both aroused and calmed him. "Don't ever let anyone call you names," he told her abruptly, his tone now serious. "You're not worthless. Pio— Mr. Beaucaire—didn't mean to say that. He certainly had no right to abuse your honor."

Her face turned red and she seemed stunned. After

several stammering attempts to speak, she finally managed to say, "You make me feel important."

"Believe in yourself. You must always consider yourself the most special person in the world." He smiled thinly. "Of course, there are times when one can take such arrogance too far. But I doubt you'd do that."

"I don't know how to be arrogant at all." Her voice trembled. "But thank you. Thank you a lot. I bet you're a great doctor. You know how to make people feel better just by talkin' to them."

Leave. Leave this second, he told himself.

"You're a very good patient." He forced himself up, cursing silently. In a few weeks he would be on his way to west Africa to serve eighteen months at the hospital and university in Abidjan, Côte d'Ivoire. He had put off his military service until now, and he had chosen to fulfill it by working and teaching in the former French colony rather than by serving in the army. He had no time for this distressing fascination.

Amy Miracle stirred awkwardly and then gazed up at him. He reeled from the open adoration on her face. "I'll never forget what you did the other day," she murmured. "Sticking up for me, I mean."

Pleasure flashed through him along with bitter self-reproach. He was not like his father, not a self-centered bastard who put impulsive ideas ahead of responsibility. Sebastien knew what he could accomplish with this shy young woman, this strange little Miracle, if he wanted, but he wasn't going to do it.

"I'll leave you to enjoy your lunch," he told her. "It's been very nice meeting you."

Disappointment dimmed her eager expression; then she looked down, becoming polite and withdrawn. "It's been nice meetin' you. Maybe I'll see you again, if you come back to pick grapes."

I'll make certain not to do that, he thought to himself angrily. "Perhaps. Adieu."

"Adieu," she repeated softly, drawling the word, making it both funny and sad. He gazed at her for a moment, hypnotized, then shoved the disturbing response from his mind and walked away.

❦

Pop was asleep when she got home from work, as usual, propped up on orthopedic pillows in his and Maisie's bedroom with the door open and the window air conditioner running full blast. On one wall was his circus shrine—photographs of himself when he worked for Ringling Brothers, yellowing handbills from shows long past, and a 1952 movie poster advertising "the Greatest Show on Earth," in which he had been an extra. There was a picture of him with Jimmy Stewart, and on it was an autograph that said, "To Zack, the greatest clown on earth." And low on the wall there was one small, crinkled photograph of Zack with Amy's mother.

Tall, redheaded, and gorgeous, Ellen Connery Miracle had been a Rockette at Radio City Music Hall before joining the circus as her brother's assistant in a trained-dog act. Two years after she married Zack Miracle she died giving birth to Amy. Occasionally he liked to remind Amy of that fact.

Maisie sat in the living room watching soap operas from her favorite chair, a plaid recliner she'd bought at a flea market for a hundred dollars. She wore overalls over one of Pop's white T-shirts. Her mostly gray brown hair was pulled back from her placid face by a dime-store headband. On her generous lap was a large grocery bag filled with green beans. She peeled strings from the beans, snapped them into neat pieces, and rocked contentedly, her attention riveted to the action on *The Guiding Light*.

Maisie was sweet and silent and not particularly smart or pretty, which were all assets as far as Pop was concerned. They were the reasons she and he had remained happy together for the past ten years. Maisie let Pop rule the world. She even made excuses for the marijuana plants he grew in the back rooms. He had a bad back. The dope was for medicinal purposes. Just like the booze. Amy understood all that and felt sorry for him, but it didn't make life easy.

She waved at Maisie and started toward the kitchen for a glass of water. As she walked wearily through the living room Maisie mumbled and rubbed her forehead as if trying to remember something. "Oh, year. Charley called. He's got to work tonight. He and his daddy are taking a truckload of pullets to the plant in Jasper. He said he'll be by at six tomorrow to carry you to church."

"Thanks, Mams." She went to her bedroom and locked the door, then leaned against it, her eyes shut. She put her straw hat on the room's dresser and dropped her sweaty, dirty clothes to the floor. Her body felt hot and confused inside; she was sad, restless, elated, and afraid.

On her bed was Pop's daily list of chores, made out in his sloppy, bold script. The unforgiving length of the list made her angry, and she shoved it onto the floor then stood, naked, and gazed around her room as if seeing it for the first time.

The furniture was still discount-store castoffs, the twin bed still creaked when she kicked it with one foot, and the walls were still covered with posters of movie and television stars. In one corner her fold-out stereo sat on an old trunk that had belonged to her mother. In a cardboard box beside it were Amy's comedy albums and the soundtracks from Broadway musicals. On the dresser sat the tiny black-and-white TV Pop had given her for Christmas three years before. That was the best Christmas she'd ever had.

Moving woodenly, she went into her tiny bathroom and took a shower. When she dried herself she scrubbed the towel over her body for a long time, her hands almost frantic. She threw herself across the bed and rolled onto her back. Shutting her eyes, she draped one arm over them, then put a hand between her legs. Such unadorned need had never surfaced in the daytime before, and it embarrassed her. Then images of Dr. de Savin destroyed her control and she stroked herself until her ache burst into such desperate pleasure that she arched upward and bit her arm to keep from crying out.

Shivering, she hugged herself and stared at the ceiling. There was so much more to want from the world than she had ever realized.

THREE

S ebastien did not pride himself on his bedside manner. But then, he excused himself, there was a strong element of macho reserve in all cardiac surgeons. So many operations meant life or death for the patients, and success was measured, quite literally, in the whisper of a heartbeat.

He gazed without pity at the fat, florid little woman who was crying. She dug pink fingers and manicured nails into her bedcovers. Her face was screwed into a childlike visage of misery. "I'm going to die," she wailed. "I just know I'm not going to survive my bypass operation."

Sebastien clasped his hands behind his back. Standing beside her bed, he trained his gaze on a mauve flower appliquéd on her robe. "There is that risk in any kind of surgery. I can quote success statistics, but I can't give you guarantees."

From the corner of his eye he noticed the cardiac counseling nurse glaring at him. She grasped the patient's hands. "Mrs. Spencer, your prognosis is excellent. You really shouldn't worry."

"B-but Dr. de Savin said—"

"Your chances of having a successful operation are very high," Sebastien told her. "You'll die if you don't have the surgery. Think of it that way."

Mrs. Spencer's eyes widened. She stared at him in horror. "I don't want to think of it that way!"

The nurse patted her hands. "What Dr. de Savin meant—"

"Was that you have no choice but to have a bypass," Sebastien interjected. "That is simply all there is to it, madame, and you would serve yourself much better by calming down. I'm here to explain the clinical procedures, which are actually very reassuring. We are going to make an incision—"

"I want a tranquilizer!" Mrs. Spencer thrust the nurse's hands away and jerked the bedcovers violently. Huge tears carried a flood of mascara down her cheeks. "I don't want to hear about incisions!"

Sebastien turned impatiently toward the nurse. "Bring Mrs. Spencer five milligrams of diazepam. I'll come back to see her in half an hour."

He strode out of the room. The nurse followed, her hands jammed angrily into the pockets of her blue blazer. Cardiac-counseling nurses didn't wear uniforms so they connected with patients on a more casual, comforting level. Sebastien thought their efforts frivolous.

"Dr. de Savin," she called softly, her voice tight. "May I speak to you for a second, please?"

He halted. "Yes?"

She looked furious. "You need some sensitivity training, Doctor."

"I'll leave the hand-holding to you. I have no interest in playing word games with hysterical patients."

"Can't you imagine how frightened that woman is?"

"No. Frankly, I avoid using my imagination in such morbid ways. That's why I'm such a good surgeon. I know how to direct my energy. Now get Mrs. Spencer a pill and call me when she's ready to listen."

"All right, Doctor."

He turned to leave but caught her obscene gesture from the corner of his eye. He knew that she hadn't meant for him to see it, and that if he reported her, she'd be fired. But he was more amused than offended. "You're not the first, madame." He glanced back at her startled expression before he walked away.

Smiling thinly, he went upstairs to the Cardiac Critical

Care Unit and entered a row of glass cubicles. An eight-year-old boy had been brought in the day before suffering complications from open-heart surgery to correct a congenital defect. Electrodes were taped to his pale skin. Tubes carried various medications directly into the veins in the boy's spindly arms. The clear tube that drained the child's catheter dangled from one side of the bed. Around him various machines beeped and gurgled and clicked.

Sebastien got the child's chart and went into his cubicle. He glanced at the boy without saying hello then begen reading. Working with children was very difficult. He had a troublesome soft spot for anyone who was young and defenseless, because he remembered his own forced maturity. Annette and Jacques, so many years younger than he, had nicknamed him *le général*. He had disobeyed their father at every turn and caused many family uproars by spending his summers with their mother's rough-hewn people, working the sardine boats along the Brittany coast.

When he finished with the chart he bent over the boy's thin body and carefully put his stethoscope against the frail chest, where a thick strip of gauze covered the long incision left by surgery. The defect, a hole between the upper chambers of the heart, should have been repaired when the child was a baby. The boy had never been healthy.

"My name's Tom," the youngster murmured. The oxygen tube in his nostrils made his voice stuffy. "I just got transferred here from Florida. My grandma got skeered that I was goin' to die."

His attention tuned to the weak sounds of the recuperating heart, Sebastien merely nodded. He was vaguely aware the boy had brown hair and large blue eyes, and a photograph of him grinning beside a run-down farmhouse was taped to one glass wall of the enclosure. Sebastien didn't want to notice more.

Tom did not intend to be ignored, apparently. "What's your name?"

"Dr. de Savin."

"Are you gonna be around a lot?"

"For now. I'm one of the surgeons who works here."

"You talk funny."

"I'm from France."

"I nearly kicked the bucket, you know. Might still." The remark was so unexpected and so unlike something a child would say that Sebastien was startled. He listed his gaze and found mischief in Tom's eyes. "*That* got your attention," Tom said solemnly.

"I'll have to watch out for you. You think too fast."

"I got a bad heart. Have to do everything fast. Might croak."

"You've got a perfectly nice heart that's just been fixed. It works very well."

"Nope. I heard one of the doctors here say that they fixed it shitty at the hospital down in Florida."

Sebastien made a mental note to find out who had been so stupid and careless. "Well it seems to be healing nicely, regardless. Believe me. I'm a very great doctor. Haven't you heard?"

Tom's eyes brightened. "Really?"

"Really."

"Good. I'm so tired of bein' sick." The boy's voice was very soft, very weak. Sebastien found himself smoothing the child's covers and adjusting the tubes that entered his arms. "Every day you'll get stronger. One day soon you'll go home better than ever."

"Promise?"

"Promise."

"What's your name again?"

"Dr. . . . Sebastien. How about that? You may call me Sebastien."

"That's a funny name."

"It's a very old name. My mother gave it to me. It's a special name. She was from a part of France called Brittany, and Sebastien is a popular name there."

"What's so different about that part of France?"

Sebastien sighed. How could one easily explain to an eight-year-old about Celts and druids and mysterious megaliths, rugged seacoasts and mystic forests, and Arthurian legends? But Tom looked so eager. Sebastien groaned silently. He was becoming sentimental lately. First the girl at the winery, now this boy. He was becoming reckless.

"I'll make a deal with you, Tom. When I finish my work for the day I'll come by here and see if you're still awake. If you are, I'll tell you about my mother's home."

Tom smiled. "Okay!" Sebastien started for the door. "You wouldn't be pullin' my leg about that 'great doctor' stuff, would ya?" the boy called softly. "You're a slick dude."

Sebastien stopped in the doorway and looked back at him. "No shit," he said solemnly. With a wink that cost him more of his reserve than he'd intended, he left the room.

❦

The man's heart lay still and expectant in Sebastien's hand, its function temporarily halted so that he could repair a jagged bullet wound. Sebastien's concentration was undaunted by the scrutiny of a staff surgeon, two first-year residents, and the surgical team of technicians, nurses, and an anesthesiologist. He had performed this procedure many times; he was now the teacher, not the student.

"It is always difficult to suture this type of wound," he noted, as the residents leaned closer. "You. Ross. Watch what I do and prepare to attempt it." The young resident jumped, his forehead sweating under his blue scrub cap. He awkwardly poked the heart with his finger.

"Doctor, are you trying to murder my patient?" Sebastien growled.

"No, sir."

"Then why are you skewering his heart? Delicacy, please. Watch."

Working confidently, Sebastien began closing the wound. "Incredible," the other resident murmured. "I've never seen anyone suture so fast."

"No idle conversation, Dr. Lewis. Compliments will be gladly accepted, but later. Remove your finger, Dr. Ross, before you become a permanent part of this patient's chest. Lewis! Help me with this! Move faster! That's an artery you're mashing shut with your hand, Lewis. If you make a mistake I'll stab you with a scalpel. There. Gently, Lewis, gently—*mon Dieu*! This man will go home with your fingerprints permanently pressed into his heart!"

The resident fumbled and sweated and made little puffing sounds behind his mask. "Don't hyperventilate, Lewis. It's only a man's life. Done. Thank you." Lewis stepped back, saluted, then collapsed limply to the operating room floor. Because everyone was busy, they let him stay there. The supervising surgeon clucked at Sebastien in reproach. "That's the third one this month, doctor. Are you trying to break your record before you leave?"

"Perhaps. I have no time for mercy," Sebastien answered, his attention never wavering from his work. Why should he have mercy for others when he had none for himself?

❦

Jeff Atwater always seemed to be lost in thought, or perhaps he was silently conversing with his ego. Sebastien considered Jeff a fine psychiatrist. He was also an admitted hypochondriac, and ex-flower child, and a divorce victim who now confined his romantic encounters to females who valued a good laugh as much as good sex, and didn't want much from him otherwise. As he ambled down the hospital corridor toward Sebastien, he rolled a sucker in one corner of his mouth. He consulted on transplant cases, which were often psychologically messy for the patients involved. He was also a source of quirky entertainment, and Sebastien admired his joie de vivre.

"Doctor, oh, doc-tor," he cried in a plaintive tone, and suddenly began to stagger. He clasped his head. His sandy hair was ruffled into a maniacal halo around his head. "I'm channeling for the spirit of an ancient Egyptian psychiatrist named Jungthra. Jungthra says you're suffering from a repressed desire to wear polyester leisure suits and go bowling."

"I believe that Jungthra has me confused with someone else."

"Impossible. Jungthra knows all. Now look, I'm taking Susan Roy—she's that big blonde from admissions—to the mountains Saturday, and you're going with us." Jeff jabbed the purple sucker at Sebastien as he came to a stop. "I found out that you're not on call until after six Saturday night, so you've got no excuse. We'll drink champagne and let Susan drive. Or maybe we'll let Susan drink champagne and hope she'll attack us. A ménage à trois. See, I can speak French, too. Look, seriously, going to the mountains with us will be good for you. Somebody's got to provoke your hedonistic tendencies."

"Doctor, has anyone ever told you that you have an obsessive need to manipulate and control people?"

He gave a fiendish laugh. "Yes, but they were tied to my laboratory table at the time. Now stop stalling. You're coming with us on Saturday."

"I need to finish making my arrangements for leaving the country."

"Why? All you have to take to Africa is a change of clothes. You have no life outside your work. Ouch." Jeff pressed one hand to the side of his neck. "I've been feeling a lot of pain here, lately. I've got to get it checked out."

"Probably a tumor," Sebastien told him. "Malignant."

"Oh, thanks, thanks a lot, you cold bastard." Jeff grinned at him. "We'll come by that gangster mausoleum you call a home at eight A.M."

"Are you hijacking me to any place in particular?"

"We're going to find someplace that has good barbecue and 'le air unpolluted.' You'll love it."

"I think I'd rather lie out in my courtyard and develop an ugly sunburn."

"Hah. You're one of those driven types who'd have to be strapped to a lounge chair by force. Eight o'clock. Listen to a shrink who grew up in California, dude. You've got to mellow out."

"*Quelle barbe*," Sebastien said. For added emphasis he affected a yawn and made a classic French gesture of boredom by scrubbing the back of his fingers up and down one side of his face.

"I think I've been insulted. See you Saturday." Jeff chortled as he wandered away.

❦

It was a perfect summer night. The crickets were singing, the moon was full, and the wheat grass gave off a sweet fragrance that mingled with the scent of the warm night earth. Seated on a blanket in the middle of a field, Amy leaned into the circle of Charley's arm and tried to concentrate on what he was saying.

"My folks would let us live with them for a couple of years, and by then we ought to have enough money saved to buy a nice-sized trailer," he told her. "We'll put it up next door to Mama and Daddy. You know, they'll be good baby-sitters. I figure we'll need them to baby-sit by then." Charley pulled her closer and whispered, "I'll pray for our first baby to be a boy, but I won't be upset if it's a girl. We'll just keep tryin'."

"Oh, Charley, it all sounds . . . friendly. It really does." She wanted to make him happy, but she was so confused right now that she was afraid to say much else. Marrying Charley was a good option; her best one. Until lately it hadn't frightened her. Now she had a strange sort of frustration and anger in her belly, and she didn't know what caused it.

Charley Culpepper was the only boy she'd ever known well, so she assumed that he was typical. If their relationship wasn't filled with romance, it didn't bother either of them too much. She rarely saw him more than twice a week, and then it was for church on Sundays and Wednesdays. But Charley was working hard to put away money for trade school, so she expected to see little of him.

He was sweet and simple and knew exactly what he wanted his life to be, which gave him a stability that she craved. He prayed a lot, and she prayed with him, though she couldn't get into the spirit. She'd told him enough about her father's moods so that he'd understand why she didn't invite him into their home very often. Charley prayed for Pop's redemption and told Amy that she was a good daughter for wanting to save her father's soul. With Charley she felt safe.

She twisted toward him. Charley was pleasantly average in every way—average height, average build, average good looks. He had thick blond hair and a smooth, round face that would always be boyish. Amy wrapped her arms around his neck and kissed him. He kissed her back, and slid his hands to the waist of the white shirtwaist dress she'd worn to church.

She ducked her head beside his and nibbled his neck above the collar of his crisp plaid shorts shirt. He smelled of spicy cologne and diesel oil. "Comeon, Charley, comeon," she whispered, stroking the front of his shirt with uncertain movements of her hands. He grunted softly when she kissed him again and finally opened his mouth.

Her breath was short, but not from excitement; instead she fought to prove that Charley could make her ache the way Dr. de Savin had. She could easily picture herself being stroked by Dr. de Savin's large, confident hands. She could not, however, picture herself taking part in his life. She could easily picture herself taking part in Charley's.

"Please, please," she murmured against his mouth. Amy pulled Charley's hands up to her breasts. He had touched them many times through her clothes, and now he stroked and cupped and kneaded them with the same fervent routine he always used. She could predict his next move.

The more he touched her, the less she felt. Before, it had been exciting to have his hands on her; now she was searching for some other feeling, and it wasn't there. Trembling, she reached for the front of his tan slacks and rubbed the hard ridge of flesh under the cloth. He gasped in surprise.

"Charley, if we're talkin' about gettin' married, wouldn't it be all right—"

"No, hon, no."

She hitched up the flowing skirt of her dress and straddled him before he could protest. Deliberately settling atop his groin, she pressed her cotton-pantied crotch against him and wiggled. "We could get some . . . some condoms, and it'd be safe."

He grabbed her arms roughly. "Amy, you stop this. I don't understand what your problem is tonight."

"Charley, please, I've gotta know how you'd feel—"

He pushed her off to one side. "I want you to be a virgin when we get married!"

"I know you didn't want to go too far before, but if we might get married—"

"I say no, and I mean no! And that's that."

She grew very still. She'd never forced the issue before, but her anger had been simmering all along. "Charley, are *you* a virgin?"

"In my h-heart!" he sputtered.

Amy stared at him. "Like the president? You only lust in your heart? Give me the facts on a part about a yard lower than your heart, Charley."

Even in the moonlight she could see the consternation on his face. "You watch your mouth! I can't help what I did before I found the Lord!"

"Maybe I should go lookin' for the Lord tomorrow so that I can do what I want tonight! How come boys have the corner on second chances?"

"It's different with girls. Why do you think I love you so much, hon? You're one of the few girls around who's kept herself pure!"

Understanding stunned her. "You want to plant your seed in fresh dirt, and I'm about the only unplowed field left!"

He groaned in disgust. "That's a stupid thing to say! I want to be a good husband for you. What's wrong with that?"

Amy suddenly recalled a scene from one of her favorite movies. It was so easy for her to become lost in fictitious lives because they were so different from her own. Except now, now she felt exactly like Katharine Hepburn in *The Rainmaker*—frustrated, all alone, and terribly afraid of what fate was planning for her. She gasped for breath and clutched her chest. "Take me home, Charley. I'm suffocating. I don't know which way to turn."

"I think you need a good night's sleep. You're hysterical." He helped her up. But when he let go of her to gather their blanket she ran, her hands on her throat. She reached his jacked-up Volkswagen with its sheepskin-covered seats, threw herself into the passenger side, and covered her face.

"You've been out in the heat too much," he said seriously, as he drove back through the field to a paved road. "You'll be all right."

"S-sure. Sure."

At home she squeezed his hand in farewell and walked

quickly indoors. Before she could reach the sanctuary of her bedroom Pop came out of the living room, where he had set up his canvas and paints and gin bottle for the night.

"I'll be needin' you this weekend," he told her. "Gonna work a festival up in the mountains. Maisie's sewing you a costume for it."

Amy gasped for air. "Why?"

"It's one of those medieval fairs. I'm gettin' paid to do a routine. I need you to drive. And I want you to work the routine with me. Go change out of your Jesus clothes and come back. I want to practice what we'll be doing."

"Oh, Pop, please, I don't mind drivin', but don't make me perform—"

"The least you can do is help me when I tell you to."

"But I'm terrible at it. All you do is get upset every time I work with you. I never do anything good enough for you!"

"The only thing I know to teach you is how to work your ass off and not look for sympathy. Now get the lead out. I'll be waitin' in the living room."

She gazed at him with simmering hostility, a new and daring reaction. Her sense of being trapped grew into a hard knot that made her stomach hurt as she went to change clothes.

❧

The fair was set in a community park in the midst of the woods. Around the perimeter was a recreated medieval village that looked to Amy as if it had been built with cheap plywood and a loose regard for historical detail. The village housed artists and craftspeople, along with a number of food concessions controlled by the local organizers. The village's "residents" were a troupe of seedy-looking actors, singers, puppeteers, and other entertainers.

Pop was a big hit as the rat-juggling man. And she was the rat-juggling man's sidekick. As usual, she was nervous.

"Oh, yes, oh, yes," Pop bawled in a wonderfully absurd Cockney accent. "I juggles the little varmints, I does. Watch 'ere, now, take a look-see." He was dressed in a tunic of grubby rags cinched with a wide leather belt; his lanky legs were covered in black tights and his hair was shoved under a shapeless leather cap. He had wrapped his old tennis shoes in rags, so that he shuffled around like an old man. With aplomb he went into a comic routine that was heavily dependent on the acrobatics of six black bean bags adorned with whiskers and tails. The rats tended to go flying with madcap uncertainty into the audience that had gathered around; escaping, they were, Pop complained.

Amy's job was to scurry after the wayward rats calling, "Hey, you little da-vils, come back 'ere!" After wrestling them into submission she tossed the rats to Pop again, for more acrobatics. At the end of the performance she pulled a leather bag from her belt and begged the audience for "a few coppers to help w'the upkeep of such fine, trained ani-muls." She wore the outfit Maisie had put together with musty scraps—an off-the-shoulder blouse made from a faded muslin sheet, a ragged skirt that dragged the ground in back, and one of Pop's old belts with the money bag tied to it. She had decided to go barefoot, and by midday her feet were filthy. She felt very much in character.

"You're doing a good job today," Pop told her when they finished with the crowd. Then he chucked her under the chin and nodded with satisfaction.

Ecstatic, Amy kissed him on the cheek. She relaxed a little as the two of them walked around the grounds looking for another good spot to perform. Pop milked the strolling crowd for laughter and money, barking corny jokes in his corny English accent and doing sleight of hand for charmed youngsters. Every time he introduced her as the rat-juggler's daughter he clapped a hand to her shoulder and squeezed affectionately.

This was how he'd been before the back injury, the retirement, the drinking, the dope. She remembered him from those times in her early childhood with adoration. Today he loved the crowd, and when he loved the crowd, he loved her. She hurried along beside him, grinning.

At their next performance Amy dove into the audience with gusto, wailing at a rat and pouncing on it like a deranged monkey. The silliness was exhilarating; Pop's good mood made her feel bold. People were guffawing at the grimy rat-juggler, not at her. She tossed the black bean bag to Pop and he caught it with a flourish, then completed his juggling act by heaving all six rats into the air and catching them one by one in his cap.

"Thank you, luvs, thank you," Amy said to the group of about two-dozen people who were applauding. She went through the crowd holding out her money bag to receive tips. "Now if you could just spare a few coppers to keep these here fine ani-muls in training—"

She looked up into Dr. de Savin's dark, amused eyes and dropped her money bag. "Hello, mademoiselle ratcatcher," he said.

Amy fell to her knees and began retrieving a few coins that had spilled. Humiliation burned in her veins as she saw the scene from a horrible new aspect—herself dirty, silly, and begging for money—not fake money but the real thing. When he knelt beside her she couldn't meet his gaze.

"We seem to have a knack for finding each other under unusual circumstances," he added politely.

"Yeah."

She stood quickly and focused all her attention on brushing dirt from her skirt. He stood also. By darting quick glances at him while she dusted herself she saw that he was dressed in topsiders, casual slacks of a light camel color, and a white golf shirt with the collar turned up and the tail out. It had a fancy emblem on it—oh, God, it was probably his family crest.

He put out a hand and picked a twig from her skirt. She noticed the heavy gold watch that gleamed on his wrist. He was as stylish as a model in a magazine, but she couldn't imagine that big, angular body standing patiently to be photographed. He always seemed ready to move.

"You're very entertaining," he told her.

"Yeah."

"I'm here with friends, but they've gone over to watch one of the other acts. I'll tell them that they should have seen yours."

"Thanks." What could she say to him? What did a person say to a fantasy?

She turned toward Pop and saw the grim set of his mouth. Her dawdling had let part of the paying audience escape. Amy's heart sank. "Pop, this is Dr. de Savin—"

"Who's this 'Pop' bloke?" he parried quickly. "Me name's Willie. Willie the Rat Juggler." He came forward and stuck out one sweaty hand. "Pleased to meet you, m'lord."

Dr. de Savin shook his hand and nodded, his bearing so polite and gallant that Amy sighed. Being around him caused her pulse to race and made her acutely aware of being too young, too ignorant, and too plain.

"Dr. de Savin's family owns the winery," she told Pop. "You know, the place where I work—"

"Now, m'gurl, my little ratcatcher, what do you mean? And what're you talkin' in such strange English for?"

Amy shifted in silence and stared at the ground.

"What do you have to say, ratcatcher?" Pop prodded.

She turned wearily to Dr. de Savin. In his expression Amy found compassion. *He understood. God, he understood.* Her chin lifted. She was willing to die for him at that moment. In her best English accent she said, "It was nice seein' you again, m'lord."

He took her hand and bowed over it. Then he kissed it. His lips felt warm and firm on her skin. Weak-kneed, she smiled at him. He said solemnly, "You're a very fine rat-catcher, but you have to stop wearing that strange greenery behind your ear." He reached beside her head, brushed her earlobes with his fingertips, and drew his hand back holding a twenty-dollar bill clasped lightly between his fingertips. Slowly he tucked the bill into her money purse.

"That's a nice bit of work you do there, m'lord," Pop commented eagerly. "You could be one o' the finest pick-pockets in the village."

"It's just a little hobby I acquired to keep my hands limber."

Dazed, Amy didn't know whether she felt embarrassed for taking his money or elated over his attention. A little of both, she finally decided. When he nodded to her one more time and walked away, she thrust the money bag toward Pop and kept her eyes trained on Dr. de Savin. He melded with the crowd around the food concessions, but he was so tall that she could easily catch glimpses of him.

"Hey. Hey. Dammit. Kid, get your thumb out of your ass."

Pop's sharp voice drew her back to reality. "Yes, sir?"

"What's the deal with that guy?"

"No deal, Pop. I hardly know him."

"Get to know him better. He's loaded."

She scowled at the ground, hating the way Pop could take the shine off of a wonderful moment. "You goin' to lunch, Pop?"

"Yeah. Comeon."

"I think I'll just sit out here and watch the people."

"Suit yourself." He headed for a tall wooden fence that had been set up to keep people from sneaking into the fair without paying. Amy watched him open a gate and disappear into the area where the actors parked their cars. Pop's old Buick waited there, a cooler and a picnic basket in the trunk. Pop would enjoy a joint and a six-pack of beer.

She walked to a dogwood tree off by itself and sat down wearily in the shade. The July day was broiling hot, and she pulled her skirt up to her knees. Stretching her bare legs out, she leaned against the dogwood's slender gray trunk and searched the crowds for Dr. de Savin. To no avail. Amy shut her eyes and tears burned their corners. Stupid daydreams. She was going to marry Charley. She was going to raise Culpepper babies and Culpepper chickens. Each time she and Charley made love she was going to smell like diesel fuel afterward.

"What? She rests? Where are her rats?"

She jerked her eyes open and found Dr. de Savin looking down at her. He knelt, his manner brusque, and handed her a cup filled with ice and a soft drink. From the items balanced in his big hands he gave her a napkin, a roast turkey leg, and a cup of coleslaw with a plastic fork laid carefully across the top. Then he sat down and arranged similar fare on his crossed legs, though his cup contained one of the dark, imported beers being sold at the concession stands.

"You shared your lunch with me the other day," he explained.

Amy sat forward, tried not to fidget nervously, and smoothed her paper napkin as if it were fine linen. "You're probably the nicest person I've ever met."

He hesitated over a sip of his beer, watching her closely and with quiet pleasure. Then he put his cup down and said, "I've never thought of myself as being particularly likable. Thank you for the compliment."

She laughed under her breath. "I can't imagine somebody *not* liking you."

"Oh, I suppose I'm fit for decent company." His voice was droll. "But there are a great many ratcatchers who'd turn their noses up at me."

"Not this one." She was so flustered that she knew she'd say something *really* dumb if she weren't careful. She took a swallow of her drink and forced herself to nibble the turkey leg. "Thank you for the . . . the tip."

"I hope it didn't embarrass you. I consider it a fair price for such marvelous entertainment."

"Pop and I were just doin' old circus stuff with a new twist."

"In my country the circus is revered. It's an art form. You're an artist."

"Oh, boy, is *that* what I look like?" She gestured toward her outfit. Her hair, cut in a short, feathery shape with bangs, was wrenched into a queue at the base of her neck. She untied the leather thong that held it and hurriedly ran her fingers through the auburn locks.

"Yes. You look like an actress playing a part. What you do requires a great deal of talent. Didn't you hear people laughing at you?"

"Aw, they laugh because the act's so silly."

"You must set very high standards for yourself, mademoiselle, because you can't accept a compliment for anything you do."

She twisted the cup in her hands and pretended to study it. "I'm sorry."

"Don't be sorry for everything!" His voice held gentle rebuke.

She started to speak, then pressed her fingertips to her mouth. "I almost said I'm sorry, again. It's a habit, I guess.

I'm"—she chuckled as he arched one dark brow expectantly—"oh, you're making me want to say it all the time!"

"Make a promise to yourself. Promise you'll say it no more than once a day. Perhaps in time you can wean yourself from saying it except when it's really needed."

"It's needed a lot. I'm always in trouble."

"Oh? What do you do that's so terrible?"

She thought for a moment. "I'm not sure."

He studied her with narrowed eyes and frowned. Amy gulped down a piece of turkey without the least notice of how it tasted. Fumbling for something to do, she stuck her hand into a pocket on her skirt and retrieved a video-game token someone had passed off as a quarter. Holding out a hand for his scrutiny, she deftly rolled the token over her fingers and then made it disappear. She swooped her hand forward to his shirt collar and drew it back holding two tokens. "Want to play Space Invaders?"

His serious expression softened immediately. To her utter delight he laughed—a beautiful, masculine sound that made her quiver inside. "What else can you do?"

"I can do card tricks, and juggle, and make balloon animals. Pop taught me how, so I could help him at kiddie parties." Inspired by his attention, she flipped the token and caught it on the tip of one finger. "It's easy stuff."

"I can't imagine such skill coming *easily*. Teach me." He leaned forward eagerly and held out his hand.

Amy placed the token on his fingers and then, cupping his hand in both of hers, showed him how to maneuver it. He bent his head close to hers and she thought her heart would stop. Dazed, she knew only that touching him created an obsession to touch him all over.

They sat there for nearly an hour, their conversation low and private and laced with laughter, the tokens becoming graceful in his hands as she showed him how to make them obey. Pop came back from lunch and stared at them approvingly, then went into his rat-juggler voice and told her, "Come along, luv, n' leave the young lord to his business."

Dr. de Savin became brusque and reserved again. "You haven't eaten yet," he noted, gazing at her untouched food.

"Neither have you. Here. Take mine. I'm not hungry."

"No. I have to get back to Atlanta. I'm on duty at the hospital tonight. I told the people I'm with that I'd meet them at the gate after lunch." He stood and held out a hand. Amy took it, and he helped her to her feet.

"Anytime you want help with your magic tricks, you can find me at the winery," she said, trying not to sound too desperate. "Here. Take this video token so that you can practice." She brought it to her lips with a flourish and kissed it. "I give it my magic blessing. It won't let you down."

He took the token solemnly. "Thank you."

She looked into his eyes and forgot shyness. For the first time she studied them long enough to know that they were golden brown with black rims. The brows over them were dramatic wings. His eyes were very private, but startling in the depth of emotion they could express. Right now they were somber, almost sad. He stepped closer to her and murmured, "You have a way of making a person feel happy. It's a very great talent, and one that you should cherish. *Adieu.*"

Amy watched him leave. *I love you*, she thought with the deep, perfect conviction of a lost soul who had finally found the way home.

FOUR

*S*ebastien thought about Amy Miracle often over the next few days, remembering her charm when she performed with her father and growing increasingly suspicious that her father was responsible for draining every bit of her self-confidence. The girl's natural ability as a performer was obvious; her appealing, comical voice and gamine face could make a stone wall laugh.

After his rounds one day Sebastien took the token she had given him—he had tucked it in a compartment of his wallet like a good luck piece—and returned to Tom's cubicle. Propped up on pillows and surrounded by medical equipment, the boy looked forlorn. But his eyes widened with curiosity when Sebastien pulled a chair to his bedside and sat down. "More stories?" Tom whispered eagerly.

"Look." Sebastien held the video token in front of him, passed a hand over it, then presented both hands to Tom to show that the token had disappeared. "Magic."

"Neat!"

"I learned this trick from a girl who plays with rats," Sebastien told him solemnly.

"Oh, bullshit."

"Such language! I think we'll have to give you a new tongue as well as a new heart."

Tom giggled a little, the sound barely audible. "Tell me what she did with rats."

Sebastien described last Saturday's events in great detail,

and as he did he again felt the peacefulness that had fallen over him as he sat with the girl. He could easily recall the gentleness of her hands on his as she guided the tokens between his fingers, her head so close to his that her hair had brushed his cheek. He could hear her voice as she relaxed and it became husky, with a pleasing and sultry tone to it.

He told himself that his fascination with her was merely vanity; when she looked at him he saw the yearning in her eyes. He told himself that he would like to indulge her yearning out of pure masculine lust.

He talked to Tom until the boy fell asleep, glanced through the cubicle's glass wall to the nurses' station beyond, and when no one was looking he held the boy's thin, unfurled hand for a moment. He left the token in it, the same token Amy Miracle had given him.

Sebastien was the son of a woman who had prayed to the Catholic saints but had kept a keen eye tuned to the more ancient reassurance of her Celtic heritage. Mysterious forces worked in her world, swirling around people and changing their lives. He honored her memory by choosing to believe that he had given Tom a bit of Amy Miracle's magic.

❦

Amy knew there was trouble when she got home from work one afternoon and Pop was wide-awake, waiting for her in the kitchen. She was tired and covered in the fine red dust of the vineyard. Laying her sweat-stained straw hat on the kitchen table, she waited nervously. Maisie stood in the corner, her back against her homemade ceramic chickens on the wall. Pop slumped at the kitchen table, one hand clenched and the other wrapped around a can of beer.

"Charley came by," he said slowly.

Amy stiffened. "I guess he told you."

"That you're not gonna see him anymore."

"Yeah. That's right."

"You think you're gonna live off me the rest of your life?"

"No. I'll get a job over in Athens. And I'll find someplace to live there."

Pop lifted his hand from the beer, made a fist, and flattened the can with one violent smash. Foam spewed in all directions. "What the hell kind of job can you do? You only open your mouth when somebody forces you to. You're so damned lazy—"

"I had a paper route from the time I was eight till last year. I've been a baby-sitter more nights and weekends than not since I was old enough to get the jobs. I've found summer work ever since I turned fifteen. I do everything you tell me to do around here. That's lazy?"

"You think any of that counts for shit? You gonna pay your bills over in Athens with that kind of work?"

"I'll find jobs. I'll work twenty hours a day if I have to."

"You'll end up broke and begging me for help! I won't be responsible for you! To hell with it! You get your ass over to Charley's tonight and make things right!"

Amy began to tremble. "No."

He leapt to his feet. Veins stood out in his neck. Maisie clasped her chest. "Do it, Amy, please!"

Gripping the edge of a counter for support, Amy shook her head. "No."

Pop's face contorted with a fury she'd never seen before, because she'd never had the nerve to back-talk him before. "You're outta here! You're out today!"

"Please, Zack, don't do this," Maisie whimpered.

"You promised that I'd have a year after I turned eighteen," Amy reminded him, horrified.

"I didn't think you were gonna go piss-head crazy on me! What's happened to you? Get out on your own and see how you like it! You've got a little money in the bank! Go live on it!"

"You promised!"

Pop hurried out of the kitchen, hunched in a way that said his back hurt. The cramped posture made him move with apelike menace. "Out! Out! I'll show you!"

Amy and Maisie ran after him. Maisie made a keening sound of fear as Zack lurched into the living room and snatched his revolver from the coffee table. He entered

Amy's bedroom. She clutched the door frame behind him, ignoring Maisie's garbled pleas to come away.

"Leave my stuff alone! I'll pack it myself! Don't touch my stuff!"

Her father waved the revolver. "You got nothin'! It's in my house—it belongs to *me*. I'll show you what the real world's like!"

He pointed the steel-blue pistol at a wall covered in movie posters and fired. The crisp explosions deafened Amy; their sound waves pushed terror through her skin. Maisie screamed.

When the revolver was empty Zack slung it into a corner and began clawing the wall with his fingers. Amy wailed in despair. "No, Pop!" She tried to get in front of him, like a mother hen protecting her chicks.

He shoved her aside. "Take this trash with you!" He grabbed at the dog-eared movie posters she'd bought for a dollar each at flea markets, recreations of classic Three Stooges ads, Mae West, the old film comedies, Katharine Hepburn and Cary Grant in *Bringing Up Baby*.

Amy's vision clouded with fury. He was violating her sanctuary, when she had asked only for a chance, for respect. She screamed at him until her throat ached, while he threw open her closet door and dumped clothes into the center of the room. Without thinking she grabbed a fly swatter from the window ledge. She brought it down on his shoulder.

He made a bellowing sound of disbelief. Maisie shrieked from the doorway when he turned and swung one fist. It glanced off of Amy's cheekbone, sending her sprawling across the bed. Shock obscured the pain as she stared up at her father. It was the last insult. Despite all his moods, he'd never hit her before. "I hate you! I've always hated you!"

"I hate you, too! Get out of my house! Out!" Breathing heavily, he pushed her cheap stereo off its makeshift stand. Then he jerked the bedspread from under her and slung it to the floor. With one swipe of his arm he cleared her dresser onto the spread. The tiny television set bounced on the floor with an ominous cracking sound.

Crying, Amy scrambled off the bed and hit him again with the fly swatter. The next thing she saw was his hand slapping forward with the dresser mirror poised like a Ping-Pong paddle. Then the mirror crashed upward on her chin, and she felt the sharp slice of glass. The mirror shattered and Amy's jaw clicked together with a force that sent explosions of light through her vision.

She staggered back and dimly heard Maisie screaming at Pop to stop before he killed her. "All right, all right," he shouted, but there was a note of fear in it. "I didn't mean to hurt her!" Then Maisie dragged him from the room, and the next sound Amy heard was the door slamming.

Her legs collapsed and she sank to her knees on the floor. She stared at nothing for a few seconds, but when her head cleared she rose and numbly packed a knapsack with all it would hold. She took a towel from the bathroom, because blood was streaming down her neck. Her face throbbed all over. She sat on the windowsill and made herself breathe slowly until she stopped feeling sick to her stomach. Then she hitched the knapsack over her shoulders and climbed out the open window.

❧

Sebastien was cramming every bit of activity into his last two weeks at the hospital. At four A.M. he had wakened without an alarm and read medical journals in bed, with a percolator of coffee on the stark, black-lacquered nightstand and a dish of warm apple tarts on his lap.

By five he was outside in nothing but his running shoes and blue jogging shorts, his long, purposeful strides taking him past the giant magnolias and perfect lawns of other townhouses, the most exclusive ones in surburan Atlanta. At 5:45 he stopped at the ivy-covered building that housed the complex's spa-quality gym.

There he allowed himself one reckless indulgence. He taped his hands, donned boxing gloves, and spent the next thirty minutes pummeling a weighted bag. It was dangerous to risk his hands, but he was careful. If medicine was his wife, then boxing was surely his mistress, and he loved both. In his teens he had won a few amateur titles, and had even talked about entering the ring as a professional, much to his father's disgust.

But boxing had never seriously sidetracked his dream of becoming a doctor. He was satisfied knowing he had all the right qualities to be a great boxer—the self-discipline, the ability to endure pain, the aggressive anger.

By six-thirty he had showered, shaved, and dressed in custom-tailored gray trousers, a gray-blue golf shirt, and handmade leather loafers. After he arrived at the hospital he would trade the outfit for baggy surgical scrubs and comfortable running shoes. At 6:35 he drove past the guard at the complex's jasmine-covered entrance, a briefcase beside him on the Ferrari's seat.

By seven he had parked the Ferrari in the staff lot behind the sleek granite tribute to fifties' architecture that was Gregory University Hospital. Less than an hour later he was in an operating room on the fifth floor, preparing to assist a prominent senior physician in a cabbage—a coronary artery bypass graft, or CABG.

It was the first of five surgeries in which he would take part during the next nine hours. In between and afterward he made his rounds, both alone and with other physicians, and attended a meeting with the head of cardiac surgery.

He managed to visit with Tom for a few minutes, and told him tales of the ancient Breton forest, Broceliande, where King Arthur's Merlin had been—and still was—imprisoned by enchantment. Tom was speechless with intrigue. Sebastien found himself looking forward to telling the boy more.

Following a quick supper in the hospital cafeteria he walked in the dusky summer evening to a small auditorium in the university's medical school complex, where he spent the next three hours attending a seminar on artificial hearts. University researchers had implanted the experimental units in several calves, and their success was a source of growing excitement among surgeons and cardiologists.

He walked back to the hospital at midnight and checked on several patients again, particularly Tom. The boy lay sleeping, his chest rising and falling harshly, his arms tied to the bed frame, his life tied to the machines around him by umbilical cords of plastic that fed into his veins. Amy Miracle's token lay on the stand beside his bed.

As his last duty for the day Sebastien sat down in a small lounge reserved for physicians and, with a strong cup of coffee in one hand, began reviewing patient charts. Five minutes later he was paged to the phone. An acquaintance had asked for him downstairs, in the lobby. Amy Miracle.

He found her standing in the shadows between the recessed lighting in one corner of the hospital's opulent lobby. Sebastien was both worried and annoyed. He had tried to remove himself from temptation, but it had followed him. He decided to scold Amy for letting her infatuation get out of hand.

But after he looked closer he was too puzzled to do more than study her odd appearance as he crossed the lobby. She was hiding beside a potted plant, and she didn't step forward when she saw him. It was the middle of the night, but she was wearing her funny black sunglasses. A bright red scarf was wrapped around her head and neck, swallowing all but her eyes, nose, and mouth.

"Can I help you?" Sebastien asked, frowning as he stopped in front of her.

"I didn't mean to get you out of the operatin' room!"

He realized how he must look in his green scrubs. "You didn't. What's wrong?"

She glanced about as if afraid someone would overhear their conversation in the deserted lobby. Then she said in a soft, weary voice, "I need a doctor. I was hopin' that you could help me." She paused, biting her lower lip. "I've got money. Cash. I can pay."

"What is wrong?"

"I, uhmm, I cut my chin. I just need it stitched up. I thought it would stop bleedin' on its own, but it didn't."

"Come. Sit down." He took her hand. It was cold and trembling. He led her quickly to a sofa and sat down beside her. "Let me see." She pulled back a little as he tugged the ridiculous red scarf down. A makeshift bandage as wide as his hand covered the underside of her chin. Plastered over the gauze was a clumsy shield of clear packaging tape. The gauze was so bloody that it was beginning to leak between the strips of tape. Gently he peeled the gauze away. Underneath was a deep, curving cut nearly two inches long. "*Mon Dieu*! Why didn't you go to an emergency room?"

"I don't want to answer any questions."

"What sort of questions?"

"Never mind. Will you sew it up for me? Please? Without tellin' anybody?"

He pressed the bandage into place again and watched her struggle not to wince. Lifting her sunglasses off with a catlike flick of his hand, he studied the ugly bruise beside her right eye. The outside corner of the eye was swollen shut. From the looks of both eyes, she'd been crying. Now she ducked her head and shielded her bruised face with one hand. "Don't ask. Can you sew up my chin, or not?"

"What are you afraid of? Are you in trouble with the police?"

"No." Obviously frightened, she leapt to her feet. "Nevermind. I'm sorry I pestered you."

"Stop. Calm down." He grasped her hands and tugged. "Sit. Tell me what's wrong. I'll try to help."

She wavered, looking tragic and confused. Gently but firmly he pulled until she sank onto the couch again. "My dad . . . hit me," she whispered, every word filled with shame. "But I hit him first. What if somebody tells the police? I don't want him to go to jail." Her voice broke. "But I don't want to go to jail, either."

"Oh, Miracle, that's not what would happen." Sebastien was silent for a moment, fighting anger and a sense of protectiveness that startled him with its intensity. "Did you hurt him, I hope?"

"I don't think so. I hit with with a f-fly swatter." She laughed sharply on the last two words, the sound a little hysterical.

"A fly swatter? That's how you hit him first? And he did this to you, in return?"

She nodded. "He was mad at me. He's never hit me before."

"What provoked him this time?"

"I . . . aw, hell. This sounds like one of my stepmother's

soap operas. I hate it. *The Young and the Embarrassing.*"
She stared at the floor and shut her eyes, then took a deep
breath. "I broke up with my boyfriend. Pop thought that
was a dumb thing to do."

"Why?"

"He thinks I'll be a burden to him if I don't get married. I
tried to tell him that I'd take care of myself, but he didn't
believe me."

"You have left home, then?"

"Yeah. Oh, yeah." She managed to chuckle, but fear
shivered in it. "For good. I've got a little money saved.
Tomorrow I'll go up to Athens and get a motel room. Then
I'll look for a job. A night job. I'll keep workin' at the winery,
too, until the harvest gets done."

"Where will you stay tonight? Do you have friends?"

"Yeah. Uh huh." When he looked at the knapsack sitting
on the floor nearby then scowled at her, she crumpled and
admitted, "I want to save money. I'm gonna hang out at a
Waffle House all night. If I keep buyin' coffee and pie,
they'll let me stay."

Sebastien stood and brusquely pulled her to her feet. "I
have a guest room at my home. Why don't you stay there
tonight?"

"You're kidding."

"Oh? Do you fear for your reputation? Should I fear for
mine?"

"No! God, I just meant . . . I didn't expect it." Tears
pooled in her eyes. "You don't need a hick teenager
around."

The tenderness he felt for her was a dangerous thing,
and his impulsive offer already worried him. "Mademoiselle, I've had a long day. I'm not in the mood to play polite
games. Do you wish to come home with me or not?"

"I'm sorry. Thank you. I will. Come stay at your house,
that is. God, I'm sorry—"

"One more 'I'm sorry,' and I'll sew your mouth shut." He
retrieved her knapsack and slung it over his shoulder. "I'll
go upstairs and gather a few items I'll need to care for your
chin." He tapped the knapsack. "I'll take this with me, so I
know you'll be waiting when I come back."

Her shoulders slumped. She nodded. "Thanks for every-thing."

"Tell me, why did you decide not to marry your boy-friend?"

Her chin, with its bloody, haphazard bandage, lifted, and her expression hardened. "That's private."

"Ah. I probed until I found a backbone. *Bon*." Nodding his approval, he walked away.

❦

Even in her dull, wounded state she was openly curious about his home. Her interest was a healthy sign; Sebastien encouraged it to distract her. After he cleaned and stitched her chin she took a shower and changed into a wrinkled sundress, then wandered around beside him, her good eye as unblinking as a cat's. His bedroom and study were upstairs in the town house; below were the kitchen, two guest rooms, and a spacious living room that opened onto a small courtyard filled with pearl-gray lounge chairs and a manicured jungle of houseplants.

She stared at the living-room's interior walls, made of translucent glass blocks lit from inside so that they glowed. A floating staircase to the upper level dominated a corner of the room, and its streamlined metal railings gleamed in the light of white globes set on white walls. She walked among oblong tables of sleek, blond wood and unyielding chairs of spare lines.

There were a few pieces of heavy, sculptured Depression glass, framed black-and-white posters advertising prize fights that had been fought long before Sebastien's birth. Amy touched a beautiful sideboard of black enamel and chrome, then the tall, laminated cabinet of a vintage radio-phonograph. She picked up a 1935-model telephone from the cradle of its wide pedestal base then listened carefully, as if fearful that it was only an object d'art. "Okay. I hear a dial tone," she said.

Sebastien realized how cold and strange his home must look to her. He found himself hurrying to justify it, some-thing he'd never done before. "This is a style from the thirties," he explained. "Some people call it art deco." He smiled wryly. "But we purists call it Depression Modern. It takes simplicity to the level of art. But to many people it's very forbidding."

She frowned, lost in thought. Then she brightened and said, "I know where I've seen this kind of place before! In a Marx brothers movie!"

"I beg your pardon. I've never been called a Marx brother."

"I didn't mean—"

"Don't apologize. It's a fascination I have trouble explaining myself. I suppose I like the style because it's so uncomplicated and unemotional—it reminds me of a hospital." He shrugged. "Such atmospheres are my life."

She shook her head. "No! I meant . . . I've seen rooms like this in lots of old movies. It makes me think of Fred Astaire and Ginger Rogers. It's romantic."

"Big Band music. The swing."

"W. C. Fields in *The Big Broadcast of 1938*."

"Jazz and blues."

"Eleanor Powell and Busby Berkeley. Dagwood and Blondie."

He applauded. "Clark Gable. Mae West."

"Everything back then was so—so sophisticated, but innocent." Her tired eyes lightened with humor. "Except . . . you know what?" She gestured around her. "In a lot of movies the *villains* lived in places like this. Real modern, real elegant." Her voice became absurdly solemn. "Especially the wicked women."

"The wicked women?"

"You know. Fast women. Gangsters' molls! Now the *good* women"—she clasped her chest and pursed her mouth primly—"always lived in places with lace curtains and chintz upholstery."

Sebastien chuckled heartily. She was right. "Then I suppose you're a gangster's moll . . . temporarily."

"Nah. You be Fred, and I'll be Ginger. Got your dancin' shoes?"

Sebastien realized he was smiling at her. No one had ever looked beneath the facade of his home. "Come along, Ginger. I'll show you the kitchen."

Once there Amy silently examined modular white cabinets and white countertops that swooped around the room. She ran her fingertips along the white venetian blinds above a kidney-shaped metal sink. "No dust. I knew it."

"I have a rather compulsive maid."

She sniffed delicately at the herbs growing in ceramic pots along the windowsill, then studied the gleaming copper pans hanging over an elaborate gas range and grill. "You probably cook something besides hamburgers in this place."

"Yes. I'm a very good cook. What Frenchman isn't? Are you hungry?"

She shook her head. In the bright overhead light he saw all the exhaustion in her body and in her pale, bruised face. "I think I'll just go to bed."

When she swayed a little he took her elbow and guided her down a hallway where the unadorned cream-colored walls raised spareness to new heights. She stopped to gaze at metal-framed photographs of old cars and whimsical inventions. "Most people put up pictures of their families. You put up pictures of *things*. Me, I put up pictures of movie and TV stars. Strangers. I guess that's as bad."

He didn't quite know what to say to that, since she hadn't sounded sarcastic or insulting. Did she think that he was lonely? unloved? unlovable? Before he could answer such disturbing insight his eyes caught an edge of blue under the face of the plain little wristwatch she wore. "What is that on your skin?"

"What? Nothing. Just a birthmark." She backed toward the door to the guest room, a coolly elegant place of white lacquered furniture and white satin bed coverings.

"My payment, mademoiselle, for stitching that stubborn chin of yours, is to see what is tattooed on your wrist."

She halted, frowning, then jerked her wristwatch up an inch and stuck her arm out. "It's a heart with the letters of my last name around it in a circle. A friend of my dad's put it there when I was about five years old. She said it was a charm against evil. She was a fortune teller in a carnival. I didn't ask for it, okay? I'm not a biker or anything. It's the only tattoo I've got, okay? I try to keep it hidden."

"No need to be so defensive." He grasped her hand and studied the crudely etched heart, which looked deflated. It bothered him to think of a child being permanently marked by superstition; then he considered the fact that his mother's prayers to the saints and her astrology had marked him in a less visible but equally potent way. "You need a transplant."

She shivered under his touch but didn't pull away. Her fingertips pressed into his palm with disarming warmth. "I'll trade you," she said softly. "Heart for heart. Scar for scar."

Shaken by such unexpected power, he watched her silently as she withdrew into the plush confines of his guest room.

❦

He was seated at the island in the center of his kitchen at five the next morning, groggily drinking a cup of thick black coffee, when Amy tiptoed in. She was dressed in denim shorts, a T-shirt, and sneakers. She carried her straw hat and sunglasses. He was dressed in a short robe of blue silk. She halted abruptly at the sight of him lounging on a tall black bar stool with his long, naked legs idly crossed and the robe gaping open to reveal most of his chest.

"I'm sorry—I mean, excuse me," she managed to say, blushing.

"Come in. I thought you'd sleep late."

Sebastien rearranged himself into a more formal posture and pulled the robe closed. Underneath the cool silk he grew so hard that he ached, not an unusual condition for him in the presence of a desirable female, but dangerous in combination with his emotions for this one. Contentment gathered in his chest—for no other reason than she was looking at him with shy fascination. Even battered and sad her face had a piquant charm; she was certainly not beautiful, but he could hardly take his eyes off her.

She sat down across the counter from him and put her things on the cool stove top nearby. "I can't sleep late. I have to leave in thirty minutes if I'm gonna make it to work on time from all the way down here." She slapped a hand to her forehead and winced. "I forgot! My bike's over at the hospital! When will you be leavin' for work?"

"You didn't go to bed until after two, and your face is very swollen. How can you possibly make an hour's drive on a motorcycle, in your condition?"

"Hey," she said sharply. "The world doesn't hold out its hand to lazy people. I'm on my own now, and I'm not gonna blow it."

"I admire your courage. But I'm putting you on sick leave for today. I say so, and I'm your doctor. I'm also your employer, remember? Sick leave with pay. Now go back to bed." He gestured toward a waffle iron beside the stove. "Or have breakfast, and then go back to bed."

She clasped her hands and stared at them stubbornly while blinking back tears. Considering her swollen right eye, the effort was painful to watch. Her chin was pink where he could see the beginnings of his stitches. She hadn't complained at all during the course of his work.

"This is a sink-or-swim thing," she whispered, her voice quivering. "My bein' on my own, I mean. I can't take your help." She laughed. "Ol' Beaucaire will think the worst about me if I call and say I'm with you."

"He'll think what I tell him to think. That's the privilege I enjoy for being his employer, not his employee."

"I can't—"

"No work today, Amy. Now answer correctly: 'All right, Sebastien.' "

"Sebastien?" she whispered, her eyes lighting a little. "You don't mind if I call you by your first name?"

"It would be terribly formal for you to call me otherwise now that you've seen me in nothing but my robe."

"Nothing but—" She covered her eyes gingerly and chuckled. "One of us is embarrassed, and buddy, it *ain't* you."

"Now, about breakfast—"

"All right, *Sebastien*, I'll stay put for now. I better go get some sleep." Relieved of her courage, she looked as if she might suddenly droop over the table. "I'll call . . . a taxi later on. Get my bike from the hospital. Go up to Athens and find a good motel."

Sebastien reached over and took her hands. A knot lodged in his throat. Courage. This morning she was forging ahead on courage alone, more of it than he had ever expected. "You're a very strong, very determined person," he told her gruffly. "Very ancient for your age. *Bravo!* But you must also be wise. Listen!" He shook her hands for attention, because her eyes were shutting even as he spoke. "Be wise. Accept help when you need it." Sebastien sighed at the irony of his giving advice that he never took. "Stay here again tonight."

He sat back, wondering what he meant to do with this incredible young woman, and whether he could keep from hurting her. "I'll be gone until after midnight. You won't be bothered. Stay here," he said again, sealing her fate.

"I'm so scared. So tired. Confused. Such a baby!"

"No. Anyone would be afraid. We'll talk about your future later. Now go and rest."

He went around the counter to her, guided her off the stool, then picked her up and carried her to the guest room. From the unrumpled state of the bed's pearl-white sheets, he doubted that she had slept much. No surprise in that, her father had thrown her to the wolves and she was terrified. Holding her close, Sebastien kissed her hair.

"Everything will be fine, Miracle," he whispered.

She nodded against his chest. "Trust . . . you."

Not too much, he cautioned silently, and putting her to bed, tucked the covers around her, then quickly left the room.

FIVE

Sebastien had finally gone too far. This flagrant attention to a girl who was no more than a field worker was unforgivable.

Pio Beaucaire swung his heavy office chair to face the wall of photographs. The images of elite old-world culture were his shrine. The de Savin vineyards. The fifteenth-century château. Le comte de Savin stood in front of it proudly, as a man who knew the value of duty and tradition should. He ruled with a iron fist because he understood that honor, discipline, and obedience were the hallmarks of nobility.

Pio gripped the arms of his chair. His family had served the de Savin's for generations. It was a proud service, a loyal service. He and the comte de Savin respected each other's positions in the world. They shared a very French love for order and continuity.

The time had long since passed for Sebastien to recognize his place in the order of society. The eldest son of the de Savin family had always headed the family businesses. That Sebastien had denied his duty for so long was a tribute to his willpower. He was headstrong, but that was a good trait. Pio loved him and was proud in a way. When his spirit matured—was tamed—Sebastien would be a credit to his father's name. Why *le comte* had not crushed the rebellion when Sebastien was a boy had always bewildered Pio. He had certainly allowed no rebellion from the younger ones, Annette and Jacques. Jacques, unfortunately, had been worthless from birth.

Pio supposed that *le comte* had made concessions because of the tragedy. A man who had lost one son was inclined by sentiment and necessity to tolerate faults in the only valuable one who remained.

But not much longer. While nothing could alter Sebastien's commitment to spend the next two years in Africa, after that he must not be allowed to ignore his responsibilities at home. No one—and particularly not some unsuitable young woman—must encourage him to return to America.

Sebastien was unpredictable. This timid young *poule* might mean nothing to him. But then again, she was not his typical kind of woman. That might be ominous. The *comte* must be informed of this situation immediately. He would know what to do, Pio felt certain. He always did.

❦

Two days later Amy was still living in Sebastien's home, and he was leaving the hospital each night at nine so that he'd have a few hours to enjoy her company before bedtime. Little by little she became more open about herself, and he learned about her father's drinking, his moods, his past as a circus performer, his tyranny. She was much more than the sum of her timid parts. She loved to read, had keen intuition about people, was a loner like himself, and above all, was a sharp observer of the world around her.

She was also an anxious daydreamer with a whimsical way of recreating that world. At breakfast one morning she placed a croissant to her ear as if it were a seashell and said solemnly, "I hear Paris." He laughed until tears came to his eyes. One evening she wandered around his living room stroking the steamlined fixtures and sleek lines, then observed, "Everything in this place looks like it's headed somewhere in a hurry."

Most disconcerting was the way she viewed him. When he spoke to her she listened avidly, but with her head cocked to one side as if she were trying to make him fit the rest of her world, which was slightly atilt.

Three nights after leaving home she called her father. She received a vague apology but no invitation to return. Afterward she went to a lounge chair in the little courtyard and sat there silently, surrounded by hot summer darkness, until Sebastien coaxed her to talk. It was not that she had wanted to go home, she explained, but she would have appreciated being asked.

Sebastien sat on the edge of the chair and put his arms around her. She made a sad, satisfied sound and carefully rested the unhurt side of her face on his shoulder. When he began to stroke her hair she cried out and, with the quick, deadly adoration of the inexperienced, kissed him on one corner of the lips. He shivered as if he'd never been kissed before and knew that he had to move away from her immediately or forget common sense.

"I didn't mean to make you mad," she said in a small voice, when he was standing across the courtyard staring into the stars above its whitewashed brick walls.

He twisted around and straightened formally. It was time to stop their charade of togetherness. "This Friday is my last day at the hospital. I could have left a month ago; my fellowship ended officially in June. But I stayed because I had no interest in taking a month's holiday before I left the United States." He paused, watching her eyes widen with understanding. "A week from this Friday I'm leaving for Africa, to work in a hospital there. And I won't be back."

After a stunned moment she bent her head. Her hands knotted against the cool gray material of the lounge cushion. "You think I was expectin' you to keep takin' care of me? Is that why you're telling me this?"

"Yes."

She lifted her head and looked at him. Tears slid down her cheeks, but her eyes were angry. "I'm not stupid. I know how to love somebody without thinkin' that they're gonna love me back."

Sebastien studied her. She would have made a fine surgeon; she knew how to cut to the heart of the matter. His brilliant logic deserted him; her scalpel had excised rational thought. "You're very wise, then," he told her finally. "That's the best way to love."

"No, it's not, but it's all I've been able to manage so far."

"You may find as you grow older that you prefer your relationships to be one-sided—in your favor, of course. They're much simpler that way."

"No, no." She scrubbed tears from her bruised face and winced. "It's sad to live like that." Vaulting to her feet, her control fleeing, she said, "Good night."

"Good night," he told her grimly. Confusion and self-rebuke were not emotions he liked to feel.

She gazed at him, her expression stern. "Don't you ever get hurt?" He nodded. Her hand rose carefully, and one fingertip traced the scar under his chin. "Before you leave maybe you'll tell me how you got this," she murmured. "You and me are sort of a matched pair, now. I feel sorry for us both."

He stayed on the balcony for a long time after she went to bed, his emotions in chaos. A reckless voice whispered, *Take her with you. Teach her everything you know. Let her teach you everything you've forgotten.*

Lifting his fingers to his scar, he cursed. *No,* Sebastien thought with bitter resolve. What a fool he was for involving himself with Amy, a vulnerable young woman who would never fit into his world. He would not become his father, ruthless and selfish, ready to ruin a life just to satisfy a moment's whim. He would not be doomed to watch the magic die again.

🦋

He was ten years old, and his life was wonderful. "*Maman!*" he called in an imperious tone. He was important and well loved, and he knew it. "I want you to go skiing this afternoon! Antoine and Bridgette and I are going to teach you!"

His mother turned from the astrology chart that she had spread across a handsomely carved desk. Behind her a large window gave her a Renaissance halo of sunshine. The snow-draped Alps rose craggy and majestic in the distance. Snow crowded the window ledge outside, and far beyond stood the white winter forest. Sebastien had never seen anything more beautiful than his dark-haired mother posed before the window.

She smoothed a hand down her plain white sweater, pausing for a second to touch a gold crucifix on a thick chain. Her fingers also brushed across the tokens of her most important saints—more than a dozen of them—spaced along the links of a second gold necklace. Then she tugged the hem of her navy skirt over her knees before finally laying her hands in her lap, signaling him that she was ready to listen patiently.

Maman was a wonderful listener, though she often looked confused when he told her about his studies at school. Maman was very old-fashioned; she had stopped going to school when she was only a little girl. She was so old-fashioned that she never wore slacks, even at home with the family. Sometimes Papa sent clothes from the design houses in Paris and made her wear them, but never slacks. At times Papa's comments about her clothes caused her to cry.

But today she seemed happy. She smiled at his attempt to draw her from the chalet. "No shush-shush for me, Sebastien." Her Breton accent lay heavy on the first syllable of his name. No one he knew spoke French the way Maman did, or made up new words such as *shush-shush*. No one practiced astrology or prayed to so many saints. Papa called her a Catholic witch, but Maman was no witch. Maman was special.

"I'll teach you to be modern, Maman," he assured her now. Laughing strangely, she came to him and fussed with the lint on his brightly colored sweater. He was nearly as tall as she, so she didn't have to bend much to kiss his forehead.

"Modern I will not be," she answered. "I am not smart enough."

"Yes, you are!"

"I am smart enough to be a good mother, yes?"

"Yes."

"Plenty for me, then." She hugged him close and he smiled against her soft shoulder.

~~Antoine and Bridgette bounded into the room then and~~
joined forces with him. Maman *would* come to the slopes
with them this afternoon, if only to watch. Papa would be
so pleased to have her there, they were certain. Perhaps he
would stop spending so much of his holiday with his old
friends in the village.

"I'll go and watch," she finally agreed, "if the younger
ones don't need me."

"Oh, Maman, the babies have fine nannies to look after
them," Bridgette said with mild impatience. Sebastien
goosed his sister and made her squeal. She was sixteen
this year, and *someone* had to keep her from becoming
too arrogant.

"Fiend!" she yelled at him, but grinned a second later.
"I'll ask Maman's saints to make you sprain your ankle on
the slopes."

"Sssh. My saints are kind," Maman said firmly.

Antoine, eighteen and nearly as tall as Papa, grabbed her
around the waist and whirled her until she laughed, much
to Sebastien and Bridgette's delight. "Then ask them to
make all the girls notice how handsome I am!"

"It would indeed take the saints' help for *that* miracle,"
Bridgette observed. Sebastien laughed as Antoine chased
her from the room. They were wonderful, his older brother
and sister. Everyone knew that Antoine was Papa's favorite
because he was the eldest and would head the businesses
someday; but Antoine never acted like the favorite, and
Sebastien loved him for that.

He loved fiery Bridgette, too, and his tiny sister, Annette,
who was four, and his younger brother Jacques, even
though Jacques was a very noisy baby. Sebastien felt lucky
to have such a fine family and such a wonderful life, filled
with travel, hobbies, and school, though Father was away
in Paris too often and Maman talked to herself oddly at
times, when she had been at their château in the Loire for
too many months without seeing Papa.

Several hours later they piled into the small van Papa
kept at the chalet for skiing excursions. Antoine drove;
Maman sat beside him, wrapped in a pretty fur coat, her
dainty legs and feet protected by tall boots. Sebastien sat

in the backseat next to Bridgette and amused himself by staring at her tight ski sweater until she threatened to wring his neck.

As Antoine drove down the winding mountain road to the resort at its base Maman stared silently out the van's window and seemed to daydream. Thirty minutes later they reached the cobblestoned parking area outside the great lodge, at the center of an exclusive little shopping district.

Philippe de Savin, tall and handsome, walked out of the lodge as they crossed its stone terrace. With him were several people whom Sebastien remembered vaguely from parties at their house in Paris. Antoine suddenly became brusque and whispered to Sebastien to hold Maman's hand.

When Sebastien did so he found it trembling. Alarmed, he looked over at his mother's pale, strained face. She was staring at one of the women among Papa's friends. "*Madame la comtesse*," she said softly. "I didn't know you were visiting."

The woman nodded without smiling, then turned and walked away. Papa looked angry. His other friends abruptly said that they had to finish their argument about the Americans' President Kennedy—some admired him, some didn't. They would settle the disagreement over hot rum inside.

After they left, Papa lowered an icy blue glare on Maman. He looked so strong and certain all the time; Sebastien wanted to be like him, but wished that he weren't so stern. Maman's hand clenched Sebastien's until it hurt.

"*Here* you invited her?" Maman asked in a bitter voice. "Where the family would be?"

Papa frowned harder. "Go back to the chalet, Gwenael."

He pivoted in his very formal, soldierly way—Papa had been a resistance hero during World War II—and walked back across the terrace. When he disappeared into the lodge Maman seemed to shrink and sag. Sebastien gazed from Maman's tragic eyes to Bridgette's tearful ones and Antoine's furious glower.

"What is it?" Sebastien demanded. "You all know. Tell me. What's wrong with Papa?"

~~Antoine grabbed him by one shoulder. "Come. We'll~~
bring Maman some hot chocolate. Bridgette, you and Maman sit down at a table."

Sebastien protested by dragging his feet as his brother
pulled him toward the lodge. Looking back he saw Bridgette, her arm around Maman, heading to a chair.

"What is it?" Sebastien asked again, and wrenched away
from Antoine's grip. "I'm old enough. Don't treat me like a
baby."

Muscles flexed in Antoine's clenched jaw. "So be it. I
learned about Papa when I was only a year older than you."
They went inside the lodge through enormous double
doors carved with Alpine landscapes. The room was filled
with plush chairs and game tables. Waiters moved regally
among patrons dressed in beautiful ski clothes. Other
skiers stood around a large stone fireplace in the center of
the room. The place smelled of wood smoke, fine liquor,
and money. Papa and his friends were not in sight.

"Here. Come here." Antoine led Sebastien aside. They
watched the crowd. "Listen closely and try to understand.
Maman loves our Papa more than anyone else in the world,
even more than she loves us. You'll realize that when you
get older and see her through a man's eyes."

"Of course she loves Papa! And he loves her!"

"No. He is ashamed of her because she comes from
common people. He thought she could fit in with his
friends, but she never learned how. She's no good to him
as a hostess. She can't help him entertain his important
business contacts. All she can do is raise children. But he
won't leave her, because he knows that she would never
give him a divorce. Maman is old-fashioned. In fact, sometimes I don't think Maman even lives in the same century
with us."

"You're lying! Lying! Why would he be ashamed of her?"

Antoine shook him roughly. "She was just a fisherman's
daughter he met on a holiday during the war! She was a
good Catholic girl who wouldn't screw him unless he
married her! He thought he was going to die at Normandy,
so the marriage wouldn't matter. But he didn't die—and so
there he was, stuck with an ignorant little Breton girl not fit

to be more than a servant. Our maman. And me, a son he didn't expect. So he made the best of it!"

Sebastien shoved him away. "How do you know all this?"

"Grandfather told me before he died. He was a cruel old man. He wanted to divide Maman from us children by making us feel ashamed of her. He said she trapped Papa into marriage. I've never told anyone this, but you. *We are mistakes*, do you understand? Papa loves us in his own way, but he doesn't love Maman, and under different circumstances he would never have married her. He stayed with her out of duty and gave her more children to keep her mind off her loneliness! *So we are all just the result of Papa's mistake.*"

Sebastien could scarcely comprehend the idea. Maman, unloved? Himself, unloved? *A mistake?*

"I don't like how Papa conducts his affairs," Antoine declared. "This time he's been too careless."

The *comtesse* strolled from a back room, and men turned to study her as she went to a table and spoke with the people there. Antoine made a sound of disgust and started forward, gesturing for Sebastien to follow. The *comtesse* saw them approach and stiffened. She ran a lovely hand, beautifully manicured, over hair the color of wheat and toyed with the ends that curled in a perpetual flip atop her shoulders.

"Hello again," she said warily, as Antoine and Sebastien stopped in front of her.

Antoine gave her a mocking bow. "*Madame la comtesse*, I would like to present my brother, Sebastien. He is no longer a child."

"What nonsense is this?" the *comtesse* asked impatiently.

Antoine turned to Sebastien. "Little brother, I present to you *madame la comtesse*. I went to bed with her when I was fourteen, but now she sleeps with Papa. She is the best-known of Papa's whores."

The *comtesse* slapped Antoine quickly and efficiently, as if she'd had great practice in slapping people who insulted her. Sebastien stared at her in shock. Papa had put his *zob* inside someone beside Maman? And his betrayal was another source of her unhappiness?

"If you ever speak to my maman again I'll kill you," he told the *comtesse*.

She laughed sharply and glared from him to Antoine. "I have no need to speak to your maman. Someday you boys will understand why your father needs me. He honors his mistakes. What more do you want?"

"She's not a mistake, you whore! And neither am I!" Sebastien yelled. The room went silent. Heads turned. Philippe de Savin strode out of the back and moved swiftly through the crowd. His patrician face held an expression so fierce that people leapt out of his path. The *comtesse* stepped aside as he came to Antoine and Sebastien.

"You disgrace me," he told them in a soft, deadly voice. "Take your mother and go back to the chalet. I'll see you both before bedtime in my study."

"Let the punishment fit your conscience," Antoine told him. "But leave Sebastien out of it."

"No," Sebastien said. He was close to crying with fury. "I don't care what he does or says to me now." He looked at his father evenly. "I hate you." Then he turned and walked outdoors with a measured, dignified gate. Once outside, however, he broke into a run and headed straight to Bridgette and Maman. "We'll go home and have hot chocolate," he told them, his voice trembling.

Maman gazed at him in horror. "Oh, no, no."

He hugged her. "It's all right, Maman. I love you. I love you."

Antoine reached them a second later. Stiff and silent, he directed everyone to the van. Maman huddled in the front seat and buried her face in her hands. She remained frozen and stonelike, until they were halfway up the mountain. Then she snapped her head up and gazed fixedly out the window. "Stop, Antoine. Stop at that curve. I want to see heaven."

Sebastien traded a bewildered look with Bridgette. Antoine parked the van on the side of the road. Everyone got out, watching Maman worriedly. "Heaven, Maman?" Antoine asked.

"Oh, yes, yes! Come and see!"

Antoine took her hand. They walked up the road to the curve. On its outer rim was a narrow ledge. The lip of the ledge was guarded by a low wooden barricade; beyond it the mountain plunged several hundred meters to a grove of trees.

Moving as if entranced, Maman staggered through the snow and stopped close to the barricade. She raised her voice in the old Breton language, which only she understood; it was no more French than a Welshman's tongue, to which it was related. She appeared to listen, then squared her shoulders. Wearily she lifted her hand to the blue sky, the mountains, and finally to her children, as she turned to face them.

"I asked Saint Yves-of-the-Truth to put the right where it should be and the wrong where it should be. And he has answered me. Content I shall be. Come here, my loves."

Sebastien and Bridgette clambered through the snow to her, and she engulfed them in her slender arms, along with Antoine. All of them cried, even Antoine. Maman laughed too brightly in the midst of it. "Let your maman do something useful, for once. Let me drive the rest of the way to the chalet."

"Maman," Antoine began with gentle reproach.

"Sssh! Let her drive!" Bridgette said firmly.

Sebastien nodded. "Yes!"

Antoine gave in with a tense shrug. Maman went confidently to the driver's seat of the van. Antoine settled on the left beside her. Bridgette took a place in the backseat again, but Sebastien climbed over the seat and sat on the floor of the storage area, where the skis were stacked. He needed to think about everything he'd heard at the lodge, and he wanted privacy to do it. He felt as if he was bleeding inside.

Maman started the car. But then she twisted in her seat and held out her hands to Antoine. "My firstborn," she said tenderly. "Your papa and I made you during the war. We made you three days after we met. We made you the night after we were married in my parish church."

"Yes, Maman," he said awkwardly.

She twisted toward the back and took Bridgette's hands. "My first daughter. I wanted a girl so much that time, and the saints gave me such a beauty!"

Bridgette patted Maman's hands. "I love you, too."

Next Maman stretched her hands out to Sebastien. He stood up and reached over the seat, feeling frightened for reasons he didn't understand. Her dark brown eyes gleamed at him. "And you—you are my magic. I gave you my grandfather's name. You're the only one Papa would let me give a Breton name. Sebastien. It was the name of a saint, you know."

"Maman, let's go home," Sebastien urged.

She nodded. "Yes. Yes!"

Sebastien sat down on the floor again and wedged himself into a corner behind the seat. He didn't feel as old as he had at the lodge. Right now he wanted to hide like a child. Maman put the van in gear and stepped on the accelerator.

The unexpected jolt threw Sebastien into the skis. He fought for a handhold as they poked him sharply. The tires squealed on the road. Bridgette made a horrified sound as the van skidded. Sebastien crashed into the wheel well with a force that knocked the breath from him. Dazed, he heard Antoine shouting, "No, no, no, *please*!"

Sebastien slammed into the back of the seat as the van hit the barricade. Bridgette's keening screams filled his ears, but for one second the momentum slowed. Then wood shrieked as the barricade split open. The ragged pieces clawed at the sides of the hurtling van like fingernails on a chalkboard.

Sebastien fell in strange directions. The world had turned upside down. Something sliced across his chin. He threw his hands out mindlessly and hit the handle of the van's back doors. Suddenly he looked up into blue sky. He was flying, but when a cloud surrounded him he came to a stop.

Half conscious, he lay still for a minute. His own violent shivering made him aware finally that he lay on his back in a snowbank. He lurched into a sitting position as his senses returned. The front of his white ski jacket was covered in blood, and when he touched a hand to his chin he felt a deep gash.

Far down the hillside the van was crushed between two trees. It lay on its side, a mangled hulk. Sebastien started toward it—falling, crawling, feeling nothing but terror.

"Maman! Antoine! Bridgette! Where are you?".

He circled the van, staring at its slowly revolving wheels. And then he screamed. Where the windshield had been, Antoine hung half out of the van, face-up, his body bent as if giant hands had snapped his backbone like a twig. His arms dangled beside his head, and he was covered in broken glass and blood. "Get up! Get up!" Sebastien begged. Antoine's eyes remained unblinking, blank.

Sebastien staggered to where the van's underside lay exposed, dripping oil and fuel into the snow. He climbed atop the vehicle and looked through the hole where the side door had been. The seats were crushed together, and the van's roof was flattened against them. Bridgette was twisted inside the wreckage, but one of her arms hung free. The hand fluttered as if an unseen puppeteer were jerking it crazily.

Bridgette was alive! Sebastien climbed inside as best he could. He yanked at the seats and searched with frantic eyes for his sister's face. But when he pulled a torn piece of upholstery aside he saw what had happened to her head, and he knew that she couldn't be alive. The hope inside his chest died, along with all other emotion. Numbly he climbed from the van and looked around. A dozen meters away Maman lay sprawled in the snow. With her fur coat twisted around her she looked like a small, broken animal.

When he reached her he slumped to his knees and touched her ashen face. Her eyes were shut. A bright red trickle of blood snaked from under the hair at her temple, making a puddle in her ear. Another streamed from one corner of her mouth. He wiped at it with the sleeve of his ski jacket. "Maman," Sebastien whispered. "I'll take care of you."

She opened her eyes wide, as if startled. Her lips moved

soundlessly. He bent over and put his ear against them. "Forgive, forgive, forgive," she murmured.

"An accident, Maman! It was an accident."

"No. I had to do it. Forgive me, Philippe, forgive me."

"Maman, it's Sebastien. Papa isn't here."

"No, Sebastien is dead, too. All of them I killed, Philippe. I had to take them with me. I saw the *Ankou* with his scythe and his coach. He came for me and them, too. He demanded them. I gave them to him."

Terrified, he shook her. "I'm Sebastien! The *Ankou* didn't get me! I'm alive!"

"Sssh, sssh. He will return if you protest." A froth of blood rose in her mouth and puffed gently with each word she whispered. "Saint Yves-of-the-Truth has placed the blame for everything on me. I take my punishment. Forgive."

"Maman, *don't* die. Don't. I forgive you." Sebastien put his arms around her and cradled her head. "I'm Sebastien. I'm alive. I'll take care of you. I won't let you die." He huddled over her in the snow, patting her face, sobbing, fiercely repeating his pledge. She stared at him. Her eyes were still on him an hour later, when the first people came to help.

"Your maman has gone to sleep. Let her rest," someone said, as a stranger closed her eyes.

Sebastien had stopped crying long before. His mind was filled with a confusion so terrible that it froze his grief. He sat back and looked at the rescuers in bitter, black rage. Fools. She wasn't sleeping, she was dead. She had killed Antoine and Bridgette, and then she'd let herself die. He hated her for it, but he loved her, too. Only one thing was clear—Papa was to blame, and Papa would pay for his *mistakes.*

In the weeks and months afterward everyone commented on his courage. They marveled at his control, at the way he continued to be strong, never crying, never asking for the least bit of sympathy. He became intensely protective of little Annette and Jacques, but where before he had been very loving with the servants and with Pio Beaucaire, he became reserved.

Papa's grieving attempts at friendship filled Sebastien with contempt, and he eventually told Papa with ruthless pleasure that Maman had driven over the ledge on purpose. Papa said he didn't believe that, but the truth shone in his eyes.

Despair and anger consumed Sebastien. It was not safe to love people; they could kill you because of it; even your Maman could kill you. Guilt tortured him for years. Why hadn't he died, too? Maman had insisted that he couldn't escape, and yet he had, at least for a while. He would have to be very, very worthy of their sacrifice, to atone. He would punish Papa at every opportunity, but more than that, he would punish himself.

Finally, out of the torment and the shriveled emotions that nearly crippled him, came one bright, obsessive goal—he would mend people. He would save so many lives that he could make up for not saving the ones that had counted most to him.

SIX

*S*ebastien de Savin was going so far away that he might as well have never existed. Amy's thoughts were dark and desperate as she sat on the white satin bedspread and traced the quilted imprint of a flower, flowing and abstract, a designer's fantasy. Dressed for work, she frowned at her denim shorts. One hand rose to tug angrily at the cheap white blouse she wore.

She pictured herself older, beautiful, wearing wonderful clothes. She stepped from a long black limousine into an alley of screaming, waving people. Sebastien, looking handsome and worldly in a black tuxedo, took her hand and walked beside her.

Real kind of you folks to come to the premiere of my movie, she called, waving one hand regally, with all her fingers clamped together like Queen Elizabeth. *My escort? Why, he's a doctor. A French doctor. And let me tell you, folks, he worships the ground I walk on.*

Her daydream ended with the sound of Sebastien's brisk, formal knock at her bedroom door. Amy jumped up and ran to it, her heart hammering. *See, folks? He can barely stand to be away from me.*

He stood in the doorway adjusting a silver cufflink on one sleeve of a crisp dress shirt. His gray trousers were sharply creased. The leather of his soft gray dress shoes gleamed. His hair had been brushed until the heavy, coffee-colored locks gave off a burnished sheen. Only the faintest of beard shadow shown on the carefully shaved planes of his cheeks.

She caught her breath at so much understated perfection. He didn't need somebody like her. Remembering how she'd tried to kiss him last night was humiliating.

"Hi. What'sa matter? Morning," she mumbled, overwhelmed by this towering, elegant presence. Then she blurted, "You look like you ought to be posing on a little platform in the men's wear department. Nice suit. Who died?"

He frowned, seeming surprised and at a loss for words. It amazed her that she was able to startle him at times. She supposed he considered her weird.

"Good morning," he replied finally. "I'm dressed this way because I have a meeting with the surgeon who supervised my training. I suppose you'd call it a farewell interview. *Finis.*"

Despair knotted her stomach. *He's leaving. Forever.* "Hmmm, did you want to talk to me about something? Is anything wrong?"

"Yes, we need to talk. Nothing's wrong. You always assume that something is wrong."

"Life is safer if you spot trouble ahead of time."

"Ah. Perhaps I agree. But don't always assume that the trouble is your fault." He ran a hand over an obstinate wisp at the crown of his dark hair. It was a habit of his. Every morning at breakfast she watched him try to tame the sprig. She loved that little cowlick. It almost made him a regular person. "May we talk, for a moment?" he asked.

Amy shivered. "Talk? Where? You want to come in?" She gestured clumsily behind her, then realized she was pointing toward the bed. Confusion and sorrow made her grimace; despite everything, she felt a smooth, deep need flowing through her body because of him.

He jerked his head toward the hall. "Come to the living room, please."

Her breath pushing harshly inside her lungs, she followed him there and sat on an unadorned black chair that glittered like wet coal. He went to a white sofa and gracefully folded his tall body onto the sharp angles.

She was embarrassed to look at him, afraid she'd cry.

She stared at a piece of Steuben crystal on the coffee table between them. "Are you lookin' forward to going to Africa?"

"Not really. The Ivory Coast is an affluent country, and Abidjan is a progressive, modern city, but the hospital there can't compare to those in Europe or America. But I have to serve my time in the national service, and working in west Africa is an appropriate way to do it."

"Oh. I guess I pictured you out in the jungle somewhere, fighting off lions."

"No. Abidjan is a very comfortable place. But I will also be treating patients at the rural clinics. Life there is more primitive, I assure you."

"Whack a lion or two for me," she told him, her throat tight. "And say hello to Tarzan. Uhmmm, look, don't worry about me. I didn't mean to be so dumb, last night." She started to rise. "Well, I'm off to the grape mines."

"No. No more. You've been fired."

She sank into the chair again and stared at him. "What?"

"I've fired you." He was not a man to waste words. She had already learned that about him. He was an important person; important people didn't dawdle. He leaned forward, rested his elbows on his knees, and stared into her eyes. "You have other things to do." He assessed her openmouthed expression warily. "Are you listening?"

"Like my life depends on it."

"I want you to prepare to attend the state university this fall. I'm going to pay your way."

She was aware of her mouth moving, but no sound coming out. She felt a miserable little laugh tickle her throat. Finally she said, "That's an expensive way to get rid of me!"

"I'm complimenting you, Amy, not insulting you."

"You always give scholarships to strangers?"

"Do you know how little the money means to me? The cost of sending you to school is such an unimportant amount to me that it's no sacrifice. So don't flatter me with your righteous indignation. *Strangers?* Is that what we are? I assumed we were at least acquainted, and occasionally friendly."

"If you want me to get out of here and leave you alone,

you don't have to pay me off! Just say, 'Get out, kid, you're pesterin' me!' "

"You're not 'pestering' me, although I admit that this conversation is beginning to sound like one of your bad American television shows. Are we actually bickering over a simple gift?"

She made a choking sound. Her voice dropped in an attempt at control. "Why do you want to do it for me? You don't owe me."

He reached across the coffee table and grasped her hands. "I don't want you to struggle hopelessly when all you need is a little help to make a good life for yourself. I've seen what that kind of unfairness can do to people."

"I'm gonna be somebody important. I don't need charity."

He said something dire-sounding in French. His large, supple hands tightened around hers in rebuke. "Is this how you repay my friendship? With accusations? You want to torment me?" He began to sound suspiciously melodramatic. "You want me to go off to darkest Africa and be distracted by worrying over your fate? I could be captured by headhunters through sheer carelessness—all because I was thinking about your poverty!"

She squinted at him shrewdly. "Headhunters? In a city?"

"Progressive headhunters."

Amy snuffled, disgusted but also amused. Her shoulders slumped. "College. You'd spend all that money for somebody you hardly know?"

"*Mon dieu*! Stop playing the martyr! You've slept under my roof for the past three nights! You came to me for help when you were hurt and homeless. You kissed me last night and said some very personal things to me."

"I'm not a martyr! I'm . . ." She fumbled, a torrent of frank words battling eighteen years of cautious silence. "I'm . . . confused." Amy pulled her hands away from his and covered her face. "I don't want you to feel sorry for me. I don't want you to feel guilty or responsible. That's the way people feel when somebody's just a chore to be taken care of. I want . . . oh, God, this is awful. I'm

babbling. ~~You're like some kind of Dr. Kildare~~ and I'm
Gidget with brain damage."

"Stop, stop," he commanded. "You're simply younger
than I am, that's all. Much younger. You haven't had a
chance to find out who you are, yet."

"So do you know who you are?" She raised her head and
eyed him fervently. "Who are you, exactly?"

He stiffened, looking wary. "A surgeon. A very good
surgeon."

"And what else?"

His expression darkened. "Games! This is pointless!"

"Are you happy with your life? Are you lonely? What do
you do for fun? Don't you want somebody to love you?
Don't you want to love somebody? Don't you ever want to
go sit on a hill somewhere and howl at the moon?"

"What does this have to do with my paying your way to
college?"

She leaned toward him. "What kind of person doesn't
want anybody to care about him, even when the person
who cares about him wants only to—to care about him,
that's all! What kind of person uses money to avoid getting
involved with other people?"

He vaulted to his feet and sliced the air with a fierce
wave of his hand. "Enough of this ridiculous posturing! I
have no use for 'being involved,' as you put it. I have no
time. I've offered to pay for your education. Be wise and
accept the offer, and don't expect sentiment along with it!"

Amy gasped. Why hadn't she thought of it before—she
could stay in touch with him this way. Of course! She'd
have to let him know how school was going. He wanted to
do something impossibly wonderful for her, because *he
didn't want to forget her.*

Shaking, she jumped up, too. "I accept. God, I accept.
Nothing like this has ever happened to me before, that's
all." She jammed fluttering hands into her shorts' pockets
and struggled not to trip over her own tongue. "I'll make
straight A's. You'll see! I know I can do it! And I'll write to
you all the time and tell you what I'm studying—"

"No." He drew himself up and looked at her coolly. "I'm
not your guardian. I'm not your warden. Once I leave the

country, you're on your own. It's up to you to manage wisely with what I give you."

"I thought you'd be interested—"

"No. I really won't be." His face was set in hard lines that made him look older and more forbidding. He went to a chair and retrieved the gray jacket that matched his pants. Slipping his arms into the tailored material, he gave Amy a brusque nod. "I think you should spend today making some phone calls. Request your academic records from high school. Call the university admissions office and ask for an application. You can have it sent to this address. After I leave for Africa, you may stay here until you leave for school. I'll have someone assist you with everything you need."

"Okay," she said in a small voice. "I don't know how to thank you. I guess . . . you don't really want me to thank you. I don't think you care whether people are grateful to you, or not." She raised bewildered eyes to his harsh, impatient ones.

His mouth tightened and he looked away. "When you're older, you'll understand that gratitude can be a very demanding emotion. Save it for the people who appreciate it." He paused. "There is only one thing you can do for me."

"Sure. What? Anything."

"I want to take you by the hospital this evening to see a patient of mine. A small boy. He's heard about you. I'd like for you to perform some of your sleight-of-hand tricks for him. Will you do that for me?"

Perform? Her mouth went dry with dread, but she nodded fervently. "Sure."

"*Bon.* I'll come back to pick you up about dinner time."

"Sure." She was overcome and could only look blankly at Sebastien. He was going to pay for her college education. He cared about her in some odd, protective way that confused her. He thought so much of the hokey carnival shtick Pop had taught her that he wanted her to entertain one of his patients. But after he left for Africa next week he never wanted to see or hear from her again.

She sank down on the chair. He was watching her closely. He took a beautiful silver pocket watch from his trousers and checked the time. He seemed reluctant to leave. "Are you all right?" he asked.

Amy lifted her chin. "I'm fine. I'm gonna be the first person in my family to go to college. This is a great day. When I get to be president, I'll send you an invitation to the White House. You better come."

"You'd make a terrible politician."

"Why?"

"Because you're too honest." He gave her a pensive, heart-stopping look, and she nearly bawled. "And you let yourself care about people too deeply. Good-bye. Be ready about six or so."

He left. After she heard the front door close behind him with an authoritative click, she forced herself to go into his elite kitchen and fix a huge breakfast. She sat down and stared at it, not eating a bite. She was learning from him. She was going to be tough and determined and successful . . . at something, certainly not politics or, she added firmly, any other kind of show business. She was going to be serious and dignified and very, very important.

Then she'd find him and make him wish he had cared.

❦

He would never forget the way she looked at this moment. Despite his resolve to be aloof, Sebastien bent closer as Amy folded one hand over Tom's and lifted the weak, pale fingers gently, fitting a coin through them, over and then under, in a slow imitation of her own skill.

"When you get out of this joint you'll be able to impress all your girlfriends," she assured Tom. "Either that, or they'll call you Ol' Fast Fingers. You'll be able to wave and pick your nose at the same time."

Tom's eyes glowed. "You're gross." His voice was a wisp of sound. "But funny."

She chuckled. Her hands trembled a little; she had admitted on the way to the hospital that performing made her sick with fear. Sebastien had murmured a platitude about courage while thinking privately that she was only suffering this torture to please him.

She brushed one sweaty palm over the skirt of her

ancient sundress and doggedly worked with Tom, her
charming, mischievous face set in lines of tension, though
she smiled at the boy constantly. When forced into contact
with other people she had an easy, loving way that capti-
vated them.

Tom's weary, intrigued eyes rarely strayed from her face.
"Talk some more," he whispered. "I like to hear you
squeak."

Color flamed in her cheeks, but she made a grimace of
comical dismay. "I donated my real voice to Minnie Mouse."
She put her hands alongside her head like mouse ears and, in
perfect imitation of a flustered Minnie, said, "Ooooh, Mickey,
I couldn't help it. Tinker Bell flew right into the ceiling fan.
Now we've got tinkle all over the house."

Tom smiled, for him, a tremendous effort. Sebastien
congratulated himself for bringing Amy to entertain the
child. He had wanted to show her what her talent could
accomplish, unfettered by her father's browbeating. He had
wanted to give Tom a moment of pleasure. He felt that he
had accomplished both.

"I think we'd better let you rest now," he said gruffly.

Tom's smile faded. His solemn gaze fell on Sebastien.
"You're going away. I overheard one of the nurses babbling
on the phone. She talked real low, but I got good ears."

"Hmmm. All right, then. Yes, I'm going to work in Africa."

"I don't want you to leave." Tom's chest moved harshly,
and he winced.

"You're getting well. You'll hardly notice that I'm gone."

"Bullshit."

"Your tongue is *very* healthy." Sebastien stepped forward as
a rasping sound edged into Tom's breath. "I should make you
apologize for using such language in front of a lady."

"Aw, bullshit," Amy interjected. She grinned, then stood
by the bed looking from him to Tom curiously. "Hey! I
know we haven't got much visitin' time left, but what if I
show Tom a card trick—"

"No," Sebastien said, his voice low and calm despite the
fact that Tom's color was rapidly changing from pale to
chalky. He studied the child's half-shut eyes and laid a
hand on Tom's arm. Fear. It jolted him, but he made his

voice light. "Now what are you up to, *mon petit*? Testing these machines again?"

Sebastien glanced at the monitors around the bed while casually reaching for a stethoscope. Tom made a mewling sound. "Something's wrong."

"No. You're tired from our visit, that's all." While he listened to Tom's chest he glanced at Amy. She stepped back from the bed as if sensing a problem, her hands clasped in front of her.

"I'll take my fanny outside," she said too cheerfully.

"Sebastien," Tom cried urgently, and gasped. His frightened eyes stared up into Sebastien's. "Don't go. I feel bad."

"I wore him out," Amy murmured, her tone full of horror. "I made him talk too much."

"No." Sebastien bent over the child and cupped his face. "Calm down. You're all right."

"I hurt."

A chill ran down Sebastien's spine. He nodded at Amy. "Go to the waiting room. Through the double doors beyond the nurses' station. I'll be there in a minute." She didn't move, and when he looked at her again she was studying Tom with tears in her eyes. "Out, I said." Her sentiment unnerved him, made him realize he, too, was upset.

She nodded jerkily. "See ya, Tom."

The child's eyes remained focused solely on Sebastien. "Don't go to Africa. I love you."

Sebastien fought an impulse to take his hands off the boy's face. He could deal with anything but this. "You love your grandmother. You love your friends. But me? You hardly know me. You don't need me very much. You'll see."

"You don't understand." Tom's voice was anguished and breathy. He struggled for air.

"Ssssh," Sebastien crooned. Without appearing hurried he pressed the nurse-call button.

"What are you scared of?" Tom demanded. "Can't I . . . love you . . . even if I'm kickin' the bucket?"

Sebastien shivered. His guard undone, he gazed blankly at Tom. Amy still hadn't left the room. Now she made a soft sound of distress. Sebastien shut his eyes. Why had these two troublesome people come into his life at the same time? He was surrounded by love for which he hadn't asked. And they wanted him to love them in return, which he simply couldn't afford.

"Sebastien." Amy was obviously struggling to say something. She faltered, hugged herself, then stepped close to the bed and bent over Tom. The boy's eyes flickered toward her. "Tom," she said softly, "Dr. de Savin is sad to be leavin' you. He just doesn't know how to say so. He's sort of like a turtle who won't come out of his shell because somebody hit him on the noggin once."

"I . . . a turtle . . . *mon dieu*," Sebastien said. "What foolishness!"

"Like a turtle," Tom whispered. Then he looked at Sebastien, his anxiety fading visibly. "Okay. I . . . love you. I understand. You're a turtle."

A nurse stepped inside the cubicle. Sebastien gestured to her to stand by, while he continued to speak with Tom. "You're a very troublesome patient, you know, and your Minnie-Mouse friend has been a mischievous influence—"

Tom's eyes rolled back. Alarms sounded from the machines attached to him. Sebastien whipped the sheet from Tom's body. "Amy. *Get out*."

She made a horrified sound and backed from the room as the nurse rushed past her. Sebastien studied the heart monitor near the bed. There was electrical activity, but no regular heartbeat. The nurse called a code for the emergency team. Sebastien planted the heel of one hand on Tom's unmoving chest. He began CPR and continued it while people filled the room, along with a crash cart bearing a defibrillator. Routines were followed precisely. Procedures were attempted. They failed.

I won't let you go. You can't die, Sebastien told Tom in silent fury, the despair rising in him. The potency of it frightened him; he had let himself become close to Tom, and now he was paying the price.

For the third time he shocked Tom's heart with the defibrillator. The lines on the heart monitor leapt, found an erratic rhythm, and clung to it. Nurses and residents kept working and watched in breathless silence, an almost palpable atmosphere of hope pervading the cubicle. Sebastien ground his teeth and stared at Tom's ashen, lifeless face. *Damn you, have the courage to fight. Don't be a coward.*

He passed a hand over his forehead and found a sheen of sweat there. Shame nettled him. He was cursing a sick child for being helpless. But the fury, his own helpless rage, would not let go.

"We're losing him again," a nurse said. "No pulse."

Sebastien stepped back. "Let's get him to the OR. I'm going to reopen him."

In the operating room he opened Tom's chest and found what he had feared. Several sutures from the previous surgery had not held. Blood poured from Tom's heart, flooding the chest cavity, soaking Sebastien's hands.

"He's bleeding out. He's gone," a resident said.

"No." Sebastien issued soft, fierce orders. Hands moved around his, helped, obeyed, tried to match his skill and failed. He cursed the heart silently, bit the inside of his mouth until it bled, fought to remedy another surgeon's poor work, while blood streamed everywhere. But he was winning. He could *feel* it.

There was no dramatic moment when life changed to death, just a slow defeat that pulled every ounce of energy from Sebastien's body. Finally, it was time to stop pretending that death had not come. Sebastien stood in stunned silence, with his hands still inside Tom's chest. Dully he stared at the carnage that had once been a wonderful little boy. He stepped back, blood dripping from his gloved fingertips. "I guess we can close now," someone said wearily.

A few minutes later Sebastien went back to Tom's cubicle, where the photograph of him—grinning on a sunshine-filled day—promised all the future an eight-year-old could want. Several residents followed him, curious about his mission. He ripped the photo down and tore it in two.

"Nice attitude," one of the doctors muttered. "Real professional."

Sebastien grabbed him by the shirt front and was drawing back a fist when the others latched onto him. The resident looked terrified.

Sebastien turned the resident loose and shrugged off the restraining hands. He went to the table beside Tom's bed, jerked the drawer open, and took Amy's video token. No one was brave enough to ask him what he was doing. Or to comment when he went back to the operating room and kissed Tom on the forehead.

❦

Amy forced herself to sit down and stop pacing around the waiting room. People shared the room with her; people pretending to watch *Hill Street Blues* on the television set in one corner, pretending that they weren't nervous.

Amy shivered. This was the big leagues of waiting rooms. She checked her watch. She'd been in here for an hour. Something awful must have happened. Her fears were confirmed a few minutes later, when Sebastien appeared in the doorway. His beautiful suit had been replaced with green surgical scrubs, rumpled and baggy. His hair looked damp, as if he'd had a shower.

His face was set in a strained, impatient expression. He beckoned her briskly even as she hurried over. "Let's go."

"What happened?" He smelled of antiseptic soap, and the skin of his face was red, as if he'd scrubbed it very hard. Amy pressed her hands to her throat and shook her head. "Oh, no, oh Sebastien—"

"Don't cry. *Walk.*" He grabbed her hand and led her down the hall, almost pulling her.

"Where are we going?"

"As far as we can."

He tugged her into an elevator. They leaned against the wall. Amy felt the hard, hot clamp of his hand on her wrist. She was afraid, but not so much *of* him as *for* him. She'd never seen so much anger in anyone's eyes. "The little boy died," she said wretchedly.

"I lost him. He *gave up.*"

"Why do you talk about it that way? As if it were your fault? You tell me not to feel guilty all the time, but you—"

"Don't analyze me," he said in a voice full of warning. The elevator came to a stop at the basement parking level. He pulled her over the threshold and swung her to face him. "I'm not in a mood to be kind to you. I don't want your simple little sentiments."

"How about this, then?" She knew she was losing her mind, because a sane person wouldn't do what she did next. She flung both arms around his shoulders and hugged him ferociously, and when he tried to push her away she held on. And then she stomped on his foot.

He made an ominous sound, lifted her by the elbows, and pinned her against the concrete wall beside the elevator doors. He looked furious, disbelieving, and desperate. "Are you insane?"

Her teeth were chattering. Her feet dangled against his legs. "Bingo. Stop it! Stop it, Doc! I feel like a real small sumo wrestler."

"What do you want from me?"

"I want to make you happy. I want to go wherever you want to take me. Anytime. Forever."

His anger shook them both. Between gritted teeth he said, "I'm not taking you with me when I leave for Africa. You're too young. I don't want to be bothered with you. Do you understand? *I will never take you with me.*"

"I *said* wherever you want to take me. *Anytime.* Forget about the forever part. Stop arguing. We only have a week. Doc, I'm sorry about Tom. I'm so sorry—"

"Be quiet! Do I look like I need your sorrow? Do I look like I care?"

She was crying now, big tears sliding unnoticed down her cheeks. "Yeah."

"Dammit! Don't cry!" His throat convulsed. He put her down, his fingers tightening on her arms. "Don't, don't—"

"Doc, it's okay, it really is. It's okay for you to cry, too."

"It's useless! Nothing is helped by it!"

"So what's the big deal, then?"

He shut his eyes and swallowed harshly, struggling for control. "Your logic . . . evades me, evades the issue—"

"The issue is simple. People die. You can't die for them. You hurt. You cry. After grieving you feel better." She struggled out of his grip and slid her arms around him again, then put her head in the crook of his neck. "Aw, Doc, you're such a sweet guy, and you don't even know it."

He shuddered and took her in a harsh, desperate embrace, his hands digging into her back and shoulders. She held him like that, standing in the muggy, dim recesses of a stark place, and listened to him cry.

She knew that she was an adult now; she had no fantasies about him changing his mind and taking her along when he left for Africa. She didn't deceive herself that she could bridge the gap between their ages and cultures, or their status in society. But for now, he was hers.

He pressed his cheek against her hair. She drew one arm from around him and lifted her hand to the tears on his face. He was very still and accepting as she stroked them with her fingertips, even angling his face so she could reach both sides.

But when he spoke, his voice was bitter. "Is this your idea of making me happy? This is a rather fascinating first for me."

"Doc, you're so dumb sometimes." She cupped his face in her hand and patted it gently.

"Enough. I'd hate it if anyone beside you saw me like this."

"I'll take that as a compliment."

They walked swiftly to his black Ferrari, their hands entwined so tightly that Amy's fingers ached. When she was seated in the passenger side, he leaned across her and grasped the seat belt, then jammed it into its clip.

"Put yours on, too," she said.

He stroked a hand down one side of her face, brushed his fingers over the small bandage on her chin, but ignored her order entirely. Amy felt a sad, poignant exhilaration as he jerked the car out of the parking lot and sent it rushing into the blue dusk of the summer evening.

They were silent while driving through urban streets draped in dogwoods; Amy clung to the armrest and watched Sebastien's expression of fierce concentration as he whipped the powerful car onto an interstate between office buildings that glinted in the setting sun.

He was not driving toward his town house. She settled in the seat and tentatively rested a hand on his shoulder. When she looked at the speedometer it read ninety. Her heart thudding, Amy watched the utter confidence of his hands. Even the fury inside him couldn't destroy their skill.

A sense of safety washed over her, instinctive and unquestioning.

Take me there fast, take me there so fast that I never look back.

In an hour they reached the foothills of the mountains north of Atlanta. The night rushed black around them, and the highway was empty. "Where are we going, Doc?"

He gave a rough, startled laugh, as if disgusted with himself. "I don't know. I don't even know where we are now. How is that for irresponsible behavior?"

"Pretty nice try, Doc. But I think you can do better. If you really want to get lost, let's get off this highway and find a nice dirt road."

He did, and a few minutes later the Ferrari was spewing gravel down an alley of forest. The tops of the trees made inkblots against a sky full of stars. The road left the forest and slid between old pastures with fallen-down fences. It rose up a steep hill toward the crumbling silhouette of a chimney.

Sebastien plowed the car to a halt at the top, sluicing the front wheels into the grassy roadside. "More suggestions?"

"This is my kind of territory," Amy told him. "You gotta roam it on foot. Comeon." They left the car and she grabbed his hand. On a silent, mutual signal they broke into a run across matted grassland wilted by the summer heat.

A dizzying time later they collapsed on the slope of a valley that stretched for miles. Lights winked in the distance; cars sped along unseen country roads. A new moon was rising; Amy looked at Sebastien sitting beside her in the faint light but couldn't read any of his emotions.

"Feel better?" she asked, her voice squeaking.

"Yes. Somehow . . ." He put his arm around her, and she leaned gratefully into the crook of it. He rested his head against hers and they watched the night sky.

"Wherever Tom is, he's okay," Amy whispered. "I hope you believe that."

"Tonight I choose to believe every good thought you give me."

"Sometimes you just have to throw back your head and—"

"Howl at the moon?" He hesitated for a moment, then

gave a long, bloodcurdling yell filled with anger and pain. It reverberated through the night, silencing the insects, making Amy shiver. He did it again. When she couldn't stand it anymore, she twisted to hold him. She caught his face between her hands and kissed him.

He made a harsh sound but took everything she offered, then wound his arms around her and returned fierce, raw energy so erotic that she shuddered and moaned against his mouth. He pulled back. "I said that I wasn't in the mood to be kind to you. There is too much going on inside me tonight. It makes me reckless. This can only hurt you. Now stop—"

"You don't have to worry about hurting me, or make promises about the future, or say a lot of hokey sweet things. You just have to be yourself."

"Most women would be dismayed at that possibility."

"I never look at things the way other people do. I guess you're in luck."

He shut his eyes for a moment, as if making a decision. "Very much in luck."

He kissed her again, this time sweetly and with obvious restraint. She sagged against him. Bending her backward, he laid her on the cool, matted grass and undressed her, his hands hurried but careful. She curled and uncurled her fingers, feeling shy, feeling amazed and wanting him so badly that he had already finished removing her clothes before caution prompted her to speak. "I haven't got any, uhmmm . . . I'm not on the pill, or anything."

"I was about to ask you." He pulled his wallet from a back pocket in the loose orderly's uniform. Opening it, he retrieved a small, flat package then tossed the wallet aside.

She felt herself blushing. "Oh. Okay. You're ready for emergencies."

Reaching for her, he pulled her upright for a moment and hugged her. "You assume that I go around indulging in 'emergencies'? No. But I'm not a boy. I can't play innocent."

She nuzzled her face against his shoulder and marveled at the thought that she was naked in his embrace. "Okay. I can. For both of us."

He guided her onto her back and sat beside her in the silver-hued darkness, stroking her from breasts to thighs, running the backs of his fingers across her taut, small nipples, drawing his thumbs down the center of her stomach, spreading his hands over her thighs and lightly brushing the inner recesses with his fingertips.

"So you haven't done this before," he whispered. He didn't sound surprised or dismayed.

She covered her face and groaned softly. "You're so French."

He bent and began kissing her breasts. "In what way?"

"You don't . . . make a big deal out of these things."

"That's as it should be, don't you think? Do you want me to turn away because you're inexperienced? Or do you want me to treat you like the beautiful woman you are?"

He put one arm under the curve of her back and lifted her to his skillful, slowly sucking mouth. She had never fantasized anything so wonderful. The aura of grief from the little boy's death gentled what was happening; even though inexperienced she realized that this was not a night for grand displays. His bluntness freed her to be a little frightened without embarrassment, even as her body throbbed.

There seemed to be a direct line of sensation from her breasts to the lovely ache between her thighs. When he slipped a hand between them and eased his fingers inside her, she forgot everything but the feelings that radiated throughout her womb.

In her excitement she waved her hands about, patting his shoulders, punching her fists into the soft, rustling grass, then finally reaching into the air, every muscle in her body arching toward the sky. He lifted her upright as if she were a doll frozen in an awkward position, her legs splayed, her arms sticking straight over his shoulders, while soft moans cascaded from her throat.

His hand massaged her intimately, covered in the warm moisture she felt spreading inside her thighs. "You're wonderful," he told her. "And so incredibly sensual that you make love in the way that suits you most, without being self-conscious about it."

She grasped his face between her hands and kissed him desperately, dazed and so much in love with him she could only express it by mewling deep in her throat, like an animal that was starving. It broke his reserve. He undressed hurriedly and lay down beside her, pulling her greedy hands over his body.

"I never thought I'd want to be happy tonight," he admitted. "And certainly not like this."

They both grew still. She studied his face. The moonlight and its shadows fell harshly on his tired, pensive expression. Amy stroked his jaw. "I won't tell your secret," she murmured. "I think you deserve to be happy, even tonight."

Shivering, he took her hands and kissed them. He placed the condom in them. "Never let anyone tell you that it's safe to be careless. Always insist on responsibility. Never let a man take advantage of you."

She bit her lip and looked away. "Stop being so French! I really don't want to talk about other men. I'm not that sophisticated yet."

The stillness that settled in him made her catch her breath. When he spoke, his voice was gruff. "I am sometimes too much a lecturer. And I forget how my logic sounds." He paused, and when he spoke again he sounded dismayed. "Forgive me."

"Just . . . go back to being a horny guy," she said firmly.

He made a strangled sound. "Oh, Miracle. Come here. Touch me. You have an incredible way of cutting straight to the point."

She fumbled with the condom until finally, with graceful gallantry, he helped her with it. He moved over her, parting her legs with his knees.

She put her arms around his neck as he settled his weight on her. Amy kissed him, opening her mouth to the hot thrusts of his tongue. His lips feathering hers, he murmured soft words of reassurance as he entered her slowly.

"Oh, Doc, you're not hurting me," she answered. "I knew you wouldn't hurt me."

"I'll try not to. Now hold me. Hold me tightly, and we'll see what kind of happiness we can make in only a week's time."

Amy latched her arms around him and buried a distraught expression against his neck, but the feel of his body and then, a moment later, the sweet desperation in his kisses coaxed her sorrow away. His darkness was frightening but irresistible, and she let it surround her.

SEVEN

*T*here was so little time left. Only a few days.

Sebastien listened to the low, seductive music of a Debussy prelude on the bedroom tape deck. The light of a bedside lamp made a pleasant sensation of heat on the side of his face. Across his room the time changed on the Tiffany clock atop his dresser: 4:02. In an hour or so the darkness in the corners of the room would take on the gray tint of approaching dawn.

But for now the night was still and eternal, and Amy lay under his arm, her back against his chest. She held his hand and stroked it with slow, lingering fingertips, unhurried, satiated, as he was, yet unable to stop caressing him. He burrowed his face into the hair at the base of her neck. Every sensation was vivid; the scent of her hair, the taste of her skin, the velvety side of her breast rubbing against his bicep.

The sheet felt like a caress on his lower body, and he remembered the playful, fumbling attention she'd given him with her mouth. *I didn't mean to bite you, Doc. I was thinking about oysters.*

Oysters. It was the first time he'd ever laughed at the expense of his testicles. He cupped his hips and legs closer to hers, and she sighed.

"Doc?" Her voice was husky, a private whisper liquid with emotion. "Do you ever feel like you're going to cry because it feels so good?"

He struggled for a moment, then gave up. What need was there to pretend with Amy? In her adoration, there was acceptance. She had no cynicism, no preconceived ideas about how a man and woman should withhold powerful information in bed. "Yes," he admitted. "Sometimes it's that wonderful."

"When you do it with me, I mean?"

"Yes. Of course that's what I mean."

"Doc?" She brought his hand to her mouth and kissed his fingers. The tension in her grip radiated through his body; she was quivering. "Do you think, after you leave, that you'll find somebody else, someone you'll want to do this with? I mean, do you think you'll find someone else right away?"

He held her tighter and shut his eyes. "No."

She exhaled wearily. "Good. I didn't want to think you would."

"Let's not talk about the future."

"Just one more thing. How . . . how are we going to say good-bye? I mean, where?"

"Where would you like to say good-bye?"

She turned over and looked at him. Her eyes were so tragic that a lump rose in his throat. No matter how right he was to leave her behind, he would always regret it. He had found himself reacting to life in a more open, more emotional way since he'd met her, and he knew he'd lose that ability when he left her. He reminded himself that he didn't enjoy being dependent on another person, and how foolish it was to be this vulnerable.

But when she gave him a lopsided smile he couldn't help but kiss her. "Funny Miracle. Where would you like to say good-bye?"

"In bed. After we make love one last time." She shook her head, tears brimming in her eyes. "But I agree, let's not talk about it anymore." She slid down and nestled her head against the center of his chest. "That music makes me think of children playing in a field full of flowers. What's it make you think of?"

"Autumn, with a cold, fast wind pushing the dead leaves through a forest."

"Oh."

He kissed her hair. "Too depressing, hmmm?"

"No. It suits you. You always look at the dark side of life."

"And *you* have a great deal of optimism for one who has had so little encouragement. Don't ever let it go. Don't ever let anyone keep you from following your dreams. You can be anything you want to be. You can have anything you want, if you never stop working for it."

"You don't know how much I want." She slid her arms around his neck, hugged him, and said no more.

"Learn the difference between what you want and what is best for you," he whispered against her ear. "That's the hardest lesson of all."

"Have you learned it?" She tilted her head back and searched his face desperately.

"Yes." He could see by the sorrowful expression on her face that she wouldn't ask him to explain; that she knew she wouldn't like the explanation. "Stop, Amy." He repeated the words, feathering them over her mouth. "No more thinking about the future."

"Make me stop," she ordered softly, her fingers sliding upward into his hair, then holdng him while she lifted her mouth to his.

"You are learning," he said, when she let him catch his breath. "You're learning very, very fast."

❦

Jeff Atwater stood on the chief of cardiac surgery's desk and made a toast to Sebastien, who had always impressed him as being his exact opposite. "Farewell, Frenchy. May the natives be friendly, the work interesting, and the karma good."

Sebastien bowed slightly. "Working with you has been an enlightening experience. Thanks to you, soon after I arrived here I learned all the slang for street drugs and many useful obscenities."

Jeff bowed back. "You're goddamned welcome." He got down from the desk and sipped from his cup of herbal tea as one of the cardiac residents made a farewell toast, a

rather timid one. Looking around, Jeff wasn't surprised to
find only a few people in the office. While the staff considered Sebastien brilliant, they didn't like him. He was too
young, too confident, too French. French surgeons tended
to rely on logic more than statistics. That drove American
surgeons nuts.

Jeff liked Sebastien because he was brutally honest, the
honesty part of a strict personal code. The man had integ-
rity. His arrogance held no hint of petty prejudice. Women
were both intimidated and fascinated by him, but he never
treated them like easy prey. He never promised more than
he gave. Jeff respected that, although for himself he believed women deserved every callous thing a man could to
to them.

As people began dispersing Sebastien called him aside,
looking more serious than usual, but distracted. Jeff wondered how much the child's bloody death had upset him.
Everyone on the staff of the transplant unit was talking
about the pitiful event and Sebastien's violent reaction.
Interesting that reaction, Jeff thought. Surgeons were such
perfectionists.

"I need to ask you for a rather involved favor," Sebastien
told him. "I hate to impose on you, but you're the only
person I can turn to."

As he explained, Jeff listened in solemn silence. Afterward he nodded sagely. "Fascinating. How can I pass up
the opportunity? See you at your place for dinner tomorrow
night."

He watched Sebastien leave the room, moving with a
long, confident stride as usual, nodding majestically to the
people who bid him good-bye, his manner indicating he
found the whole sentimental business awkward and unnec-
essary. This was a man who would probably spend most
of his life alone, because he had all the warmth of a cold
steel wall. Jeff had always been in awe of his self-suffi-
ciency.

That was why, as he mentally replayed their conversation, he felt stunned and disappointed. What kind of power
did this girl have over him?

Later, when Pio Beaucaire called to introduce himself

and ask for Jeff's help, he thought the coincidence was promising. He wanted to meddle in Sebastien's life, and here someone was asking him to do just that.

❦

Jeff chewed on a grape sucker and waited in the atrium of the trendy hotel restaurant. He disliked places that reminded him of his own greed. Impatience brewed inside him, though he cultivated an appearance of calm. Stress was an ailment suffered only by establishment types. He told himself that he hadn't lost his individuality. At the bottom of his dress shirt, loosely knotted blue tie, and tan slacks, his feet were encased in red socks and leather sandals.

He was a product of a fading era. He'd spent most of the turbulent decade of the Sixties as a tow-headed, jug-eared, lanky bookworm in the middle-class atmosphere of his parents' orange orchards, south of Los Angeles. But a latent sense of adventure caught up with him finally, and he experienced the seventies in college at Berkeley, floating on a cloud of drugs most of the time, waggling the peace symbol at everyone, and living in a commune.

A few bad experiences with hallucinogens and the discovery that he liked to make money had convinced him to sober up, and he'd gotten his M.D. degree, then gone into a psychiatric residency.

Which suited him perfectly. He was a master at using people, at charming them, at deciphering what they needed and feared. He liked power, especially when it concerned women, and the only time it had served him badly was when he married a sloe-eyed fashion model who spelled her name Aleze when it was really Alice. That pretention alone should have been enough to warn him, he thought later.

But he had been obsessed with her, and during the first six months of their marriage she had returned his adoration with an intensity that couldn't have been more real. They settled cheerfully into a cheap duplex in suburban L.A. When her career began to take off and she made the cover of a leading women's magazine, he had been so proud.

She spent his modest resident's income with abandon, a problem he could dismiss because he loved her so much. Their life revolved around glorious escapades in bed. When she gave him gonorrhea he was stunned. His magnificent Aleze was one part fashion model and nine parts prostitute, a profession she practiced from a nicely furnished apartment overlooking Sunset Boulevard.

After the divorce he had pulled up stakes and moved across the country. Having recently celebrated his twenty-ninth birthday, he stared into a mirror in the hotel lobby and wondered if his hair was receding as fast as he suspected. Oh, well, as long as he got everything else he wanted from life, he could live without hair. What he wanted was simple: money, professional prestige, and the chance to take revenge on as many women as were foolish enough to give him the opportunity.

He winked at his reflection. *Misogynist.* It had a nice ring to it.

"Monsieur Atwater?"

Jeff turned at the sound of the accented voice. A stocky man gazed up at him with limpid, solemn eyes. His robust face and white hair gave him the grandfatherly appeal of a clean-shaven Santa Claus, a corporate Claus in a double-breasted gray suit.

"Mr. Beaucaire?"

"Yes." They shook hands. "Thank you so much for agreeing to meet with me."

"No problem. Let's go inside." Jeff controlled his curiosity until they were seated at a table in the restaurant. "You said on the phone that you'd heard Sebastien mention my name over the past two years, and that's why you contacted me?"

"Yes. You seem to be a close friend."

"You're an employee of his?"

"Of his father's, actually. I've worked for the de Savin family all my life. Sebastien is to me as precious as a grandson. That is why I have come to you for help. Because I love him. Because his father loves him even more, and his father sent me to America to watch over him."

Jeff couldn't imagine Sebastien de Savin needing anyone's guardianship, but Beaucaire's sentimentality touched him. He was definitely distraught. "Why come to me?"

"Sebastien does not become friends with many people. You must be a fine man."

Jeff grinned, enjoying the praise. It was true—only an expert at manipulating human relationships could get beyond Sebastien's reserve. "What can I do for you, Mr. Beaucaire?"

A waiter appeared. They ordered drinks, and for no apparent reason the dapper Beaucaire began elaborating on de Savin history. It was like listening to a lecture on European civilization all the way back to Charlemagne. By the time Beaucaire finished, Jeff realized his point. The de Savins weren't just any family; they were one of the oldest lineages in Europe, and Sebastien was dawdling with a girl whose illustrious family history could probably be traced no further than the night grandpa met grandma at a hoedown.

"It shouldn't surprise you if I say that Sebastien has been involved with several women since I've known him, and each of them came away with freezer burns when they tried to get too close," he told Beaucaire.

"But this one . . . she is crafty. She is unique." Beaucaire spread his large, ruddy hands on the linen tablecloth in a gesture of appeal. "You can reason with Sebastien. I'm asking you as his friend to speak with him about this."

"But he's going to Africa soon. He'll leave her behind."

"Who knows for sure? This girl, she might appeal to his sympathies. She is poor and ignorant and tries to appear helpless. Her provincial charm may remind him of his mother, you see. I am absolutely certain that such thoughts influence his judgment."

"I doubt that Sebastien is looking for a mother figure."

"No, of course I don't mean it that way! But you see, his *maman* was a pitiful little thing, and she died in an automobile accident when he was a boy. It affected him greatly. No one has understood him since. His father has tried so hard, but without success. The *comte* de Savin is heartbroken over the situation, and he is growing older. He is not well. He wants to have his eldest son's love. He fears that Sebastien will never come home."

"And you want me to intervene in Sebastien's relationship with this girl? I admit it's a strange infatuation on his part, but I'm afraid you overestimate my influence with him. In fact, no one has much influence over Sebastien."

"This girl does, obviously."

"Hmmm. I wish I could help you, but—"

"Sebastien's father wishes to employ your professional services."

The conversation halted. Jeff studied Beaucaire in astonishment. "You mean pay me to assess the situation and make a report, without Sebastien's knowledge?"

His eyes never leaving Jeff's, Pio Beaucaire leaned forward and said in a careful tone, "There could be a great deal more to it than that. The *comte* de Savin would like your evaluation of the problem, certainly, but he would also be interested in your continuing *supervision* of it, as well."

Jeff traced a line of moisture on his martini glass while he weighed ethics and friendship against his bank balance. "You'll have to be more specific."

"Fifty thousand dollars now. Fifty a year from now, and a hundred when Sebastien returns to France, in two years . . . if he returns alone, and the girl is no longer a problem."

Jeff's mental scales slid heavily to the side of his bank balance. He hadn't been out of medical school long enough to acquire a champagne income, but he had a helluva taste for it. He watched his finger tremble on the martini glass. "Two hundred thousand dollars to intervene in a problem that will probably take care of itself, as soon as Sebastien leaves for Africa?"

"The *comte* is a cautious man."

"And an extravagant one."

"Only where love for his son and his family heritage are concerned."

Jeff drank his martini in one swallow. "I'm not sure I can do what he wants. This is a tad outside the bounds of professional ethics."

"He would be hiring you as a private consultant. No one

other than you, he, and I would ever know. And he really doesn't care how you accomplish his goal. You'd have complete freedom. He would never ask you to violate your honor."

"There's no guarantee I could succeed."

"Of course. He understands. Do your best, and if you fail, you'll be fifty thousand dollars richer, regardless."

"I'll have to think about this offer." He had already thought about it, accepted it, and begun spending the money, but he didn't want to sound overeager. "I promise you," he told Beaucaire, clasping the older man's hands, "that I'll try to help, even if I don't take the *comte*'s offer."

"Bless you."

Jeff gave him a reassuring smile. "Believe me, I'm an *expert* at dealing with manipulative women."

❦

Jeff was in a sour mood by the time he arrived at Sebastien's town house that evening. From the entrance foyer he sniffed the scent of fried chicken. Fried chicken. He'd learned to recognize the heavy, greasy aroma in every two-bit diner he'd ever entered in Atlanta. It was pervasive and uniquely Southern, lard sizzling around bloody fowl. It made him want to stuff his nose with tofu.

"You're letting her cook for you?" he demanded of Sebastien.

Sebastien studied him shrewdly. "You don't like this situation."

"I just didn't peg you for the domestic type."

"You're very astute."

"Did I get this right? She's only eighteen?"

"Yes. That also is not my type, I think you know."

"I *thought* I knew. Frankly, you've left yourself open for a lot of problems, pal."

"Hmmm. I regret requesting your assistance. I won't have you insult her. Let's forget that I asked—"

"No, pal, let's not forget. If you want someone who knows how to handle hysterical females, you've come to the right man. I'll give her the old big-brother treatment and ruffle nary a feather on her fledgling wings. But I tell you, I'm a little surprised."

"No more than I. Come and meet her." Something dark and warning rose in Sebastien's eyes. "And by the way, my friend, she is the least hysterical female you will ever encounter. Don't patronize her."

Jeff followed him through a curving hallway past his stark art deco living room and into the kitchen. He swept a quick, professional assessment over the girl who looked around hastily from her place at the stove.

Her eyes disappeared behind her lashes as she gave Sebastien a vivid smile. It became uncertain when she looked at Jeff. The smile tugged at the large Band-Aid on her chin. She'd been smacked by her father, Sebastien had said. Jeff's case studies were full of patients who'd suffered abuse. They were emotionally vulnerable and desperate to find security. She was the kind who'd prey on a man's protective instincts. No wonder Beaucaire was worried.

He could understand her appeal. There was an intriguing mixture of merriment and caution in her face. She had a goofy, endearing smile. Auburn hair curved gracefully around it in a short style with feathery bangs. Her jeans and plain white T-shirt showed off long legs and a decent ass. She had an adequate set of knockers.

But she was just an odd, timid-looking eighteen-year-old. Yet she'd managed to move in with Sebastien and convince him to pay her way through college. Jeff watched with hidden amazement as Sebastien went to her and took her hand. He drew her forward, not with obvious affection but with solemn consideration that said even more. The man as treating her like an equal, it seemed.

"Amy, I'd like to present Dr. Atwater. Jeff Atwater. Jeff, this is my house guest, Amy Miracle."

Jeff stuck out a hand. "Hi ya."

"Hi." She shook firmly but briefly. Color flamed in her cheeks. She stuck her fingers into her jeans' pockets and stared at a point at the center of Jeff's sport shirt.

He tried to draw her out. "So . . . you're cooking dinner, I see. Do you like to cook?"

"Sure."

"Fried chicken, right?"

"Yeah."

"Smells great," he lied. The girl had about a five-word vocabulary. What else did she have, besides a mouth that could probably suck chrome off a tail pipe, or some other incredible sex skill that held Sebastien's attention?

"What else is that I smell cooking?" he asked politely.

"Turnip greens."

"Great. My favorite. So . . . you're planning to go to the university this fall, Sebastien tells me."

"Yeah." She hugged herself, met his eyes for a second, then looked as if she might sway from one sneakered foot to the other. Sebastien moved past her to pick up a glass of wine from the island at the center of the kitchen. In passing he stroked a hand over her shoulders. The gesture might have been meant to reassure her. If it was, it worked, because she relaxed visibly. Jeff found the silent communication disturbing; it was so intense for two people who were completely unsuited to each other.

"What do you want to study?" he asked her.

"I'm not sure."

"For the first two years she'll be in a basic liberal arts program regardless of her major," Sebastien interjected, pouring amber liquid into a fluted wineglass. "She has plenty of time to decide on a major."

"Oh, I'll study something respectable," she added quickly. She sounded determined, almost adamant. "Maybe I'll become a lawyer."

Now that she'd managed a full sentence, Jeff did a double take over her voice. Besides having a pronounced drawl, she sounded like she was just coming down from a hit off a helium balloon. Cartoon characters had voices like this, not real people.

Recovering his train of thought, he told her, "Pick a more respectable profession than the law. Like stealing used cars or robbing old ladies. Why in the world would you want to be a lawyer?"

She turned beet red. "Well, I, uhmmm—"

"Ignore him. He has some personal reasons for disliking lawyers," Sebastien explained. Once again he rested a soothing hand on the girl's back. She shot him a look filled with the kind of devotion one sees in an adoring pet— totally focused and sincere. Jeff cursed silently. A kid with an infatuation. This had more potential for causing Sebastien trouble than he'd expected.

Sebastien handed him a glass of wine. "One of the best zinfandels you'll ever taste."

Jeff made a dramatically derisive sound. "Domestic or imported?"

"Imported. And a de Savin label. What more is there to consider?"

"My man, I should take you to the wineries in California sometime. After you sample a little of the home brew you'll lose that arrogant French attitude."

"California pretensions do not make classic wines." Sebastien included the girl in the repartee, nodding to her.

She grinned at him, abruptly open and unabashed. "We had better appear what we are, than affect to appear what we are not." She spoke as if reciting.

Sebastien actually laughed, the unusual sound aimed solely at her. "You remembered. La Rochefoucauld."

"I was listening real hard when you read that to me." She chuckled, and they shared a private look that hinted at intimate conversations. Jeff sighed. God, this was ludicrous.

Jeff plunged ahead. "Well, Amy, if you and I are going to be housemates for a few days, I guess I better warn you. I'm bringing my collection of Ray Charles albums over here. I hope you can stand to hear 'Hit the Road, Jack' three or four times a day."

She looked startled. "House . . . mates?"

Sebastien's expression became dark. He shot a rebuking glance at Jeff. "Let's go outside and talk."

The girl's cheerfulness faded. She seemed to contract, and by the time they reached the courtyard and sat down in wrought-iron chairs, she appeared ready to disappear into the plush gray pillows.

Sebastien held her gaze with unwavering, though not angry, eyes. "After I leave on Monday, Jeff will stay here with you. He'll help you make arrangements to attend school. He'll make certain that you find a place to live on campus."

She studied Sebastien in silence, her mouth an anguished line of control. "You think I'll waste your money, Doc? You think I need a chaperone?"

"No. I think you need a friend. There's a lot you don't know. Jeff will make certain you don't have any trouble."

Jeff restrained a sardonic smile. Of course this babe could waste the money if nobody kept her under control. Women had that inclination anyway, regardless of age. His ex had left him owing twenty-thousand dollars in credit-card charges.

Jeff lifted a ladybug from its struggle on the slick tile floor to a safe spot on the leaf of a philodendron. That was the limit of his compassion for a female of any species.

"All right," the girl said. She looked at Jeff, having regained enough of her dignity to eye him with a frown. "But I want you to know . . . I want you to understand, Dr. Atwater, that I don't need much help. I'm not some kind of charity case you gotta feel sorry for." She looked at Sebastien. "I want you to be proud of me someday."

He was visibly moved. "I'm very proud of you already. I know you'll do well."

"And maybe we'll meet again."

"Perhaps."

Jeff gave them both a sympathetic smile, the one he used on delusional patients. They couldn't see how pathetic this situation had become, and how dangerous. No wonder Sebastien's father was concerned enough to send Pio Beaucaire in search of professional help. The fact that Sebastien had *asked* him to take care of the girl eased Jeff's guilt. This duty promised the perfect blend of personal and professional satisfaction.

The two hundred thousand dollars, of course, was merely a fringe benefit.

❦

Sebastien placed the green silk scarf next to her face. "See? This is your best color. Exactly the color of your eyes."

Amy stared into the oblong mirror atop a display case. She was too distracted to concentrate on her face, with its frown and stitched-up chin. Instead she looked at the reflection of a fantasy world behind her. Neiman-Marcus. She'd heard about this place. It was like being in church and made her want to whisper.

Sebastian, even dressed simply in charcoal-gray trousers and one of his white polo shirts with a tiny de Savin crest on it, radiated style in a way that said his money was old, very old. Sales clerks had stared pointedly at him, then at *her*, when they'd entered the store.

"Are you listening?" he asked.

"Sure." She looked at herself reluctantly. "Green. Okay. I'll remember." She chuckled.

"What is it?"

"I never knew a man could be so good at picking out clothes."

"The best clothes designers in the world are men."

"But they're gay."

"Not all." He looked at her wickedly. "Perhaps I'm gay."

She burst into laughter and covered her mouth. Amy shook her head at him emphatically. "You're not even *cheerful*."

He sighed and laid the scarf over the shoulder of her T-shirt. It looked silly against such an ordinary background, she thought. But then, she looked silly shopping in Neiman-Marcus. "This feels wrong," she told him, her humor fading. "Can we go now?"

He gestured at the bags piled around their feet. "We're not finished."

"Doc, I can shop by myself . . . later." She pointed to the green scarf. "Don't worry. I'll buy everything in green. Even my underwear."

"I thought you enjoyed getting out of the house."

"I can get out all the time after you leave. I'll *want* to get out."

Subdued, they stood in silence, sharing a bittersweet look. He tossed the scarf onto a counter, then reached for her hand. "I hoped to postpone the inevitable. When we return I have to begin packing."

A long, ragged breath slid from her throat. "Oh."

"I can't put it off any longer. It's fairly simple—I'll only take clothes and personal items. Pio—Monsieur Beaucaire—will arrange to close up the house and sell everything."

"Just like that? You won't keep anything?"

"There's very little that's important to me here."

Including me, she thought sadly. "What about your cars?"

"The Cord will be shipped back to France." He shrugged, unconcerned. Amy knew she'd never understand what it felt like to be that rich. He reached into a pocket of his slacks and removed a set of keys, which he placed on her palm. "I thought perhaps you'd like to have the Ferrari."

He led her out of the store, while two clerks trailed them carrying her new clothes. Amy said nothing after his announcement about the car. When they reached it she gave the keys back. "I can't drive it. Not right now, anyway. You drive."

He nodded. After they were seated inside the Ferrari's plush interior, with the bright, hot sunshine of the August day beaming through the open top, he took her face in his hands and looked at her carefully. "Don't you want the car?"

She shrugged, finally. "Sure."

"Don't overwhelm me with excitement. Try to control yourself."

Amy took a deep breath. "I'd rather have a one-way plane ticket to Africa."

She watched the impulsive words register on his expression, making his eyes turn cold. "That's impossible."

"Why?" She had to ask. She had to know, even if the question made him furious. "I wouldn't cause any trouble. I'd do anything you wanted—"

"I want you to stay here and attend school."

"But if you care about me so much, why—"

"The subject is closed, Amy."

"No, no!" She shook her fists at him. "How can you be so wonderful to me . . . how can you give me all this stuff and take me to bed and touch me the way you do and not ever want to see me again?"

"I told you from the beginning it would be this way. Nothing has changed. Don't ruin our last two days with this childish questioning."

"Don't call me a child! You can't—you can't *screw* me like I'm a grown woman and then talk to me this way. I don't care if you're eleven years older than me. You're not even thirty!"

"I am an eternity older than you are. And I'm not taking you with me to Africa. Now do you want to hate me and be angry for the next forty-eight hours, or will you accept reality?"

"Doc, why?" She was pleading with him. "Am I so awful that I'd embarrass you?"

He grabbed her hands and jerked them lightly, his expression strained. "No. I promise you, it's not that. If I took you to Africa you'd be bored and restless. You would resent me for the hours I work. You'd feel homeless in a strange country—you can't speak French, which is all you would hear in that part of Africa, except for the native languages— and you'd have no friends." His voice curled around her like a whip. "You'd come to hate me."

"Tell the truth. I'm too young. I'm not educated enough. I'd never fit in with the kind of people you come from."

"You *are* too young. You *do* need more education . . . you deserve it. And yes, you'd never fit in, but I don't *want* you to fit in with other people. I want you to be what you are, because it's wonderful. I've seen what happens when someone who has a unique spirit is forced to change."

"You're trying to make it sound like you're leaving me for my own good."

"I am. Listen to me, Amy. You're an adult. I'm treating you like one. Now act like one. Do what's best for your future: Stay here and go to school."

Her defiance sagged. It was useless to argue with him. She'd make a complete fool of herself and ruin what was left of their time together. But Amy asked grimly, "Do adults sleep together and then deliberately forget they ever met? Is that what it means to be an adult?"

He sat back in his seat, drained of fight as well, and rubbed his forehead. "Sometimes."

"Does your mama know about this?"

"My mother is dead. I told you that the other night, remember?"

"It was a joke, Doc. You missed the point."

"You see? Half the time, I don't even understand your humor. You'd get tired of explaining it to me." He fumbled the Ferrari keys, dropped them, and cursed viciously under his breath. Amy watched him in dull surprise. He wasn't angry with her, he was angry with himself. The realization made her reach over and grasp his hand. "I'll act like an adult," she assured him. "But I'm never gonna forget you."

He sat still, his eyes burning into hers. "You will. I promise."

"I won't." She took the key and jabbed it into the ignition. "Let's go. And be careful driving my car home."

❦

She stood in his bedroom helping him pack, smoothing her fingers over each shirt, stroking each book, studying the family photographs in their simple sterling silver frames because each was a lifeline to his world. His sister and brother looked a great deal like him, though both were younger and his brother had a cocky, almost insulting smile.

His mother, standing in front of a flower garden in an old, faded picture, gazed out at the world with a shy smile, dark eyes peeking from under arched brows. She was such a delicate, whimsical-looking person that she could have been an elf who'd just popped out of the marigolds for a second to have her picture made. Amy felt immediate empathy with her. Here was someone who seemed out of place. Must have been a trick of the camera.

She turned the picture frame in her hands, reluctant to put it down. On the back was written, *La comtesse de Savin. 1957.*

"What do you find so fascinating?" Sebastien asked gruffly, moving over to her from his dresser.

She pointed to the name. "What does *La comtesse* mean?"

"It's one of the old titles. No one pays any attention to them now. My mother never used it."

"But . . . you mean, this is like a royal title?"

"Something of that nature, yes. But it's worthless."

"You—you're *royalty*?"

"Only in the most pretentious circles," he said with a sardonic smile. He placed shoe boxes in a trunk.

"Do *you* have a title?"

He clicked his heels together and bowed. "Viscomte de Savin, at your service."

"Should I curtsy, or just get in my pumpkin and ride away?" At his puzzled scrutiny she explained, "Like Cinderella. You know, when the party's over, the coach turns back into a pumpkin?" She wrapped his mother's photograph in a sheet of bubble plastic and placed it into a box, her hands trembling.

Sebastien put his arms around her. "Come with me. The party isn't quite over."

He guided her to the courtyard, and they shared a lounge chair, holding each other and watching the sun set in a balmy, purple-streaked sky. A little while later they undressed and she made love to him there, sitting astride his thighs with her knees buried in the chair's thick cushions.

He gripped her hands tightly and held them against his chest as she rocked over him, her eyes half-shut. Amy felt him moving inside her like an ache of sadness. She wasn't interested in pleasure tonight; closeness would do, being as close to him as she could get. She bent over and put her arms under him, held him to her as his hands went to her hips and stopped her.

"Be still," he told her gently. "Put your head on my shoulder. Yes. Like that. The other need is unimportant."

Later she lay beside him and he cupped her breasts in his hands. He watched his fingers move over skin still imprinted with the fine pattern of his chest hair. He lifted her right hand and kissed the lopsided heart tattooed on her wrist.

"I'm gonna have that tattoo taken off someday," she assured him.

"No. It's not shameful." He kissed the line of stitches under her chin. "Not shameful."

She touched her forefinger to the more prominent scar on his chin. "Will you tell me how you got this?"

He nodded. He related a very brief story about the accident that had killed his family and injured his face—how their van had slid off an icy mountain road when he was ten years old—and Amy listened with sad fascination. He spoke of the deaths unemotionally, and she decided that he hardly remembered them, it had all happened so long ago.

She helped him finish his packing. He stacked the suitcases, boxes, and trunks in the hall foyer. The town house seemed unchanged. He'd taken a clock here, a few special books there.

He cooked dinner for her, but neither of them ate much. Amy cleaned the kitchen, wearing only his white undershirt. He sat at the counter, checking notes he'd made about his travel plans, but sometimes when she glanced his way she found him watching her. Amy finished at the sink and stood, gazing blankly at the line of ceramic pots filled with herbs on the window ledge.

"These'll die," she said wretchedly. She realized that she was clenching her hands together until her knuckles ached.

Sebastien came to her and stroked her hair. He wore nothing but snug blue jogging pants, and when she rested her head against him she smelled the scent of her inexpensive perfume on the bare skin of his chest.

"Why don't you take the plants?" he said.

"Thank you." She put her arms around his waist and held him tightly.

"Put on some clothes. Let's go for a walk. It will help."

They walked in silence through the summer night. Amy's senses were dull with misery; she could barely stand the poignant sweetness of the air, filled with the scent of flowers and newly mown grass from manicured lawns. The lights of the town houses shone through expensive draperies, happy and bright, and so much in contrast to the dread inside her that she couldn't look at them.

"Jeff Atwater will come by in the morning at nine," Sebastien told her. His hand tightened around hers, but he looked straight ahead. "Before I leave for the airport."

"Okay."

"My flight leaves at eleven. I'll only be taking two of the suitcases. Pio Beaucaire will send someone for the rest tomorrow afternoon."

She halted him with an urgent little motion of her hand and looked up at him wearily. "Please, don't talk about this anymore—"

"You should stay busy. Jeff and one of his *many* ladies will be taking you places . . . to dinner, to concerts. And you'll be getting ready to attend school in less than a month."

"Okay, Doc, okay. And what will *you* be doing?"

"Working. I report to the hospital as soon as I arrive in Abidjan."

She met his gaze somberly. "And in a couple of years you'll be going back to France?"

"Yes."

Amy nodded but said nothing. She was learning when to speak up and when to keep quite. A small plan began to burn inside her, making tomorrow seem less terrible: In a couple of years, when she was older, better educated, and respectable enough, she was going after him.

❦

Morning came too soon, bleak and unrelenting. Sebastien showered slowly, hating to lose the scent of her body. What would Amy bring to his life, if he gave her the chance? Was he foolish to turn his back on the one person who made him feel capable of love?

But how could you bear to condemn her to your lifestyle? She should be in college; she should be developing her own independence and self-worth, now that she was away from that bastard of a father who'd cowed her.

As he dressed he stared into the mirror over the bathroom vanity, seeing his haunted eyes clearly. *In two years, when I leave Africa, perhaps I should come back and see her.*

He'd leave her alone until then. He'd let her decide if playful, light-hearted boys her own age were more appealing. He'd let her get a taste of what her newly expanded world could offer, how many choices. And then, if she still thought that she loved him, and was seasoned enough to understand the pitfalls, perhaps. . . .

He went into the bedroom. She sat on the side of the bed hugging a pillow to her chest, her head down. She was dressed in her jeans and a new light, pink blouse and new jogging shoes, unspoiled white. She looked like a college student, and that helped him keep his resolve. He crossed the room and sat down beside her.

Suddenly there was a lump in his throat. He was glad when he didn't have to speak right away because she dropped the pillow and put both arms around him, pressing her tear-streaked face against his neck. "The last time was wonderful," she murmured. "I wanted to say so before you went to take a shower, but I was afraid I'd cry again. I look like I've got frog eyes, as it is."

"But they're beautiful frog eyes. And you have lovely green skin."

She laughed shakily. "There's hope for your sense of humor. Keep working on it." When he hugged her fiercely she made a tragic sound. "Dr. Atwater's here," she whispered. "He's hanging around in the kitchen. He said he'd take me to breakfast after . . . after, you know."

"I'll speak to him on my way out."

A convulsive little shiver ran through her at those words. "I don't want breakfast. But I'll go. I'll be all right. I'm as strong as you are, okay? And I'm gonna make you proud."

Sebastien laid his face against the top of her head and shut his eyes. He never prayed; he wasn't certain that he was praying to anyone or anything in particular now, but he found himself asking silently, *Please let my decision be the right one.*

"You can make anything you want of your life," he told her. "Do that for me. You're very special. Don't ever let anyone tell you otherwise again."

"I'll try not to. And you . . . Doc . . . Sebastien . . . please don't look at the dark side of things so much. I'm afraid for you." She wiped her eyes roughly. "I sound like a kid who's seen *Star Wars* too many times. But you've gotta fight the dark side of the force, okay?"

"Yes. I'll try." He kissed her, trying to savor the last, vivid contact as long as he could. Then she raised her lips to his eyes and forehead, kissed his cheeks, the tip of his nose, and finally the scar on his chin. "A matched pair," she told him, drawing one fingertip from his old scar to her new one. "I'm glad."

He struggled for a moment. "I'm glad, also." Sebastien took a deep breath and tried to let it wash the regrets out of his chest. "It's time, Amy."

She caught a sob in her throat and kissed him again. He bent her back on the bed, his hands shaking a little as he stroked her face. When he gently pulled her arms from around him she turned over quickly, her head bowed against a pillow, her hands knotting in the silk casing. "I can't look. Good-bye. Good-bye. I love you so much. I always will—"

"Amy, don't," he said gruffly, then bent forward and pressed a hard kiss to the crown of her head. "You give so much happiness to others. Now go and find some for yourself."

He left the room, closed the door behind him, and stood for a moment with his eyes shut. Walking away from her was the hardest thing he'd ever done. Compared to that, admitting that he loved her was easy.

TWO

EIGHT

S eated on the floor of her tiny dorm room, Amy bent over a book and gnawed the end of her pencil, trying to concentrate. For Sebastien's sake she would even suffer through algebra.

She had learned a lot about survival during the past seventeen months, a different kind of survival from the cringing, don't-notice-me-please behavior of the past. She had become more confident. She had amazed herself by her ability to make good grades, to talk to strangers, to manage her life without anyone's supervision. She had learned that a person could get up every morning and carry through every day despite grief.

She called Jeff Atwater anytime she needed the advice of an experienced person, and he was always eager to help. He phoned often just to chat with her, and she loved their easy camaraderie. He regularly drove up from Atlanta to visit, and they held long discussions about her past, and Pop.

Jeff had helped her see how she'd let Pop's problem ruin her own self-image. With Jeff's guidance she had even grown secure enough to endure holiday dinners with Pop and Maisie. But those were the only times she could bear to see them.

Good old Jeff. She had come to like him a lot. She glanced eagerly at her watch. A few minutes later she was surprised to hear footsteps stop at her door. Someone banged on it lustily. "You can't keep her prisoner in there!

I know you've got the princess! Now let down this draw bridge!"

Laughing, she bounded to the door and flung it open. Jeff stood there, a bright-red poinsettia tilting toward her from the cradle of his arm. "You're here an hour early!"

"It's Christmas season, m'lady. You shouldn't be studying.' He glared at her. Over snug jeans and a colorful sweater he wore a jacket that seemed to have been fashioned from a Navaho blanket. "Grab your coat and let's go eat. I'm starving. Oh! A flower for you." He thrust the poinsettia at her with mock shyness.

Amy set it on her tiny dresser, stroked the brilliant leaves, then smiled at him. "Thanks. You made my day."

He peered inside the room, studying the half that had been cleared of her roommate's possessions. "Did you lose *another* one?"

"Yeah. She was flunkin' out, so she went home early for Christmas." Amy pulled a heavy raincoat over her jeans and sweatshirt, then jammed her door key and wallet into the coat's pockets. "Is it something about me? Am I bad luck? Why am I always alone?"

He pulled her into the hall and shut the door. "Because no one should have you but *me*," he said with glorious lechery, and swung her around in a circle until she was breathless and laughing.

She hugged him. "That's right. I'm all yours." Arm in arm, they marched down the hall.

After dinner at a restaurant in town, they walked the block back to campus. In a park near the adminstration building they sat under the stately, leafless oaks and watched twilight ignite the street lamps.

"Elves are responsible for that," Jeff announced.

"Yeah, and Santa Claus is complaining to their union about the overtime." She clenched her hands against the calves of her legs and tried to sound casual. "I guess Sebastian didn't send you a Christmas card or anything, huh?"

Immediately Jeff's mood changed. It happened every time she mentioned Sebastien. "Has he *ever* sent me a card or note, Amy?

"No, but—"

"In almost a year and a half has he ever written or called to ask how you're doing?"

"No, but I keep thinkin' that—"

"Amy. Sweet Amy." His voice became cajoling. He put one hand on the back of her neck and rubbed circles with his fingertips. He always did this to her when she mentioned Sebastien. "He's not interested in you, Amy," he murmured.

"For now."

"For good."

Jeff's gaze locked with hers, and he moved so close that she could feel his breath on her cheek when he spoke. "You're going to forget about Sebastien. He's not coming back. Accept that. Say it, Amy. Say, 'There's no future for him and me together. I have a life to lead without him. He's forgotten me. I won't hold onto unrealistic ideas about him.' Say it."

His tone hypnotized her. He sounded so sad. But she shook her head. "He belongs to me in a special way. I'll never forget him."

"Amy. Don't hurt yourself with fantasy."

Each time Jeff got into one of these soft-spoken moods it made her burn with confusion and fear. What if he were right? But she never agreed with him. Jeff, rather than get mad at her, would only rub her back or her neck a while longer and continue speaking, his voice always low, sometimes almost a whisper. Like now.

"You deserve to be happy," he told her. "I understand your loneliness. I understand what it means to have needs, normal, guilt-free needs. You miss Sebastien because you want to be touched, to be held."

"I know you understand. I can talk to you about anything. But having 'needs' isn't the same as needing just one person."

His fingertips soothed the back of her neck. They felt marvelous there, keeping her hypnotized, keeping her eyes riveted to his. "Trust someone who's been lonely, sweets. Some needs are too important to ignore."

His gaze trailed down to her mouth. A jolt of surprise hit her, and then deep wariness. "You want me to kiss you?"

He smiled, reassuring her. "Just to prove that you can kiss someone besides Sebastien. If you love him so much, you won't feel anything for another man."

"Even as green as I am, I know that it doesn't work that way."

"Are you afraid? Adults aren't afraid to push their limits."

His teasing tone provoked her. After all, he wasn't serious. He was just good old Jeff, Sebastien's friend. Her friend. Her heart thudding against her rib cage, she leaned forward and pecked him on the lips. "Did it."

"Like it?"

"I wouldn't trade ice cream for it. Comeon, let's go. I told you I'd buy you a Frosted Orange at the Varsity."

"You didn't give me a fair chance."

His fingers clutched gently at the nape of her neck. He pulled her to him and twisted his mouth on hers. Memories of Sebastien's kisses came alive with exquisite detail. Shutting her eyes tightly, she kissed Jeff back. It was so easy to pretend . . . and so easy to bring back all the pain.

"Stop," she begged against his mouth. She jerked away from him, trembling.

He lifted his hand and stroked her cheek. "See?" he said gruffly. "There's nothing to be ashamed of. It's a normal human need. You have to let someone show you how easily it can be satisfied. Then you'll stop hoping for the impossible."

She scooted away from him, miserable with herself for feeling anything at all. "Fake sugar is worse than no sugar at all."

Jeff's ragged breath made puffs in the chilled air. He seemed a little unnerved, himself. "Fake sugar?" His hand dropped to his knees. "You've crushed my lumps, Amy." He shook his head and laughed. The disturbing mood faded. "Okay. Lesson ended."

She scrambled to her feet. Tears stung her eyes. "Maybe you're not the kind of friend I thought you were."

Jeff got up quickly. "I'm your pal, and don't you forget it." When she pivoted and started to walk off he grabbed her by one arm. Before she knew what was happening he had his arm around her shoulders and was hugging her against his side. "I apologize, sweets." His voice became absurdly pitiful. "I'm an old man of thirty-one, just trying to have a little fun before all my teeth fall out."

"Or some woman punches 'em out." Amy frowned up at him.

He clasped his chest with his free hand. "Forgive me, fair lady, forgive! Thou dost read too much into this old man's gallant attempt to make you happy."

She felt a little foolish. Maybe she had overreacted. "Okay, okay." She slipped away from him and shrugged. "But no more lessons."

"No more," he promised solemnly.

❧

Amy grabbed at ner newspaper and her book bag as the lurching bus threw her against her seatmate. She grumbled under her breath. She had a ton of homework to do, she'd been sick to her stomach all day in anticipation of a book report she'd had to give in her English literature class, and her latest roommate had just been expelled for setting a fire in one of the men's dorms. That made four roommates in six quarters. Two juvenile delinquents kicked out and two pledged to sororities. Her loneliness had a sharper sting than usual.

She stared out the window. She and the girl next to her swayed with all the other damp, bedraggled students as the bus chugged up a street ascending one of the university's interminable hills. It was impossible to drive the Ferrari around campus. Parking was difficult, and she always worried that the car would be vandalized or stolen. She stored it in a garage in town.

Poor little thing. Can't drive the expensive sports car to class. Amy chastised herself. She had it good. She had plenty of money. She had everything she could possibly want. Sure. Amy watched cold rain drizzle down the bus window. Tugging her gloves off, she shoved them into the pockets of a quilted jacket. Then she folded the student newspaper, *The Red and Black*, to the classified section. The ad leapt out at her like a rescue beacon:

ROOMMATE NEEDED, LOVELY OLD HOUSE ONE
BLOCK FROM CAMPUS. ARE YOU A SERIOUS
STUDENT? CONSERVATIVE? EASY TO GET ALONG
WITH? INTO HEALTH FOOD, PHYSICAL FITNESS,
HOME, MOM, AND APPLE PIE? *THAT'S
DISGUSTING. STAY AWAY FROM ME.* BUT IF
YOU'RE LOOKING FOR AN ADVENTURE IN
(CHEAP) LIVING, CALL MARY BETH.

Startled, Amy laughed. This person had a way with words,
a sense of humor—and an attitude problem. She made a note
of the phone number and called the intriguing Mary Beth as
soon as she returned to her dorm room. A masculine voice
that engendered images of thick, red necks and steroid abuse
told her that Mary Beth would be back from choir practice at
the synagogue at any minute; then it politely gave her directions to the house and volunteered that the room rent was
only a hundred dollars a month.

The house had seen better years. In fact, it had seen
better decades, probably before World War II. Amy parked
the Ferrari next to a cracked sidewalk under a walnut tree
that leaned sideways like a drunk trying to whisper a secret.
Parked nearby was a bright red Honda Civic with a lot of
dents. The license tag said BIGTYM. The bumper sticker
said Born to be Bad.

Her palms sweaty, Amy crossed a balding yard and climbed
concrete steps to a veranda that had recently suffered somebody's idea of a paint job. She pulled back a warped screen
door and knocked on a scratched wooden door.

Within a few seconds it was slung open by a small
blonde in jeans and a kimono, a cigarette dangling from
her lips, sock-clad feet planted wide apart on yellowed
linoleum. Her hair was a perfect Farrah Fawcett mane; her
face was serious enough to be beautiful despite its cheer-
leader cuteness; and when she lifted one hand to scratch
under one arm with all the aplomb of a truck driver, she
flashed magnificent nails lacquered a peach color.

Amy's dread increased. She had nothing in common
with this person. "I, uhmmm, I called about the ad . . . the
housemate ad."

"You must have talked to Harlan. He was just passing through on his way to football practice." Out of the little blonde came a voice of disc-jockey depth and blue-blooded debutante vowels. "Well, come on in, honey. Wait—you're not a freshman, are you? I'll take ax murderers and dope dealers before I'll waste time with any more dumb-fart freshmen."

"You're in luck. I'm a sophomore. I've been living in Brumby for the past six quarters. My last roommate was a first-quarter freshman. She threw up on my bed one night. I never did that to anybody when I was a freshman."

"You obviously have style. Six quarters in Brumby?"

"I lived there over the summer, too."

"Jeez, and you don't have any inclination to nibble cheese and twitch your whiskers? What a rat hole. Okay, so haul it in and sit it down, so we can talk. By the way, I'm a sophomore, too."

"Listen, I'm uh, I'm not Jewish. Is that okay? The person on the phone said you were at the synagogue, and I thought maybe you wanted a Jewish—"

"You afraid I'll make you eat matzo balls or something?"

"I'll give 'em a try. Sure."

The blonde peered at her closely. "I'm Jewish on my mother's side of the family. The other half of the family are whacked-out Christian fundamentalists. The combination keeps me totally confused. So I try to eat a lot of kosher food, and I don't dance or gamble during Jimmy Swaggart sermons. My grandmother Rose calls me a shiksa and my grandmother Melanie calls me a JAP. My parents don't care what I am as long as I'm perfect. It's a bitch."

Amy began to smile. "I'm not anything. So whatever you are is okay by me."

"Be something, sugar! Be a rebellious shiksa JAP like me! But be proud of it, no matter what!" The blonde waved a hand. Amy followed her into a living room strewn with battered furniture. "Salvation Army brand. Great, huh? Wait till I get it all arranged. I just moved in a week ago."

They sat down on a plaid couch. "Okay, so here's the sob story. I got kicked out of my sorority for being too liberal. That's what happens to you when you join NOW, the NAACP, and the ACLU all in the same quarter. My parents cut off my allowance for being kicked out of the sorority. See, sugar, I broke a three-generation legacy. So now I'm a rebel debutante. But I'm going to be the next Barbara Walters, so I don't give a shit. Except I have to pay my own bills until the network calls. I got a four-oh average and I study as hard as I party. I rent this place and you'll rent from me. Still interested? You gotta pay utilities, too."

Amy nodded blankly, hynotized. It all made sense. Somehow, it all made sense. Not much else had in all the months since Sebastien's departure. "Okay. Good," she told the girl. "I'm on my own, like you. And I'm ambitious, too. I'm majoring in international business. I'm planning to work in France after I graduate. Oh, and I'll pay utilities."

"We'll be ambitious bitches together, then." The blonde stuck out her hand. "Mary Beth Vandergard. Welcome to the big time, sugar."

❦

Amy moved in that weekend. Mary Beth came outside to gawk at the Ferrari. "Shit, why don't you just buy yourself a house?"

"I'm not rich." Amy carefully lifted a box from the passenger seat. It contained the herbs Sebastien had given her. She held the box close to protect it from the February chill and started inside. Mary Beth marched along beside her.

"Sugar, those better not be dope plants."

"They're herbs. I don't . . . I don't use drugs." Amy looked at her anxiously. "Do you?"

"Oh, I've been known to smoke a joint at a party now and then. But I don't want the shit in my house."

"That's fine with me."

"So how'd you get the Ferrari?"

"It was a gift."

"From who? Your parents?"

"No." They entered the house.

"Sugar, you need to loosen up. Talk. Comeon. I'm a journalism major, okay? You can't escape my probing, incisive questions." Mary Beth chortled. "Also, I may be little, but I can beat the shit out of you if you don't cooperate."

"Do you know that you've said 'shit' three times in the last five minutes? A record?"

"Not even close."

Amy frowned as she carried the box of plants down a long hall to the back, where she had a big, musty-smelling bedroom across from the kitchen. She loved the room; it was hers alone. She didn't want to share it any more than she wanted to share her memories. She had spent months thinking that she was going to wither and die from missing Sebastien, and she was only now beginning to feel better. This summer she was going to France. She only had a few more months to wait.

"I'm really . . . you see, I'm really not much of a talker," she insisted, hating herself for feeling awkward around someone her own age.

Mary Beth crossed her arms over the front of a football jersey that bore Harlan's number and sighed impatiently. "Okay, Amy. Here's the scoop. I'm a nosy broad, and I talk too much, but I know how to be a good friend. I don't want a housemate who's going to treat me like a fucking land-lord instead of a pal."

Amy clenched her teeth. "Why didn't you get one of your friends to move in here, then?"

"Because I needed rent money to help pay my bills this month, and none of them could move that soon. Besides, they're all dweebs. Their idea of a good time is a binge-and purge party. I wanted to meet somebody new. Somebody with goals." She shook a finger. "But I don't want a damned clam living here. No introverts."

Amy dropped the box on the bed she'd bought the day before at a discount furniture store. "Everybody in the whole world isn't like you, you know. Some of us have trouble talkin' about ourselves!"

"God, when you get mad, you squeak. What a great voice. My speech professor would puke with despair. He couldn't ever change that voice."

"Look, you've called me a clam, you've made fun of my voice, and you've basically admitted that you only gave me a room here because you need money in a hurry. Would you like to just stomp on my self-esteem and get it over with?"

"I knew it! I knew it! If I got you pissed off you'd be fine!" Mary Beth threw both arms around her in a hug. "Nobody stays around me for long without learning to defend themselves."

Startled, Amy stood for a moment, thinking about what Mary Beth had said. Then she began to laugh. Mary Beth plopped on the bed and belched, looking satisfied. Studying her in growing wonder, Amy decided that she might be a blessing in disguise.

❦

"You're living with a sociopath," Jeff said bluntly. He walked around the living room looking at Mary Beth's Grateful Dead posters. Then he picked up a switchblade she'd left on the coffee table. "I suspect that she's a classic case of borderline personality disorder."

"She's not violent," Amy assured him. "And I like her. She works part-time at one of the local radio stations as a reporter and disc jockey. She's going into broadcast journalism. I hope you get to meet her sometime."

"I'll continue to avoid that pleasure if at all possible."

"Come see my room. It took me weeks to get it fixed up the way I want it."

They went down the hall to her bedroom. He took a couple of rangy strides into the center of it and stood, looking around with a droll expression on his face. "Are there walls under all these posters of France and Africa?"

She smiled. "I like posters. Besides, the wallpaper has holes in it."

He looked even less pleased and gestured toward a bedside table made from a pair of orange crates, then at the towels she'd stuffed into the window casements to keep out drafts. "Why are you living like this? Sebastien gave you enough money to have an apartment and be comfortable. What are you spending it on?"

Amy stiffened with pride. "I'm saving it. I'm gonna give as much back as I can."

The look of surprise on Jeff's face bordered on insulting. "So how's your social life?" he asked abruptly.

"What social life? I'm taking an overload every quarter and making straight A's. I spend all my time studying."

"Why are you doing that? You ought to be partying and making C's."

"I want to get a *great* job after I graduate." She knotted her hands inside the pockets of a corduroy skirt and went to a window hung with homemade curtains. Under a gray wool sweater her shoulders hunched with tension. "I gotta graduate and get on with my life."

"And then what?"

"I'm gonna get a job in France."

"Amy, come here." He held out his arm. She eyed it warily but stepped inside the brotherly curve. It closed around her like a vise. He gave her his hypnotist's stare.

She shook her head. "Oh, no, you don't. Don't go all glassy-eyed and syrupy on me."

"You know that you want to forget Sebastien. It's all right to forget. He's forgotten you."

"No."

"Think about it, sweets. A man like him . . . can't you imagine how many women he's, hmmm, dated after all these months?"

She made a mewling sound of despair. "Yes."

"There. Good. Reality." He kissed her, flicking his tongue over her compressed lips, sinking it inside her mouth when she gasped. The wet, probing heat frightened her because it was so easy to accept. Wanting it didn't mean she had forgotten Sebastien, she realized. In fact, the kiss made her want Sebastien more.

Bewildered, she swiveled out of his arms and moved across the room. "Did Sebastien ask you to look after me this way?"

"Yes."

"He did not."

Jeff was silent for a moment, his blue eyes holding her green ones with so much sincerity that dread curled through her. "He told me to do whatever I thought best."

"That didn't include puttin' these moves on me."

"For God's sake, Amy, don't you understand? He didn't *care* whether it included that or not."

She sat down on the bed and buried her face in her hands. "He did care." She had to believe her own reality, not Jeff's. "You better go. I got some thinkin' to do."

Jeff came over and lightly touched her hair. "You need me," he whispered. "I'll call when I get back to Atlanta. We'll talk about this some more." She shook her head. "You need me," he repeated, trying to hypnotize her. "I'll call." She remained hunched in confused silence as he sauntered out of the house.

❦

Mary Beth, annoyed with Amy's studying to the exclusion of everything else, convinced her to try out for a Neil Simon play at a local dinner theater. "Sugar, all you have to do is read the lines in that goofy, wonderful voice of yours, and you'll get the part," Mary Beth assured her. "And it will do your self-confidence a shitload of good."

"I'm a business major. *International* business. And I'm making great grades at it, too. I'm going to do something respectable and work in Europe."

"Yeah, you're a business major who listens to comedy albums and watches reruns of old television shows all the time. Admit it, sugar, you're not meant to walk around in a pin-striped suit with a copy of *The Wall Street Journal* under your arm."

"Va te faire foutre."

"Oh, indeed? Getting uppity now that you're studying French, are you? I went to a private high school, sugar, and I know *all* the French obscenities. So get stuffed, yourself."

"Business may not be exciting, but I know I'd be good—"

"Oh, stop it. You're just a chickenshit introvert."

"I . . . you . . . if that chip on your shoulder was any bigger you'd need a back brace to get through the day. And sometimes I get tired of your foul mouth."

"Chickenshit."

"I'm fighting a war of wits with an unarmed person."

"Coward. Shy little sugar-tit."

"All right! I'll audition!"

🍃

Seated at a rickety table in the darkness of a cotton warehouse that had been turned into a stage and dining area, Amy squinted at the students around her. Most of them were drama majors, judging from the conversations she overheard. They were poised and nonchalant; a few looked her up and down then turned away, obviously unconcerned. She felt foolish for competing with them. Her legs began to quiver, and perspiration soaked the underarms of her green shirtwaist dress. She propped her elbows on the table and hoped desperately that her dress would air-dry.

What a great horror movie this would make. Killer armpits. The armpits that flooded Tokyo.

Amy clenched a copy of the audition monologue that the director's assistant had given her. She noticed that most of the other students had brought their own copies of the play.

The director began calling people. Amy's mouth went dry. She tried to concentrate on the other student's performances. They were incredibly polished. They held nuances of emotion that she'd never even considered. They were professional. She heard her own name. Someone laughed. Miracle.

Oh, this was bad, very bad. She hadn't even gone to the stage yet and people were making fun of her. Every ego-bashing remark Pop had ever made to her echoed in her head. She forced herself to the stage, not feeling the floor beneath her feet, her senses frozen from fear of ridicule. This wasn't the circus. This wasn't a carnival or a children's party. This was the *theater*. Shakespeare and Olivier and Broadway and audiences who didn't throw coins after the performance or spit up their ice cream.

Dimly she knew that everyone was staring at her, waiting. She felt too hot. She held her copy of the audition piece in front of her like a shield and watched it tremble.

"Take a deep breath and give it a shot," the director said. There were some barely stifled giggles in the audience. She heard *those* as if they'd been amplified a million times.

She squeaked her way through the piece, not knowing or really caring what she read. The director stopped her halfway. Somewhere in the dark distance between her and the audience he stood up and said, "Thank you. Good night."

"Good night" meant "Get lost," she'd already heard someone explain. Amy stole a glance at the people around her as she left the stage. People craned their heads to watch her. They had bewildered expressions, as if they weren't quite sure how to classify what they'd just seen and heard.

Her face felt as if it were on fire. She bolted into the cool evening air and ran to the Ferrari, then threw up beside the rear bumper. She slumped against the car and rested her head against the smooth black metal. *Doc, I'm sorry. This is one thing I can't do. I'm never going up on a stage again.*

❦

She and Mary Beth and Harlan drove to Florida during spring break. Daytona Beach. It was a madhouse filled with college students from all over the Southeast. Amy wore an ordinary white maillot to the beach and was surprised when boys whistled at her.

The attention pleased her and bolstered her confidence at the same time that it made her nearly sick with loneliness. She didn't want to be ogled by these guys; they were just kids. She had sampled something that they were incapable of offering, and she couldn't forget it.

Mary Beth hauled Amy and Harlan to a wet T-shirt contest on their last night in town. Sitting in a club packed with eagerly waiting males, Mary Beth drank six vodka stingers and Harlan drank four. Amy drank one and stopped. She felt disoriented and depressed.

When the contest started Mary Beth shoved her bra into Amy's hands and went up on stage with two dozen other girls. She wore only tight cutoffs and a Grateful Dead T-shirt, and her breasts bounced merrily. Harlan grew morose as the emcee started spraying the girls with a hose and the audience started cheering.

Mary Beth proudly thrust her plastered chest into the spotlight. She won first prize and twenty-five dollars. Harlan was embarrassed and grumbled about Mary Beth's morals all the way back to the motel. Amy was sorry to be sharing a room with them. Mary Beth stripped to her panties and got into one of the double beds.

"Can the lecture," she told Harlan. "I wouldn't protest if you entered a wet jock-strap contest. Life was meant to be experienced, sugar. Now shut up and go to sleep." Harlan left his clothes on and flopped down beside her.

Amy turned out the lights, pulled the tail of her T-shirt out and removed her shorts, then slid into her bed and lay there in the dark listening to Harlan and Mary Beth mutter to each other. She was stunned when the mutters turned to soft slurping sounds. Then she heard a zipper open, followed by Harlan's grunts as he pushed tight denim shorts off the lower half of a 250-pound body.

Amy turned her head and saw the faint pinkness of Harlan's naked butt as he rolled on top of Mary Beth. Her sense of honor wouldn't let her watch the rest; she pulled a pillow over her head and turned on her side, facing away. The sounds filtered through anyway—soft moans, the bed thumping the wall, ragged breaths, and finally simultaneous gasps.

As crude and silly as the whole event was, it turned her loneliness into a hot, aching desire to be touched, and suddenly she understood how any attractive man could serve a woman's purpose at a moment like this, or vice versa. She muffled her soft sobs in the pillow and whispered Sebastien's name.

❦

The old wound was now just a fine, crescent-shaped scar, mostly hidden under her chin, with only the front tip visible under close inspection. Mary Beth liked the scar. She said it and the tattoo gave Amy an air of mystery and a sinister appeal. Amy decided to make fun of it, rather than let it embarrass her. She was learning to protect herself by making fun of a lot of things.

Pop never mentioned the scar. He didn't this time, either. He treated her like a distant relative who dropped in to visit, which depressed Amy more than his bad temper had. At least when he had been mad at her, she'd felt noticed.

For her Easter visit he wore a yellow flannel shirt and his best brown slacks. He propped his elbows on Maisie's prettily set kitchen table and dangled a beer between his hands. Amy sat adjacent to him and stared at the pink roses on the china. Maisie bustled around, bringing casseroles to the table, humming a gospel tune, her mind much farther away than her body.

"You're dressing like one of those preppies," Pop commented. He nodded at Amy's herringbone blazer, pleated blouse, and long plaid skirt. "I thought college kids were supposed to be hippies."

"It's the Reagan era, now, Pop. everybody's going conservative." She studied the graying auburn hair that lay on one of his shoulders in a thin braid. "But hey, I always liked the Willie Nelson look."

"Raise hell and live the way you please.'"

"Sing with Julio Iglesias. It gives me the shivers."

"You're making fun of Willie."

"No, I'm making fun of Julio. He looks like a lounge lizard. Or since he's Spanish, like a lounge *iguana.*"

Pop laughed. It startled her. She couldn't recall when she'd made him laugh at a joke. Despite the thread of distrust and bitterness that always underlay her feelings for him, she couldn't help but be pleased.

"College has made you more fun to talk to," he told her.

"Fun is my middle name these days. So, how's the art world treating you, Picasso Pop?"

"Lousy. Haven't sold anything in three months.'

"Power company cut us off last week," Maisie interjected. "I had to sell off fifty of my hens to catch the bill up. I fussed with that man out at the power company, but he wouldn't give me any more time."

Amy frowned over this news and was about to ask more questions about their bills, when Pop asked abruptly, "Heard from the Frenchman?"

Amy cleared her throat and answered, "Nope," in a nonchalant voice. It still angered her that stories about her and Sebastien had gotten to Maisie through Pio Beaucaire's secretary. She rattled the ice in a glass of tea and hoped that dinner would be ready soon. She wouldn't feel like eating if Pop pursued this subject.

"Well, I'll say this for him," Pop continued, nodding. "He stole the milk, but he paid for the cow. Can't ask a man to do more than that. I mean, if you had to go live with some foreigner, I'm glad he was a generous one. And he didn't knock you up, so there was no harm done. I just don't understand why he picked *you* out of all the girls who worked at the winery. He wasn't some kind of pervert, was he?"

Maisie gave Amy a sympathetic look and plopped another casserole in the center of the table. "Amy wouldn't have nothin' to do with a homosexual. That man was probably just shy. You know, some men are scared of girls who sound too smart. Amy suited his nature, that's all."

Amy took a swallow of tea. She very calmly set the glass down. She arranged Maisie's pink, embroidered napkin in her lap and folded her hands on top of it. She was going to be very pleasant, eat her dinner, and compliment Maisie on her cooking. She had reached an important point in her life, and it made her calm. Deadly calm.

"Pop, do you know how much that car I drive is worth?"

He snorted. "More than this double-wide and the chicken house put together."

"Right. Well. I'm gonna sell that car. Then I'm gonna buy me another car—something ordinary. I'm gonna give you and Maisie the rest of the money. I want you to be comfortable. I don't ever want to worry about you and wonder if you're able to pay your bills." Her voice kept a low, casual timbre, for once. She nodded to Pop. "Because I'm not ever coming back here."

That announcement pretty much ruined dinner. Amidst all of Pop's snide comments about her attitude and Maisie's pleas for her to give them some money but not abandon the family, Amy remained unyielding. She'd pay the debt for what, if anything, she'd done to deserve being unloved and made to feel unlovable. Now she could move forward, toward a time when somebody could love her and she could love herself. It was another step toward Sebastien.

NINE

*S*ebastien rented the top level of a spacious duplex in an exclusive section of Abidjan, a place where chauffeured cars cruised down streets lined with fruit trees, and gardeners tended yards filled with tropical flowers. His downstairs neighbors were a university professor and his family. The professor had left the Senoufo tribe as a very young man and gone to France to attend college.

Though middle-class, middle-aged, and very European in dress and manner, he proudly bore the whiskerlike scars of the Senoufo on his face, and he had taught the traditions of his tribe to his children.

To Sebastien the Ivory Coast was like that professor, a fascinating mixture of cultures. Thatched huts existed in the shadow of skyscrapers and resort hotels; huge freighters slid along the surface of the great inland lagoon that fronted the city, while only a short drive away monkeys chattered in the rain forests.

It was a country of ancient ways and dark mysteries, which suited his nature, but he was anxious to finish his service and leave. Owing to the natives' lean diet, there was little heart disease here. Except for an occasional congenital defect or injury, he had few opportunities to practice his specialty. Because there were so few doctors, each had many duties, so he did everything from lance abscesses to deliver breech babies.

Now he dropped to his haunches beside a cot in a village

home and probed the thick scar that crossed the man's belly from hip to hip. The pink ridge, swabbed clean with alcohol, made a startling contrast to the patient's dusty black skin. Sebastien nodded with approval at the results of the work he'd done a month ago. This was surgery at its most primitive, and yet somehow most satisfying.

"Tell him his wound has healed well."

The robed interpreter who hunkered next to Sebastien relayed that message. The patient, a young father of five, sat up on his mat-covered bed frame and slapped his bare chest lustily, then zipped his pants up. He said something and grinned.

The interpreter began to smile. He drew one dark hand over his mouth to hide it. "*Monsieur le docteur* has made the patient's wife very happy," the interpreter said in precise French. "He says that his penis works very well again."

"It should, now that his abdominal muscles have lost their soreness. Ask him if he's had any more fights with the fellow who did this."

The victim listened to the interpreter solemnly, then nodded. "They still feud," the interpreter told Sebastien. "It's a family quarrel. They may continue for years."

Sebastien frowned. "He'll end up dead, and waste my efforts."

"But for now his stomach is healed and his penis works. What more is needed to make a man happy?"

"I envy your attitude." Sebastien nodded farewell to his patient and stood up. The man's house was part of a government project to upgrade life-styles in the remote villages. Built of concrete, with dirt floors covered in straw mats and screened openings that served as windows, it was grand by local standards. His wife and children looked healthy, though thin. They perched on a bench in one corner, watching Sebastien with fascination.

Sebastien studied the man's grin for a second longer. He loved the idea of fitting people back together, mending them in the most elemental way. Only a surgeon received such clear proof that they *were* mended. The proof sat, smiling, before Sebastien's eyes, neatly healed. He allowed himself few moments of victory here on the Côte d'Ivoire;

there were few to be had. It was a very French attitude to
admire the aesthetics of a scar and be concerned that it
didn't mar the beauty of the body.

Work had been his salvation since he'd left America. It
forced him to forget everything but the day-to-day business
of keeping people healthy and alive, a venture not so easily
accomplished in a place where doctors were few and
resources slim. It demanded a dedication that left Sebastien little time to consider his own past, his loneliness, his
restless hopes for returning to America, to Amy.

Shrieks filled the air outside the tiny house. A wiry,
chocolate-skinned matron burst into the room. The patient's wife and children huddled and covered their heads.
The patient scurried over to them and watched the old
woman worriedly.

She glared at Sebastien, who bowed slowly, along with
the interpreter, who held out his robed arms in supplication and began trying to calm her, while attempting to
decipher the angry stream of Baoule that poured from her
mouth.

She stomped her sandaled feet. The force of her fury
made a large leather bag swing wildly from the leather
strap over her bony, bare shoulder. The bright cloth draped
over the opposite shoulder slipped down, revealing a pen-
dulous breast. She jerked the cloth back into place without
a glance and continued berating Sebastien. Inside her
cotton shift was a regal body filled with wrath.

"This is the village medicine woman," the interpreter
explained when she finally paused for breath. "She says
that you are sneaking into her village to doctor her people
without permission. After you left last time she had to
purify everyone you touched. Your rudeness is making the
spirits unhappy."

Sebastien was well acquainted with the customs of the
major tribes, but he avoided patronizing such nonsense
whenever he could. This time, however, tradition had
caught up with him. He bowed to the medicine woman
again. "I would be honored if she will forgive my rudeness."

The interpreter translated. She spat and answered with
obvious disgust. "Madame Toka says you—"

A tall man ducked inside the house and straightened ominously, his gray boubou swirling around him. He jabbed a finger at Sebastien's patient and muttered something. He and the man began arguing in loud voices.

"This is the man who cut him," the interpreter yelled to Sebastian.

Madame Toka stepped between the two feuding men. She added her commands to their verbal melee. Sebastien stared at the chaos and enjoyed its entertainment. The interpreter began tugging at his arm and yelling that they should leave.

Sebastien shook his head. "I intend to protect my handiwork."

The intruder pulled a short knife from a pocket in his robe. Shoving Madame Toka aside, the man advanced on Sebastien's patient, who cowered.

Sebastien took one long step forward and swung a fist at the attacker's head. He felt the dull sting of his knuckles connecting with bone, but he also felt pleasure. It was rarely so easy to find an outlet for his anger and frustration. The man swung drunkenly and slashed at him. Sebastien sidestepped the knife's downward arc, but it caught the right side of his chest at a point just over the breast-pocket button of his khaki workshirt.

The heavy blow was like a hammer striking. Grimacing in pain, Sebastien slammed his fist upward into the man's jaw. The man's eyes rolled up and he sank to the floor. Sebastien staggered back, numbly raising a hand to the tunnel of fire that had burrowed into his chest.

If he'd been stabbed through a lung he might not live long enough to reach the hospital in Abidjan. He would die in his Land Rover on a dirt road surrounded by alien forest. He would never see Amy again. He feared that consequence most of all. But when he looked down at the hand he had plastered over the right side of his chest, there was no blood. Slowly he drew the hand away. There was only a rip in his shirt.

Madame Toka made purring sounds. Her eyes wide, she came to him and peered closely at his chest. Sebastien fumbled inside his open collar and retrieved the long silver

chain he wore. At the center of it was the video game token
Amy had given him. The token now bore a deep dimple in
the center.

Madame Toka grasped the whimsical piece of metal and
stroked it with her fingertips. She crooned to it. The interpreter's breathless words finally penetrated Sebastien's
amazement. "She says you are blessed, Doctor! You are,
you are! How amazing!"

Sebastien passed a hand over his forehead. He was
sweating with relief. This meant nothing, of course. Sheer
luck. A small miracle. Miracle. It pleased him. It pleased
him so much that he threw back his head and laughed for
the first time in months. Amy would be flattered by this
story. He could barely wait to tell her.

"*Gris-gris*," the medicine woman said, still stroking the
token.

"She's very impressed. She says that this is your sacred
charm," the interpreter explained. "Your *gris-gris*. She says
that some important spirit must be looking after you."

Sebastien's chest ached. He would have a terrible bruise
where the knife had sunk into Amy's video token. He
rubbed the spot, distracted. "Nonsense."

But he gently removed the cheap, dull bit of metal from
the medicine woman's fingers. Protective of his private
faith, he slipped the token back inside his shirt. It slid into
place with a comforting warmth against his skin. He was
too much his mother's son to ignore a sign from the spirits.

❦

"Pio, we have a distinct problem." Frowning at the path
in front of him, Jeff walked along beside Pio Beaucaire
with his head down and hands shoved into his trousers
pockets. Pio had the same distracted look. They walked
the perimeter of the de Savin vineyard, both of them
oblivious to their surroundings. Ordinarily Jeff would have
reveled in the dark greenery sprouting on the trellises and
the fresh springtime scent of the air. "I'm afraid that in the
past few months I've developed an even more self-serving
reason for helping you."

Pio clasped his hands behind his back as they walked.

"Everyone has selfish reasons for everything he does, dear boy. I'm not surprised to hear you admit yours. What is it?"

Jeff exhaled wearily. "Sebastien was right, I'm afraid."

"Right about what?"

"Amy Miracle. She's unique."

"*Mon dieu*! Not you, as well."

"Oh, I don't have any illusions about her. I certainly wouldn't let her near my bank account."

"A man has far more vulnerable areas than that."

"Not this man."

"But what makes her so special?"

Jeff spread his hands. "She's . . . she's just so damned determined to be taken seriously. And things have always gone so badly for her. I have to admire her courage."

"Those are not reasons to love her."

"I didn't say that I loved her. But . . . God, she's still a kid. She just turned twenty. She hasn't sharpened her claws yet, and that's appealing. I wouldn't mind liking her intensely for a while."

"Hmmm. Well, I'm pleased, then. You are even more inspired to help me do what's best for her, and best for Sebastien."

Jeff grunted. "I don't know if it's what's best for her, but that's not really important. I'd leave her happier than I found her—or at least wiser."

"And she is agreeable?"

"She is *vulnerable*," Jeff countered with a grin. "And that's nearly the same thing." Becoming serious again, he shook his head. "Pio, I don't want the last payment on our deal. This is the end of it. I don't think she's going to cause you any problems. I don't want to be a spy anymore."

"My God, you're joking, aren't you? Now is not the time to become sentimental. Do whatever you wish with the girl. You'll still get your money. All you have to do is keep me informed of her whereabouts and intentions."

"No. I'm sorry. I can't do this any longer. I don't have much guilt, Pio, but I *do* admit to some. Sebastien calls me every few weeks. And every time I make it sound as if Amy's so busy that she never mentions him. But this time he told me that he's planning to come back to the States and see her when his duty is over in Abidjan."

Pio sighed. "I'm not surprised. His father says that he's ignored several inquiries from hospitals in France. Sebastien could have a position on the staff of the finest private hospitals in the country, but he has refused to make a decision."

"Amy sold the Ferrari."

"No!"

"She won't tell me why she did it. Or what she wanted the money for."

"She has plans, that one! She is going to leave school and chase Sebastien! You wait and see. As soon as he's finished in Africa, she'll be after him."

"I suspect that you're right. I didn't want to tell you this before, but she's been planning all along to find a job in France as soon as she graduates. That's almost two years from now, however."

Beaucaire rammed both hands through his white hair. "*If* she stays in school."

"Precisely."

"I will phone *le comte* immediately. He will know what to do. He always has ideas. You can't desert us now."

"I've been offered a very good position on the staff of a drug-and-alcohol rehabilitation center in California," Jeff told Beaucaire. "I have to leave in about six weeks."

The man's shoulders slumped, but after a moment he held out his hand. He and Jeff shook solemnly. "Excuse me," Beaucaire said. "I have plans to make. I wish you'd reconsider."

"I want privacy. I have my own plans for Amy and myself."

"Can't you tell me—"

"No. What little honor I have has finally risen to the surface."

"Forgive me if I do what I must, without your help." Pio pivoted stiffly and walked away.

❧

"Amy, there's some old geezer here to see you. He looks like a fat Lorne Greene. Ask him where Little Joe is."

Amy looked up from an economics book. Mary Beth lounged in the doorway to her bedroom. "Who is he?"

"Says his name is Mr. Beaucaire. *Mister*, right? No first name. And he gave me an ugly look. Like I ought to be scrubbing toilets somewhere. Go see him. He's in the living room."

Amazed, Amy hurried there. Mr. Beaucaire stood by a window, staring at Mary Beth's menorah on the sill. His black suit gave him an especially imperious air. Why had he made the long drive to the campus? He'd never shown any interest in her before. She fought her shyness and crossed the room to him confidently, smiling. "Hi there. It's nice to see you again."

He lifted pale eyes to her in surprise, then swept them over her baggy shorts and T-shirt. Finally his attention returned to her face. "Forgive me for taking so long to visit."

She gestured awkwardly toward the sprung sofa. "That's okay. Have a seat. Please, I mean."

He settled slowly onto the couch. Her nerves humming, she forced herself to sit in a chair without fidgeting. He cleared his throat. "Tell me about your studies."

"I'm majoring in business. International business." She hesitated, then rattled off several sentences in French. His expression remained neutral, but she thought disdain flickered in his eyes. She halted, shrugged, and smiled. "Well, I've got a lot more to learn. I know my accent is terrible."

"After you graduate you hope to work in France, hmmm?"

Amy wasn't certain that she should announce that fact. "I haven't decided for sure." She couldn't restrain her question any longer. "I, uhmmm, I guess that Sebastien is doing fine in Africa?"

Mr. Beaucaire smiled. "Yes. Very well."

She sat forward on the chair, her hands clasped tightly in her lap. "Do you talk to him very often?"

"Frequently."

"Will you tell him that you came to see me?"

"Of course. I'm sure he'll be glad to hear that you've used his gifts wisely. The Ferrari . . . you are enjoying it?"

She bit her tongue. She didn't want anyone telling Sebastien some cock-eyed version of the truth. She wanted to explain to him about the Ferrari herself. "It's wonderful, yeah."

Mr. Beaucaire's chuckle was sinister, somehow. "And you have plenty of money left from the amount Sebastien gave you?"

"Oh, yes, more than half of it! Tell him . . . tell him that I'm not living high on the hog."

"I beg your pardon?"

"That I'm not wasting his money."

"Ah. I see. Yes."

She clenched her hands. "Would you mind telling me about him? About the kind of work he's doing? What's it like in the Ivory Coast? Where does he live . . . in an apartment or a house?"

"Oh, who knows about Sebastien? He isn't one to talk much about frivolous things. I'm sure he has a nice home, and I'm sure that he rarely sees it. He's always working. His work, you see, has always been the center of his life."

She leaned forward, anticipating. "Yeah, you're right. He probably doesn't do anything else. He's probably pretty bored with Africa, I bet. I bet he doesn't *ever* take time to enjoy himself."

"Oh, I wouldn't say that." Mr. Beaucaire reached inside his suit jacket and retrieved a photograph. "This is an old friend of his. She has gone from Paris several times to visit him."

Amy rose and took the picture. After a second she managed to concentrate on the stately young woman in it. "What's her name?"

"Marie d'Albret. Her family and Sebastien's were neighbors. He has known her all his life."

She raised her eyes to Mr. Beaucaire's. Though he tried to look sympathetic, she saw the victory in his face. "Is this why you came here? To show me a picture?"

"I feared that you had misconceptions about the doctor's intentions toward you. I just wanted to make certain that you understood his situation. He and Marie are very close. When he returns to France, I wouldn't be surprised if they marry."

Amy laid the photograph on the couch. Then she backed away from it carefully, watching Mr. Beaucaire. "I guess you've done what you meant to do. You can leave."

Mr. Beaucaire tucked the photo into his jacket pocket and stood. He nodded to her. "You've enjoyed quite a bit of generosity from Dr. de Savin. But it would be foolish for you to expect more."

"Why should I believe you?"

"You believe me, but your pride won't let you admit it. Tell me, did you honestly think that the doctor would remain interested in you? Don't you know what sort of girl you were to him? He was kind to you and gave you this chance to better yourself. Do *not* harbor fantasies about the future." He strode into the hall. "Good-bye, mademoiselle."

Amy waited until the front door clicked shut behind him. Then she turned blindly, her eyes full of tears. Mary Beth leapt out of a doorway down the hall, glowering. "Old bastard. I eavesdropped on the whole thing." She came to Amy, stood on tiptoe, and put an arm around her shoulders. "Comeon, honey. Let's go for a walk. And then we'll eat ice cream until we explode. Or maybe we'll go find some tender, unsuspecting high-school boy and abuse him. Wouldn't that be fun?"

Amy whispered. "I am somebody important. I don't deserve to be unhappy."

"There you go, honey. You don't need this shit."

"I'm going to see Sebastien in France, right after he gets home. If he's not interested in me, he can tell me so himself."

After giving her a stunned appraisal, Mary Beth said something pithy and obscene. Then she sighed heavily. "I *like* watching Juliet poison herself over a Romeo who couldn't care less. It's educational."

❧

Jeff was leaving for California. Amy congratulated him on his new job and tried to appear pleased, but halfway through dinner she halted with her fork posed over a plate of chicken chow mein and blurted, "I wish you were staying here. What am I? A train station? All I do is watch people come and go in my life. I'll miss you. I'll miss you so much."

"Amy, that's the greatest compliment you could give me."

"You didn't have to drive all the way to Athens and take me out to eat just to say good-bye. But you did, because you're terrific. I can't scarf down my chow mein and act nonchalant. I feel like I'll never see you again." She jabbed her fork into the food and looked at Jeff despondently.

He reached across the table and took both of her hands. His fingers stroked her palms. "Did it ever occur to you that I hate to leave you?"

Her withering emotions took a little life from his remark. She *knew* that he cared about her. Not much was certain in the world, but Jeff's friendship was a sure bet. Right now she needed his support in every way he could give it. "What's really wrong?" he asked.

"Sebastien is seeing some *woman*." She told him about Mr. Beaucaire's visit.

Jeff's expression went from amazed to thoughtful. "Better a woman than a *man*." He squeezed her hands gently. His gaze held hers with compelling sympathy. "I'm sorry, sweets. I really am."

"Thank you for not gloating."

"Why would I gloat? I don't like to see you hurt."

Emotion filled her throat. Jeff. Good old Jeff. "Could we get out of here? I can't eat. I'm suffocating."

"You're just hyperventilating."

"I know, I know. But I'd rather do it in fresh air."

He paid their bill and they left. On the sidewalk of one of Athens's quiet, small-town streets Jeff put his arm around her and she leaned against him. They walked through the spring night.

"I've got a great idea," he told her. "I'll get a room at one of Athens's *finest* motels. I'll hang around town for a couple of days, and we'll live it up."

"I'd like that."

"What say I get a room now, and you come with me? We'll order some pizza and watch cable TV."

"That sounds okay. Sure."

Inside Jeff's new Mercedes sports coupe she put her head back on the passenger seat and shut her eyes. She now owned a small blue Ford, cheap but friendly. She missed the Ferrari because it had made her feel close to Sebastien. The day she had sold it she spent an hour sitting quietly in the driver's side, her senses tuned to the memories of a fast night on a dark road with him.

Sometimes she couldn't stop thinking about him, and every moment played on her emotions with sharp awareness; but at other times a soothing blankness washed away all thoughts but those of the present. She wasn't fooled by it. She knew that the memories hid just behind a wall of fatigue, but she appreciated the respite. She felt blank right now.

As he drove, Jeff reached over and took her hand. "You're learning a valuable lesson, sweets," he said softly. "I know it hurts, but in the long run you'll be smarter because of it."

"I love him. I always will."

"You may always love Sebastien, but you won't hurt when you think about him. The mind has a wonderful way of losing touch with painful stimuli. Trust me."

She decided not to tell him that she'd be visiting France in late summer, to find Sebastien. Deep down she feared that everyone was right, that she was being foolish. Her determination seemed more hopeless than ever before. "Dr. Freud, I may be naive, but sometimes I think you don't know diddly squat about how to love—really love—somebody."

He chuckled with fiendish intent. "Ah, but I know the mind. The psyche. The intellect. The dark little corners where only the bravest mice go."

"My mice are running around like chickens with their heads cut off."

"What a charming analogy. I'll have to remember it."

He drove to one of the motels on the highway outside of

town. It was the kind of place that catered to business people and well-heeled football alumni. Amy was impressed by the cable TV selections. Jeff sprawled on the king-size bed and picked up the phone. "A giant pizza and a six-pack, all right, sweets?"

"All right." She sat at the foot of the bed and studied his prone body with dismay. Jeff seemed threatening this way; she couldn't quite put her finger on the reason. She frowned and got up, then prowled around the room. She put her big cloth purse on the dresser and pretended to look for something inside, while she darted glances at Jeff in the dresser mirror as he placed their food order.

His jogging shoes, soft, faded jeans, and rumpled red T-shirt made him look less like a thirty-one-year-old doctor and more like a graduate student close to her own age. His blondish hair was marching back from his forehead, but the disheveled look of it flattered him, gave him a mad-scientist appeal that suited his personality.

Cupping the phone to one ear, he tucked a pillow under his head and flopped one foot over the other. His position accented the impressive mound that lay at the base of his belly. Amy lowered her gaze to her purse, uncomfortable with scrutinizing him that way. She stared at her cold, pale hands and wondered why being here with Jeff should upset her.

They ate pizza and watched television in companionable silence. She stayed on the far side of the bed, her legs curled under her. He made clucking sounds of disapproval because she wouldn't drink more than one beer. "I'll have to drink the other five," he said and moaned.

"Better not. You've gotta give me a ride back to the house."

He wiped his hands on a napkin, studied her in silence, then said softly, "You don't really want to go, do you?"

She dropped a half-eaten slice of pizza back into the box and sat very still, frowning at Jeff. "I don't love you."

"I didn't ask you to. But you like me. And I'm crazy about *you*." His eyes were intense, but he smiled. "Crazy. An appropriate choice of words."

A cry of confusion and torment rose inside her. She pressed her hands to her mouth to suppress it. Shaking her head, she whispered, "Having sex doesn't mean anything to you, does it? It's as ordinary as brushing your teeth."

"Yes, but you should see how well I floss." He set the pizza box and beer on a nightstand, then rolled toward her and propped his head on one hand. The other hand snaked across the bed's coverlet and rested on her knee. His fingers stroked her lightly through her jeans. "Give yourself permission to be happy. There's no reason to feel guilty. You've been faithful for so long. Sebastien never expected you to live like a nun. My God, sweets, adults don't make those kinds of demands on each other."

When she put her head in her hands and groaned with frustration, he continued, speaking in his low, cajoling tone. "You're finished with Sebastien. Let go, Amy. Be an adult and *let go.*"

She caught a sob. Crying silently, she didn't protest when he sat up and pulled her into his arms. He brushed his lips across her hands then nuzzled her ear, whispering, "It's like riding a horse. If you fall off, you have to get right back on."

She wiped her eyes. "But on a new horse?"

"Whatever it takes to get you back in the saddle." His nimble fingers went to the buttons on her pale cotton shirt. "Sebastien would understand. He'd approve. He wouldn't care."

He wouldn't care. Amy numbly watched Jeff's fingers part her shirt and stroke the inner curves of her breasts above her bra. He dipped his head and kissed her there, his mouth firm and sure. "I've wanted you for a long time. There aren't any lies in what I'm telling you. I really believe that I know what's best for you. Trust me, Amy, trust me. You can start to feel better. I can make you feel better. It's as simple as this."

He slid a finger inside her bra and rubbed a nipple until it hardened. Desire slid through her. She felt breathless and sad, aroused but detached. It was good to be touched, to be wanted by a man. Sebastien had taught her the power and beauty of satisfaction, then left her hungering for it, alone.

She raised her hands to Jeff's shoulders and explored the smooth movement of muscle over his lanky frame. Her

head swam with guilt, confusion, sorrow, desire. Shutting
her eyes, she accepted reality.

❧

This night was not going as planned. Usually following
sex Jeff dozed—relaxed, gloating, victorious. Usually his
partner curled herself to his side and sighed with happiness.

His partners did not stare at him unblinking while he
was in the midst of a magnificent performance. They didn't
fake their excitement with little humming sounds that
reminded him of a sewing machine at low speed. And
when he finished, smiling, waiting for a compliment, they
did not just thank him brusquely, roll over, and pretend to
fall asleep.

"It won't work," he said grimly. "I can feel your vibes.
You hate me."

"I don't hate you." Her voice was hoarse with misery.
"You did just fine."

"Why, thank you." Troubled about the depth of his
concern for her, he cursed silently but pulled the sheet
aside and moved close to her. Tucking the cover around
them both, he curved himself against her back and but-
tocks. She was cold and trembling. Jeff put his arm around
her waist. He cupped his hips so that his penis wouldn't
bump her. "I'll keep that dastardly villain away from you,
fair damsel," he teased, his throat tight. "Now stop regret-
ting what you and I did."

"It was fine. Just fine."

" 'Fine' seems to be the word of choice tonight. What
happened? At first, I could swear that you wanted this."

"I did. I thought it'd be a good substitute for the real
thing."

"Ouch. I see." His sense of rejection climbed higher. He
hadn't realized how much he'd wanted to please her.
Determined, he stroked her face with the backs of his
fingers. Her eyes remained shut, but tears crept from under
the lids. "It may take time for you to relax," he told her.
"It's all right to feel ambivalent about me right now."

"You sure are good-natured and patient." She turned

onto her back and gazed up at him. Distress made dark smudges under her eyes. "And I don't want to hurt your feelings. You're so nice."

He cupped her chin. "Listen to me. The next time will be great. I promise."

Her eyes clouded. "I don't think—"

"Sssh." He kissed her. *God damn you, Sebastien. Get out of her mind. There. See how she opened her mouth for me? All I need is patience.*

"Jeff, don't," she said, and turned her head away. "I'm trying, but it doesn't work. This isn't right for me."

Wounded and growing angry, he scowled at her. His patience began to fray, but he spoke calmly. "How would you like to live in California?"

"What?"

"Come with me. Live with me. Enroll in college out there. We'd have a great time, sweets. You'd love California. Especially San Francisco. I'm going to buy a house near the bay." He tried to intrigue her by describing the state's attractions. He told her about Hollywood, Los Angeles, Malibu, Disneyland. He mentioned that some of his patients would be television and film people. He'd make contacts in the entertainment business. She might get to meet some of her favorites.

His speech raised no shred of interest in her. "I can't leave here," she said gently. "This is where I told Sebastien I'd be."

Jeff felt a muscle ticking in his cheek. "What difference does that make? He doesn't care where you go to school."

"I told him I'd be in school *here.*"

"I thought we settled all this." He wanted to shake her. His voice rose. "You were making progress. You can't backslide now. *You are never going to see him again.*"

She began to squirm under the clamp of his arm. Her eyes flashed defiance. "I might! At any rate, I won't run off where he can't find me!"

"And if you do see him again, and he hasn't forgotten you, are you going to explain why you fucked his best friend?"

They both froze, those words hanging like a knife be-

tween them. Her chest rose with short, strangled breaths.
"He wouldn't look at it that way."

"The hell he wouldn't. European men are very possessive. If he cares about you at all—which I doubt—he'd be
disgusted to know that you're in bed with me. Take a sniff
of the air, sweets. That's sex you smell. There's no way you
can pretend that this didn't happen."

Horror filled her eyes. He had struck a chord. "I'd explain
. . . somehow," she insisted, but her voice was hollow. She
twisted away and pulled a pillow to her chest, hugging it,
her body hunched.

Jeff raised himself to a sitting position and glared at her.
But a sense of shame stabbed him, and his head began to
throb with tension. *Repressed guilt*, he admitted with a
bitter smile. He rubbed his temples. "Don't worry, sweets."
His voice was leaden. "Sebastien will never find out about
this unless you tell him. Your secret's safe with me."

"But the damage is done," she said brokenly. "And it
was my fault."

Jeff flicked the light off. The darkness complimented his
bleak mood. For the moment, he loved her, and he was
sorry for hurting her. He rested a hand on her shoulder.
"You didn't do anything wrong. And I'm sure that Sebastien
would understand."

But she no longer trusted him. He sat in the darkness
giving useless comfort and listening to the soft sounds of
her defeat.

❦

For the proper effect, it was vital to keep one's voice
pitched at the level of casual conversation. One could not
reveal the satisfaction that had been spawned by a private
investigator's report. One could not hint that risks worth
taking had paid off handsomely. Or that even a smart young
man, such as Dr. Atwater, could play into a crafty old man's
plan. After Pio added a few half-truths and outright lies *le
comte*'s plan would work out perfectly.

When Pio heard Sebastien answer the telephone he
gathered himself for a perfect show of nonchalance. "Sebastien, hello! How are you, my boy?"

"Pio?" Sebastien's deep voice conveyed wariness even over thousands of miles. "Is everything all right? Why are you calling?"

"My boy, it's not as if I never call you."

"Ah, but Pio, the reasons, the reasons." Now Sebastien sounded more amused than suspicious. "What are you up to?"

"All right, suspect a harmless old man, if you will." Pio laughed. "I call with good news. The girl . . . Amy. You don't have to worry about her anymore."

"Oh? How is that so?"

"She's sleeping with Dr. Atwater!" Pio spoke with Gallic earthiness. Affairs, after all, were nothing about which to be shy. "They have been lovers for a long time, I suspect!"

"Where did you come by this information?"

"From Dr. Atwater, of course. It is no secret. He's asked her to go to California with him. I don't know if she'll do that or not. But she sold the Ferrari you gave her, so that must mean she expects to move."

"When is he leaving?"

"Soon. In two days, actually."

"I will be there before he goes. You locate him for me."

"Sebastien, no. The girl has made her choice. You left her to her own devices, so what did you expect? She is young . . . she has no patience for waiting. It is beneath you, a grown man, an important man from an important family, to let your energies be diverted by her."

"Tell Dr. Atwater that I expect to see him."

Pio sighed. "All right, my boy, if you insist."

"I have plans to make. Good-bye."

He hung up without waiting for Pio's response. Nodding, Pio slowly laid his receiver back on the cradle. He sat back in his chair and rested his hands on his stomach. Sebastien would not get permission from his superiors to leave his duties, even for a few days. *Le comte* had already made certain of that. And Sebastien would soon have diversions to take his mind off the girl. *Le comte* had made certain of that, too.

Pio sighed, relieved. It was good to see *le comte*'s world being put right, finally.

TEN

*T*he medicine woman knew that something about him had changed. She hiked up the shoulder drape of her dress, spit red kola-nut juice into a can, then sternly jabbed a finger at Sebastien's shirtfront. Her bright cloth turban wobbled with each dismayed shake of her head.

"She is very surprised and displeased that you're not wearing your *gris-gris* this time," the interpreter explained. "She says without the magic charm your medicine won't do the villagers any good."

Rather than frown at Madame Toka, Sebastien frowned at the woven mat on which he sat. He and she had enjoyed a pleasant professional relationship; he'd listened patiently as she'd offered her opinions on treating everything from bee stings to cancer. He wasn't going to quarrel with her now over a ridiculous bit of metal he'd once worn around his neck.

He'd seen a great deal of needless suffering and death during his time in the Ivory Coast; it had taken a toll. He had become tougher than ever, less gentle, less able to tolerate human frailties, including his own.

"No compromise," the interpreter whispered.

Sebastien gestured toward the gifts that lay in front of her kneeling place. "I suppose this month she doesn't need her supply of cigars and candy."

"She is strong-willed," the interpreter said.

Madame Toka eyed Sebastien with birdlike shrewdness. She clasped her heart and spoke in hushed tones.

"Madame asks, 'Why are you sad?' "

"Sad? She is mistaken."

"Humor her. When she decides something, there's no point in arguing."

"All right. Tell her that I'm sad because I've been disappointed by someone I love."

When the interpreter finished, Madame Toka gestured dramatically, then opened up her conjuring bag filled with small-animal skulls and shells, spread them on the floor, and consulted them. She began speaking with solemn assurance.

Sebastien's interpreter hitched his white *bou-bou* up a little and leaned forward, hands planted on crossed legs. "You are disappointed in yourself as well, she says."

She was very perceptive. Sebastien nodded. "I demanded too much. I gave too little in return. I waited too long because I didn't have enough faith. But the mistake is made now and can't be changed." He couldn't even get permission to leave this damned country for a few days so that he could try. Fate was against him.

"The *gris-gris*," his interpreter reminded him. "Madame won't let you treat anyone unless you wear it."

"Tell her that my magic is here." He held out his hands. "And here." Sebastien pointed to his head. "And there." He pointed to his medical kit and the case of supplies sitting beside him on the hut's wooden floor. "I don't need any help from a *gris-gris*."

She spoke, spit again, then pointed to the empty spot between the breast pockets of Sebastien's khaki work shirt. The interpreter sighed. "She says your magic has to be in your heart as well as everywhere else. It's no use arguing with her. If you want to treat the villagers you'll have to wear your necklace."

Sebastien bit the inside of his cheek and fought the sour, short-tempered impatience that threatened his control more and more lately. Waiting for his attention was a child who had been gored in the stomach by a bull, a pregnant woman suffering from toxemia, at least a dozen people infected with venereal disease, and other villagers with assorted minor ailments.

"Tell Madame Toka that my *gris-gris* no longer holds magic for me," he instructed. "Perhaps she can give me a new one."

But his diplomatic maneuvering fell flat. The medicine woman spoke at length this time, and finished by smugly shoving away the gifts. "Madame believes that you are in danger without your protective charm," the interpreter explained. "She says you are a strong man who draws the attention of jealous evil spirits. She can't have you working around her people in that condition."

"Ah. I see. I might contaminate them. I'm infested with demons. What nonsense."

"*Monsieur le docteur*, I've never heard you make light of the people's religion before. I'm a Muslim, but even I don't look down on the beliefs of the villagers."

"I apologize. The heat is severe today. It bothers me," Sebastien hadn't noticed the heat any more than usual; he was merely offering an excuse, while he considered the absurdity of the situation. He was wasting time over his own ridiculous wounds when he could be treating the wounds of others, an infinitely easier task. And why was he arguing? For his pride's sake, and no more. His pride over a brief affair that a grown man should dismiss with a sigh and a shrug. *C'est la vie*.

Sebastien nodded to the medicine woman. "Madame Toka, if you consider my *gris-gris* important, then I will wear it."

The interpreter told her, and she nodded back to Sebastien, then smiled. Sebastien went to his truck, searched in its glove compartment, and returned to Madame Toka's hut carrying the long silver chain and its charm. He hadn't quite been able to bring himself to throw them away. He knelt in front of Madame Toka and held the charm out for her to see; she waved her hand over it and said something.

"She feels the magic. It's still there," the interpreter noted.

No, Sebastien told her silently. He grimaced at the faded video token that Amy had given him so long ago. The cheap finish was worn off of it; it was dimpled from the knife attack two months ago. It was hardly recognizable as the shiny trinket he'd once loaned to a dying child. But indeed, it was powerful. It had kept him celibate for almost two years. It had kept him enchanted. No more.

But to placate Madame Toka, Sebastien slipped the chain around his neck again. He was startled when a distinct sense of comfort came over him from the slight pressure of the token against his chest. Madame Toka nodded sagely. Sebastien ignored her but didn't protest. Slowly he touched the cheap, tarnished metal. Today was his birthday. For a moment he did not feel quite so alone, and for that, at least, he was grateful.

❧

Sebastien moved forward, angling between people, taking energy from the challenge of the crowd at the airport. He tapped his folded sunglasses in the callused palm of a hand that was darkly tanned from the equatorial sun. And he scanned the in-coming passengers.

He was spending half of his working days in the villages and half at the hospital. One day a week he lectured at the university. He had come directly from a visit to one of the villages and was wearing baggy white trousers and a native shirt of indigo-blue wax cloth that hung to his thighs.

When his sister appeared at the far side of the room she spotted him immediately. Their eyes connected over the heads of the crowd, one tall person to another. Sebastien braced himself before Annette reached him, her dark hair flying and her zaftig figure pushing aginst the confines of a rumpled white dress suit. She laughed as she dropped her travel bag and flung her arms around his neck.

"Sebastien! What has become of you? You look like a calypso singer! I wish that Papa could see you! He'd stop thinking that you should be a businessman!"

"Perhaps I'm bored with my conservative image." He staggered from her size and enthusiasm but hugged her happily and returned the kisses she pecked on his cheeks. Annette, big, blustery, a powerhouse of intelligence and charm, was absolutely determined to head all the family businesses. Sebastien approved. The only thing standing in Annette's way was their father's unending determination to put Sebastien in charge.

She stepped back and scrutinized his face. "You can wear a native shirt but you can't change your image," she said, frowning a little. "You'll always be The General to me. You look tired. And thinner. And too solemn, as always. But then, I'm becoming rather solemn myself these days."

"She's trying too hard to please the old man," a petulant male voice interjected. "But aren't we all? God, this place is awful. I hope you've got a car waiting. I want to get to the hotel and take a bath. Why didn't you warn us that it would be like this? Shit!"

The whining roused Sebastien's temper even before he frowned past Annette at his younger brother, who had just arrived behind her. "You look like a man now, Jacques. But you complain like a child."

Sebastien stared sternly into eyes that were lighter than his own but just as stubborn. He and Jacques hugged, briefly, stiffly.

"You talk like Father," Jacques retorted. "I've always said that you'd turn out to be just like him."

Annette stepped between them. "Brothers! I don't think you two know how serious your teasing sounds!"

"He's in shock from seeing me," Jacques said. "Since it's been three years."

"Ah, but you've avoided me and devoted all your time to leading the life of a decadent college student," Sebastien answered. "I've been waiting for you to outgrow it."

"I've been waiting for you to develop a sense of humor."

Annette clapped her hands firmly. "Enough!" She looked nervous and distressed.

Sebastien put his arm around her, sorry for letting his disapproval of Jacques upset her. Annette was going through a bad time; with her prestigious record from one of France's most esteemed business schools she could have had her pick of corporate positions. Instead she had gone to work for their father, and so far he had given her little more than secretarial duties.

"Come. My car's close by," Sebastien told her and Jacques. "This is a terrible place for a family discussion."

Jacques hooted. "But we're a terrible family." Thin and muscular, with a face more boyish than Sebastien's had ever been at twenty, Jacques was a beautiful young animal. He wore tight jeans and a T-shirt bearing the seal of the Sorbonne, from which he had recently been expelled. He ran both hands through hair that he'd had lightened from dark brown to a reddish mink color. It curled in soft waves against the back of his neck. "We came to talk to you about the old man," Jacques announced. "Shit. Let's get it over with."

"Not here!" Annette ordered. "We're standing in the middle of bedlam, and we haven't even gotten our luggage yet." She grasped Sebastien's arm. Her smile had returned, but it was too bright. "Besides. I have a surprise for you."

"Oh?"

"Your surprise left her bag of books on the plane and had to go back after it," Jacques noted. "God knows that she couldn't survive without her books."

Sebastien gave his sister a wary, questioning look. "What is this surprise?"

"It's not a what, Sebastien, it's a who. Someone I know you'll enjoy seeing again."

"There she comes," Jacques added. "One of the truly intellectual people of the world. But she has all the vivacity of a rock."

Puzzled, then profoundly pleased, Sebastien started forward. 'Watch out. The widow wants a new husband," Jacques called in warning.

Sebastien met the black-haired, blue-eyed, extremely beautiful woman and clasped the hand she extended with regal aplomb. He took the black leather tote that held her beloved books. Though their families had been neighbors in Paris and he had known her since childhood, he didn't hug her. Marie d'Albret was a close friend of Annette's, but she never invited public displays of affection, even from Annette.

He was shocked when she looked up at him now with eyes that brimmed with greeting, then put her arms around his neck and kissed him on the mouth. Perhaps Jacques was right—the widow was anxious for a new husband. But even that wouldn't account for such a dramatic change in behavior.

"Don't look bewildered," she teased, stepping back and straightening her shoulders. "I wanted to get away from Paris for a week. I asked Annette if I could come along. Do you mind?"

Sebastien took her elbow. He didn't mind if she had ulterior motives. Everyone had ulterior motives. Even Amy, he thought with a swift stab of anger. Here was a beginning, a direction, a way to fill part of the void. He had not thought about Marie in years, but suddenly he wanted her to erase his sentimental disappointments. "I don't mind at all," he told her. "You have perfect timing."

🍂

Their father had been diagnosed with skin cancer. Sebastien stood stiffly in front of the window of his sister's hotel room. He found himself studying a palm-lined plaza many stories below while another part of his mind dealt with an excruciating mixture of emotions. Behind him on a damask-covered couch, Annette huddled in dignified misery. Jacques lounged on the floor, hands latched behind his head, bare feet crossed casually, his face a mask.

"It's not fair," Jacques murmured. "The old bastard should die fighting something he can see."

"He isn't going to die!" Annette exclaimed. "The doctors think they removed all of the melanoma. They took the birthmark off his neck and sent him home. His chances of surviving are very good!"

"The old man should die in a way befitting a grand old veteran of the war," Jacques insisted. "He should die at the office doing what he does best: ordering his assistants around like soldiers and kicking German bankers in the ass."

"Not the Germans," Annette corrected. "We're counting on them to invest in that factory we just bought in Marseilles."

"Pardon me. I don't have your aptitude for putting business ahead of feelings."

"You don't have any aptitude for anything that involves using parts of your body above your waist," she teased. "But believe me, little brother, you'll pay attention when I turn that factory into a successful venture."

"May I remind you that it will belong to Sebastien if the old man dies? You're only the old man's daughter, remember? And I'm only the old man's extra son, the one who doesn't matter."

Sebastien had heard this kind of talk too many times to feel more than dull disgust. "I will give it all to you. I've never wanted it."

"Father doesn't care what you want," Jacques retorted. "Now he's going to die and leave everything to you, just to spite your uncaring attitude."

"So how do you two expect me to react to his illness? Do you expect me to run home and play the dutiful son? I doubt that he is in danger of dying. He will use any ruse to get me home."

"Father isn't calculating," Annette insisted. "I know he can be distant and stern, but I respect him, and you should too—"

"You don't know him the way I do. Either of you. You're both too young."

"For God's sake, Sebastien, what did he do then that he doesn't do now?"

"I shouldn't really need to explain why I have no affection for a man who treats his children like chattel to be spied upon or ignored."

Sebastien walked to a bar and poured himself a stiff drink of brandy, slamming the bottle down when he finished. He had often debated whether to tell Annette and Jacques the truth behind the deaths of their mother and siblings. But he couldn't do it. They didn't remember anything about her, but they cherished the idea of her. They even thought that Father had loved her. Sebastien would never take that away from them, or her. They would never know that they had only been the result of their father's *mistake*.

"What does he want from me now?" Sebastien asked. "Why does he want to see me?"

"To talk to you about taking over the businesses," Annette said wearily. "He doesn't give up."

Jacques continued to stare at the ceiling, his face impassive, but his voice tinged with sadness. "His own mortality frightens him, I suspect. And it isn't out of the realm of possibility that he loves you, you know. You've always been his favorite."

"No. I've been his eldest surviving son, whch made me the favorite by default. Antoine was his favorite. *That* is the sort of thing I remember, and you don't."

"You're jealous of a brother who died almost twenty years ago?" Annette asked.

"No. Never. You cannot understand why not, because you never knew Antoine. Or Bridgette. You never knew how different the family was before they died—before our mother died."

"You're saying that Papa changed after their deaths? Of course he did; he was nearly destroyed with grief! I love him for the way he cared about them!" Annette jumped to her feet. "I knew you'd be sullen about this. But now I see why! You *are* jealous! All these years you haven't had the honesty to admit it! You're jealous of our dead brother and sister, and you hate Papa for the way he withdrew from the family after they and Maman died! You're a bitter, petty person, Sebastien, and now you won't even admit that you've been too harsh on Papa! You won't go to see him when he needs you!"

Sebastien looked grimly at his sister. "I'm glad that you love him. He doesn't deserve it, but it makes *you* happy. Just don't ask me to love him."

"You cold bastard! I can't believe you'd continue this feud now! Don't do this, Sebastien! Don't do this to the family!"

Jacques sat up, scowling. "She's right. If you try to mend things with him, maybe it will be better for all of us."

"No. It won't. This is wishful thinking."

"You absolutely refuse to go see him?"

"Yes."

"You'll be finished here in a few months. What then?"

"I'm going home. I've already had invitations from several surgeons who want me to join their practices."

"But surely you'll go see the old man when you get home?"

"No."

"Not even if the cancer returns?"

"Not even then."

"You're awful," Annette said, her voice low and vibrating. "You want Papa to suffer for his faults, but you refuse to admit that you have any faults yourself. I'm tired of your arrogance. It's not fair! Papa wants you to take over the businesses and all you do is throw your hatred in his face! While I *love* him, and he doesn't care! Get out! Get out of my sight!"

"I will call you this evening," Sebastien told her calmly, though he was upset at the way this visit had degenerated into a fight. "Perhaps tomorrow we can—"

"I'm going home. On the first flight I can get."

He went to her and grasped her shoulders. "Annette, I won't pretend to love our father, not even to make you happy. But I don't want you to accuse me of motives—"

"I despise your pride! I despise *you*!" She flung herself away from him, dark hair flying around her face.

"Annette, try to accept the way I feel—"

"Heartless bastard!"

"You'd better leave," Jacques said, rising and coming to her. "I can't say that I don't agree with her, but I'll try to calm her down."

Annette burst into tears and covered her face. "Father could be dying of cancer! But Sebastien doesn't care!"

Sebastien hesitated for a moment, thinking about the past, analyzing the unforgiving bitterness of a small boy who had cradled his mother's bloody head and watched her die begging his father to forgive her for deliberately killing herself and their children. Then he remembered his father's mistress, *la comtesse*, who had come to the funerals. She had stayed at their home in Paris the night afterward, and he felt certain she had not slept alone.

Sebastien touched Annette's shoulder. "I'm sorry," he

murmured. "But you're right about the way I feel toward our father. I don't care if he dies. And I'm certainly not going to make it more pleasant for him by pretending to care."

He left the room to the sound of Annette's sobs and Jacques's muttered obscenities.

❦

Marie was formal and solemn, not prim in the way the nuns had intended to make her at school, but of a serious nature that rebuked the world for being frivolous. Her exquisite heart-shaped face and willowy figure rescued her from a look of severe reserve, and she was beautiful despite the tailored black dresses that she had favored all her adult life.

Sebastien had last seen her three years earlier at her wedding to an English financier. Her husband's death in a boating accident the past fall had added an appealing aura of sorrow to her dignity.

When he took her out to dinner she talked of neutral subjects, and in his troubled mood he was glad simply to sit and listen. There was nothing passive about her reserve, nothing hesitant. She spoke slowly and without flirtation; she was almost placid, except for her habit of stroking a graceful hand along the long strand of pearls she always wore.

She owned a day-care facility, a very exclusive one where the fees were high and the children of the rich were taught by the most advanced methods. She was intent on making the world safe for intellectuals, starting with the youngest. Sebastien wasn't certain that he approved of formal schooling for mere toddlers; he preferred to let them enjoy their innocent ignorance for as long as possible.

But Marie's dedication impressed him, as did her independence. Her father was the chief administrator at Sainte Crillion, a hospital of great renown situated in one of the wealthiest suburbs of Paris. She could have lived handsomely on family money and her late husband's wealth, but she didn't.

"My father asked about you before I left to come here,"

she told Sebastien. "He hopes that you'll contact him. He practically spied on you the entire time you were working in America."

"I know. Several surgeons told me that they were acquaintances of his. I suspected that they were reporting on my progress.'

"That doesn't annoy you?"

"Your father is no tyrant. I respect him. I was flattered."

"He is so impressed with you, Sebastien. The department of cardiac surgery at his hospital is becoming very prominent, I'm sure you know. Father has spoken to the department's chief surgeon about you. They'd love to have you on staff there. Would you be interested in meeting with him when you return to Paris?"

"Of course."

She looked pleased, smiling at him under darkly lashed eyes nearly devoid of makeup. Her black hair was twisted atop her head in a soft, simple style. Like many French women, she gave the natural look a distinct elegance.

He found himself wanting to know more about her, wanting to explore the personality that viewed life with such cool control. She was self-absorbed and made no apologies for it.

"You know, we share many memories," he told her. "I recall a time when you were tutoring Annette in the violin, practicing together at our home. I was preparing to enter the university and you refused to speak to me because of it."

"I was envious! All of the servants kept talking about you—Oh, he's so advanced for his age! I wanted to compete with you! And, you must understand, I was terribly infatuated with you. You were only two years older, but you seemed so confident and so mysterious. There was an air about you, even then, of great purpose. I wanted to be part of that purpose, whatever it was."

"And now?" he asked, propping his chin on one hand. A waiter brought coffee, and she smiled slightly while she stirred cream into hers.

"Now?" she repeated, her eyes settling on his with businesslike challenge. "Annette says she's going home tomorrow. Jacques says he's staying for a few days to make you uncomfortable. What do you think I should do?"

"Do you know why my brother and sister are angry with me?"

"Yes. Annette told me."

"Do you think they're right?"

"I think that you're one of the few men in the world who never lets sentiment interfere with principle. And that, my dear Sebastien, is why I'm still fascinated with you. Now, what should I do? Go home, or stay here?"

Sebastien held out his hand. She placed hers in it, cool and still. "Stay here," he answered. "Definitely."

❦

That night he took her to his apartment and to bed, where she surprised him with the ferocity of her needs. She suited him, with her pragmatic tenderness and unhesitant requests, offering her slender, small-breasted body to him much more easily than she would ever offer love.

He was happy that she stared at his body in awe; happy that she writhed under him, clawing his back with her long, carefully manicured nails; happy that her needs were easy to satisfy. He was frantic for a woman's touch after being alone for so long; abstinence made it easier not to think about Amy, at least during the most heated moments.

When Marie came, calling the name of her dead husband, Sebastien was only mildly perturbed. She apologized quickly, and he assured her that he understood. They both realized the truth—this was not about love but about something much simpler and safer. They were perfect together.

ELEVEN

*A*my wandered into the kitchen, an economics book under one arm, huge circles under her eyes, her face gaunt. "Cheese toast with pickles. At *midnight*. Ugh. Are you pregnant or something?"

Mary Beth chortled. "If I were, the kid'd be wearing a coat hanger by now."

"You're like *totally* gross."

"Nice Valley Girl impression, bitch." Mary Beth grinned at her. "I made extra cheese toast for you. And here's a glass of milk. Now sit down and eat. Your half-Jewish mother commands it. How are you feeling?"

"Better. I think I'll be able to sleep tonight."

"Don't tell me you *miss* that Atwater jerk. I never even met him, but I know the type. He's not worth missing."

"I don't miss him. I'm glad he's in California. I hope he never comes back."

"Then stop feeling guilty over what happened. The guy preyed on you like a fox on a rabbit, sugar. You never had a chance."

"This rabbit didn't hop too fast. I *let* him catch me."

"So you're human. So what? Let's cut classes tomorrow. It's summertime. We should be sunning our tits, not work-ing."

Amy sat down at their battered table and wearily propped her head on one hand. "Nah. When I lay in the sun, I think too much. My mood starts to smell like a dead fish."

"A good deodorant would take care of that."

That made her smile. She grabbed a pickle slice from a small plate and threw it at Mary Beth. "I like the delicate way you treat my feelings."

Mary Beth dodged the pickle and laughed. The poor kid was too nice. *Somebody* had to look out for her. She sank her teeth into a piece of toast and ripped a bite free with predatory pleasure.

❦

Amy hunched over a soft drink in the cafeteria of the student center. She had just gotten her grades from a quarter filled with accounting, management science, and economics. Only through agonized efforts had she come out with straight B's. It galled her to lose her A average; all this time she'd submerged herself in the pursuit of a perfect grade-point average. It had become her holy grail, something she could present to Sebastien if she ever saw him again, proof that she was smart enough and determined enough to be loved.

She was halfway to her degree, but now she admitted a disturbing truth: Business administration was as exciting as watching Mary Beth's latest boyfriend blow bubbles in his chocolate milk, which he was doing right now with great gusto.

Beau was another athlete; a member of the track team, lean and rangy where Harlan had been bulky and squat. Mary Beth made no excuses for her puzzling taste in men. "I don't need an intellectual fuck," she had once explained. "I want my men hard, I want 'em sweaty, and I want 'em dumb." Beau qualified.

Mary Beth, dressed in a pink tank top and overalls, threw both sandaled feet onto the cafeteria table and reared back in her chair, watching Amy. "Business isn't for you, sugar," she announced. "You can recite all of Joan Rivers's best jokes and make 'em funnier than she does. You act out your dumb Broadway songs when you think I'm not around. Oh, hell yes, don't look shocked. One time I peeked through your keyhole and *saw* you doing the soundtrack from *The King and I.*"

"Oh, no. I'm so embarrassed."

"Hey, you make a great Yul Brynner."

"That stuff's just for fun."

"You ought to switch your major to drama."

"No! No way!"

"So this fall you're going to take another miserable quarter of business subjects, and I'm going to have to watch you be sexually unfulfilled, introverted, a workaholic, *and* depressed over your grades. I think I'll strangle myself with one of my many fake gold necklaces."

"I'd be glad to help you strangle yourself."

"Say it. Comeon. I've been coaching you for months. Say it. Let me have it, sugar."

"Oh, all right. *You're a heartless slut.*"

Beau laughed and snuffled milk up his nose accidently. Or on purpose. It was hard to tell.

Mary Beth grinned at her. "Bravo! You're ready to progress to your next stage of therapy, which means finding a good boy and getting laid."

Amy straightened angrily. "I've *told* you why I don't want to date anyone. I don't want to talk about 'getting laid.' Sometimes, Mary Beth, you're really cruel."

Mary Beth looked apologetic. The reality of Mary Beth Vandergard, outcast debutante, was that she often embarrassed herself and was so aggressive that she scared most people off. And she didn't like that about herself.

She pulled her feet down and leaned across the table, her eyes somber. "Sugar, you're going to get your little heart busted all to hell. I think you're the dearest person who's ever learned to put up with me, and I don't want to see you get hurt. Please, *please*, forget about this French doctor and get on with your life."

"I can't. You don't understand how it was between us. I have this feeling, this intuition, that he wouldn't mind seeing me again. I'm going to France next week and I'm going to find him. Don't you see, Mary Beth? If you love somebody this much, you have to believe that he loves you back, even if he didn't say so. At least, there are some things I have to talk to him about. Explain some stuff."

Mary Beth arched a blond brow wickedly. "I oughta hold

your head against the TV set so Oral Roberts can have at you. He'll slap you right between the eyes and yell, 'Heal,' and you'll be fine."

"I'm going to find Sebastien," Amy repeated, nodding firmly. "And *then* everything will be fine."

❧

Amy parked behind the château and went into the square concrete building that housed the winery offices. The plump little woman behind the receptionist's desk beamed at her.

"Lord have mercy, look at you. Maisie said you'd gone off and gotten real grand, and she wasn't kidding."

The woman's admiring eyes scanned Amy's flowing white skirt and cowl-necked blouse. Amy swallowed hard and forced herself to act nonchalant. "Is Mr. Beaucaire around? I'd like to talk to him, if he has a minute."

"Well, shoot, I'm sure you could talk to him if he were still here. But he went back to France a week ago, and we've got a new manager. You remember Gordon Thompson, don't you? Mr. Beaucaire promoted him."

Amy sat down limply on a couch.

Suddenly the door opened, and a small sweaty man came inside, wiping his forehead with the back of one hand. A Panama hat was propped on the back of his grizzled hair. His face had a perpetually sour expression. Amy recalled Gordon Thompson well. One of the vineyard assistants, he'd been a tyrant.

"Mr. Thompson," the receptionist called cheerfully. "Look who's here to see you." As she explained Amy's visit Amy stood up and forced herself to smile at the man. He examined her, frowning.

"Didn't you get fired?" he asked sharply.

"No. I . . . I had some personal emergencies, and I had to quit."

"Wait a minute. Wait one minute. I remember what was going on with you, because Mr. Beaucaire was mad about it."

"I wasn't in any trouble. Look, all I need is Mr. Beaucaire's—"

"You shacked up with Dr. de Savin."

Amy could feel her face growing hot. "Dr. de Savin was my friend—"

"Yeah, right. And now you're trying to hunt him down, I bet. Look, I know how Mr. Beaucaire felt about that situation. There's a name for girls who take advantage of their jobs that way. You just haul your hot little ass out of here."

"I don't think Dr. de Savin would want you to talk to me this way. I don't care what you think of me, but I'm sure *he'll* care, because we're good friends. In fact, I'm going to visit him in France next week."

The new manager smirked at her. "Oh? You're gonna visit him and his *wife*?"

The last word was a sledgehammer. Amy stared at him in a dumb shock. *"What did you say?"*

"I said *wife*. Dr. de Savin just got married. He married some woman he'd known all his life. A French *lady*. So I guess you and him aren't such close friends anymore, huh?"

Her mind was frozen. "He wouldn't get married. He wouldn't."

The receptionist cleared her throat awkwardly. "It's sure true. Mr. Beaucaire told me all about how they had a nice Catholic ceremony down in Africa. Mr. Beaucaire was invited to it."

"Guess you didn't get an invitation, huh?" Thompson asked.

Fierce pride welded her bones together so that she could stand still. "Well, shoot," she said dryly, "You give a man the best two weeks of your life and two years later he forgets you're alive."

Thompson looked puzzled. "Huh? He forgot a long time ago."

"That's the joke, see?" Amy smiled at him. "Whoops." She peered at his head. "I better slow down. I guess the traffic's a little heavy in there." A harsh hand was clawing inside her. "So the doc got hitched? An African wedding. Hmmm. Must have been hell trying to rent a loin cloth to match his tux."

"I got a snapshot," the receptionist told her, staring at

her oddly. She opened a drawer. "Mr. Beaucaire gave it to me because I wanted a picture of him. It's at the wedding. It's got Dr. de Savin and his wife in it."

Amy marched over to the desk and studied the photograph. She stared at the woman she had first seen in the photo Mr. Beaucaire had shown her. "She's got a nice smile. I like the way her eye teeth curve down into little points. Funny how you can't see her reflection in the mirror."

"What the hell are you talking about?" Thompson asked.

"Nothing. Hey, the doc looks great, for a guy who just married one of the undead. She's gonna be a real drag at the beach. Not to mention that embarrassing little problem with garlic."

Thompson snorted in disgust. "Next time you go fishing for the big ones, you better use fresh bait. Now get out of here."

Amy walked slowly to the door. With her ice-cold hand resting on the knob, she turned back. A list of Mary Beth's best obscenities ran through her mind, but they weren't her style. And Thompson's insults didn't matter to her anyway. Nothing mattered except the knowledge that Sebastien was beyond her reach forever. "Thank y'all for the information," she said softly, and left.

❦

"Sugar? Amy? Poor honey, comeon. Comeon now." Mary Beth sounded wretched. She tugged at Amy's arm. "You can't sit in the backyard all night. And I'm afraid you're gonna set yourself on fire."

"Roasted in lighter fluid. What a way to go."

Hiccuping between sobs, Amy dropped another poster onto the pile of ashes, squirted liquid from a small can, then struck a match and tossed it. Blue flames engulfed the poster only inches from her updrawn feet. Amy took a swig from a bottle of wine. "We now say good-bye to the lovely province of Normandy."

In seconds Normandy was indistinguishable from its charred predecessors. Amy leaned back, wiped her arm across her eyes, then reached for another poster from the trash can she'd carried outside. "We now say good-bye to—what's this one—" she squinted in the dim light from the back porch, trying to read the poster, "the Alps. Good-bye, Alps."

Mary Beth took the poster away from her. "Time to go inside, firebug. You can finish this tomorrow."

Amy dropped the wine bottle and hugged her knees. She cried raggedly, her head tilted forward. Mary Beth sat down beside her and draped an arm over her shoulders. "It'll get better, honey. I've been dumped by some of the biggest heartbreakers in Atlanta, so I know what I'm saying. After a while you feel fine again, and then you go out and kick some poor innocent guy's ass to get even with men in general."

"I don't want to get even. I still love him. I'll always love him."

"I guess you better drink some more, then." Mary Beth retrieved the bottle and looked at it. "Oh, God. You bought de Savin wine. What are you trying to do—rip your heart out?"

"It feels like I already have." She rocked back and forth. "What do you do when you know there won't ever be anybody else as wonderful?"

"You promise yourself that you'll never love anybody that much again. And you hope you're right, because it's not worth all the trouble."

"Never again. But he was worth all the trouble. I swear that he was."

"He must really have been something special, then, I envy you."

Mary Beth began crying, too. She put her head against Amy's, and they held hands. Amy shut her eyes. *Never again.*

❧

It was one of those nasty days that sometimes struck northern Georgia in the cusp of late autumn. The temperature hung just below seventy-five degrees, the sky was a deep, clear blue, and the air smelled like dried wildflowers.

There was no excuse for staying inside. Amy dipped one

hand into the box of cereal that was balanced on her stomach, while she stared dully at the television set. Her bare heels were a little numb from resting on the arm of the couch for too long; she crossed them at the ankle, right over left, the most monumental decision of the day, so far. A corn flake fell on her T-shirt, and she let it stay there.

Mary Beth came in and punched off the TV. "No more bellyaching," she announced. "I'm out of sympathy. You've been like this for more than three months. Are you going to pass *any* of your courses this quarter?"

"Not unless somebody uses a big grade curve. Like maybe half the circumference of the earth."

Mary Beth threw herself into a squeaky chair they'd purchased at a garage sale. Her rose-hued nails rapped imperiously on its scarred arms. "Well, at least you're not bawling over your damned herb plants anymore. Or burning posters of France." She sighed. "Now you're just concentrating on proving that you're worthless."

Amy set her cereal box on the floor, turned on her side, and hugged a throw pillow to her chest. "Yeah, it's straight from here to a career as a game show hostess."

"Very cute, very cute. You've developed a real smart mouth. Why don't you put it to good use? Come down to the radio station this afternoon and work. All you have to say is, 'Good afternoon. The Bulldogs bark for WDIG FM. Rock'n'roll classics, all day, everyday.' "

"Do I have to say that on the air?"

"No, you have to say that on the *phone*. They need a receptionist."

"Will I get paid?"

"Are you kidding? The place is a suckhole. Only a handful of people get paid to work there, and even they're selling their blood on the side to make ends meet. Students don't get paid. They get valuable work experience."

"As a receptionist?"

"You gotta start somewhere, sugar. You hate business school. You love TV. That means you'll at least *like* radio. What have you got to lose? Look, forget about the French doctor, okay? You're not trying to impress him anymore. Just make yourself happy."

Amy sat up wearily and stared at the floor. "I'll always try to impress him," she murmured. "Even if I never see him again."

"Great. Fine. Impress anybody you want to. Just *do* something impressive."

Amy rubbed her forehead. "*Good* afternoon," she muttered. "The Bulldogs bark for WDIG FM, rock'n'roll classics, all day, every day."

Mary Beth did her debutante's tea-party applause, tips of fingers primly patting the heel of the opposite hand. "Quite nice, dear. We'll be the only station in town with Olive Oyl for a receptionist."

"I won't ever have to talk on the radio, will I?"

"Nah. There's lots of work behind the scenes. Maybe that's what you could do. You just might enjoy yourself."

"Mary Beth?"

"Hmmm?"

Amy touched Mary Beth's arm. "Thank you for putting up with me. And for caring. For a heartless slut, you're a wonderful friend."

Mary Beth's large hazel eyes filled with tears. "You've got bad taste. I like that in a person."

❦

Amy found, to her shock, that she loved working at WDIG. It was a shoestring operation set up in a tiny old house a few blocks from campus. Parker Poodit, owner, manager, advertising rep, and midmorning disc jockey, lived upstairs. He looked like a leftover from a long day at Woodstock. He was going bald, had a graying blond beard that hung to his collarbones, and favored tie-dyed T-shirts, leather sandals, and turquoise jewelry. There was always a faint smell of incense and Aqua Velva around him.

Parker was a mellow man; unfettered by union rules and barely within the bounds of FCC regulations, he viewed his one-station broadcasting empire as a center for grassroots rebellion. Rock and roll brought in the ordinary listeners; Parker's weird commentaries brought in the fringe. He had been the only sports announcer in the history of Bulldog football to come out in favor of gender-identification tests.

Mary Beth was the afternoon D.J. She became a different person when she sat at the mike talking in her husky, dulcet-toned drawl. Amy saw the tough-talking good-old-girl evaporate; in her place was a serious young woman who knew how to make the news sound solemn and dramatic. Her work behind a microphone was probably the only thing in her life that Mary Beth took seriously.

Amy progressed quickly from receptionist to general gopher, fetching tapes and albums from the library—a big closet off of Parker's kitchen—to the studio, typing copy, and eventually learning how to set up program schedules. She even dabbled in the technical end of the work and learned how to edit tape.

She finally decided to switch her major to communications, with an emphasis on radio-TV-film production, over a pizza at a hangout in town. Mary Beth put a candle in the center of a glob of mozzarella. After she lit it she proclaimed solemnly, "Here's to the future famous producer. May she be happy and find a new man. Hell, may she find an old man. Any man. She's spending a lot of time staring at cucumbers these days."

Amy shook her head in benign disgust but laughed as if she were having a good time. She'd gone out on a few dates, nothing serious, each one ending with her half-heartedly kissing the guy. She blew out Mary Beth's candle and wondered, *Oh, Doc, how long is going to hurt like this?*

🥭

Parker Poodit ran into the station office—a converted living room with much-abused desks and chairs—and screamed, "We've got Elliot Thornton! I'm going to interview him on the morning show next week!"

People jumped up and began asking questions. Amy dropped the program log she'd been filling out and gave Mary Beth an excited look. She had a ticket to one of Thornton's sold-out shows at the Peach Pit, a big club in town.

"How'd you do it?" someone asked Parker.

He slapped his beard happily. "I called his booking agent and told him that we were the only station in town that ever ran an uncensored interview with Hunter S. Thompson. Get this place cleaned up! Somebody get a mop! Take down that poster of Elton John!"

Mary Beth reared back in a lawn chair, stroked her blond hair thoughtfully, and announced that Elliot Thornton had all the comic subtlety of a geek with a hormone problem.

Amy threw a pencil at her. "He's great at visual humor! He can stand on stage and just peel a banana, and people laugh! I've seen every appearance he's ever made on Johnny Carson. He won *Showtime's Big Laugh-Off* hands down. And I just read in *TV Guide* that he's only twenty-seven."

"What are you, the head of his fan club? Geeks for Thornton?"

"You obnoxious blond terrorist. Elliot Thornton is very all-American, a real guy-next-door type. That's why he's so popular. Everybody feels comfortable with him."

"Yeah," Parker Poodit interjected. "He looks like he takes a bath every day."

"He's also sexy," one of the female staffers noted. "I think he's adorable."

Outnumbered, Mary Beth shot everyone a bird. "Suck some saccharin."

Amy laughed. "Well, I want to see him up close."

"He'll eat you alive."

"He sounded nice in *TV Guide*."

Mary Beth groaned. "Sugar, his publicist makes sure he sounds nice. Ten bucks says you're too shy to squeak one word to him. And that if you do, he turns out to be a jerk."

"You're on." Mary Beth had known that she'd rise to the bait. It dawned on Amy, with a measure of relief, that it was good to feel so much anticipation again. She grasped at the new attitude, nurtured it, and buoyed her courage. She was going to be someone who wasn't afraid to speak up, even to Elliot Thornton, just to prove she could do it.

❧

She had no morning classes the day of the interview, so she went to the station around dawn and sat in the booth, handing wire copy to a student who read it in between playing Beach Boys' music for the early bird listeners. The engineer, a burly man who wore his hair in dread locks, made lecherous faces at her from the control room, and she mimed absurd reactions of shock. It was a game they'd played before, and it pleased her that she could make him laugh so hard that his hair jiggled.

An hour later she went to the kitchen, one of the few parts of Parker's house that had remained in its original form, and brewed a big pot of coffee. From upstairs came the sounds of running water; Parker must be awake and washing his beard for the big occasion.

Outside the open front door birds sang in the oak trees and cars whispered by on the narrow old street, their tires making a muted *whoosh* as if the dew had dampened noise. From somewhere came the rude rumble of a different motor; as she poured a cup of coffee she vaguely categorized the noise as a motorcycle.

It grew louder. Sipping her coffee, Amy wandered to the front door and leaned against the frame. As the motorcycle roared around a curve her hand rose to clutch the front of her white pullover. She watched in horror as the rider braked and the big Harley slid sideways into a curve. It bounced onto the sidewalk and careened across the lawn, while the helmeted rider let out a howl of amusement or terror, Amy wasn't sure which.

When the Harley plowed into a towering hedge of red-tipped photinias, the rider sailed into the foliage, and Amy ran, tossing her coffee cup onto the ground. By the time she reached the man he had turned over. She looked down anxiously. His arms, inside a faded Michigan State football jersey, were spread wide as if he were lounging on a couch of burnished red leaves. His gold watch, encrusted with stones that might be diamonds, was caught on a branch. He was moaning and chuckling at the same time.

She peered at the handsome, jaunty face inside the helmet. Blood-shot blue eyes met her gaze, then roamed over her, necessitating a comical craning motion of the head that owned them. They weren't as jaunty as the face; in fact, they looked a little embarrassed.

"Baby," he said solemnly, "I came early to save you from boredom. But I'm afraid I've been . . . am-bushed."

Amy was so intrigued that she didn't have time to feel shy. "Bushwhacked," she corrected.

He laughed, the sound charming but sheepish. Shy? Was he shy? Amy wondered.

He cleared his throat, eyed her sternly, then flipped the chin strap on his helmet. "Get back. I've taken the safety off. My head could explode at any minute. Until two hours ago, I was indulging myself at a wild party in Atlanta." He flung his arms about, warding off invisible people.

"Better stop flapping. Turkey-hunting season starts early around here."

His arms froze in midair. He sputtered in amazement and stared at her closely. "Are you for real?"

"Real enough. I work here at the station."

"Over eighteen?"

"By three years."

"Born with that crazy voice?"

"Yep. Your eyes look terrible."

"You ought to see 'em from my side."

"Lee Marvin said that line in *Cat Ballou.*"

"What are you—the joke patrol?"

"Nope. Actually. I'm a big fan of yours."

"I think I love you."

She rolled her eyes in mock disgust but couldn't help smiling as she helped Elliot Thornton out of the photinias.

❦

The Peach Pit was crammed with little tables, and the little tables were crammed with well-dressed students. These were people eager for a future of condominiums and BMWs. Amy studied what she could see of them from her vantage point in the wings of the Peach Pit's intimate stage.

"Come to me, baby boomers," Elliot Thornton muttered beside her, as he checked his blue blazer in a mirror. "I'm your next king, baby boomers, your next king. Come to me. Be mine. Come to me."

He spoke the words as if they were a mantra. Amy watched him in fascination. He swiveled toward her, then slicked a quivering hand over sandy-brown hair that was fashionably short but comfortably mussed. "Baby boomers, baby," he said, smiling at her in a tight, nervous way. "I'm going to own them." He snapped his fingers in a silent, manic rhythm.

Elliot Thornton, Kansas City native, childhood asthmatic, Michigan State graduate in education, and outrageously spoiled only offspring of a dentist and a lawyer, was obviously scared to death of going on stage. Amy could see a blue vein throbbing in his all-American cheek.

He needed her to be his assistant tonight, to hang around with him and soothe his nerves. He'd said so at the radio station that morning, after a crazed, brilliant interview with Parker.

He'd said so again during a lunch of hotdogs and onion rings at the Athens Varsity. He'd said so once more on the card that came with the pink roses that were delivered to her house after she returned from her afternoon classes.

She was needed. She was the calm one. She could barely believe it. She was thrilled.

Amy patted his arm. "What you've got out there tonight are *Southern* baby boomers. Hush-your-mouth-and-pass-the-quiche types. I call 'em Hush Yuppies."

A grin cracked his tense expression. "Hush Yuppies, Hush Yuppies. Hmmm. That's great, baby."

"Thank you, *baby.*"

"Ready, Mr. Thornton?" the emcee asked, stepping out of a hallway that led to the back of the club. The emcee was a tall black guy who traveled the regional college circuit doing bad impressions of Jimmy Walker and opening for comics who had a much brighter future than his own.

"Yeah." Elliot wiped a bead of sweat from his forehead. "And hey, you shouldn't call me Mr. Thornton."

"Thanks."

"*Massuh* Thornton will do just fine."

The emcee grunted like Mr. T. "I'll chew up your ass and spit it in your ear, white boy."

They shook hands cheerfully, and the emcee went on stage. He worked the crowd with professional control, and

Amy was mesmerized. She loved watching from this view-point; she loved the curious, respectful glances the wait-resses gave her and Elliot as they walked past on their way to the kitchen; she loved the undercurrent of anticipation in the audience because of Elliot. She loved being Elliot Thornton's assistant, for whatever it was worth.

He was nice. He hadn't put any moves on her, so even though Mary Beth had voiced the opinion that he was looking more for a piece of ass than an assistant, Amy felt comfortable with him. There was, after all, only one man who had the power to overwhelm her good sense, and she hadn't seen him in almost three years. He was in France, with his wife. She had dreamed about him again, one of her painful, erotic, desperate dreams, only the other night.

The emcee finished his routine to respectable applause. Elliot paced back and forth in a space no more than a yard long, practically pivoting in a circle. Amy discovered that her heart was pounding with excitement, as if she were the one going on stage. This was so perfect, being part of the anticipation without suffering the terror.

"Please welcome Elliot Thornton!"

As cheers and applause flooded the stage and swept back into the wings, Elliot grabbed her in his arms and gave her a dry, compressed kiss on the mouth. His body was as tight as an overwound spring. "I'm going to be top dog, baby. Wish me luck."

"Arf."

"God, you're perfect."

He left his real self behind and sent a new persona into the spotlight. It was the Elliot Thornton she'd seen on *The Tonight Show* and cable comedy shows, the nonchalant wiseguy with hands shoved casually into the pockets of his pants, his mouth set in a confident smirk. "Well, hello there," he said into the mike, with a look of boredom so grand that people began to laugh. "What we have here is a room full of southern baby boomers. I see a lot of hush-your-mouth-and-pass-the-quiche types. Yeah. Southern yup-pies. *Hush yuppies.*"

The laughter swelled, mixed with applause. Amy stood in the wings with her mouth ajar. Surprise gave way to delight. He had liked her comment so much that he'd put it into his act! And he'd made it funny!

Two shows later, tired but giddy with joy, she went to Elliot's motel room with him and a group that included the emcee, the club manager, and a few students who worked part-time at the club. The manager brought along sandwiches and beer, which he spread on a table. People produced small bags of grass and began rolling joints. Elliot was the first to finish eating and light up.

Carrying a soft drink, Amy secluded herself on the room's balcony and pretended to be interested in a dark, deserted parking lot and a hill covered in kudzu. She frowned in consternation. The sweet smell of pot and the burnt-grain scent of beer would always remind her of Pop's bad moods. She didn't like what drugs and booze did to people.

But a part of her craved acceptance from Elliot, and that part remembered what it had been like to stand in the wings with him and then hear him tell her joke on stage. *That* was the drug she needed, that and the comfortable looniness of his world.

"Hey, baby, what have asphalt and kudzu got that I haven't got? I'm smooth and hard. I can grow on you."

Elliot stepped outside and swaggered to her, twirling the tip of an imaginary mustache. He didn't have the joint anymore, and Amy studied him in pensive confusion. "I don't do drugs," she said slowly.

His amusement fadded, and he looked down at her thoughtfully. "You could be good for me," he said as if speaking to himself. His attention shifted outward again, and he asked, "Why don't you quit school and come to work for me?"

Amy shoved her soft drink onto the balcony railing then grasped the rail for support. "That sounds great. Thanks. Thanks a lot. But I've gotta finish college." She thought privately, *I can't let Sebastien down.* And then, hurting, she corrected it to, *I can't let myself down.* "I'm the first Miracle who ever went to college. I can't quit. . . . What kind of work?"

"I don't know. I guess it's time I hired a secretary. Let's try this. 'Take a letter, Ms. Miracle.' "

"I'd like a vowel, please."

He groaned and drummed a rim-shot in the air. "But seriously, folks—"

"I want to get a job on my own, without anyone doing me a favor."

He grabbed his head with both hands and yelled to the night sky, "Why is she so difficult? Women are supposed to do anything I want them to do now that I'm rich and famous!"

"You're not that rich and famous yet."

"She's stabbing me in the heart! My ego is deflating! I'm melting! Melting!" His voice became high-pitched. "Melting, melting! I'll get you, Dorothy!" His knees buckled slowly and he sank to the balcony floor. "You, and your little dog, too!"

Amy laughed helplessly. He was one of the few men she'd ever seen who could be ridiculous and yet charming. He was a handsome clown, but a puzzling one. He was six years older than she, but it didn't feel that way. She felt as if he needed someone to take care of him. On the other hand, she understood this kind of man, she'd grown up with this kind of man.

"I guess we should just see what happens," she told him. She wasn't naive anymore; she didn't daydream about impossible futures. "I mean, you're gonna be in town a whole *two* days. And then you're going to New York. Might as well admit that I'm a passing fancy, bub."

"Her cynical tone of voice wounds me," Elliot said to an unseen audience. On bended knee he grasped her hands and kissed them. "I honor a mere college student with my affection and she taunts me. Me, the next superstar of comedy. Oh, woe. Woe. Such arrogance."

Amy sat down cross-legged in front of him and, keeping her hands in his, returned his warm, insistent grip. "It's not arrogance, ol' boy. It's self-defense. Just be honest with me, okay?"

Subdued, he settled quietly beside her. "Okay. Maybe I'll see you again after tonight, and maybe I won't. I like you a iot, baby. You're definitely unique. I'd like to know you better. That's all I can guarantee."

"That's enough."

"Let's sit here and talk, for right now. In a little while I'll chase the party vultures off. And then maybe we'll do some of this." With comical lechery he poked his forefinger through a circle made by the opposite forefinger and thumb. "Or maybe some of this." He contorted his fingers in absurd ways and wiggled them. "Or even some of *this*—"

"You stole that from Steve Martin."

He frowned in exasperation. "Have you memorized every comedy bit in the business?"

"Not all. I'm still working on the early Milton Berle shows."

He put his arm around her and kissed her. There was nothing electrifying about it, no burst of shivers inside her and no desperate greed to have him, as there had been with Sebastien. But it was pleasant. Very pleasant. It was enough.

The next morning she woke up lying on her side with Elliot draped across her as if he'd tried to crawl the width of the bed and she were the obstacle that had stopped him. Amy maneuvered onto her back, and he began to snore. His face was buried in the sheets. One arm was flung upward so that his forearm lay between her breasts and his hand nestled against her chin.

"Sleepin' with you is like mud-wrestling with an octopus," she told him.

Amy studied his naked body, and her own. Tears slid from the corners of her eyes, and she wiped them away quickly.

He was sweet and funny and gentle. She was happy to be here with him, and she hoped this wouldn't be their only time together. She shut her eyes and covered them with the heels of her hands, forcing back more tears. There was a sense of letting go, of saying good-bye, of putting useless daydreams aside and replacing them with memories that could be cherished instead of regretted. *Oh, Doc,* she thought sadly. *Adieu.*

THREE

TWELVE

*J*ust as Sebastien had suspected, Philippe de Savin was not in danger of dying. In the two years following his surgery he remained in good health, according to the various medical tests that were performed on him regularly. He continued his regimented life of running the family businesses, marshalling exclusive social events, and spying on Sebastien.

Sebastien wasn't surprised at the surveillance, and it gave him vicious pleasure to ignore it, and his father. That he now found himself waiting in the anteroom of his father's business offices was due to a remarkable turn of events.

One of several secretaries in the room answered a softly buzzing telephone. "You may go in, now," she told him. Sebastien nodded to her as he strode past and through a set of heavily paneled doors. Entering a room where the heavy carpet silenced his footsteps, he stopped in the light of tall windows and watched his father rise from a desk. Looking into Philippe de Savin's angular, lined face with its thick cap of white hair, Sebastien saw himself in thirty years.

"So you've finally come," his father said, his mouth hard and amused. "Hoping that your sister's reports of my good health are inaccurate?" He slipped a finger into the collar of his shirt and pulled the material down to show the lurid pink indentation on one side of his neck. "I appreciate your concern. However late it may be."

"I have no need to see you. I need only inquire about you from all the people who watch me at your request."

Philippe de Savin settled his tall, long-limbed body into a leather chair. With his fingers resting lightly on the arms, he seemed secure in his superior status. "They say you'll be appointed head of the new transplant unit. They also say, however, that you've made enemies among the other physicians."

"I'm not in favor with people who cling to old techniques, no. When tradition harms patients, I say so."

"I approve of your aggressiveness. It would serve you well here." He raised a hand and gestured gracefully at the surroundings.

"Annette is doing brilliantly."

"She is madly in love with Giancarlo Costabile. She'll marry her Italian airplane designer and bear his common Italian children. She has chosen her life."

"No, *you* have chosen her life, without consulting her, as usual. Whether she marries Giancarlo or not, she wants to head the family corporation. Let her. Women do such things now, as well as marry and have children. Annette would be an excellent chief executive."

"It isn't a daughter's place to take charge. It is the eldest son's place."

Sebastien laughed curtly. "Still the same argument. And always pointless. You seem to think that I'll throw away my career someday and come to you, begging to be a part of your dynasty."

"Hardly. But I have other expectations." His eyes were fathomless, but a knowing smile hinted at private plans.

Sebastien went to a wall filled with photos of the de Savin businesses and idly studied the display. "Scheme if you want. I don't worry about it."

"You've become even more self-assured. So proud. But how is your life, really? I hear that your wife prefers the company of her friends and that the two of you share few interests."

"We share enough. We respect each other."

"So when will you take a mistress? Or have you already? It's really a very practical way to run a marriage."

"I enjoy your quaint description of disloyalty. I don't need a mistress. I barely have time for a wife. My work is everything." He paused, then pivoted toward his father, smiling thinly. "Well, not quite everything. I have a new interest that surprises me with its charm. I didn't expect to be so taken with it. Marie and I are going to have a child."

Philippe de Savin sat forward, his fingers clasping the chair arms, his blue eyes intense. "I'm going to be a grandfather?"

"Typical, you look at it solely as it affects you. Yes, you're gong to be a grandfather."

Philippe rose from his chair. Sebastien was surprised to see his father tremble. The sheen of emotion in the older man's eyes shocked him so much that he took a step backward. His father crossed the room and halted so close that he could almost touch Sebastien. He held out both hands. "You came here to tell me this as a gesture of truce."

Sebastien reeled. His father's unexpected vulnerability confused him, repulsed him, then made him angry at the swift tug of sympathy he felt. "I came here to tell you because Marie asked me to do so. She believes a child should know its grandparents. You will be invited to visit after the baby comes."

"Son, I am honored—"

"Were it up to me, you'd never see your grandchild. I don't intend to take part in your show of dubious sentiment. I'd prefer that the next generation of de Savins never be exposed to you. I won't have any more of my loved ones destroyed by you."

Philippe slapped a fist into the opposite palm. His moment of softness evaporated in fury. "How many more years will you go on making sacrifices at the altar of your mother's insanity? How much longer will you hate me for no reason?"

Sebastien walked to the doors, his hands clenched by his sides. "Your blindness crippled this family. But it will not cripple my children. Perhaps you and I are both getting a second chance to prove ourselves. Good afternoon."

"To prove *what*, Sebastien?" His father strode after him and blocked his way. "I did nothing wrong. *You* did nothing wrong. Terrible accidents happen in the world without blame."

"It was no accident. There was blame."

"You know what I mean. Your mother was an accident, a mistake, a misguided soul, a simple-minded and confused woman incapable of adjusting—"

"If you ever let my child suspect that you feel that way about its grandmother, I'll kill you." Sebastien's voice was low and utterly serious. "Do you understand? I'll kill you."

He left his father standing in grim silence, both hands out in a supplicating gesture that came more than twenty years too late.

❦

Annette's wedding was planned abruptly, owing to the fact that Annette was pregnant, a circumstance that delighted Giancarlo and depressed her, she confessed to Marie.

"She will be happy once the baby arrives," Marie told Sebastien as they dressed for the ceremony. "It's just that she fears that your father will pressure her to curtail her work." Marie patted her swollen stomach, at five months showing generously under the pleated black dress she wore. "She'll be happy."

Sebastien finished knotting the silk tie that matched his double-breasted suit. He frowned at himself in the long, gilt-framed mirror of their bedroom, privately hurt. "I shouldn't go to the ceremony. She doesn't want me there."

Marie settled in a chair near the bed and laughed lightly. "She didn't include you in the attendants. So? She feels threatened by the birth of our child. But she didn't include your brother, either. Surely such things are insignificant. Don't tell me you're hurt. I don't believe it."

Marie's pragmatism was her charm, but there were often times when he felt that he was conversing with a stranger.

The baby was their most intimate connection, and they were both excited about it.

She rose and went through an open doorway to the stone balcony that overlooked a small courtyard and garden. The house they kept in this exclusive Paris suburb was solemn and stately. Marie had chosen it, and Sebastien was indifferent to it.

"What is this?" she called a moment later. "Are you decorating the shrubbery for some special holiday?"

Sebastien walked outside. She stood beside a flowering shrub set in a container of thick stone. Bright sunlight glinted on the silver necklace she pulled from a leafy branch.

"I must have left it there when I was going through a box of photographs yesterday. It's something I carried when I was working in Africa."

She lifted the worn video token and studied it. "Was this the magic charm you mentioned? The one the villagers expected you to wear?"

"Yes." Feeling that something very private was being violated, Sebastien took the necklace from her rather abruptly.

"You needn't snatch it away." She gave him a bewildered look. "It isn't like you to keep memorabilia. Why this?"

He smiled sardonically. "Perhaps I don't want to lose my magic."

Marie dismissed the notion with a delicate sniff. "Throw it away."

"No."

Her fair complexion reddened a little. "You're being silly."

"Allow me. It's a first."

"Such nonsense."

Doc, don't you ever want to just sit on a hill somewhere and howl at the moon? "Marie? Have you ever howled at the moon?"

Her eyes widened in astonishment. "No."

"I thought not."

Marie gave him a rebuking look and swept past him. "You're in a peculiar mood. Come. We have a wedding to attend. ~~Do what you wish with your magic charm.~~ But please don't become maudlin."

"I hardly think I'm in danger of that. A patient called me 'pitiless and acerbic,' only yesterday. See? You can relax."

"I dislike your sarcasm."

"I dislike it, myself." Sebastien went to an enormous armoire and opened a drawer at its base. He dropped the necklace atop precisely folded handkerchiefs bearing the de Savin crest. His fingers lingered on the medal for a moment. He murmured under his breath, "Someday, Marie, we really should howl at the moon."

❦

Sebastien didn't see his brother at church. He looked for him during the reception, a huge affair in the garden of a fine restaurant near the Champs-Elysées. Jacques had been attending art school in Amsterdam for the last two years, and rarely returned to Paris.

Sebastien finally glimpsed him in the crowd dressed in pastel hues. He stood out like a raven among canaries in his black leather pants and a black sports jacket. He turned, a thin cigar clamped in his mouth. His gaze met Sebastien's, he smiled, and with the awful flash of teeth still showing in his gaunt face, he made his way across the garden.

By the time he stopped a pace away, Sebastien had recovered enough to speak calmly. "Come with me."

"And greetings to you, too, dear brother. I was planning to find you if you didn't find me first."

Jacques followed him to a corner where a trellis draped in vines sheltered them from scrutiny. Sebastien stared at his brother's ashen, emaciated face. "What's happened to you?"

"A bout with a stomach ulcer, that's all."

"Who are your doctors in Amsterdam? What have they said?"

"They've said they'd like their bills paid. Could you loan me some money?"

Sebastien was silent, disbelieving. He knew the size of the trust fund that Jacques had received at eighteen. Each of them had been given such a fund. It was an enormous amount of money. "You couldn't have—"

"Ah, but I did." Jacques threw the cigar on the perfect carpet of grass and ground it viciously with the heel of his black boot. "And I don't need a lecture on my irresponsibility. All I need is a loan. To pay my medical bills and my tuition. Consider it a grant to support the arts." He blithely named an amount.

"That's not a grant, that's an endowment. It's ridiculous for you to remain in school, wasting time."

"Look, will you give me the money, or not?" Jacques's cheek twitched.

The movement produced a tightening that made the skin look frail and translucent. Sebastien's heart twisted. Suddenly he remembered a whimsical, daydreaming little brother scorned by their father for interests he didn't perceive as masculine. Sebastien remembered a cheerful shadow who had idolized an impatient older brother.

"I'll give you a loan as soon as you have your doctors send me your records."

"Shit. You've got Father's skill at coercion." Jacques lifted trembling hands to scrape at hair that looked thin and dull.

"You've asked Father for money, too?"

"Of course not. I'm asking you. Shit. I thought you'd be easier. I should have known better. And I can't ask Annette. Her husband dislikes me, so at the moment she wouldn't give me a centime."

"I only want your medical records. That's not a terrible trade."

"Such unselfish, unquestioning love. To hell with you."

He started to leave, but Sebastien grabbed him by the arm. "If you want to waste your life, I won't pay the way. What have you done—sniffed a small fortune up your nose? I won't help you fund a drug habit."

"You won't help me at all. But relax, brother. I don't need it. I was just seeing how much I could take you for. Testing to find out if your balls are still made of steel."

Sebastien shoved him away. "I have no pity for whining and weakness. But come to me like a man and I'll listen to you."

"I *am* a man. I am. Goddamn you." Tears brimmed in his eyes. Jacques jerked his arm from Sebastien's grip and stumbled off. Sebastien watched him leave. Marie came over, frowning.

"Jacques looks terrible. Is he in trouble again?"

"Yes."

"What are you going to do?"

"Nothing. His lack of control is not my concern."

For a moment, before he realized that Marie was looking at him closely, he grimaced at the coldness of his words and wondered if he were being strong, or merely cruel. And when had he begun to sound so much like his father?

❧

The nursery was becoming the focal point of their home. Every evening when Sebastien returned from the office or the hospital he found the signs that workmen had once again been altering the room to suit Marie's excited plans. It was as if carpenter ants were making daily pilgrimages and leaving their trailings for him to find.

The room was now done in soft gray and ivory, hardly traditional nursery colors, but not surprising in view of Marie's nature. They gave the place dignity. Surrounded by such colors and furnishings of Victorian wicker, their child would develop eclectic tastes, she vowed.

Sebastien and she were happier and closer than they had ever been. During her sixth month they went to Sainte Crillion's outpatient clinic together. Marie had scheduled a sonogram.

Sebastien sat down beside the cushioned table where she lay propped on pillows, her tailored maternity blouse pulled up to expose her rounded stomach above a dark skirt. Filled with anticipation, Sebastien playfully thumped her belly with a forefinger. "This melon is ripe, I believe."

She looked embarrassed. "I beg your pardon."

"When I worked in America, in the South, people were always in the markets during the summer, thumping enormous green watermelons. Thumping watermelons is really quite a regional custom, it seems."

"It is *not* summer, and I am *not* a watermelon."

"You are not smiling, and you should be. Even a water-melon should have a sense of humor."

"Sometimes, Sebastien, I think you consider yourself funny. You really aren't, my darling, and you shouldn't try to be amusing."

Frowning mildly, he sat back while the technician, a pleasant little woman, prepared to begin. He *had* a sense of humor, he told himself. He could remember times with Amy when he had laughed with a deep, belly-tugging joy that had made him feel clean inside. More than that, he recalled making Amy laugh in return. . . . But why was he thinking about her when his wife waited to share a child with him?

"Oh, look, Sebastien!"

Marie's exclamation drew him out of his pensive reverie. Sebastien leaned forward, watching as the technician moved a sensor over Marie's abdomen and an X-ray-like picture flickered on a video monitor. With all his years in medicine, with all his knowledge of sonograms and what to expect, still the sight of his own baby awed him. This little one he could love. This little one he could protect.

"It's a boy," the technician noted, smiling. "Large. Very handsome, too. We've obviously caught him in the middle of a nap. Maybe he'll move, in a second. In the meantime, I'll try to show you a picture of his heart. To see it beating is a marvelous—hmmm. His position is making it difficult to locate. This little one is going to test my skill, I see."

As the technician continued to move the scanner and make exasperated sounds, Sebastien straightened rigidly in his chair. His attention never left the murky screen.

"I'm gong to ask Dr. Reginau to have a try at this," the technician said in a carefully nonchalant tone of voice. "He's much more skilled than I." She avoided looking at Sebastien and hurried from the room.

Marie raised up on her elbows. "Sebastien? Is something wrong?"

Because he didn't want to believe it, he answered no. Sebastien stared at the screen, then at Marie's stomach.

She lay back but grasped one of his hands. "You're

freezing cold. What is it? You know how to read a sonogram. What are you afraid of?"

Slowly he raised his eyes to hers. She shivered. He
squeezed her hand tightly. The words hung in his throat
like shards of ice. "She can't find the heartbeat because
there isn't one. The baby is dead."

❧

Labor was induced, and a few hours later Marie expelled
the fetus. She didn't want Sebastien present for the pitiful
event, and he didn't protest. Dr. Reginau, the obstetrician,
came to him afterward and said all the appropriate things:
There was no obvious abnormality, no obvious problem
with the pregnancy, no reason to think such a thing would
happen again. This was just nature's way of correcting a
mistake.

Your father honors his mistakes.

My mother is not a mistake, you whore.

The words came back to Sebastien with startling vivid-
ness. That was when he hit Marie's doctor. When Reginau
was being helped to his feet by several shocked nurses,
Sebastien told him that his child had not been a mistake,
by nature's standards or any others.

There would be repercussions because of such uncalled-
for violence. He had struck a fellow physician, and a
popular one, at that. He had struck a physician at the same
hospital where he himself was on staff. Where he hoped to
become head of the proposed transplant unit.

Marie lay in a private room, sedated, attended by her
mother and Annette. She gave Sebastien a glazed look and
told him to go home, that she didn't need him. He was
relieved to hear it. He spent the night walking the boulevards, his bruised hand throbbing.

❧

Marie had the workmen come back and put a lock on the
nursery door. Then she bolted it and kept the key in her
jewelry box. She told Sebastien that she didn't want the room
opened again until she brought a baby into it. He had never

seen her distraught and depressed before, and his efforts to soothe her were complicated by his own depression.

It was typical of their relationship that she didn't really want to share her grief with him, and he didn't know how to share his with anyone, including her. So they retreated into their work. She moved into another bedroom temporarily, preferring her privacy. He lay in their big, canopied bed each night, exhausted from another twenty-hour day, and stroked himself roughly. At those times he rarely thought of Marie but instead saw a piquant face with expressive green eyes and a scarred chin.

Three months passed in that way. Life began to feel normal again, although normal was not as it had been before. And then, one cold winter night just after one, the police came. Two detectives stood stiffly in the downstairs hall. The older of the two, a grim-looking veteran, spoke brusquely.

"Doctor de Savin?"

"Yes."

"You have a brother named Jacques?"

"Yes."

The younger man shifted and cleared his throat. "We're sorry to tell you that he has . . . been found . . . dead."

Sebastien took a step back and rested a hand on the banister. He stood very still, his shoulders stiff, his head up. "You must be mistaken. My brother isn't even in Paris. He's living in Amsterdam."

The older detective, looking as if he'd been through this sort of scene a thousand times, rubbed his neck above a sweat-stained shirt collar and sighed. "No, Doctor. He had plenty of identification. It was with him in his hotel room. A guest reported hearing a gunshot. An officer went to investigate."

They are simply mistaken, Sebastien thought firmly, "This person you found, he was murdered?"

"No. It appears to have been suicide."

"That is not something my brother would do."

The older detective grimaced. "Doctor, we have a note. It was written to you. We're keeping it at the station. If you'd come with us, we can show it to you. And the body, as well."

After a silent moment, Sebastien found his voice. "I see." He turned smoothly and started up the stairs. "Let me tell my wife some delicate lie for the moment, and then I'll go with you."

"Very good."

Sebastien heard the younger detective whisper to the other, "No brotherly love lost here, it seems."

They took him to the police station and showed him a note written on hotel stationery in Jacques's sweeping script.

I WAS NOTHING TO YOU BECAUSE I WAS NOT ANTOINE OR BRIDGETTE. I WAS NOTHING TO FATHER BECAUSE I WAS NOT HIM. ONLY ANNETTE LOVED ME FOR WHAT I WAS. I HAVE HONOR. I AM A MAN. I'M STRONGER THAN YOU, BECAUSE I HAVE THE COURAGE TO DO THIS.

Sebastien read the words a dozen times. *What courage, you coward?* he demanded silently. *What honor? What code of honor tells you to die?*

"Do you know what he might have meant?" one of the detectives asked.

"No."

"Did you know that he was sick?"

Sebastien looked up, frowning. "I suspected that he had a drug habit. What do you mean?"

"There was no evidence of drugs in the room."

"Then what was there?"

The younger detective fetched a pamphlet from Jacques's belongings. "Perhaps it means nothing." He handed it to Sebastien.

"Acquired Immune Deficiency Syndrome—Facts and Fallacies."

Sebastien stared at the title. It absorbed him. It brought back his conversation with Jacques at Annette's wedding. It ripped at his conscience.

"Are you all right, Doctor?" someone asked. Then, "Bring the doctor some water. Doctor? Would you like to call someone else in your family? Someone who can come to the station? Or a friend, perhaps? Here. The water."

Sebastien tossed the pamphlet on a table and waved the glass of water away. "I'd like to see my brother's body."

They took him to the morgue. The chief medical examiner was very blunt. "The body has a nasty head wound," he warned, as an assistant wheeled a sheet-draped gurney into a room with walls of stained concrete and floors dotted with drains.

Someone offered Sebastien a pair of yellow rubber gloves. Sebastien shook his head. The medical examiner coughed awkwardly and said that he couldn't allow him to touch the body without them, under the circumstances.

Sebastien took the gloves and slid them onto his hands. These were not a surgeon's gloves, meant for the artistry of life; these were the sort of gloves one wore to handle filth and death.

The drape was pulled back, and he stepped close, deliberate and silent, feeling as if he were in a dream. The gloves were appropriate. The thing on the table, with its misshapen head wrapped in bloody plastic, was only an obscene imitation of Jacques's beauty.

Sebastien pushed the plastic away and looked at his brother's face, then stroked his fingers down the silent artery in the throat, convincing himself. At the edge of his brother's blood-stained T-shirt he found an ominous lesion.

"A typical sarcoma related to the syndrome," the medical examiner interjected. "Probably, that is."

"Yes. Yes." Sebastien's voice was low and hollow, for Jacques alone. "What you did took courage. It took honor. I wish I had known." He laid his fingertips on Jacques's lips.

"You and your brother were very close," the medical examiner said with sympathy.

"No." *Not until now, when there's only a secret to share, as there was with our mother. Forgive me, forgive me.* "I want the nature of his illness kept from the rest of the family. Will that be possible?"

"I don't see why not. We're very good at misplacing information that would otherwise shame the surviving relatives."

Sebastien turned Jacques's face toward him and looked into the empty eyes. *There is no shame, little brother.*

He had spent so many years frowning at Jacques. He wanted to give him a smile now, but he was afraid it would ruin his control. His love for Jacques wasn't lost at all. It was bottled inside his chest, cold and hard, where it hurt more than anyone could imagine.

❧

Annette was openly devastated by Jacques's death. She was six months pregnant, the same as Marie had been when she lost a baby, so Giancarlo whisked her away for a vacation in Tuscany after the funeral. He was a charismatic man, too much so, Sebastien thought. Annette was almost slavish in her devotion to him. But in this case, Sebastien was grateful that Giancarlo took her away from Paris and its memories.

Their father went through the funeral mass with an aloofness that contrasted with the subtle air of frailty about him. Sebastien felt only weary indifference for him.

A few nights after the burial Marie came into their bedroom. Sebastien was standing at a window, trying to lose his thoughts by looking for the faint stars that pierced the haze in the night sky.

She stopped behind him and kissed him on the back of the neck, running her hands down his bare torso to the waistband of his pajama bottoms. He felt her nipples pressing against him through the sheer lace of her nightgown.

"Let's do something to help us forget the past week," she whispered. "It's been so long since we've had sex, my darling. I'm ready to start again. And I should be very fertile right now."

"Have I become nothing but a means to an end? Could you make the request a little more romantic?"

"Oh, Sebastien, don't be moody. I know I've been distant, but it's because I've been depressed all these weeks, and so have you."

"Ah, and having recently buried my brother, I'm cheerful?"

She ran her hands over the front of his pajamas, caressing him through the material. "Come to bed. You of all people should know that grief has its limits. We'll do something positive—we'll make another baby."

"It seems that you've avoided me until your obstetrician said it was safe to conceive again. Did you think I was happy in here alone every night? Is our sex life now solely devoted to creating a baby?"

"Stop it!" She moved around in front of him, her eyes fierce but her hands still massaging between his legs. "We have a wonderful sex life. We've both enjoyed ourselves. It's always been a purposeful sort of pleasure, so why should it be any different now?"

He stared at her for a moment, growing angry and yet also feeling his body react to her stimulation. "If you want sex from me tonight, you'll have to work for it."

Her eyes glittered with challenge. "All right, my darling." She untied his pajamas and jerked them down, then knelt down in front of him and took his growing erection in her mouth.

Sebastien trembled at the wet heat and the hard sucking of her lips. She was right. It was easy, and why should he care if it were even more emotionless than in the past? He wanted a child, too.

He grasped Marie's rich black hair and pulled her away from his rigid penis. "Enough. We wouldn't want to waste good sperm, would we?"

She smiled, her mouth wet, and quickly helped remove the pajamas from his legs. He lifted her to her feet and dragged her to the bed. The instant she climbed atop it he pressed her down and tore her gown in two.

"Yes. That's just fine. Whatever you like," she murmured, putting her hands behind her head and drawing her knees up.

Sebastien thrust into her and wondered if her slick welcome came from a tube of lubricant. Then he closed his eyes and shut her out completely, only feeling the connection between their bodies. He burst inside her with a furious orgasm that left him shuddering. When he opened his eyes to look at her, she nodded approvingly.

THIRTEEN

"*W*e are doomed," Mary Beth said dully, "to live in dumps and work for the Parker Poodits of the world forever."

Amy began to laugh. "But the people we meet are so darn interestin'. Come look out this window. I think the Ripple Man is trying to hit Frank up for another dollar." Their neighbor Frank, a very dapper jazz musician who resembled Sammy Davis, had innocently stepped onto the old building's tiny lawn to repot his houseplant. "Frank is shaking his head. Now the Ripple Man is peeing on Frank's begonia."

Mary Beth snorted. "I dislike living in a neighborhood full of derelicts, artsy-fartsy types, and men with very smooth cheeks and very short hair. I dislike being bohemian middle class."

Amy leaned back in her chair and smiled at the irony of life beyond college. The bohemian Mary Beth had worked hard in the past year to change her image. Her wild blond hair was now straight and short. It curved around her face like parentheses, the blunt ends swinging inward just below her chin. She'd thrown out her bargain-military wardrobe and begun dressing in tailored suits. Around their colleagues at WAZF, UHF channel 16, Atlanta's smallest independent television station, Mary Beth Vandergard was now Elizabeth Vandergard, newswriter, news producer, and sole anchorwoman for WAZF's sole newscast, aired every weekday evening at six.

It wasn't hard to get ahead at WAZF. And there wasn't much about the place to intimidate someone fresh out of college. Which was why Amy had been content for the past year. She'd progressed herself, starting as a production assistant but zooming through the haphazardly staffed ranks to a producer's job. She now commanded an impressive staff of two and enjoyed an annual income that was almost one-thousand dollars above minimum wage.

"It'll get better," she told Mary Beth. "This is great experience. Everybody our age is supposed to suffer while learning the ropes."

"Bullshit. Deborah Norville is already working for a network affiliate. It's not fair. For God's sake, she was in the same production classes as me! We made the same grades! And I can enunciate better than she does!"

"She's three years older than we are."

"No excuse. I don't intend to be known as the 'other' blonde who came out of the university! Norville will eat my dust one day. Wanna know why? Because she's Miss Ice Cream and I'm a bitch, and the public is more fascinated by mean blondes than by nice ones."

"Interestin' theory."

"No brag, just fact." Mary Beth put a cashmere scarf around her neck and swept a long white alpaca coat over her slacks and blouse. "I'm off. Off to edit tape for my soon-to-be-acclaimed show on candy making." She sighed. "I wish I could title it, *Lick This, Sucker.*"

The news was not a high priority at WAZF, and the whole city knew it. The station was best known for its wrestling shows. Mary Beth rolled her eyes. "Have a nice Friday off. I'll see ya on Monday. Don't be too wild with Mr. Comedy."

"I won't be wild. I might be semi-weird, though."

After Mary Beth departed Amy tossed a jacket over her sweater and jeans. She left the apartment carrying a canvas tote and her purse, then drove to the airport through a murky winter morning. She picked up the ticket Elliot had left for her and took a flight to Chicago.

He was waiting for her, in body at least, at the gate. She

found him slouched in a chair, snoring, his head thrown back and his denimed legs flung open. Large black sunglasses covered his eyes. Under a red ski jacket he wore a wrinkled flannel shirt with a crushed paper coffee cup tucked in the pocket.

Amy bent over him and sniffed. As she suspected, the scent of mint mouthwash puffed from him with each breath. He was as ridiculous as a kid trying to hide his drinking, and not nearly as successful. He smelled like a big mint julep. Frowning, she kissed his upper lip and woke him up.

"Huh? Baby, baby!" He engulfed her in his arms and pulled her onto his lap. "Salvation has come at last." He kissed her repeatedly as she wound her arms around his neck.

Amy removed his sunglasses and peered at his bloodshot eyes. "Let me guess. You finished your last show then hung around the club until about four, then you and every guy who could still walk went to the owner's place and partied until dawn. Right?"

"Wrong. Some girls went, too." He grinned. "But I fought them off when they started rubbing their breasts against me."

"Do you know that when you sleep sitting up you throw your legs apart and look like a dead frog?"

Looking toward heaven, he groaned. "I fought off the groupies to save myself for *her*?" But he was chuckling as he said it and ran his hands up and down her back. "I've got a great hotel room. No cheap digs for the hottest comedian on cable. You're going to love this place. My God, I can't believe we haven't seen each other for three weeks. That's a record. I knew I was getting too lonely yesterday when I was watching the *Flintstones*. I started fantasizing about Betty Rubble."

She chucked him under the chin. "Well, Barney, I missed you too." Amy loved the welcome in his eyes, and she knew that he wasn't lying about his loneliness. Elliot was faithful. When they met she hadn't expected him to be faithful, but after a year with him she was convinced that he meant it when he said he didn't have other women.

Elliot had held onto most of his solid midwestern values, and he was so sensitive to the feelings of other people that he was like a piano string that vibrated from every sound near it. His observation-style comedy was built on the resonating tones of the world and the people around him.

But the dark side of such sensitivity made him restless, fearful, and moody. He needed Amy most when those demons plagued him. She took care of him, she made him stop partying long enough to rest, and she gave him a quiet, secure place to which he could retreat.

Now that he was emceeing a monthly showcase for comedians on one of the cable channels, he was hot, and making big money. He headlined at the best of the big clubs in New York and Los Angeles, and the owners of the smaller comedy clubs that had begun springing up all over the country were begging his manager for bookings.

He was riding the crest of an exploding demand for comedians, and he deserved the rewards. If he played too hard—way too hard—at least he worked hard, too. He was a workaholic nomad. People in the business said that Jay Leno was the only big name who traveled more. Most comedians dreamed of being successful enough to quit the road, yet Jay and Elliot thrived on it.

But Amy had met Jay, and Jay was a quiet, mellow person with none of Elliot's manic traits. And compared to Elliot, he was a homebody. Elliot didn't even own a home. He didn't have a car. He said frequently that he had his work, and he had her, and that was enough. She knew that he had his booze and his dope, too, but she did her best to fight them.

Amy had learned a lot about her own strength and confidence during the past year. She made a great nurse-maid behind the scenes. It was a trait that bolstered her value at the television station. Being a producer at WAZF meant doing a lot of mother-hen work. She was proud of her ability to protect Elliot more than anyone else could, even his doting, indulgent parents.

She steered him to an airport café and got him a large carton of milk. He sipped from it obediently as they walked out of the terminal, then handed her the empty container when a group of people recognized him and asked for autographs. Amy hailed a cab and tossed her bag in the backseat. She glanced at her wristwatch and marked five minutes, knowing that Elliot would get restless if she let his fans adore him too long. When time was up she angled through the crowd and reminded him that he had a meeting to attend.

Elliot gave the crowd a resigned look. "This lady keeps my appointments. Sometimes she even makes me go to them."

He wrapped his arm around her as they made their way to the cab. Amy enjoyed the attention, though she was no longer awed by her status as Elliot's girlfriend. It was impossible to keep a man on a pedestal once you'd been privy to most of his bodily functions. Even in the most routine moments of his day Elliot loved an audience. As far as he was concerned, she ought to be impressed by his special talents. For one thing, he produced more gas than the Alaskan pipeline.

At the hotel he flopped on the bed and pulled her down with him. "Showtime, baby," he said with sloe-eyed lechery, his face tired but flushed with excitement. "I've got the microphone set up for you already."

Warmth and need slid through her, but she tweeked his nose. "I don't do requests."

"Do whatever you want. I'm helpless."

"Hopeless, you mean." She undressed him hurriedly, touching his lean, lightly haired body with appreciative hands, knowing that her happiness with Elliot came from acccepting each moment without question. When she finished removing his clothes he rolled on top of her. "I think one of us is still dressed, and it's ruining my good time."

"So undress me."

"How? You've got a man on top of you."

"Use those big floppy things at the ends of your arms." Mashed pleasantly beneath him, Amy wrapped her legs around his hips. His body was hard and inviting between her thighs; his smile held genuine affection as he began unbuttoning her jacket.

She looked forward to spending the next two days in bed

with him. Even more, she looked forward to spending the next two nights at the club with him, where she could absorb the magic that made people laugh.

❦

Atlanta Talks was taped on Friday afternoon at four. At quarter past one Dan Chapman called, frantic. He was a fatuous ex-weatherman and he hosted the show. He'd been hit in the mouth by a baseball while coaching his grandson's Little League practice. Amy learned later that he'd actually been punched by a taxi driver named Zbrowski, who had objected to one of Dan's Polish jokes.

A substitute host was needed for the show, and Amy sought out Mary Beth. Amy explained the dilemma, then put her question bluntly. "How would you like to interview two plastic surgeons about thigh sucking?"

"Do I have to be nice to them?"

"No."

"All right, I'll do it."

And so, at four o'clock on a windy spring afternoon, a phenomenon was born. Mary Beth poked, prodded, and slashed the two doctors until they were stammering in shock. By the time she finished with Dan Chapman's golf buddies, they had not only been humbled into admitting the hazards and cosmetic complications of liposuction but had also impaled themselves on the issue of treating women like imperfect pieces of meat.

After the show aired on Sunday night, fifty-seven viewers called. Thirty-six demanded that Mary Beth host the show from then on; nineteen insisted that the station fire her; one reported that she and he had been sisters in a previous life, and one threatened to kill her.

WAZF had never had a bigger or more passionate response to an on-air talent. The next week Elizabeth Vandergard became the juicier Liz Vandergard, and *Atlanta Talks with Liz* moved to Monday mornings at ten, replacing reruns of *Gilligan's Island*. Within two months it became WAZF's most popular and profitable show. Amy and Mary Beth came up with topics that rivaled the network talk fests. Amy reasoned that Atlanta must have its own supply of

bizarre, fascinating, ~~and obnoxious people anxious to joust~~
with Mary Beth on television. She was right. She found
them. Mary Beth interviewed them. Sometimes they survived the interview with their dignity intact. Not often.

Within six months the station tripled the show's budget
and let Amy bring in a studio audience for the tapings.
There were discussions of syndicating the program.

Amy reveled in the success and the raise that came with
it. Mary Beth accepted celebrity as her due, and bought a
racing-green Jaguar that her salary, even with her own
raise, could not begin to support. Her latest boyfriend, a
second-string running back for the Atlanta Falcons, paid
off the car note as a present for Mary Beth's twenty-sixth
birthday.

Amy, after some thought, invested her extra money in a
night course at Georgia State. She studied advanced French
and began to plan a trip to Paris. She wasn't going to
search for Sebastien; this would simply be a vacation, she
told herself.

Elliot complained about her plans. Why roam around
France when she could spend time with him, in the clubs?
He sulked for two weeks over the issue. When she finally
threatened to strangle him he decided to be a good sport.
He sent her a set of luggage with her monogram on each
piece. He offered to pay for the whole trip—if she'd stay for
only three days. She sent the luggage back and told him
that she was paying her own way. Elliot was puzzled and
angry.

In the back of her mind there was the tiny thought that
perhaps, just perhaps, she would take a side trip to the
Loire valley and find the winery Sebastien had bought,
according to a piece on him she'd read in a Paris newspaper she bought regularly at a bookstore. There was certainly no harm in that. She squirreled money away and
waited.

❦

Amy woke as if by a sixth sense. Raising herself on one
elbow, she shivered and pulled the blanket over her bare
shoulders. So people in Minneapolis called this *spring*

weather. Spring in the Arctic, maybe. And Elliot loved a
cold room. He liked to burrow into his security blankets
then wrap his arms and legs around her. She often felt as if
she were smothering, an ugly sensation that made her
wake sometimes in panic. But this time she woke because
he was gone. Amy huddled under the blanket and squinted
through the dark hotel suite at a strip of light at the base of
the bathroom door.

The door shouldn't be shut. Immediately suspicious, she
pulled one of Elliot's undershirts on and tiptoed across the
room. Listening at the door, she heard sniffing sounds. A
bleak feeling filled her stomach. She pounded the door
with a fist. "Are you auditionin' for a nose-spray commercial in there?"

There was sudden silence. Then Elliot sang out, "Yeah!
And I just got the part!" From the noises that followed, she
determined that he was hiding his evidence. Fear brought
cold perspiration to her forehead. When he opened the
door he grinned down at her, naked, his brown hair disheveled and his eyes looking too blue, too bright. He pecked
a forefinger toward the majestic erection that protruded
from the base of his belly. "Check it out. All for you."

She shoved past him and went to the shaving kit he'd left
near the sink. A quick perusal turned up the vial of white
powder. "Do you want to ruin yourself? I can put up with a
lot of things, but not *this*. This is dangerous, Elliot."

"Baby, sssh." He came up behind her and stroked her
shoulders. Their gazes met in the mirror over the sink. "I
barely touch the stuff, baby. I swear."

"Good Lord, you were using it *in the middle of the night.*
Why?"

"I just wanted to give you a fun time." He flashed a
charming smile. "After the way I fell asleep when we got to
the room, with my dick dead to the world, I thought—"

"I don't want a fun time that way." She took the vial,
opened it, and flushed the contents down the toilet.

When she looked over her shoulder he was watching her
with open-mouthed dismay. He snapped his mouth shut
and shrugged. "That's why I need you, baby. You look out
for my best interests. Too much, sometimes."

Tears slid down her cheeks. She slammed the empty vial into a trash can. "Do you want to end up like Belushi and a dozen other guys you've known?"

"Ah, baby, lighten up. Everybody who plays the road uses a little coke. All the travel, all the pressure . . . you know how tired I get. The coke is just a little dance I do with myself sometimes, to feel better." He looked down at his fading arousal then pulled his face into exaggerated lines of distress. "Now look what you did. King Kong went back to sleep."

"Elliot, promise me that you won't use coke." She faced him and clutched his hands. "I care about you, you overage delinquent. I worry about you."

He took her in his arms and held her desperately. "You're the only person who sends me postcards reminding me to take my vitamins. You're the only one who tells me when I'm being an asshole. You're the only one who understands how afraid I am, of so many goddamned things. Of not making it in the business. Of not being the best. Of being nobody. You understand. I've never said this before, but I love you. I mean it."

Stunned, she stood rigid within his embrace. Finally she slumped against him. "I love you, too." It was true in a fundamental way she didn't want to examine closely.

He whispered against her ear, "No more coke. I promise."

Amy shut her eyes and nodded, not believing him and not knowing what to do. For no logical reason she thought of her trip to France. The desire to go there, to escape, to be part of a fantasy, overwhelmed her. She decided to take the vacation even sooner than she'd planned. Her life was twisting in directions that frightened her, and for the moment, at least, she wanted to turn it toward the past.

❦

The innkeeper gestured broadly, a long loaf of bread in one hand. She looked very Gallic in her distress. *"Vous ne pouvez pas aller piqueniquer aujourd'hui. Il fait un temps de chien!"*

Amy took a moment to decipher the impassioned words

and was proud when she managed easily. She answered in halting but correct French that she couldn't let the rainy weather cancel her outing because this was her last full day of vacation. She had to take the train back to Paris in the morning and then leave for America.

The woman grumbled maternally but wrapped the bread in plastic and placed it in a knapsack along with cheese and a small bottle of wine. Amy tucked her hair under the hood of a bright yellow raincoat and gazed anxiously out a kitchen window that framed a picturesque garden shrouded in mist. Why had she waited until the end of the week to make this excursion? Now the weather had turned cool and wet, and the prospect of riding a bicycle several miles in it seemed foolish.

But she knew that she couldn't go home without seeing the estate that Sebastien had bought after he married. Of course, he had a home in Paris, too, and that was undoubtedly where he and his wife spent most of their time. The press covered his life in great detail. He was very famous now. Amy made some inquiries and learned the house was in an old, exclusive part of the city. She hadn't visited it. Her pride, along with a sense of embarrassment, wouldn't let her. She wasn't going to lurk on the street outside Sebastien's home like some kind of pitiful fanatic.

But she *would* allow herself to lurk outside his country château. Troubled, Amy glanced down at her oversized raincoat, borrowed from the innkeeper's tall daughter. She felt ridiculous.

"You are having doubts," the innkeeper said, watching her shrewdly. "Good. Don't go. I'll make you a cup of tea and we'll eat some sweet biscuits with marmalade."

Amy shook her head. As much as she disliked this compulsion, she wanted to give into it, to expel it by indulging it, just once. *"A tout à l'heure. Merci."* Taking the knapsack, she hurried through a back door into the dreary morning.

❦

Her heart in her throat, Amy brought the bike to a halt in front of a massive stone entrance flanked by walls of tall, sharp hedge. Through a filigreed iron gate a cobblestone drive wound along terraced slopes covered in tulips and hyacinths. In the distance, among perfect lawns and ancient groves of birch, stood a small but breathtaking château. Amy had read about it in a guidebook, but the description hadn't warned her that she would feel so awed. So this was the country estate Sebastien had bought for his wife.

Staring at the château's round white towers capped with spires, the peacock perched lazily atop a stone fountain, and the vineyards stretching along the hills beyond the main grounds, the last of her fantasies crumpled. They mocked her for thinking that she had ever been an important part of Sebastien's world.

Trembling, she reached under her slicker and opened the nylon bag attached to the belt of her jeans. She removed a large pair of sunglasses and covered her eyes. Pulling rain-dampened hair over her forehead, she tried fervently to disguise herself. There was almost no chance that Sebastien was here, but still. . . .

"*Bonjour,*" a scratchy voice called to Amy from somewhere in the tall shrubbery near the gate.

Amy jumped. A stout woman emerged carrying a woven basket filled with cut flowers. She wore a clear plastic raincoat over a stern black dress; a uniform, Amy guessed.

"*Bonjour,*" she responded. "*Pardon, s'il vous plaît. Je reviens tout de suite.*"

"Ah. American. I recognize the accent."

"Yes. A tourist. Do you mind if I stand here for a minute and look at the château? It's so beautiful."

"We don't give tours here."

"I know. I just want to stay at the gate."

The woman stepped closer, studying her. "Of course, you are welcome to look through the gate. You must be very dedicated to make your tour on a day such as this. But why are you wearing those glasses?"

"Uhmmm, I have an eye condition. My eyes are sensitive to the light."

"You are so young to have such a thing. Are you a student?"

"No. I work for a television station as a producer. I'm here on vacation." Feeling awkward, she nodded toward the basket of flowers. "Are you a gardener here?"

The woman laughed merrily. "I might as well be, I come out here so often. No, I am the head housekeeper."

Amy took a deep breath. "The people who own the vineyard . . . do they actually live here?"

"They live in Paris, but they visit frequently. They're here now. But they're getting ready to drive back." The house-keeper cocked her head toward the château. "I hear an automobile engine. Perhaps they are leaving now."

Amy's breath evaporated. Her heart raced and she felt dizzy. Here. He was here, close by. She, too, heard the car engine. Fear and elation washed over her. Sebastien mustn't know that she was here. It would be too humiliating for her. But if only she could see him, get just a glimpse of him. . . .

"Move from the gate, please," the housekeeper told her.

"Sure." Stepping with numb precision, Amy wheeled the bike into the tall grass a dozen feet away. She was standing in a ditch before she realized it, with a puddle of water creeping inside her cloth walking shoes.

But her attention was riveted to the gate, which slid back on both sides with majestic slowness when the house-keeper reached inside a control box and pushed a button. The approaching car seemed to take forever. Amy strained her eyes, staring at the place where it would appear. She would have only a second, as it slipped past, a second to merge memories with the present.

But the low-slung black vehicle purred halfway through the gates and came to a stop. Amy clutched the bike's cold handlebars. She bled inside as if he had left only the day before, instead of almost five years ago. Sebastien opened the driver's side—the side nearest to her—and climbed from the car.

He wore a long trench coat that billowed open as he stood up, revealing dark slacks and a light shirt, open at the collar. His charcoal-black hair was disheveled, his expression dark and angry. He was thinner, older, with a tension in his face that gave a cruel slant to his features. She recorded all that in the back of her mind while silently chanting his name.

He didn't look her way, didn't realize that she stood there, watching him. With forceful strides he crossed behind the car and went to the housekeeper, who smiled despite his imposing attitude. He nodded to her brusquely and took a handful of flowers from the basket.

Amy glanced toward the car. Through the open door she met the stern gaze of a woman dressed in a dark maternity blouse and skirt. His wife. A book lay open on the woman's lap. A pillow cushioned the back of her neck, and her black hair draped over the white case in a smooth river. She was in the early stage of a pregnancy, judging by her barely evident stomach. Which child—their first? their third? They had been married almost three years.

Amy's attention jerked back to Sebastien. He came to the driver's door and, bending over, handed the flowers to his wife. He adjusted a side mirror, his hands moving with impatient force. For one heartbreaking moment he seemed about to turn toward Amy. She had no idea what she'd do if he looked at her. She was frozen in a maelstrom of conflicting emotions—sorrow, jealousy, a need to call his name, the horror that he would look at her and know who she was, the horror that he would drive away and never know.

He didn't turn toward her. He got back into the car and shut the door so hard that the window rattled. He threw the car into gear. Amy lurched forward one step but brought herself to a halt, pride stabbing at her. His wife frowned at her, then cupped the flowers to her face and leaned back on her pillow, shutting her eyes. His wife.

The car pulled away with the nearly soundless precision of a mechanical work of art. Amy watched it until it rounded a bend in the road. She felt as if every organ inside her body had been rearranged.

"Mademoiselle?" the housekeeper called, then called again. "Would you like to come to the house? It is starting to rain again. You can wait in my quarters until it stops."

Wait in the servant quarters. Hide beside the gate, in a ditch. Be nobody. Be nothing. Be absorbed by wanting what can't be had. No. No more.

Amy found her voice. "Thank you, but no. I can't stay. I have a long way to go. It's a real long way to where I'm going."

And I've got a lot to do if I want to get there.

❦

When she walked off the plane in Atlanta, Amy found Mary Beth waiting. Mary Beth wasn't supposed to be waiting. She wasn't the sentimental type who'd greet a pal at the airport after only a week's absence. Amy stopped in the aisle and stared at the grim expression on her roommate's face.

"Let me guess. We've been evicted from the apartment for hosting that lingerie party. I knew the vice squad would get us for buying underwear with zippers in it."

Mary Beth slipped an arm around her shoulders. "Honey, I hate to tell you this—"

"Who died?" An ominous feeling turned Amy into stone.

"Your stepmother."

Amy sank onto a railing beside the aisle. *Maisie.*

❦

True to her nature, Maisie had died without fuss. She had simply fallen off the top of a 30-foot ladder while adjusting one of the vents in the ceiling of her chicken house. Her head had struck a concrete block that she'd propped against the ladder's base. The coroner said the fatal hemorrhage was probably quick.

There was only one note of drama, but a perfect one, one suited to Maisie's love for the tabloid newspapers she'd bought every week at the grocery store for as long as Amy could remember. Amy strangled on a hysterical urge to laugh as she stared into Maisie's coffin, surrounded by the cloying scent of gardenias and the antiseptic funk of the funeral home. She could see the tabloid headline in her mind: *Fowl Play—Maniac Chickens Maul Owner's Dead Body.*

She gulped her bile. The mortician had done a terrific job of fixing the damage. Maisie appeared to have no more than a bad case of acne. But of course, beneath her eyelids there were no eyes.

Swaying, Amy clutched the side of the coffin. The room was empty. Maisie's church friends had visited earlier, judging by the guest book on a stand by the door. The carpeted-and-brocaded silence made Amy's skin crawl. She touched Maisie's hand then drew back, jolted by the coldness and hardness.

This was her first experience with the death of a family member. She'd only been a baby when her mother died. Her thoughts flew back to Sebastien, wondering how he had been able to stand it when his family was killed in the car accident. How had he felt when he'd seen their maimed bodies? And later had he stood over their coffins and been sickened by this awful imitation of life? How in God's name could a little boy deal with such a thing? How, then, could he go into medicine as a career, knowing that his whole life would revolve around the sick and dying?

Amy fought a rush of loneliness and confusion. Touching Maisie's hair, she whispered, "Love you, Mams."

She turned and stumbled from the room, winding the fingers of one hand into the skirt of her dress, holding numbly to her purse with the other. Pop was slumped on a claw-footed sofa in the hall. Even dressed in his best brown suit he looked like a long-haired bum who'd just wandered into someone's nice parlor. He gazed at the patterned carpet beneath his feet and didn't move.

"Come on, Pop." Amy bent over him and touched his shoulder. Tenderness rose inside her, but fear held it in check. She spoke without emotion. "I'll fix you some dinner."

"Don't need it."

"Let me drive you home. I'll stay overnight, and we'll come get your car in the morning."

"Don't want you to do that. Don't need you. Need Maisie."

"Pop, I know—"

"I found her. I found her in the chicken house. Layin' there, her face all, all . . . I'm gonna sell the chickens."

"That's a good idea. Now come on, let's go home." She slid her hand under his arm and tugged.

He jerked the arm away and glared up at her. "I don't need you. You said you were never coming back. Too late to come back, now."

"I'm trying to help you, Pop."

He began to cry. "You hurt Maisie's feelings by not ever coming to visit. You didn't think about anybody but yourself. Mean-tempered little shit. I don't need you. You don't love me."

She stepped back, stunned by the sight of him crying. Guilt filled her, but rage grew alongside it. "I want to love you, but you won't let me."

"Twist the truth! What do you want? To give me some more money? Well, forget it, all right? Don't crawl to me and expect forgiveness."

She wanted to shake him. She wanted to scream and bury her head in her hands. *Stop looking for acceptance,* she told herself. *It never makes sense.*

"I give up, Pop. I'm not doing either of us any good here. I won't be back tomorrow for the funeral. I'm going to visit a friend, in New York."

"I don't want you here. You show up here, I'll throw you out! Get! Get out of here!"

Slowly she moved back from him, straightening her shoulders, lifting her chin, freezing inside. Her grief mingled with bitter resolve. Her life was twisting again, but now she was in control. Dignity, pride, honor—she wouldn't give them up for anyone, ever again. She was no longer a victim, or like sweet, dumb Maisie, a passive martyr. She was going to New York, where Elliot was filming a television special. She would stay with Elliot and take care of him, because she was important to him, and that meant a lot to her. But Elliot was going to take care of her, too, in ways she had just begun to plan.

FOURTEEN

Sebastien was appointed head of the transplant unit at Sainte Crillion on a January day when icicles fringed the stone fountains of Paris and added a crystal beard to the snarling stone lion who guarded the hospital's front entrance.

Sebastien's appointment was no surprise to anyone, even with his outburst of violence toward a fellow physician. The staff and his fellow surgeons had expected it to come sooner. So had Sebastien. Still, at age thirty-six, when most heart surgeons were just establishing themselves, he held one of the most respected positions in the European medical community.

"You know what some of the older physicians are saying, don't you?" Marie's father asked him on the day that the appointment was announced. "They're saying that you were selected in part because you're my son-in-law."

Sebastien continued to gaze out a window toward the boulevards below, his hands clasped behind his back. He felt calm and reflective; he was at a brief peace with himself as he savored the moment. The loneliness of his life had never seemed more justified; the barrier reef that surrounded his emotions, more necessary. Idly he slid a finger over the back of one hand, caressing the dry, overscrubbed skin that was a surgeon's trademark. "Ironic, isn't it, since being your son-in-law has disadvantaged me."

"I beg your pardon?" Christian's chair squeaked as he shifted.

Sebastien reveled in the tension. "I have my informants, too, you see. I know that my father has lobbied you incessantly to keep me from being made head of the transplant team. I congratulate you on having the nerve to ignore him. Or was it simply that you could no longer ignore my qualifications without appearing foolish?"

"You bastard. You ungrateful bastard." The older man slapped a hand on his desk. "Watch yourself, Sebastien. A man who has no friends should at least cultivate his relatives."

"I find that my relatives have ulterior motives."

"You mock my honor. You mock your father's love. He may be misguided, but is it a crime for a father to want his legacy perpetuated through his most-deserving child? He wants only the best for you: power, prestige, family—"

"I have satisfied his requirements, then. I owe him nothing. He wants what suits him best, not me."

"Oh? With all your talent and arrogance, why can't you at least manage to give him a grandchild? Why can't you give my daughter a baby?"

Slowly Sebastien swiveled his head. He met Christian d'Albret's eyes and held them until a warning had been fully and effectively conveyed. A month ago Marie had lost another baby, their fifth. Thank God, this one had miscarried very early, not like the first one or the fourth, which had both reached six months. Sebastien ground the knuckles of one hand into the other. Her specialists, having conducted every test possible over the past few years, still found nothing wrong.

Nature culls her mistakes. Sebastien winced. He and all his siblings had been mistakes, the products of a marriage that should never have taken place. If his sister had not borne two healthy children in the past three years, Sebastien would have allowed himself the morbid thought that nature, in keeping him from becoming a father, was simply correcting its error in the second generation. Perhaps the sins of the father were only visited upon the sons, the bearers of the family name.

Sebastien found himself pondering sins and curses, then angrily discarding such nonsense. He tried to concentrate

on Christian d'Albret, who was now detailing some minor
point of administration that had no importance to the
practice of surgery, particularly transplant surgery, where
the protocols were shaped by the skills and personalities
of the members of a small, elite team.

Sebastien already knew how he would run the new unit:
He would treat his doctors and nurses with respect but
demand complete dedication. Home, family, friends—all
must be a distant second to the incredibly complicated
work at hand. He expected no more of them than he
expected of himself. He never left the hospital before
midnight, and many times he didn't go home at all, catching a few hours' sleep on the cot in his office. He saw
Marie no more than two or three nights a week.

"I think that your most crucial staff problem will be
burnout," Christian was saying. "Transplant patients inspire
such personal involvement . . . and so many of them die.
You must give your staff ample means to retreat."

"I have selected people who understand the risks and
the demands, people who live for their work."

"But each of them needs a sanctuary, Sebastien. Even
you, believe it or not, need something besides your career."

"No."

Christian exclaimed in dismay and continued lecturing
him. Sebastien tuned out the sound. Marie's father was the
perfect type to head a hospital bureaucracy; it was from
him that Marie had gotten her passion for rules and her
colorless view of life.

Christian finally came to an awkward stop. When Sebastien didn't comment, he leaned back in his upholstered
executive chair so heavily that it groaned. "Forgive me for
bringing up the subject of children a few minutes ago. But
I can't help but think that you spend so much time at the
hospital in order to avoid Marie. You blame her for the
problems, and that angers me."

"I don't blame her." Sebastien returned his attention to
the window, while peace deserted him and frustration
twisted his stomach. Each of Marie's miscarriages carved a
larger wound than the last one and strained their cool
relationship even more, it was true. But he didn't fault her;

instead he felt cheated by some vindictive fate or by his own failure, some enormous failing he had only to discover and fix. "She suffers. I know how much she wants a child."

"And what will you do if she never produces one? What is there to make your marriage worthwhile besides children?"

"There will be children. Have patience, Christian."

"You will not divorce my daughter, you understand? Not if you want to keep your position here."

"Don't insult me with a limp threat. I would be welcome at any hospital in Europe."

"But there is only one Sainte Crillion, the best of the best, with a new transplant unit that could bring you worldwide recognition. No, Sebastien, I think you won't jeopardize what you've built here . . . and what you could accomplish in the future."

"I'll live my life as I wish, Christian, without your permission. But rest assured, I have no intention of divorcing Marie."

"I don't hear love speaking, I hear complacency. You and Marie—"

"Have an understanding. And it works quite well. She understands the liabilities of marriage to a heart surgeon. She has always understood that my work demands most of my time and energy. She enjoys the prestige. She has her own life."

"She is very unhappy."

"Unhappiness is the state of most lives, eh? Enough." Sebastien shrugged, trying to sidetrack the anger that was winding through the muscles of his shoulders. He shut his eyes and made himself concentrate on the soothing, silken glide of his shirt and the heavier weight of his coat. He spent more time at his boxing than ever before, and the workouts plus maturity had added bulk to his chest and shoulders. He knew that he looked brawny and intimidating—and vain, many of his colleagues claimed.

"What are you thinking?" Christian asked in a disgusted tone. "What are you feeling? I can never tell. That's a great talent of yours, Sebastien. Goddamn arrogant surgeons. So tough. They hide everything so well. And you are the best, I admit it."

Sebastien shook his head. "I am only reveling in my new position of power," he said in a sardonic tone. But his emotional state was as fierce and vivid as the torrent of sleet that slashed across the window. He was thinking of a night seven years ago on a hilltop in the moonlight, when a naive American girl had made life seem so carefree and simple.

❦

Annette had relaxed since having her children, because they put her in a position of power. Sebastien was deeply pleased to have her friendship again, though it came at his own expense. She had contributed something to the family that he couldn't—grandchildren. And her ambitions benefitted because Philippe de Savin adored them.

"You should hear how he talks to them!" she told Sebastien over lunch at her club. Gripping a lapel of her dusk-blue cutaway jacket like an orator about to make a speech, Annette leaned across her venison cutlets and winked. "He calls them Puppy and Kitten! Imagine! Papa using whimsical nicknames!"

"I'm glad that his attention pleases you."

"And I'll tell you something else." She clinked her wineglass to Sebastien's. "He's become more open-minded. He's turning the shirt factory in Lille over to me. I'll be in charge of the entire operation."

"Congratulations. You deserve much more than that."

"Oh, in time, Sebastien, in time."

When they finished lunch and rose to leave she grasped his hand. "Don't drive back to the hospital this second. Come see the children. Come to the nursery with me while I gather them up."

Sebastien agreed reluctantly. He avoided children, even Annette's. "I have only a few minutes."

"That's enough. Good God, how will you ever be a father if you can't stand children?" She frowned at him.

He decided to let her mistaken assumption pass. "So far, that question has not urgently required an answer."

"Oh, I give up! I'll never decipher you."

"Mystery is part of my charm."

"Hardly. There's no mystery, only stubborness. Come along, stone face."

The club's nursery was too bright; the cheerfulness of it weighed him down as he followed Annette into a suite of rooms filled with toys, children, and sunlight. She clapped her hands at the blond two-year-old who sat in the midst of candy-colored building blocks. "Jacques! It's Maman! And Uncle Sebastien! No, you haven't forgotten him, even though he hasn't come to see you in months."

Sebastien hid a grimace that leapt from deep discomfort. He hadn't been surprised when Annette had named her first child after their brother. He approved, in fact, but the name was never easy to hear. Little Jacques laughed and held out his arms. Picking him up, Annette kissed him heartily then thrust him into Sebastien's arms. "Now, Sebastien, you hold him while I retrieve Louise. She's in a crib in the infants' room. Try not to look so stern. You'll frighten him."

"Wait, Annette—"

"I'll be right back."

She left Sebastien holding his nephew, who squirmed and stared at him with dark eyes that grew wider with each second. The silence hummed with uncertainty; Sebastien realized that he was gripping the boy against his chest in an almost fierce hold. "You have your father's coloring, but those eyes, *mon petit*, those eyes . . ."

The child had his grandmother's big, haunting eyes. She had given those ancient Celtic eyes to the de Savins. Sebastien looked into them and saw her, remembered her dying. He saw Antoine, Bridgette, Jacques—and himself. Himself. Doomed to survive alone, doomed because he had grown up afraid to let anyone come too close again.

Doomed. He told himself it was a ridiculous, morbid notion. But suddenly the room felt too hot; Sebastien had the disturbing thought that he was being smothered by the scent of babies and the light, high laughter of the older children. His throat ached. To his horror, his eyes burned with tears.

Shocked, he held Jacques at arms' length. The boy dangled there, looked frightened, then began hiccupping.

"Stop it," Sebastien ordered, his voice raw. Jacques began to cry loudly. Calling an attendant, Sebastien set the gulping child in her arms. "Tell his mother that I had to leave. I detest cranky children."

"Sir, you can't treat a child so coldly and expect—"

"I have no time for this nonsense. Take care of him. Do your job."

She regarded him with maternal disdain. "Yes, sir."

As he walked away he measured his gait carefully so that it would not appear that he was on the verge of running.

❦

Due to the brutal schedule he set for himself as head of the transplant unit, months passed before Sebastien realized that something strange was happening to Marie. She had gradually filled every extra spot in the downstairs library with books on astrology, psychic phenomena, spiritual channeling, and other occult subjects. He found crystals tucked among the cushions of the stately eighteenth-century divan in their bedroom suite. When he passed through the somber rooms downstairs he smelled the lingering aroma of an incense so heavy it obscured the delicate scents of fresh flowers the maid regularly set about the house.

At first he found it difficult to believe that Marie, the soul of earthly pragmatism, had succumbed to a spiritual fad. He disdained the commercialized and public grasping for spiritual fulfillment, and he thought of his mother's quiet adherence to her Catholicism and the occult, her faith, lifelong and simple, potent, filled with magic.

He didn't discuss his own fancies, not certain whether he believed them himself: the longings that he couldn't name; the dreams in which he was always reaching, always searching; the moments when he paused during his daily routines, feeling compelled to listen. He couldn't shake the idea that someone who cared about him was whispering so softly that he couldn't quite hear.

Yes, he could tolerate a few harmless chimeras, whether his own or Marie's. It was only when they invaded his breakfast—a cherished tradition of thick coffee and pastries—that he rebelled.

One predawn morning he sat down in the breakfast alcove to enjoy his usual fare, but the cook, coughing with embarrassment, set out new concoctions. "What is this?" Sebastien demanded, throwing down a medical journal to glower.

"Wheat germ cereal, sir. With soy milk. Herbal tea and a slice of melon. Madame said this is what you'll be having from now on."

"Not unless I'm being force-fed through a tube inserted in my stomach. Take this away and bring me my usual."

"I can't, sir. Madame has forbidden it. I've restocked the kitchen and thrown everything away." The cook, a florid middle-aged man with classical training, seemed to be on the verge of tears. "I can't manage this health-food cuisine, sir. I'm going to resign."

"You most certainly are not. For me, at least, you'll continue to cook as before."

"God bless you, sir. Will you tell madame?"

"Yes. This evening."

Late that night when he returned home from the hospital Marie was waiting for him in their suite. He stopped in the center of the bedroom and stared at her in much the same way he'd studied his breakfast. In the course of one day she had transformed herself. Her tailored silk robe had been replaced with a shapeless wrap of mustard-colored cotton. Her long black hair had been shorn; it now lay flat and straight against her head in a style that barely covered her ears. Good-bye to her pearls. On a loop of leather around her neck hung a large, brilliant crystal.

"I decided that an abrupt change would shock you less," she said, folding her hands across her stomach placidly, almost nunlike in the new robe. "I've been planning this."

"What? To impersonate a harem boy?"

"For one thing, I'm closing my business, as soon as possible."

"Why close your school?"

"I'm going to spend all my time in personal study. Meditation. Yoga. Trust me, Sebastien. For the past five years you and I have allowed ourselves to be twisted by negative forces. That is why we haven't had a child. We must purify ourselves."

He felt a vein throbbing in his neck. "We haven't had children because one of us has some as-yet undiscovered medical problem. You don't seriously expect me to agree with your plan, do you? And don't ever tamper with my breakfast menu again."

Her expression remained benign, almost beatific. "I knew you would resist. So be it. But I intend to perfect *my* contribution to conceiving a child, so that if anything goes wrong the next time I'll know that my body and spirit are not at fault."

"Making for a convenient assumption that I'm the guilty party."

"I don't place guilt. It's a negative—"

"Stop. I really don't want to hear the jargon. Do what you feel you have to. I won't complain."

"Then you'll try to understand why I want us to be celibate for a year."

Sebastien studied her in dull fury, his chin up, his hands slowly balling into fists by his side. A dozen responses streaked across his mind—brutal, sarcastic, threatening words that he would never have believed himself capable of speaking to a woman. A brittle expression entered her eyes, and her face went white.

She shrank back, hugging herself. "*Sebastien*," she whispered. "I'll scream if you do anything."

Understanding slammed into him and made a cold shiver crawl up his spine. What had he become, that he could terrify her with a mere look? She who was as strong and hard as himself, she who could not be intimidated, was now on the verge of cowering.

It made him sick. It frightened him. He did not know himself anymore. "Do whatever you wish," he said in a barely audible tone.

She sagged. A huge sigh of relief came from her throat. 'I know how strange and cruel this must seem to you, but several of my spiritual advisers—"

"Fine." Sebastien waved a hand in dismissal. "Our sex

life degenerated long ago into brief ruttings devoid of imagination or tenderness."

"I won't complain if you take a mistress."

"How kind of you. But it would be more trouble than the pleasure is worth. Be glad that I don't have the patience or the time to seduce any woman discriminating enough to suit me."

She opened the robe and held it apart, showing that she was naked underneath. "Tonight, one last time, if you like—"

"No."

"I've moved into the guest suite in the left wing."

"So be it. Good night." He turned away and walked onto the balcony. The night air was sharp on the cold sweat that beaded on his forehead. After he heard Marie leave the suite he sat down on the balcony's wide stone balustrade and sank his face into his hands. He laughed softly, without humor, and after a while he went downstairs and across the back portico, through the small courtyard to the garage, where a black Ferrari always waited.

He drove out of the city and found the open highway under a clear sky. Only on these late-night excursions did he feel totally free, yet totally in control. When the Ferrari was soaring at its speed limit, when certain death waited on the other side of even the smallest mistake, he felt better. He told himself that he did not make mistakes, in his driving, in his marriage, in his work, in any of his choices. He had conquered himself again, at least for now.

❦

There was only one aspect of his work that Sebastien didn't relish, but its growing importance couldn't be ignored. Unlike many surgeons, he was not interested in the limelight; speaking and lecturing conflicted with his private nature. Language seemed inadequate; it made him feel trapped inside himself, his thoughts a jumble of earnest enthusiasms and concerns that he didn't know how to express.

He relegated public relations chores to one of his staff surgeons and spoke as rarely as his prominent position would allow. The requirements of his ego, which he knew with sharp

self-awareness were great, were satisfied by the attention his
transplant protocols had already begun to receive.

So he viewed his speech at the 1988 World Seminar on
Transplantation with stoic disinterest. What *did* fascinate him,
to his surprise, was its setting. He had never been to California
before, and as a limousine carried him from the airport to the
hotel he sat on the edge of the seat, absorbing San Francisco's
postcard-perfect views with more delight than he'd felt in a
long time for anything other than his work.

The next day he stole a few hours from meetings, rented
a car, and drove north into the wine country. It charmed
him. He stopped on the side of the road and walked to a
small vineyard. In the distance sat a weathered house and
barns; he hesitated by an unlocked gate in the wire fence,
planning his apology if the owner noticed his intrusion. He
knew the sacred bond between a man and the land. He
inhaled the scent of earth, breeze, and vegetation, remembering how he'd followed Pio around the vineyards as a
child, loving the outdoors.

He slipped into the small enclosure and went to the
grape trellises. Under his breath he exclaimed over the
quality of the vines; kneeling in the soil heedless of his
crisp tan slacks, he scooped dirt into one hand and admired its richness. No wonder Jeff Atwater had bragged so
about his home state.

Atwater. He had returned to this area to take a job.
Sebastien scowled. He had thought of him when he
planned the California trip. Years ago he had hated Jeff,
even though he blamed himself for leaving Amy in the
man's seductive care.

Time had softened the hatred but not the sense of
betrayal. He didn't blame Amy, from whom he had never
exacted promises. He had asked her to forget him, and she
had, and that was that. But he did blame Jeff, and he
always would.

The world was silent around him; the road empty. Birds
swooped past and insects made a pleasant hum. He lifted
his head, listening, experiencing the quicksilver, familiar
sensation that someone was calling his name. *A good
omen*, he told himself.

By the time he returned to the car he had made his decision. Before he returned to France he would hire a real estate agent to find what he wanted. He was going to buy a home—a refuge?—in this place.

❧

Sebastien couldn't tell if the mostly American audience had been impressed by his speech on heart-assistance devices or by the fact that a foreign surgeon had contributed important research. American physicians generally felt superior. At any rate, everyone in the hotel's darkened ballroom rose to applaud him. He basked in the sea of respect for a second, then stepped down from the stage and shook hands with a portly, balding man who wore an amicable smile and the ugliest plaid jacket in existence. His outfit included a string tie and cowboy boots. Dr. Adrian Johnson resembled a carnival barker, but he was actually a pioneering heart surgeon and one every surgeon in the past twenty years, including Sebastien, had idolized. He ran the cardiothoracic research program at the Pacific Heart/Lung Institute, a private foundation affiliated with Stanford University. Johnson was the seminar's chief coordinator.

"I knew that you'd knock 'em off their asses," he told Sebastien, pumping his hand. "Congratulations. Magnificent. I owe you a bottle of cognac."

Sebastien walked with him toward the row of double doors at the side of the room. "I won't hold you to a bet made over dinner. But I *will* take your suggestions concerning real estate agents."

"Hell, Frenchy, don't you know that I'll do anything to get you to California? Think about what I said last night. You'd be welcome at the institute. I think we could offer you research opportunities you"d never find elsewhere. Of course, I'd have to mellow you out a little, get you to loosen up, but other than—"

"To be asked by you is the greatest honor. But I have too much at stake in my own program."

"You're not Dr. Kildare, man. You're no good at backslapping other doctors and coddling patients. You belong in the lab."

"Dr. Kildare? Do I know him?"

"Nevermind. Just remember my offer, if you ever get the urge to transplant yourself to the States."

"I will. Thank you."

Sebastien turned toward the doors, anxious to escape the throng of surgeons converging on him. He was not staying for the seminar's final day. He had a plane to catch that evening. Someone grasped his shoulder from behind in away that was too commanding and personal. Sebastien pivoted, frowning with impatience.

Jeff Atwater looked back at him. "Dr. Livingstone, I presume," Jeff deadpanned. "It's so good to see you again. I had to sleep with several important people—most of them women—to get an invitation to this sawbones' event. But I heard that you'd be speaking, and I couldn't miss the chance to say hello to you."

Jeff had less hair but more money, judging by the fine cloth and cut of his tan herringbone suit. The angular, rubbery face had changed very little. He had gained a few needed pounds. He gave Sebastien a jaunty smile, but the expression in his eyes said that he knew the risk he had taken.

Sebastien regarded him for a moment in bitter silence. It had been five years since he'd learned about Jeff and Amy. Five years had not dulled the anger, he discovered quickly. "Do you think we have anything to discuss?"

"Nuclear waste has a shorter half-life than your memory." Jeff pointed to his blond head. "Look, I've pulled out enough hair over this."

"Excuse me. I have a plane to catch."

"I see by your expression that now is not the time for jokes."

"I think I'm reacting well for a man who once considered castrating you with a rusty scalpel. Not that the loss of your balls would have been noticeable. You have no honor."

"Can we go have a drink and talk? At least let me drive you to the airport."

"Unless there's something you care to explain, something you never bothered to explain five years ago, get out of my way."

"I wasn't to blame for what happened. Look, no woman

is worth losing a friendship over. This is ridiculous." Jeff blocked his way with deliberate slowness. "You wouldn't hit an earnest man."

Seconds later he was flat on the floor with blood streaming from his mouth. In the general chaos, as men crowded around and someone called for paper towels, Sebastien bent over him and wrapped a hand around his silk tie. Jeff stared up at him through glazed eyes, then mumbled, "Feel better?"

"I have only one question. Do you know where Amy is?"

"No. I haven't seen her since I left Georgia. I swear. What difference does it make now?"

Sebastien asked himself the same question. Trembling, he released Jeff with a little shove. "You and I have had our reunion, Doctor," he whispered in an acid tone. *"Adieu."*

He smoothed a hand across the lapels of his black suit then walked out of the ballroom and across a glittering atrium. He realized that his fellow surgeons were watching him, and he smiled thinly. Dr. de Savin was building two reputations, they would say—one for his work, another for his violent temper. Sebastien grasped the rail of an escalator and rode down to the hotel's main lobby. His mind was blank, charged with adrenaline and anger. He vaguely noticed the video monitor mounted on a marble pedestal near the base of the escalator. Announcements were scrolling upwards on the screen:

THE GOLD PAVILLION RESTAURANT WILL BE
CLOSED TONIGHT FOR THE TAPING OF THE
TELEVISION SHOW "THORNTON AFTER HOURS,"
STARRING ELLIOT THORNTON. PLEASE PARDON
THE INCONVENIENCE.

He passed the monitor without a second glance.

FIFTEEN

*T*he hotel suite was a madhouse. Amy scrawled notes on a pad atop her clipboard and recalled scenes from *One Flew Over the Cuckoo's Nest*. Shifting on the floor, where she sat cross-legged, she glanced up at the two harried young men who were yelling at each other while Elliot stood to one side, waving his arms.

"It stinks. The concept stinks!" one bellowed. "There's nothing funny about Iranian cabdrivers!"

"Not to *you*. You only think dick jokes are funny!"

Elliot bounced a soft-drink bottle off a full trash can and climbed atop a chair. "Shut up!" he yelled among the arguing writers, the red-faced producer, the muttering director, and the dozen other staff members. "We've got three hours until we tape! So *what* if a guest cancelled! This talk show is not going to be about the goddamn celebrity guests! We're not doing a Carson or Letterman rip-off! This is consumer comedy! The comedy of the masses! Interactive comedy! If you people fall apart just because we have an extra ten minutes to fill, then you don't belong on my payroll! Now shut up! Zip it! Let's *think*."

Elliot could afford to talk tough. He had his own production company now. He was executive producer of *Thornton After Hours*, and this was the premiere show. It had had the hottest press buildup of any non-network, syndicated program in years. A record number of stations across the country had bought it. It would tape at seven P.M., five nights a week, and air at midnight, eastern standard time. Unlike any other talk show, it would frequently be taped outside of the studio with impromptu audiences, the weirder the better. Studio shows would be taped at a big independent station in L.A., where Elliot's production company had rented offices.

Tonight, for better or worse, *Thornton After Hours* would make its home in the Gold Pavillion restaurant of the Alistar Hotel, one of San Francisco's grandest. During the show the restaurant would serve dinner as usual, though the diners would be carefully selected guests: a dozen people who had appeared on *The Price Is Right* without winning anything, the stage crew from *General Hospital*, a clogging team of transvestites, and various pals of Elliot's. Elliot's plan was to incorporate the quirky audience into the show. Robin Williams had promised to drop by for a brief round of anarchy.

But the anarchy had begun already. Veins bulged above the collar of Elliot's white golf shirt; his khaki trousers were stained from the cigarette ashes he kept dropping; barefooted, he curled and uncurled his toes, looking like a large yuppie bird trying to perch on the chair. "I need space," he said suddenly, his voice strained. "Amy. Yo. Five minutes."

She got up and followed him into the bedroom, where paperwork, cue cards, and luggage took all but approximately four square feet of space on the bed. She sat down on it and waited. Elliot slammed the door and leaned against it, his eyes shut. "I need a drink. A beer. One beer."

"One." She went to an enormous ice chest in a corner and returned with a can. "You're doing great."

"After the show tonight I'm going to get absolutely shit-faced."

"Thanks for the warning. I'll have the hotel install training wheels on a commode." She knew that he'd been good beyond his limits lately; she knew that if she protested too much he'd rebel. They walked a thin line between his excesses and her control. It had taken her months to learn the boundaries of her influence, and there had been some ugly confrontations during that time. But he trusted her judgment, and sooner or later he always admitted it.

He jerked the can's pop top and chugged the beer in three swallows. Sighing, he handed her the can. "Thank you, Nurse Ratched."

"You're welcome. I've scheduled your lobotomy for to-morrow." Amy faced him and began massaging his shoulders. "You know, everyone on the staff suspects that we have a quickie each time we come in here. It's bad enough that some of them think I only got my job because I'm your main squeeze. Like a rock star's chief road groupie."

"That's not true, and they know it. You work harder than anybody but me. Look, baby, you told me you wanted a job, and I gave you one. But if you hadn't pulled your weight I'd have fired you by now. I've got too much at stake to play Sugar Daddy." He chucked her under the chin. "Tough, ain't I? But doesn't that make you feel better?"

"Yeah. I don't want special treatment. Not when it comes to being associate producer."

"And assistant to Mr. Thornton," he intoned, as if reading the show's credits. His humor faded. He jammed his hands into his ruffled brown hair. "We've *got* to come up with some new material for tonight. Gimme one of your brain-storms, baby. Kick me right in the old imagination."

She walked to a window, chewing her lip and toying with the scarf at the waist of her green jumpsuit. Excitement lit her thoughts. This was the fun part. This was what she loved most—Elliot asking her, *her*, for suggestions, and then using them in his act. And now that he was going to be on national television five nights a week, he would need her contributions even more. Even his team of comedy writers couldn't help him the way she could when he was desperate.

For several seconds she watched the busy San Francisco streets far below, her mind humming with ideas. They always came so easily. "The Road Kill Café," she said softly.

"Huh? What?" Elliot moved closer, listening.

"The Road Kill Café. It has a sign by the grill that says No Food Dead over an Hour. Hmmm, let's see. Okay. The chef's motto: If it's slow, it's edible. He serves low-choles-terol specials: 'We use only thirty-weight oil.' And regional specials: 'Try our pressed armadillo!' Mystery meals: 'That sucker was mashed so flat even *we* couldn't identify it.' Food with an elegant touch: 'Try our special purée and pâté'—wait a minute, weren't those the twin sisters on *The Patty Duke Show*?"

"Yes! Yes! I *like* it!" Elliot grabbed her for an exuberant kiss. Then he stepped back, rubbing his hands eagerly, lost in thought. "Take a couple of people and go find me some flat animals. The more disgusting, the better. I'll start working on the bit with the guys. We'll expand it. God, it'll be so funny, doing it in a restaurant!"

"You want me to go out on a California highway at the beginning of rush hour and try to scoop up squashed carcasses? Why don't I just paint Hit Me on my chest and play in traffic?"

"Baby," he cajoled, looking anguished and tired. "Pul-leeeeze."

"I'll delegate the job to a couple of guys from the crew. I don't have time to go myself. I've still got to revise your interview notes and double-check the cue cards."

"Baby, I want this bit to go over big. I know I can trust you to find funny dead animals. It's important." He grabbed his head and groaned. "Oh, God, I'm getting a killer headache."

She stared at him in alarm. With his contorted expres-sion and hunched posture he suddenly seemed on the verge of agony. "Honey, okay, I'll do it. Sure I'll do it. Now you just relax—"

"I love you. I love you so much. Now let's get to work." He wiped his forehead, slapped her on the butt, then strode to the door and flung it open. "I've got it!" he shouted to the waiting staff. "The Road Kill Café! Writers, into the kitchen with me. Pronto. I need food around me while I work on this!"

He began detailing the bit to them as they hustled away. Amy came out of the bedroom and looked at the rest of the staff, who studied her with a mixture of curiosity and respect. She shrugged. "We had wild sex. It always helps him create."

Amidst their smiles she turned away, frowning. There was no reason for the resentment she felt toward Elliot sometimes, and she scolded herself. She had an exciting life because of him, a terrific job, the respect of her coworkers in a tough business, and best of all, an inside ticket to a world she loved.

She flung a big leather pocketbook over her shoulder and gestured to a pair of fresh-faced production assistants. "Guys, we have a mission. Come with me."

"Is it important?" one of them asked.

"Yeah. So important that Elliot will only trust it to me. There'll be danger, suspense, and possibly a reprimand from the California Highway Patrol." She shook her head at the inquiring looks everyone gave her. This was the life she had chosen. She wasn't going to waste time examining a small humiliation here and there. "Hey, has anybody got an extra shovel?"

❦

After the first few shows the reviewers overcame their amazement and began to write. Amy cut the headlines out and thumbtacked them to her office bulletin board.

THORNTON A SMASH—ALIEN LIFE-FORMS TAKE OVER TALK SHOW

IS "AFTER HOURS" FOR REAL? RATINGS SAY YOU'D BETTER BELIEVE IT

GET READY FOR THE ROAD KILL CAFÉ, BOWLING FOR PIZZAS, KAMIKAZE CAMERA

WEIRD TV! IS THORNTON THE NEW KING OF COMEDY? EGADS!

She circled "Road Kill Cafe." *Mine*, she thought every-time she looked at the headline, and pride would nearly swallow her.

Within two months Elliot became a household name. Everyone associated with the show was giddy with excitement. The energy level was so high that Amy worked eighteen-hour days and couldn't wait to get up each morning. Elliot corralled his binges and zoomed around on pure adrenaline.

"You know what we need, baby?" he asked one night. They were sprawled on a hotel bed, fully dressed, with cartons of shrimp chow mein perched on their stomachs.

Amy squinted at him. Fatigue weighed her down. She barely knew what she was eating. "Did I forget to order egg rolls?"

"We need a house. It's time we stopped living in hotel rooms. Now that I'm off the road, it makes sense."

"Sure. I'll call some real estate agents. I can visit houses and narrow the choices down so that it'll only take you a couple of hours to see the best ones. Then we can pick out one that we both like."

"Hmmm. How soon can you do it?"

"While you're playing in the celebrity softball game this Sunday afternoon, I guess."

He continued to mumble about houses, but she fell asleep without hearing, with one hand resting in her chow mein.

The next day he bolted into her tiny office and slapped a piece of paper down. "I made a couple of calls and leased a place in Toluca Lake. Burbank! Forest Lawn! The Hollywood Bowl! The big studios! Can't beat it for convenience, baby. And I hired a decorator to fill the place full of leased furniture, too."

"Just like that? Over the phone? What if we hate the wallpaper, or the next-door neighbors raise goats in their backyard?"

"We lease something new!"

He breezed out, while she gritted her teeth in frustration. It was Elliot's house, Elliot's money, Elliot's decision. Mary Beth called from Atlanta to chat. Her interview show was stronger than ever, and she wanted Elliot as a guest. Upon hearing the house news, Mary Beth grew quiet. Then, her tone ominous, she warned, "This is gonna be a turning point. You are about to become a full-fledged, live-in, significant other. This, sugar, is where the shit gets deep."

She was right. Once the place was furnished they had only to move their suitcases, and they were settled. Amy parked her aging Escort in a three-car garage covered in rose vines. There was a heated pool with a lava-rock waterfall and a sauna; the house was an airy three-bedroom Spanish-style, decorated inside with oversized white couches, pottery lamps, and Navajo art. It had a gym, several wet bars, a state-of-the-art entertainment center, and a sunken marble tub in the master bath.

Elliot went out the afternoon after they moved and bought himself two big black Harley motorcycles and a black-leather jacket studded with silver. She thought he looked like Eddie Haskell doing a Hell's Angel impression, but she didn't say so. Everything felt so strange.

The next morning she carried a briefcase full of production schedules outside and sat in a pink lounge chair beside the pink-tiled pool. But she couldn't work. She could only look blankly at the surroundings. "I have arrived," she said out loud. "But I'm not sure where I am." She put a Walkman over her ears and listened to Edith Piaf sing mournful French ballads, which made her feel like crying.

Elliot burst out of the house, whooping. Naked, smelling of bourbon, he pounced on her, tossed the Walkman and the paperwork aside, pulled her from the lounge chair, and stripped the black maillot from her body. "Isn't this great?"

She struggled playfully, relieved by the distraction. "I'm glad you leased a home with a privacy fence."

"Decadent Californians. That's what we are!"

"You were decadent before."

"But now I'm getting a tan!" He tossed her into the pool and jumped in after her. By the time she came up, slinging hair from her eyes and coughing, his hands were between her legs, pulling her to him. "Hitch your wagon to a star. Hmmm. Nice wagon."

"Nice star." He flipped her over and jammed himself into her from behind. Off-balance in water that was too deep for such activity, she flailed about, feeling ridiculous and trying to keep her head above water. "Elliot! Elliot, I don't want to drown like this! It would be too embarrassing!"

His rhythmic pumping quickened. A second later he groaned and stiffened against her, jerking her even tighter against him. Then he slumped over her and, breathing heavily, kissed the nape of her neck. "Fantastic. Flipper would be proud of us."

She disengaged herself and turned to face him. His hair was plastered to his head, his face was red; he grinned at her. He made a handsome, mischievous picture, but as she searched her mind she couldn't recall the last time she'd really wanted him to touch her.

"Elliot, when we make love there ought to be a laugh track. And most of the time, I don't get the joke."

He looked wounded. "Baby, we have a lot of fun."

"Sometimes I'd like to be sentimental, you know, with soft music, and candles, and a few sweet words."

He put his arms around her. "Okay. You mean everything to me, right? You work your ass off to keep me out of trouble; you take care of my business so that all I have to do is be a fucking star. And you don't ask for much in return. I love you for it."

Amy shivered. He loved her for being a dutiful helpmate. Who wouldn't love someone who gave everything and expected nothing? But she needed to take care of him, she needed to make him happy, because it made her feel worthwhile. Confused, she shut her eyes. No, she was being cranky. She had everything she could want. What was wrong with her?

"Marry me," he whispered.

She jerked her head back and looked into his eyes. "How much did you have to drink before you came out here?"

"I've thought about this for a long time. Now that everything is perfect, we should make it more perfect. Say you'll marry me. Hey, you know all my faults. What have you got to lose?"

"That's one way of looking at it. Aw, Elliot, comeon now. You're joking, aren't you?"

He frowned. "No. I expected you to be happy about it."

"I am, but it's just such a shock. We never talked about getting married before."

"Don't you want to be Mrs. Elliot Thornton? Don't you

know how much money I stand to make in the next few years? I'm going to be a comedy *mogul*. Don't you want to be part of that?"

"I'm part of it already."

"Yeah, but you always get weird when I try to buy you things. You'll live with me but you won't let me give you presents."

"I'm an old-fashioned sort of groupie."

"Look, my parents love you. They think you're a good influence on me. My father says you're a taller Sally Fields—and he's crazy about Sally Fields—with a southern accent."

"They like me," she intoned dramatically. "They really like me."

"What's wrong with you?"

She ducked her head under his rebuking gaze. "Sorry."

"Why the doubts, baby?"

"I . . . they're not doubts. I don't know what I'm trying to say."

"Say yes."

A breath shuddered out of her. Her temples throbbed. *Overwork and stress. That's all this is*, she told herself. Of course she wanted to marry Elliot. "Yes."

He held his left hand where she could see it. A large diamond solitare glimmered on his little finger. "For you."

"I already have two little fingers."

"Cut the crap! I want to be serious, for once."

The ring was beautiful; she kicked herself for making a joke. Who would have thought that anyone would be offering her a life like this? Wasn't this what she had worked for—respect, security, love? "Oh, Elliot," she whispered, tears sliding down her face. "It's great." He put the ring on her left hand. She began to sob and buried her face in the crook of his neck.

"Amy? Baby?" He stroked her hair anxiously. "Well, I guess I ought to be the strong one sometimes." After an awkward moment he added, "Is this, hmmm, *happy* sobbing?"

When she didn't answer he made soft, bewildered sounds of comfort. She continued to cry and clutched his shoulders, her control racked by the knowledge that she wanted something indefinable, something that taunted her like the shadows of wings because she still couldn't fly.

❦

The charmed progress of *Thornton After Hours* crashed to a halt. That spring the Writers' Guild threatened a nationwide strike, and every writer on Elliot's staff prepared to join it. Television executives across the country blanched at the thought of lucrative shows going on involuntary hiatus, of fall schedules dissolving.

Elliot was inconsolable. Amy woke alone one night and went to look for him. He was sitting cross-legged beside the pool with an ashtray full of joints and cigarettes beside him. His complexion was sallow in the light of the patio lamps. He gave her a droopy look as she sat down. "Gone. All my momentum. Pfffft. If there's a strike Letterman and Carson can show reruns. Months and months of reruns. I can't. I'm just a syndicated nobody."

"Elliot, don't overreact." She laid a tentative hand on his arm. He began to cry. Amy hugged him and shut her eyes, gathering courage. She'd been planning to approach him with an idea, but only if the strike came to pass. She couldn't let him go on torturing himself this way, however. "Elliot, do you think, hmmm, I know this will sound crazy, but, do you think that the show could keep going as it is now, if I helped you write the material?"

"What?" He stopped sniffling and drew back to look at her in the light of a poolside lamp. His mouth dropped open. "You?"

"Nobody would have to know. I'm not a writer, so I wouldn't be violating any union rules. I think we could do it, I really do. It won't be easy, but it's worth a try. I mean, what's the big deal with writing a monologue and a couple of simple bits every day? And we could try more ad-lib segments, send you to strange places with a camera crew and just let you react, the way Letterman does."

"You? Writing for the show every day?" Even stoned, he sounded amazed.

She scowled at him. "I've been giving you material for

years. Oh, I know I'm not as good as a professional, but you can take my basic ideas and make them work. You always do."

She could see the light go on in his mind. He swayed. He thumped his knees. "You're right! You always have ideas out the wazoo! If even half your stuff is usable, we might get by!"

"Of course we will. And think how impressed people will be, with you doing fresh material every night even though you don't have a team of writers to back you up!"

He laughed and draped an arm around her shoulders. "My secret Miracle. You'll make me a legend in my own time. I tell you what, baby, we'll plan to get married as soon as the strike ends. Deal?"

Be good and I'll reward you. Earn my love and you'll be happy. Amy shoved the troubling thoughts aside. She was getting an opportunity to do work she adored. She trembled with anticipation. "Deal," she answered.

❧

The reporter from *People* magazine leaned across the patio table, eyes fixed on Elliot. "The writers' strike has been going on for months, but you keep going, turning out fresh shows. If anything, your work has gotten *better* since the strike. People are using words like 'genius' to describe you. Where do you get your inexhaustible supply of ideas?"

"I work at it. I never stop. I'm driven, and I love it," Elliot answered, looking weary but satisfied. He glanced over his shoulder as Amy set a pitcher of tea on the table. "I have a lot of moral support from my lady, here. Thank you, baby."

She bared her teeth in a smile and glided back into the house, where she went to the main bedroom and flopped amidst dozens of notepads. She grabbed a mug of coffee from a nightstand and took a deep swallow, then rubbed her gritty eyes and tried to concentrate.

An hour later Elliot sauntered in and collapsed beside her. "I was brilliant."

"What do you think of this idea? You take a camera crew to an elementary school and interview kids."

"What's the hook? What makes it funny?"

"Didn't you ever see Art Linkletter? I've got a list of questions worked out. You ask 'em, then wait for the answers, then react."

"Like what kind of questions?"

She picked up a notepad and scanned it. "Like, 'What kind of bird is a Dan Quayle?' "

Elliot chuckled. "Not bad."

"Good. Let's get back to work."

"I can remember when Saturdays were fun."

"It's hell being a genius, I know."

He cut his eyes at her. "Testy bitch. Excuse me while I go to the kitchen."

"The percolator's full. Bring another cup of coffee, please."

"You bet."

He was gone for a long time, and when he returned he began pacing the room and talking excitedly about the interview idea. Amy looked up wearily. "What did you do— drink the whole pot of coffee? And you forgot mine?"

He laughed with a high, brittle sound that set off a warning in her brain. She straightened, scrutinizing him. She felt the pulse throbbing in her throat. "Elliot, did you snort some coffee up your nose?"

He halted and stared at her, nostrils flaring, his whole body stiff with defense. The sudden switch from laughter to fury stunned her. He jabbed a finger at her. "I am *tired* of your goddamn overbearing attitude." His voice rose to shout. "I'm not hurting anybody! I need all the energy I can get!

"How much coke are you using, Elliot? How often?"

"I've got it under control! Stop grilling me! Stop it! Stop it!" He grabbed a pottery vase from the dresser and slung it at the wall beside the bed. Amy covered her face as shards of pottery struck her.

There was a sharp pain in her hand. Shaking, she looked at the bloody cut on one knuckle. Her horrified gaze rose to Elliot's. He stood at the foot of the bed with his mouth open. He tried to speak, had trouble, and shook his head.

Nausea welled up in her stomach. Her teeth chattering,

she whispered, "If you ever do something like that again, I'll leave you."

"If you do, I'll kill myself."

While she stared at him in shock, he crawled across the bed to her. Tears pooled in his eyes. He took her injured hand and licked the blood from it. She sat there numbly, watching. "You need h-help. Elliot, you've got to talk to a doctor."

"No!" He gulped for breath. "I need *you*. I need the coke, too, but just until things get back to normal. I swear." He buried his head in her lap and wrapped both arms around her. Sobs convulsed his shoulders. "Don't leave me. I'm so tired. I'm so afraid of fucking everything up. Please, baby, please. Try to understand."

The caretaker in her was a compulsive mistress. Pity and concern overcame anger. She *had* to help him, because nobody else could. Amy stroked his head and crooned to him, crying as she did.

❧

The Laffeteria was a second-rate comedy club in West Hollywood, but it was one of Amy's favorites. She'd spent hours in every major comedy club in the country, watching Elliot work, then sitting with him and studying other comics, but there was something comforting about this tiny place.

She sat at a corner table by herself, enjoying the womb-like darkness, a pad and pen in front of her, a glass of mineral water growing tepid as she concentrated on her job, which was to scout the Tuesday-night showcase of female comics.

Thank God the writers' strike was over. She was glad for this new duty, glad to get away from Elliot and his sneaky habits that concealed nothing about his problem and depressed them both.

She propped her chin on one hand and watched as the emcee introduced a stout young woman who popped gum and told jokes stolen from Roseanne Barr. The audience, happy and unsuspecting, liked her and applauded heartily

at the end of her five-minute routine. Amy noted her name
and slashed a black line across it.

The next woman was a wispy little black doll who made
obscene comments about everything from her large breasts
to the width of her vagina. She mixed in a few bitter jokes
about race that had the audience squirming with discomfort, though people laughed from the shock effect. Amy
crossed her name off the list, too.

Everybody needed a persona, a hook, something that
made them memorable. Like Roseanne and her domestic
goddess bit, or Judy Tenuta, punk-princess. Each woman
who got up on stage at the Laffeteria tried to be unique.
Few were.

Amy found herself drawing thick, angry blocks over the
names on her list. The irony of the comedy boom was that
there were hundreds of clubs now, all across the country,
and they were begging for comics. Even the most mediocre
of tonight's performers was probably making fifty thousand
dollars a year telling bad or stolen jokes to audiences in
the boondocks.

I could do better than that. Frowning, she drew jagged
doodles on the pad. *So why don't you try it?* Dread mingled
with excitement in her chest, as if she were standing on a
high dive, wanting to leap but petrified. She pictured herself
getting up on stage and staring blank-faced at an audience
while her knees knocked and words suffocated in her
throat. No way.

Tonight there was only one comic worth watching. Her
name was Angela Poulos, and she told whimsical anecdotes about her Greek family. Nothing hilarious, but charming. The laughs were solid and the material clean enough
to go straight to television without much work.

Toting her pad and a couple of business cards that
proclaimed her the associate producer of *Thornton After
Hours*, Amy went backstage to a communal dressing room
hung with bare light bulbs and smelling of cosmetics and
fear.

A dozen women eyed her warily as she entered. She
went to Angela and introduced herself. *You got talent, kid.
Call me tomorrow. I want you to come down to the studio*

and audition for my boss. Amy smiled grimly. She felt as if she needed a fat cigar and a fedora. Angela Poulos began to hyperventilate with excitement. "Of course I'll do it. Oh, thank you, thank you, I gotta call my folks, this is incredible, I think I'm going to faint."

Smiling though she felt depressed and envious, Amy made her way back through the hovering crowd. One of the comics, a spike-haired type whose act consisted of playing a saxophone in between telling jokes about oral sex, grabbed Amy by one arm.

Ambition was stamped on the comic's face in hard lines. She looked desperate. "What'd you think of my act?"

"It's got potential. But it's not right for our show. It might work on one of the pay-cable channels, though."

"Hey, I could fix it any way you want. Did you think it was funny enough, huh?"

Amy hesitated, trying to think of a diplomatic response. "I can only tell you what works for *Thornton After Hours.* We look for acts that appeal to a wide audience. Some comics aren't mainstream enough."

"Who are you to tell me that I'm not funny, huh?"

"I didn't say you weren't—"

"Are you a comic?"

"No, but I—"

"What the hell do you know about what's funny? You come in here in your pink Donna Reed suit with your raspy little down-home voice and you think you know what's cool. Bullshit. Who did you screw to get your job?"

"Not anyone very important, or I'd be someplace nicer tonight, gettin' a better class of insult."

"Have *you* ever done any stand-up work?"

"No, but—"

"You ever *write* any comedy for anybody?"

She ground her teeth. Elliot's secret. "No."

"To hell with you, then!" The comic jabbed a finger at herself. "I've been doing stand-up for five years! I've played business conventions where men threw ice cubes at me! I've had club owners cancel my gig because I wouldn't screw 'em! I've emceed male-strip shows! I've done singing telegrams when I was so broke that I was sleeping in my car at night because I didn't have any place else to go! I've suffered to get where I am, and I'm sick of candy-asses like you deciding whether I'm funny or not! *You* haven't suffered! *You* haven't—"

Amy shoved the woman against a locker. "I know what's funny and I know what stinks. You stink. I've seen dozens like you, male and female, tellin' jokes you steal from each other between gigs at some club stuck in the back of a shopping center in Podunk, U.S.A. You think you're in show business 'cause you've got fifteen minutes of material that makes a livin' for you. You don't know squat about the traditions, and you don't want to work hard enough to be an original. *And don't tell me I don't know my job. I spent my whole life learnin' my job.*"

The comic gawked at her, face flushing deep red, chest heaving. Amy walked away while she was still in that speechless condition. In the parking lot she leaned against her car and took deep breaths of L.A.'s musty night air.

Despite her convictions, she felt like a coward. No matter how much she knew about the business, she didn't have the guts to get up on a stage.

🍎

"Where are we going?" she asked Elliot as he tugged her up the steps of the small private jet he'd chartered.

"I've told you a dozen times, baby, it's a surprise vacation. We've earned it. Now relax and quit asking questions."

There was a bouquet of white roses on one of the jet's plush seats, champagne and caviar in a refrigerator, crystal glasses, damask napkins, and fine china. When the jet reached its cruising altitude Elliot poured the champagne. "To us," he toasted, clinking his glass to hers.

Amy watched him over the fluted rim. He had kidnapped her from her Saturday-morning swim, then presented her with a packed suitcase and a pearl-gray silk organza dress that took her breath away. He was clothed in a beautiful silk suit of soft gray, with a white tie. He had hummed merrily while she put on the new dress and fixed her hair and makeup.

And now here she sat, bewildered, wary, and sipping Dom Pérignon.

"Did I pick a good vintage?" he asked, downing his third glass.

"I think so, but I don't know as much about champagne as I do about wine."

"My classy little red-neck peach." He laughed.

"You think it's funny that I taught myself how to pick a good wine?"

"No, baby, I think it's charming. I just wonder how many people who come out of the hills of Georgia speak French and know how to pick a good wine and like to read Sartre."

"About as many as want to, I guess. Watch it, boy, your Yankee prejudice is showing."

"I'm just proud of you. Proud to be with you."

His exuberance worried her. She looked out a window at a summer sky full of white clouds and tried not to brood. Less than an hour later the plane began to descend.

"Viva Las Vegas," Elliot said, watching her for a reaction.

She looked at him askance. "You told me once that Las Vegas was only good for Shriners' conventions."

He laughed. "I changed my mind."

A white limousine met them at the plane, and soon they were traveling down open highway. Nevada desert whipped by the car window. Amy clutched the roses in her lap and studied Elliot's Cheshire-cat smile. "Look," he said eventually, pointing out the window at the neon oasis rising to meet the highway. "Glitter City."

She was speechless with intrigue as they drove down the strip. "It looks just like it did in *Ocean's Eleven!* I can almost see Frank Sinatra and the Rat Pack. Hey, there's Peter Lawford."

"He croaked."

"I *know* that. Use your imagination, grinch." She twisted to face Elliot. "Where are we going? The Sands? The MGM Grand? Caesar's Palace?"

"Nah. You'll see."

The limo purred down side streets. Amy grabbed Elliot by the tie. "Where?" she demanded. "This is a threat."

He laughed. "There. Right there. Look."

She swiveled and gazed eagerly out the window. Her heart stopped. *The Elvis Wedding Chapel.* It glowed with white neon. The windows had pink shutters with little gold guitars on them. The walkway to the street was lined with people in garden-party finery—frothy sundresses and big hats on the women, pastel suits on the men. They were people she knew: Elliot's business manager and agent, people from the staff of *Thornton After Hours*, friends of hers and Elliot's, most of them from show business, some of them bonafide Big Names. And just a few feet from the curb stood Mary Beth, impeccable in a tailored suit of peach silk, her eyes hidden by black sunglasses, her mouth set in a hard line.

The limousine stopped by the walk. Amy hoped the tinted window kept the crowd from seeing her face. She felt like a fish that had just been hooked. Trapped. Frantic. On the steps of the chapel stood an Elvis imitator in a white sequined jumpsuit. The minister, she presumed.

"I promised you a wedding after the writers' strike," Elliot reminded her. "What do you think, baby?"

"I can't. I can't." She dropped the roses on the floor and took his hands. Shaking her head desperately, she struggled for calm. "I can't marry you."

"Huh? Why not? I got all the paperwork set up. I took care of everything so that this could be a surprise. What the hell?"

"Oh, Elliot, how could you do this to me, when it's been months since we even talked about getting married?"

"You've always worn my ring." The color rose in his face. His moods were treacherous these days; she held his hands tightly and tried to smile. "Elliot, I won't leave you, but I won't marry you, either."

"Why?"

"We have problems. You're a drug addict. You need help, but you won't admit it."

"You don't love me anymore."

"Would I stay with you if I didn't love you?"

The chauffeur opened her door. People outside cheered and whistled. A muscle twitched beside Elliot's mouth. He spoke between gritted teeth. "Get out of the car. We're going through with this."

"No. Elliot, please. Don't get upset. *I'll still be with you. I'll still take care of you.*"

"Ma'am?" the chauffeur said, extending a hand.

"Don't do this to me, baby," Elliot warned. "You've changed. I don't understand. Don't get cold on me."

"I'm just learning to be realistic. I can't marry you."

"Sugar?" Mary Beth's honeyed voice interrupted the tension. She stuck her head in the car and looked from Elliot to Amy. "I hope y'all are having fun in here, but Elvis is getting a little antsy." Amy could tell from the careful tone of her voice that Mary Beth knew trouble when she saw it. "How do you like Elliot's surprise wedding, sugar?"

"Get in the car," Amy ordered. "And shut the door."

"Hmmm. I suspected as much."

"If she gets in the car I'm getting out," Elliot said.

Amy reached for him. "No."

"We're finished!" He slung her hands away. "I don't need you! I never needed you!" Shoving the opposite door open, he leapt out and yelled to the waiting crowd, "You want to hear something funny? She won't marry me! But I paid for the fucking limo, so I'm the one who's going on the honeymoon!"

Amy made a horrified sound as he reached inside the car and snatched her by both arms. He dragged her out the door, and she landed hard on the street. "Have fun," he told her, then stepped over her and got back in the car. She jerked her feet aside as he slammed the door. There was a commotion and then Mary Beth's indignant curse. Amy heard the other door slam.

The chauffeur ran to the driver's side. "I'm sorry, ma'am, but Mr. Thornton gives the orders."

He threw himself into the front seat. The car roared away. It had all happened in a few seconds. Suddenly Amy was staring across empty pavement at Mary Beth, who was pushing herself up from the curb. The people behind her looked as if they'd just been caught in a vice raid and wanted to evaporate, they were so humiliated.

The moment of shock passed and people ran toward her, hands outstretched. She hurriedly got up, brushing grime from her dress, trembling, feeling sick to her stomach but bitterly determined. She had hidden behind her self-doubt long enough. She was on her own, now, and she didn't want a hand up, from anyone.

SIXTEEN

$\mathcal{M}$arie returned to their bedroom one year after her transformation into a spiritual being in search of purity. Sebastien had become so accustomed to his solitary nights that when she glided in, a coarse muslin robe belted loosely around her body, always reminding him of a noviatiate from a nunnery, he almost resented the intrusion.

Almost. It was true that some needs were basic, simple, and selfish, and the coldness within him had grown so much in the past year that he no longer cared whether there was any emotional intimacy between them. She knelt on the bed beside him, her black hair framing a face that had grown thinner from her vegetarian diet.

"It is time to try again," she whispered. She clasped her hands in her lap and regarded him with placid eyes. She seemed no more than a quiet stranger, waiting to be serviced.

She would get her wish, for now. Sebastien tossed a file of paperwork onto the nightstand. He did not tell her so, but he believed that this pregnancy would be as futile as the others. After six years of miscarriages, it was time to stop trying. If she lost this baby, he would explain to her that he no longer wanted children. He was burned out, with no resources left to confront the grief of each disappointment. And he couldn't shake the morbid sense of being cursed.

"Could we begin trying again tonight?" she repeated, watching him closely.

Without answering he got up and removed his robe and pajama bottoms. She draped her robe over the bed's ornate foot rail and continued to sit like a supplicant waiting to be blessed. Her wistfulness twisted something dark inside him—he didn't hate her, he felt sorry for her, sorry for them both.

But sentiment would not get the job done. Sentiment must be pushed aside for lust. The sight of her firm, olive-skinned body was all that his months of celibacy needed to create the blindness of desire. He knelt on the bed in front of her, watching her gaze drop approvingly to his rigid penis. He cupped her chin in his hand for a moment and studied the anticipation in her face. She breathed quickly, her lips parted. She tilted her head and let her gaze move to his mouth.

He took her by the arms and turned her so that her back was to him. She hesitated for a moment, looking over her shoulder as if she was about to protest, a frown creasing her forehead. Then she shrugged and lowered her head in a cradle made by her forearms.

With her face buried in her arms she was anonymous to him; it was better this way, and he decided that from now on, until she conceived and lost interest in sex again, he would only take her from behind, so there would be no need for either of them to pretend affection.

Sebastien lifted her hips and ran his hands across the firm mounds. Sliding his fingertips up her spine, he caressed her shoulders for a moment, then reached under her and began playing with her breasts. She moaned softly and begged, *"Ne me tourmente pas."*

No need to waste time, she meant. And why should he? He had a great deal of reading to do after he finished with her. Sebastien grasped her hips and eased into her. She swelled and tightened around him; he threw his head back and gasped at the hot glove that squeezed each time he pushed forward. Only a few seconds passed before her guttural moans became frantic. Her back arched like a cat's, and she writhed.

After a year's abstinence her movements made him feverish with sensation. In the trance of approaching release he shut his eyes and allowed pleasure to open channels in his mind. The onrush of emotion flooded him before he could retreat. He grimaced and gave a hoarse shout as he came.

Breathing heavily, Sebastien looked down at Marie, who was deadly still. Then she jerked herself away from him and whirled around, crouching on the bed, her face livid. "If you have mistresses, I don't care! But don't call their names while you're with me!"

A chill ran through him. "I wasn't aware that I'd called anyone's name. And I have no mistresses." Sebastien stretched out on his side and tried not to appear shaken. "So tell me, madam, who is this lover that I can't even recall?"

She leapt forward and slapped him solidly across the face. Sebastien grabbed her wrist in an electric snap of movement then held it rigidly. Her hand quivered in the air and he loosened his grip. "Who?"

"Amy." She snarled the name.

Sebastien felt the breath leave his lungs. And yet a sense of the inevitable taunted him. He wasn't surprised. He was only sorry he had hurt Marie. "It means nothing. I've never been unfaithful to you. I apologize for being so ungallant."

Her anger wavered. She searched his eyes for a moment, then shuddered. Her head drooped. "You have bad timing, Sebastien, that's all. I shouldn't have slapped you. But you and I, we are so alike, so pragmatic, I have always been proud of that. I dislike emotional displays. And no disruptive energy must come between us right now. Who is this Amy?"

"Someone I knew before I met you. In America. No need to be jealous."

She arched a brow in surprise. "That many years ago? What a woman she must have been!"

"Forget what happened. I wasn't even thinking about her."

"I'm not jealous. I simply don't want anyone to cloud

your focus. You're going to be a father. Our next child will live. The time is right. The planets, the mood, the signs—"

"I hope your mysticism lives up to its noble purpose." Feeling tired and distressed, he let her hand go. After a second he stroked her hair. He tried not to reveal that he wished she would leave.

She kissed the small graying spot at the center of his chest hair. Her expression was now more indignant than angry. "Good night. I have to go back to my own room and meditate." She slipped away from him and nodded politely, then took her robe from the bed's foot rail.

Sebastien nodded back. "Until our next mating session."

After she left he got up, feeling dazed, and went to the armoire across the room. He jerked its bottom drawer open and scooped stacks of linen handkerchiefs onto the floor. Underneath them was a large, lacquered box. He hadn't opened it in years. There were numerous Celtic crosses that had belonged to his mother, a Bible that Pio Beaucaire had given him, a pistol that had belonged to his maternal grandfather, and a box of the special cartridges it required.

Wedged in a crack between the base and one side of the box was the old silver token on its tarnished necklace. Sebastien ripped it from its place. He went to the balcony doors and opened them, then stepped naked into the freezing night air and hurled the necklace into the hedges across the courtyard.

Memories were more dangerous than he had realized. If he cultivated them they would only make him examine his choices, his life, himself.

❧

Pio was getting old. It saddened Sebastien to have to shorten his strides to match Pio's stiff, slow ones. But Pio was too happy to notice. Spring was here and the vineyards were rich green stripes under a magnificent sky, and Pio hummed as they walked among the trellises. They had strolled the vineyards together each spring for as long as Sebastien could recall. First at his father's estate, now here at his own. It was one of the few traditions that mattered to Sebastien. Stealing amused glances at Pio's satisfied smile,

Sebastien recognized a vintage year. What did Pio's infirmities matter when compared to that?

"Ripe. I like it when everything is ripe," Pio announced, waving his arms. He slapped Sebastien's shoulder. "This spring feels special. You watch—this will be the year you become a father."

"Marie is only four months pregnant. She's lost babies later than that."

"Such pessimism. And Marie is so positive, this time!" They halted, and Pio scowled at him. "What will become of you, if you don't have a little faith in something besides your work at the hospital?"

"Hmmm. Let's change the subject. I have a surprise for you. I've bought a small winery in the United States."

Pio snorted. "What for? Isn't owning one dreadful American winery in Georgia enough?"

"This one is my personal place. It's to enjoy. Simply to enjoy. I want you to visit it. It's in California."

"California! *Merde!* You won't even get good table wine from it!" Pio spat with such disgust that Sebastien laughed.

"I went there two weeks ago and made the final purchase arrangements. It's a wonderful place, Pio, with an old stone house that only needs some repair to be enjoyable. I plan to hire a caretaker to work the vines. They've been badly neglected, but within a few years—"

"That is not a winery. That is a charity project. What will you do with an unimportant vineyard halfway across the world?"

"Use it as another home."

Pio frowned harder. "You don't need a home in America. Your American days are long past. I'm too old to go chasing you, and I'm sure your father would send me."

"And I'm sure his spying would have as little effect as it did before." He patted Pio's shoulder. "Don't worry. I don't run as fast as I once did."

Pio relaxed. He chuckled ruefully. "You certainly kept him busy. Especially with that last escapade."

"Which of my *escapades* could possibly have become so infamous?"

"The one with that funny young woman who lived with

you right before you left for Africa. *That* one had your father worried. She was so totally unsuitable that he was certain you were going to keep her just to spite him."

Sebastien stared hard into Pio's eyes. Why was the past crowding him so much, lately? "My father knew about her? You told him?"

Pio's amusement faded. "Of course. I told him about every woman you had. You found my snooping not the least threatening. You used to call me Inspector Clouseau, remember?"

"But why her? I knew her so briefly—"

"Ah, but she was the only one you took care of as if she were a wounded bird. The only one who charmed you into supporting her, sending her to college, giving her an expensive car." Pio spoke lightly again, though there was a worried glint in his eyes. "You should have seen your car parked in front of the decrepit old house she lived in at school! You would really have questioned your decision if you'd seen *that*."

"You visited her? You never told me! I never asked you to look after her, so what business did you have with her?"

The look on Pio's face said that he'd only just realized his misstep. He made several awkward noises, then coughed. "I was curious about her. I wanted to see how she was spending your money."

"I see more in your eyes. Much more. I see the fear that you've become old and careless, and that you've told something I was never supposed to know." Sebastien grasped Pio's shoulders. *"What were you visiting her for? What had my father sent you to do?"*

"Nothing! Why does this concern you now? You left America almost nine years ago! You have a wonderful wife! She's going to give you a child this fall—yes, I have faith! You've avoided almost every plan your father had for you and you've gone your own way. You should be happy! Why this interrogation?"

"Goddamn you, Pio!" Sebastien shook him. "Goddamn you! What plot did you and my father concoct?"

The older man's face had gone white. "You've never cursed me before."

"I'll do worse than that if you don't tell me the truth! I'll fire you. You can go back to my father's estate and gloat over your victories there!"

"Fire me? Fire me?" His eyes were furious, but glistening with tears. "How can you talk that way to me?"

"How can you continue to deceive and manipulate me?"

"Honor! Loyalty! You are the heir of one of the finest, oldest families in France! You must not be allowed to ignore your responsibilities!"

"The truth, Pio! *Now.* Or get off the estate!"

Pio shoved him away and stumbled down the row, clutching the vines for support. "I'm leaving! I'm going to pack! Oh, Sebastien, Sebastien! How could you have come to this—"

He grabbed his chest and pitched face-forward on the thickly matted grass. Sebastien raced to him, broken words catching in his throat. He turned Pio's limp body over and groaned at the blue tint already staining the face, and the sightless, rolled-back eyes. Ripping Pio's shirt open, he put his ear to the unmoving chest.

The physician in him became brusque, performing emergency procedures with confident hands. The small boy in him felt helpless and choked back tears while whispering, "No, Pio, no. Pio! I won't let you go. Pio, it's *springtime.*"

❦

Pio's funeral mass was attended by several hundred people. The funeral itself was formal and solemn, in keeping with Pio's wishes. He was buried where he had been born, in a village south of Orleans. Sebastien stood at the back of the cemetery alone, having left Marie in Paris with her crystals and her meditations. A funeral radiated too much negative energy, she had said.

Sebastien couldn't agree more. He kept a hawklike watch on his father, who stood near the grave with head bowed majestically, his severe black suit accenting the grief in his posture. Sebastien didn't doubt that his grief was sincere; Pio had been his father's lifelong servant, friend, loyal co-conspirator.

When the priest finished with the graveside service

Philippe de Savin turned and caught Sebastien's gaze. His father gave him a hopeful look that hardened when Sebastien didn't respond.

Sebastien felt a muscle pop in his jaw when his father moved toward him through the crowd. He watched people step aside to let him pass, their attitude respectful but their faces shuttered. His father did not inspire sympathy or affection. A grim realization came to Sebastien: That was how the staff at the hospital regarded *him*.

"I had expected to see you before now," his father said, coming to a brusque stop in front of him. "I looked for you before the mass, and then during mass, but you never arrived."

"All that matters is that I was with Pio when he died. I despise the maudlin atmosphere of funerals. I've attended a few too many in my life."

"Perhaps for your benefit we should have had a reading from something by Camus. An uplifting passage about how absurd and unfair life is, and how we suffer because we try to change it."

"Ah, but we need not suffer ourselves. We can meddle in the lives of others and put the suffering on them. Pio and I were discussing that point just before he died. Your name was mentioned."

His father regarded him silently, his face tightening. "Not happily, it seems."

"I want you to search your memory. Go back nine years, to the time when I was preparing to leave the United States for the Ivory Coast. I was involved with a young woman who worked at the Georgia winery. You knew about her. Pio told you."

"Sebastien! You flatter me! I can't remember all of your transgressions. And certainly not from so long ago."

"I think you would remember Amy Miracle. She was a unique problem—too appealing, too different to ignore. Come now, Pio remembered her easily. He remembered visiting her at school after I left the country. I'm sure he remembered why he visited her, and what you instructed him to do about her. But he wouldn't tell me."

"There was nothing to tell. Did you badger Pio? My God, did you upset him with pointless accusations?"

"Yes, and I could cut out my tongue for doing it. He wasn't to blame—you were. I want you to give me the answers that he was too loyal to give."

His father drew back a blue-veined hand and slapped the back of it across Sebastien's face. The blow had an emotional force that was far greater than the physical one. Sebastien didn't flinch, but every nerve pulled tight.

His father's eyes glittered with fury. "You were not forced to leave your American woman behind when you went to Africa, but you did. You were not forced to marry Marie or come home to France, but you did. You made your own decisions. So there is nothing for me to tell you. God help you for making Pio miserable. He loved you. He wanted the best for you. So did I. But I've given up on you, and he never did. You killed him for caring."

Annette was now standing beside them, her hands covering her mouth in horror. "Stop it! Stop disgracing us, both of you! Everyone is staring! To brawl at Pio's funeral—it's unforgivable!"

"Forgiveness remains impossible in this family," Sebastien said softly, hatred in every word. He held his father's gaze with vicious intensity. "I made the decisions, true, and they can't be reversed, but now I know that you manipulated them—somehow. You're dead to me, do you hear? You don't exist anymore. If Marie and I have a child, you'll never see it. There will be no contact . . . and no mention of you in my home, ever."

His father gave him an icy, unperturbed smile that hinted at plans yet unveiled, then walked away.

SEVENTEEN

*I*t was easy to be funny when the alternative was being homeless. Amy scribbled notes on a thick yellow pad and ignored distractions—the noisy play of her landlord's five children, the rumble of the freeway, the clacking of the fan in the window that swirled hot night air through the kitchen.

She gnawed the cap of her pen and studied her work. *She's the kind of girl who goes to her family reunion to pick up men. Her idea of great art is a "scratch-and-sniff" ad for men's deodorant.*

Amy scanned a dozen other lines written along the same subject. With confidence born of growing experience, she decided which of her clients would be suited to the material and which wouldn't. Sometimes she felt schizophrenic trying to write gags for a dozen different comics. But she was meeting the challenge. And she was making steady money—twenty-five bucks a joke from the lesser names, fifty from the headliners—and paying her bills. For starters, this apartment—the top half of a small duplex—cost her five hundred dollars a month.

Amy sipped a glass of iced tea, fanned the tail of a floppy sundress at her sweaty legs, and continued working.

She looked up, and listened intently. Footsteps were ascending the wooden stairs to her door. She kept a handgun on the top of a bookcase across the one-room apartment. Of course, if anyone bothered her she could simply yell, and a swarm of Alvarezes would come racing up with their arsenal of weapons.

She went to the door and waited. When the careful, polite knocking came she cleared her throat and asked in a gruff voice. "Yes? Who is it?"

"Stop doing the Lauren Bacall impression and open the door."

It was Elliot. He sounded cheerful, teasing. But he had visited her in that mood before, only to switch to anger or tears after she let him inside.

"Just a second." Amy hid the gun in a dresser near her bed. Then she unlocked the door. He stood there in tie-dyed, knee-length denim shorts, a wrinkled white pullover, and unlaced basketball shoes. He held a pizza box in his arms.

"Pizza-gram," he said coyly.

"It's ten-thirty."

"I just got away from the studio. I was restless. Lonely."

"What? Nobody to hang out with? How was Miss July? Any fireworks? No cherry bombs, I bet."

"Well, well, you watched last night's show."

"I wouldn't miss seeing you interview a centerfold babe who's also an expert on explosives. Too bad she had the I.Q. of a sparkler."

"Jealous?"

"No, I just hate to see you use the show to pick up women. In the eight months since we broke up your ratio of beautiful female guests to funny skits has become *real* skewed. Stop trying to antagonize me. It's not good for the show."

He breezed past her and went to the kitchen in one corner. Tossing the pizza container atop her table, he then ambled around the room, hands on hips. "Oh, I like what you've done with the place. Plastic furniture and bean-bag chairs are *so* cool. Did I tell you that I just bought a little bungalow at Malibu? Right on the beach. With an incredible view. You really *must* drop in sometime."

She crossed her arms and regarded him patiently. "The tip of your nose looks like a tomato."

He gave a short laugh and scrubbed a hand over the swollen surface. "Cherry or Big Boy?"

"What are you doing here tonight, Elliot?"

"Making you an offer you can't refuse."

"Try me."

"So you still hate my guts. So maybe I deserve it. But you know I love you. You know that I haven't touched any other woman since you left me—"

"Since *you* left *me* sitting in a street staring at the Reverend Elvis."

"You're writing gags for other comics. Don't do that. Come write for me."

"I did that once before. Without pay or credit. Forget it."

"This time will be different. I'm offering you a job on the writing staff. You'll be our first girl member. Gee whiz, Amy, we'll let you in the tree house and give you a decoder ring and everything."

A treacherous thrill went through her. A writing job on a national show—a hit show! She could join the Writers' Guild. She'd be paid at least fifty grand a year. She knew because as associate producer she'd been privy to the writers' salaries. Her palms clammy, she searched Elliot's face. "What's the catch?"

"No catch. Just be there for me, the same as you used to."

Her hope died. "You mean get paid to be a writer but instead be your warden—slap your hands when you reach for a drink or a pill or a spoonful of coke?"

"Both."'

"And sleep with you?"

"If I get lucky. No pressure. I swear."

"Oh, Elliot." Her shoulders slumped. She pressed trembling fingertips to her mouth and dropped into a chair. "I can't watch you self-destruct anymore. I care about you, I really do, but you won't listen to me. You make me play mom and never take responsibility for yourself."

"I party. I've always partied. So what? I'm still in control."

She groaned. "Don't kid yourself. I know what's going on in your life. I talk to the people who used to consider themselves your friends. I know about your mood swings, your stupid arguments with anybody who disagrees with you, the wasted money, the slick characters who hang around the studio waiting to sell you drugs. I know about the fist fight you had with a stage hand whose only sin was to forget your glass of mineral water. I also know that you totaled one of the motorcycles up on Mulholland one night."

"You have better informants than the FBI." He began to pace the small room, no longer able to hide his agitation. "You're driving me crazy! I could deal with everything if you'd come back and do what you're supposed to do, which is take care of *me*!"

"I deserve to be more than your glorified baby-sitter. I've got talent! One of these days I'm goin' to try a stand-up act."

He halted, pointed at her, and began to laugh in loud, yelping gulps. It was a bitter sound. "Hanging around comedians for six years doesn't make you a fucking comedian! You've never even been up on a stage! There's no way you can make it on your own. Don't be a sap, baby. It's pathetic."

"Thanks for the lecture and the pizza." She stood, miserable with the tension these confrontations always provoked, and gestured toward the door. "See ya later."

He shifted from side to side, his face flushing, fury spewing from him like steam from a cappuccino maker. "You're trying to ruin me! Somebody's paying you to fuck up my mind! Who? Who wants me to screw up? Oh, I know they're out there, trying to get me! They know how important I am, and they can't stand it! Just like when I was a kid with asthma! Make fun of the geek! Make him look bad! Well, I never let 'em beat me then, and they're not going to beat me now!"

Amy backed away, her muscles stiff with horror. She wondered how long Elliot had been paranoid. She tried to speak in a soothing voice. "Let's sit down and talk about this. I'll get you a beer. How about that?"

"Don't suck up to me now! Forget it! I've had enough of this abuse! You can't treat me this way!" Spit flew from his mouth. His face was livid. "I'm getting out of here! I'll make you sorry! I'm taking my goddamned pizza with me, too!"

He snatched the carton and flung the pizza through the window into the backyard. "Put some salsa and some jalapeños on it and have dinner, you mothers!" he bellowed to whomever might be wandering the neighborhood, waiting to be insulted by a loud-mouthed Anglo-Saxon.

Frozen in place, she listened to Elliot run down the outside stairs, yelling obscenities. She heard a door slam and the patriarch of the Alvarez family cheerfully threaten to pull his asshole over his head. Elliot dissolved into garbled muttering.

She hurried to the front window and drew the curtain aside, staring down into the street as Elliot, trailed by Mr. Alvarez and his oldest son, stalked to a Porsche. He shot a bird at them and their baseball bats, and they rewarded him by pockmarking the car roof with dents. He floored the accelerator and careened out of their range.

Amy went to her bed and sat down limply. She had never been afraid of Elliot, before. Where could she get help? Who would know how to deal with him—and more important, who could she trust to keep his name out of the press? There had already been some ugly tabloid stories about the Las Vegas incident and Elliot's erratic behavior on the set.

She held her head and tried to remember the names of drug rehab centers that had been whispered to her by friends over the years. Then she thought of someone who might help her for old time's sake. *Jeff.*

❦

Jeff was nervous. He was still shocked at learning that Amy was living in California and working for Elliot Thornton. The prospect of seeing her again made him check his hair more than necessary. He hoped she appreciated the torture he'd gone through in the battle of the hair plugs. At least he had a hairline near the front of his head now, though nobody was going to scalp him for his luxurious fur.

He lounged in the brocaded foyer of a Los Angeles

restaurant celebrated for its haute cuisine. He tried not to fidget with the lapels of his Armani suit. It didn't look good for the head of staff at the most exclusive rehab center on the west coast to fidget.

When she arrived, he was speechless. How she had changed! She carried herself with great dignity, a delicate purse clasped in front of her elegant three-piece suit of crepe de Chine. The suit's muted shade of green complimented her eyes. She wore a wide gold choker and thick gold earrings. She looked at him without shyness.

She gave him a wide smile and came to him with her hand extended. He shook it and searched for a sign that she wanted to be hugged, but there was none.

Saddened but admiring, he called the maitre d' and requested a table. They were led to one of several plush dining rooms decorated with French tapestries, Louis Thirteenth chairs, and Aubusson rugs on walnut-wood floors. The tables were set with candelabra, white orchids, fine china, and Christofle silver. She sat down across from Jeff and propped her chin on her hands, projecting the comfortable aura of a person who had seen too many fashionable restaurants to be impressed by this one.

"God, you've blossomed," he said.

Her face colored, and she laughed. "So have you. You look like a wealthy and important man who shrinks important heads."

"And I have hair!"

Laughing more, she nodded. "Did you shrink your own head?"

The tension broken, they chatted about his work at the rehab hospital while an aproned waiter brought the wine she selected. Jeff found it enjoyable to be her guest, invited here to discuss the problem with Elliot Thornton. He disliked her involvement with the hyperactive smartass at the same time that he resigned himself to it. His latest relationship, with the star of a lightweight television drama whom he'd met when her daughter came to the center for treatment, was satisfyingly superficial. He knew better than to expect something similar from Amy. She had loved Sebastien despite all odds and then devoted years to taking care of Thornton, an addict. No, she wasn't the superficial kind.

As the meal progressed she grew increasingly subdued and distracted. Jeff knew that the pleasantries were a facade; fatigue settled around her eyes, and she pushed pieces of sole across the plate without eating.

"Let's talk about Elliot Thornton," he suggested.

She gave a tremendous sigh of relief and poured out a list of symptoms and activities from the recent months, ending with the bizarre episode involving the pizza. Jeff heard nothing that surprised him. Thornton's fragile moods and paranoia, plus his growing career problems, were part of the typical addiction syndrome. "You need to get a group of his friends together and corral him at home for a discussion—"

"I tried that once last year. It didn't do any good. He left home for a week and I couldn't find him. The show went into reruns and we had to lie like crazy to keep the reason quiet. When he finally showed up again he was wearing Mickey Mouse ears and looked as if someone had drained all his blood. He said he'd spent the whole week at Disneyland."

"The time has probably come for you to let go of Elliot. You just have to let him sink or swim by himself. Since you don't live with him anymore, you've made a start. But sometimes, when someone can't be helped, you have to walk away completely."

"I know." Tears rose in her eyes. "Like with my father."

"How is he?"

"I haven't seen him in four years. I call him on the phone at Christmas and the Fourth of July, though." She laughed sharply. "For my biannual doses of guilt."

"He trained you well." When she gave him a bewildered look he explained, "You're a dutiful slave. Eager to make the helpless strong again, even if it's impossible, even if you're always getting hurt in the process. You couldn't help your father, but you're determined to help Elliot. Your self-esteem is based only on what Elliot tells you about yourself, the same as with your father. If you want the five-dollar word for what you are, it's 'codependent.' "

She fixed an intense, thoughtful gaze on empty air. "Sounds like a brand of cold medicine. But I believe you."

"I get paid a lot of money to tell people the obvious."

"So tell me the obvious next step."

He took one of her hands and squeezed it hard. Maybe this time when she needed his trust he could help her instead of hurt her. "Live your own life. Do what's best for Amy Miracle, not for anyone else. Practice telling yourself that the only person you have to make happy is yourself."

Her drawl became more pronounced when she was upset, he'd noticed. Now she leaned toward him and said with about a million extra syllables, "Good lord, Jeff, that sounds cold. I think *amoebas* have friendlier lives than *that*."

"But the important question is, Do amoebas deliberately hurt other amoebas?"

She sat back and shook her head, her attention distant again. A decision tightened her mouth. "I feel my protoplasm mutatin'."

"Go for it."

Her gaze met his—sad, angry, determined. "Do I look like an amoeba yet?"

He nodded with approval. "Maybe it's just the light, but I think I see you changing."

❦

The phone was ringing as she walked into the apartment from her dinner with Jeff. She had a terrible headache, in part because she'd forced herself not to ask him if he ever heard from Sebastien.

Amy frowned at the phone and let the answering machine respond. As she dropped onto the bed the tape clicked, and a formal female voice said. "This is Lakeside Hospital in Gainesville, Georgia, calling to tell Ms. Miracle that her father was admitted today. Please contact us at—"

"Got it!" Amy interrupted, having dived across the room. "This is Amy Miracle. What happened to my father?"

"He had a severe stroke, I'm afraid."

The woman continued talking, but Amy's thoughts were already tuned to plane reservations and packing. She imagined Pop—garrulous, independent Pop—as an invalid, and it was the cruelest fate and the best revenge she could have wished on him. But she felt only a gnawing sense of love, of a deep and bittersweet regret that his unhappy life had come to this.

She didn't have to be absorbed by his unhappiness to love him. She did have to go to him. So much for amoebas.

❧

"A neighbor saw your father collapse beside the mailbox," the doctor told Amy. "It's good that it happened that way, because he got an ambulance there pretty quick. Your father might not be alive, otherwise."

Staring at her father now, a slack-faced stranger who did no more than flutter his eyes from time to time amidst a wilderness of tubes and machines, Amy wanted to ask why being alive in this condition was a blessing. "Will he ever be normal again?"

"It's hard to tell."

She was so giddy with fatigue and nerves that she almost said, *Oh, you can tell me, I'm his daughter. Rim-shot, please. It's a gag I swiped from a movie, thank you very much.* "Do you think he'll ever be able to take care of himself without help?"

The pudgy, earnest-looking doctor sighed. "Considering his poor health in general? No, I don't, frankly. I think you need to consider a nursing home."

"What's the going rate on the good ones?"

"You're probably looking at two thousand a month."

Amy gaped at him. "I've got to check my father's savings account," she finally managed to say. *Please, God, let him have saved some of the Ferrari money.*

❧

He hadn't. She didn't know what he and Maisie had done with the money, but he had only five thousand dollars in the bank at Gainesville. After talking to the manager about gaining access to the account, Amy left the city and drove out to the old place. She wandered numbly through the trailer, anxiety having given way to a blank feeling. She let herself be caught up in the eerie déjà vu of memories. The summer sunset haunted the rooms; dust motes seemed suspended in air and time.

Pop hadn't changed much of the decor; Maisie's ceramic chickens still preened on the kitchen wall, and her cheap bric-a-brac filled the living room. The only major alteration was in Amy's bedroom. Pop had turned it into a studio, and it was crammed with canvases, easels, and painting supplies.

She stood in the shadows, hating him. His clowns and circus scenes were robust, colorful, even cheerful. Because she hadn't seen them in so many years the contrast struck her as never before. He had despised his life after the circus, the back injury. And she had been just one more responsibility that he didn't want.

Amy began to shake. "I deserved better," she said aloud. Rage cleared away the numbness. She grabbed a tube of red oil paint and ran to a corner where dozens of canvases were stacked against the wall. Falling to her knees in front of them on the old pine floor, she squirted paint onto her palms then swiped it across a portrait of a smiling clown.

Low keening sounds came from her throat as she shoved the canvas aside and attacked another one, then another. She would destroy what his talent could create, just as he'd tried to destroy her. Without putting it in so many words, he'd blamed her for everything that had gone wrong with his life. Her birth had killed his beautiful Ellen; raising a child without her had put too many emotional and financial demands on him, especially after the back injury; he would have been happier with a son, whom he would have trained to be a professional clown like him.

It enraged her to think that she'd grown up trying so hard to compensate for crimes she'd never committed, and that even now Pop lurked in the back of her mind, telling her that she was no good, that no one could really love her, that she could never succeed at anything important. He'd imprinted his dark, fearful world on her so deeply that she was always wary of being captured by shapeless specters. She couldn't fight them because she couldn't name them.

And here was the evidence of his selfish lies. *His* world

could be cheerful and confident when he wanted, but he'd never shared it with her. He had hoarded these happy images and put them on canvas, leaving her with nothing but blank spaces to be filled with hardship and self-doubt.

She ripped into the next canvas, punching it with her fists, spitting on it, hating the smiling clown. Throwing it aside, she stiffened in shock at what she found behind it.

Her own portrait stared back at her. He must have painted it from memory after she'd made one of her early visits from college. She recalled the brindle sweater and soft white blouse she'd owned. It was a flattering portrait, devoid of hostility on both his part and hers.

Dazed, Amy set it aside and looked at the next one, another portrait, this one taken from an old photograph she had loved. It was a man and a tiny girl in matching clown suits. The photograph had been taken against a backdrop of half-constructed circus sets, but in the painting Pop put him and her against an empty slate of white tinged with pink.

She went through every canvas in the room. She found portraits of the mother she had known only from photos; she found portraits of Maisie; she found other portraits of herself—as a child, as a teenager, as a young woman. All were painted with a sensitive, even loving, touch.

Why, Pop, why? she wondered desperately, tears streaming down her face. *Does this mean that you didn't hate me? Is this the only clue I'll ever have?* She gathered the family portraits and carried them to the living room. As darkness closed in she turned on a lamp and arranged the portraits along the sofa, where she could look at them as a group.

She felt confused and lost; redefining Pop meant redefining herself. But she still didn't know who he was, and never would. His puzzle was maddening, unsolvable. She dialed Mary Beth's number in Atlanta, hoping for a cynical bit of advice to put the dilemma in perspective. But there was no answer. She finally recalled that Mary Beth was in New York hawking her interview show to a convention of station managers. This was the year Mary Beth hoped to go national.

She can't help you, anyway. Listen to yourself. For the first time, really listen.

Amy moved restlessly around the house, sorting through her emotional turbulence, her fists pressed to her temples. Pop hadn't destroyed her, that was the important thing. She could be whatever she wanted, despite him. How he had viewed her in his life and paintings was only *his* reality, not hers. He had never known who she really was. He had treated her one way and painted her another, so what did his opinion matter? What did anyone's opinion matter, except her own?

She locked the house, got into her rental car, then rested her head on the steering wheel and took deep breaths. She fought a smothering sensation. The summer heat seemed heavy with fear, but also with excitement.

Do it, the new voice inside her urged. *You know you can do it. It doesn't matter how he judged you. You aren't the person he created. Don't live in that person's image anymore. Find out who you really are. What have you got to lose?*

❦

The audience at Live Wire was patient on Monday nights. They had paid their discount cover charge knowing that they were going to be subjected to a stream of rank amateurs or third-rate professionals with nothing better to do between paying jobs.

Amy remembered the small in-town club from the early days when Elliot was touring and would stop by Atlanta to see her after one of his weekend bookings. He and she would go to Live Wire to watch the beginners make idiots of themselves. Elliot had loved to play the magnanimous Big Name, doling out advice and hope, getting up on stage to do a few minutes of material for the surprised, cheering crowd.

She was glad that Elliot was three thousand miles away tonight.

As she angled between people at the bar her legs quivered so violently that when she looked down she could see a tremor in the skirt of her print sundress. Her shoulders itched under the thin white jacket she'd put on to make the dress look more formal. Hives. She was getting hives.

In a little office down a hall hung with autographed photos of comics mugging for posterity, she found a squirmy little man in sport clothes who climbed over his desk and grabbed her in a hug. "How ya doin'? Long time no see! Lawd-dee, it's been years since you and the Elliot-man dropped by!"

They rocked from side to side. Her nervous stomach began to rebel. "I'm fine, Irving. Irving . . . can you put me into the lineup for tonight? Anywhere. I'll take the graveyard if I have to. I just want five minutes to do some material I wrote."

"You? Writing gags for yourself? What happened to Elliot? What's going on? You? Amy? When did this writing thing start?"

"It's a long story. Can I get into the lineup?"

"Sure! It's open-mike night. You can have all the time— Amy? Are you all right?"

"Fine. Excuse me. Thanks for letting me in. I'll be back in a minute. I just have to go throw up."

She spent the next two hours huddled in a chair in the ladies' room, alternately clutching her stomach and going over the jokes she'd listed on a paper towel. She told herself that she'd survive, even if she bombed. Bombing was part of the business. *Nobody*, not even the top comics, escaped it all the time. The important thing was to prove that she could get up on stage and not make a fool of herself. Or at least not too much of a fool.

At ten-thirty Irving sent one of the waitresses to get her. "You're on after the next guy finishes," the girl told Amy between quick puffs on a cigarette. "Hey, does this smoke bother you?"

"Nah, I always look like Dracula on a day pass." Amy splashed cold water on her wrists and stared at herself in the mirror. *You're good. You can do this.* She walked out of the rest room on wobbly legs. An eerie sense of panic rose in her chest, and she almost headed for an exit. A comic was twisting balloons into animals, and his giraffe popped two feet from her ear.

She bolted into the short, narrow hall that led directly up on stage. Trembling, she tried to take slow breaths. A stockbroker was on stage telling stockbroker jokes. The audience wasn't laughing. Soon they wouldn't be laughing at her.

The stockbroker finished quickly. Amy leaned against the wall and shut her eyes. Irving squeezed her shoulder on his way to the stage. "You okay?"

"Sure!" Her voice was an octave higher than usual, with a squeak like a reedy clarinet. She couldn't recall her first two jokes. She began to take small steps backward. With any luck, she'd be gone before Irving got the introduction out of his mouth.

But he was too fast. He bounded to the microphone. "Here's an old friend of mine who just dropped in tonight to try out a few jokes. Please welcome Amy Miracle."

Only the worst coward would run at that point. She thought about it, but her feet began moving forward. She climbed a short ramp. She stepped onto the stage's varnished wooden floor. The lights surrounded her. The applause was polite.

Somehow she ended up front and center. Her throat had a knot of fear in it. She wrapped both hands around the mike's slender metal post and simply stared at the audience, unable to speak. They stared back. After twenty or thirty seconds the waitresses stopped to stare, too.

Oh, Lord, this was hopeless. The Catatonic Comic. Someone in the dark, intimate room began to snicker. It wasn't a pleasant sound, but at least it broke the monotony. *Go for the sympathy element*, Amy thought desperately. *Just tell the truth.*

She leaned toward the mike and croaked. "Y'all terrify the hell out of me."

To her shock, they laughed. She found a bored face and scrutinized it. The man watched her with his head tilted to one side in a quizzical way, as if someone had just goosed him. *Well, go on, go on. Make me laugh.*

"Suburban people are real scary," she continued, her voice cracking. The man chuckled. Why? She hadn't said anything funny. What was this—some kind of *Twilight Zone* episode? She stepped closer to the microphone and peered over it warily. "Suburban people have their own gangs. Oh, I know—you think I'm just paranoid. But I've seen 'em. Those women in jogging suits, walking in packs, with their little headphones. Are they *really* just listening to 'Thin Thighs in Three Hundred Years?' Or are they casing your station wagon? Do you want to go out some morning and find your hubcaps missing and a Barry Manilow tape on the front seat?"

This time the laughter was no fluke. The bored man was sitting on the edge of his seat, grinning. She couldn't think about it too much or she'd freeze again. She had to keep careening ahead, jabbering about whatever came into her mind. "I'm also scared of furniture salespeople. They hang out in gangs, too. You know how frightenin' they can be. You walk in and there they are, trying to look nonchalant, leaning against the furniture, with measuring tapes hanging out of their pockets. You try to ignore them—you get real nervous, but you're trying to be cool and just walk on by. But they won't let you. It's 'Hey, mama, want to see some sofas?' or 'Check out *this* credenza, baby.' Oh, you can try to detour around them—take the long way through the dining-room sets—but they'll only laugh. They know nobody can find their way out of all those fake rooms alone."

People applauded. The man with the bored face was nodding to the woman beside him. They were both chuckling.

Amy took a deep, disbelieving breath. She knew she'd be frightened the next time she got up on stage, and the time after that, and probably the thousandth time. But obviously fear could be funny. "You know what else I'm afraid of? Big words that sound embarrassing. Like 'mastication.' What is that—having oral sex with yourself?"

The man with the bored face nearly fell out of his chair laughing. She stared at him with adoration. *Pick the toughest person in the room and concentrate on him*, Elliot often told new comics. *When you own him, you own the room.*

She owned the room. She owned her future. She could deal with the rest.

❦

"You want a *what*?" Elliot bellowed at the top of his lungs. Then he went to the soft-drink machine in one corner of his office and kicked a dent in the diet cola.

Amy had expected his reaction. Her newfound confidence didn't desert her. "I want the writing job you offered me a couple of months ago."

"Why?"

"Because I just put my father in a nursing home and I need the money."

"So you think you can crawl back—"

"I'm not crawling. Either you give me a job or you don't. I'm a damned good writer, and you know it."

"You want a favor? Go rub a lamp."

"I want a *job*. And actually, I want to be your friend again. I remember when we liked each other a *lot*. You don't have many friends left, and I'm willing to try to help you—but on my terms."

"You greedy, arrogant—"

"Here are my terms. I won't sleep with you, I won't act as your gopher, and I won't play Nurse Ratched when you're determined to get stoned, because that hardly ever worked anyway. But I *will* be your best writer and your best friend, and I'll stand by you while you get professional counseling."

"Fuck the counseling. When you're ready to live with me again, then we'll talk about the rest."

"Too bad. Bye." She pivoted and headed for the door.

"Wait!" He kicked the soft-drink machine again. His anger crumpled. "All right. You're hired."

"Good. One more thing. I don't mind working overtime at all, but I won't work nights."

"Why?"

"I have other fish to fry." She had decided to keep her stand-up routine a secret. He wasn't capable of dealing with more of the new Amy yet. She planned to work at the little clubs outside L.A., where people who knew her would be less likely to go. She had a lot to learn, and she wanted the relative anonymity of the smaller clubs in which to do it.

Elliot thrust his hands into his hair. "You've got a boy-friend!"

"No, I just want to have my nights free."

"All right, all right! Anything else? You know, of course, that you really crave my body and it's just a matter of time before we do an Ozzie and Harriet again?"

She smiled, putting sunshine on steel. "Don't hold your breath."

EIGHTEEN

*M*arie entered her seventh month—longer than she'd ever carried a baby before—and the waiting became torture. Sebastien went to her room every night and sat for a minute with his hand on her stomach, hardly believing the movement he felt inside her. They discussed the change of luck in cautious terms, always more polite than intimate, but Sebastien allowed himself a surge of hope.

Throughout the pregnancy Marie had forbidden her doctors to perform any but the most routine medical examinations; she had decided that all the testing on past pregnancies had contributed to her miscarriages. "I no longer violate the purity of my womb," she explained to Sebastien. He humored her beliefs, caring only that this pregnancy had survived.

After the child was born they would finally have a mutual interest; something worth sharing in their lives. His work had begun to seem like a treadmill on which he performed with automatic efficiency, losing track of his emotions to the point where he would sometimes resort to cafés to observe people laughing and talking in casual conversations. He rarely saw such things at the hospital or at home, and a hunger for them was growing inside him.

Marie's eighth month came, without complications. Late one night Sebastien returned home to find that she had unlocked the door to the nursery. Now she sat in a lotus position in the middle of the floor, eyes shut, lips moving in a silent chant, radiating her earnest vibrations to the empty, stale-smelling suite that had not been entered in years.

Sebastien couldn't resist imagining the suite filled with toys and baby furniture, with the tall, stern windows open to let sunlight into a pleasant world filled with his child's laughter. It all seemed amazingly possible.

The ninth month was as charmed as the rest. Sebastien's one firm request was that Marie not have the baby at home, which was what she wanted to do. In her peaceful, confident mood she agreed without protest. Nothing could go wrong now.

And nothing did. Sebastien was performing his rounds one evening when the call came from the hospital's maternity ward. Marie's water had broken during her Thursday-evening yoga class, and she'd gone straight to the hospital. Sebastien ignored the hospital's lazy elevators and ran down several flights of stairs to see her. She was sitting up in the bed of her private room, placidly stroking a crystal.

He raised both the crystal and her hands and kissed them. "I'll rearrange some duties upstairs so that I can be with you during delivery."

"No, please. You're a dear for offering, but you'd distract me. I have to focus all my thoughts." She gave him a pleading look. "Try to understand. I only agreed to come to the hospital to make you happy. Now please, let me manage the birth as nearly to my liking as possible."

"As you wish." His excitement over the impending birth drove away any frustration. After the baby was born he would no longer tolerate her aloof and possessive attitude. Before he left the room he placed his hand on her belly. Her hospital gown made a soft cover for the turgid muscle underneath. "Welcome to the world," he said gruffly.

❦

It was near dawn when Marie's doctor came into the waiting room. Sebastien pivoted from a window and stiffened the moment he saw the woman's shuttered expression. A thousand shards of fear cut through him, and his only salvation was to feign anger. "If something is wrong,

Doctor, I want to know why you've waited until now to inform me."

If there had been sympathy under the obstetrician's severely plucked brows, it vanished. "It was impossible to inform you of something I didn't know until ten minutes ago. Your wife delivered the baby without extraordinary problems. Your wife is doing well, physically. She's heavily sedated."

"The point, Doctor, the point."

The woman's chin snapped up. "You have a baby daughter," she retorted. "But she's having breathing difficulties. We've already put her on a respirator. Her condition is marginal—low pulse, poor reflexes, poor skin color. I've scheduled an EEG. I hate to say this, but I suspect that she's anencephalic."

He died inside. The horror was almost palpable. After all the years of waiting. . . . *She suffers. Dear God, I brought my daughter into a world filled with nothing but the most terrible misery.*

The perfect machine, trained from childhood to turn grief inward, asked brusquely, "If the baby is anencephalic, how much time does it have?"

"*It*? Your child?" the doctor asked in an acid voice. "No more than a week, at most. Maybe a day or two. These babies . . . it's tragic—"

"Yes, well, it's doubtful that it knows much of what's happening." He strode from the room, snapping his fingers for the pediatrician to follow. "I want every detail. Extensive blood work—"

"Just a moment!" She grabbed the sleeve of the hospital scrubs he still wore from his own work, upstairs. "We're discussing your daughter! Your own flesh and blood! What do you think you're going to do?"

He halted and very calmly pried her fingers from their grip. Her furious, disbelieving gaze clung to him. She loathed him, not that it mattered. Not that anything mattered except rescuing his daughter from this nightmare. He held the doctor's attention without blinking. He hardly knew that she was there. "I'm going to check with other hospitals," he told her, "to see if they have any babies waiting for heart transplants."

❦

The nursery for intensive-care infants was home to only one tiny patient, a dark-haired thing with an undersized head and a small mask of a face, his daughter. He looked down at her in her prison of electrodes and tubes, watching her breathe with the aid of a machine. She was blind. There was nothing behind her eyes. She was one of the cruelest contortions of nature, born with only a brain stem, the most primitive neurological center, and it was already failing its task.

He slipped his hand down into the jungle of technology and touched her gently, amazed at how beautiful she was. Her delicate hands curled and she blinked long, dark lashes, but he knew that both reactions were meaningless. She was no more aware of him than she was of herself. His legs failed him, and he sat down quickly on a stool he pulled close to the incubator.

Shaking, he leaned over her and whispered, *"Je t'aime, ma petite, je t'aime."* It was no sentimental lie. He loved her so fiercely that he wanted to be absorbed in the hopeless body and die with her.

But he couldn't indulge self-centered grief, not when she was in such torment. He cupped her head in his hand as she had a mild seizure, crooning soft sounds to her while he stroked the silky forehead with the pad of his thumb. *It won't be much longer, little one. I promise. Your father promises.*

"Doctor de Savin? I came as soon as I got your message." The transplant coordinator waited a few feet away, his clothes rumpled, his owlish eyes revealing the early hour and the tension of this unusual situation. "I've finished checking. We have a match with a baby at Jenane Saint Alz."

"The baby? Tell me—"

"Two weeks old. A congenital heart defect. Very critical at this point. We may be too late for him."

"Why?"

"He may not last until, uhmmm—" the coordinator shifted awkwardly, "until we can provide the donor."

Sebastien straightened. His daughter lay quiet again, her head still resting in his hand. There would be more seizures, much worse than this one. He wouldn't let her be tormented. There was no alternative, no guilt, nothing but the sacrifice they would make for each other.

"We won't wait," he told the coordinator. "She is no more alive than a brain-dead accident victim. I'm going to take her off the respirator. I don't think she can breathe on her own."

"But if there are impulses from the brain stem—"

"A CAT scan of an empty skull is fascinating in its perversity. I suggest that you refresh your memory."

"I know it's terrible, Doctor, but—"

"The impulses from the brain stem are meaningless."

"But what if she continues to breathe when you remove life support? That would be considered . . ." His voice faded and he shifted from foot to foot.

Alive, that's considered alive, Sebastien finished for him silently. *But only in the most pitiful way.* He fixed a hard gaze on the man, daring him to finish the statement. "I'm willing to take that chance."

The coordinator coughed and looked away. "Hmmm, Doctor de Savin, *shouldn't* we contact Dr. d'Albret? He's scheduled to return tomorrow from the administrator's conference in Nice, but I'm sure, considering the birth of his grandchild—"

"I'll call him myself."

"*Before* you proceed?"

Sebastien rose to his feet furiously, ready to fight anyone who tried to delay him. "I will make all the decisions concerning my child. As head of the transplant unit I make *this* decision. If you have a problem with that, you no longer belong on my staff."

"But hospital protocol—"

"Does not apply to my daughter. I take full responsibility. I'll perform both the removal and the transplant."

"Mother of God! To do this to your own child . . . how can you?"

How can I not? Sebastian thought. "We have work to do," he said crisply. "And no time to waste on ethical debates." He gathered his strength and sent the coordinator a look so full of warning that the man nodded jerkily and hurried away.

Power. Privilege. He would use them to full advantage today, knowing that this would probably be the end of them.

❦

By the time the operation was arranged, she had been off life support for thirty minutes. She lay on the operating table, breathing in shallow, irregular gasps which grew weaker as Sebastien watched. Without the machines she was dead already. No, she had never really lived, never sensed the world around her, never had even the most basic awareness of herself, of being loved and pitied.

Standing beside her fragile little form, Sebastien didn't let himself think about what he was going to do; later he would agonize over the memory, but for now he forced himself to look at her without emotion. He gave directions to his nurses and residents in the same low, firm voice he always used. They responded in silence, all of them subdued, many of them angry. He noted the frowns above their masks, the unnatural quiet, the way they avoided brushing against him around the crowded table.

He knew what they were thinking: that another surgeon should be performing this task; that a loving father would not be able to divorce himself from his feelings; that he viewed his daughter as a monstrosity to be used and disposed of quickly.

Five minutes later she stopped breathing. "Let us begin," he told them.

The cutting didn't affect him—watching the frail chest open more with each soft crunch of the heavy scissors—nor did the finer work of opening the pericardial sac that surrounded her heart. It was only when he saw what was left of her life making its last flutter of movement—so tiny, and yet so determined—that he almost cried.

But this, at least, will live.

And several minutes later, when her heart lay free and quiet in his hand, only waiting to be resurrected, he was at peace.

❦

Marie flung herself to the foot of the hospital bed and spat at him. "Bastard! Monster!" Sobbing hysterically, she pounded the bed's metal foot rail with both hands. "I never saw her alive again after they took her from the delivery room!"

He stood quietly, rooted to the floor by exhaustion so complete that his feet felt bolted down. He had only taken time to change his bloody scrubs for clean ones before coming to see if she was awake. She was, though still groggy from the sedative. He told her what he had done, expecting the worst reaction, knowing that their marriage was over, and only sorry that they had not ended it before birthing a tortured child.

"How could you?" she screamed. "You killed her! You didn't even wait for her to die before you mangled her as if she were no more than a laboratory experiment!"

"She was never alive, not in any sense we consider human."

"Not human in *your* ruthless world! Not human when you wanted to use her for your work!"

"Another baby is alive because of her. That was the only contribution she could make. Don't you understand? She had dignity and worth. There was a reason for her to be born, because of what I did. *She was not a mistake.*"

"Stop rationalizing! You didn't love her, and you couldn't wait to be rid of her! Well, now you can be rid of me, too! I despise you! I'm leaving you!"

"I don't know why we've put up with each other for so many years. Convenience and practicality, I suppose. You don't have to leave. Keep the house. I'll go."

"Go! Go straight to your place in hell! It was the blackness in you that kept us from having a child! You should have died with your mother all those years ago. You were meant to die! I thought that I could conquer the evil auras around you, but no one can. She doomed you, and all you will ever see are the shadows of life!"

There was truth in what she said, but not enough truth. Sebastien turned to leave. "My mother was only a victim of my father's selfishness."

"Oh, let's talk about your father. Yes, yes, fine timing, Sebastien." Marie gave a shriek of laughter. "I thought you were so perfect for me. I didn't want to love anyone after my first husband died. And you didn't care about being loved. Perfect." She surged forward, chin thrust out, eyes glittering. Her voice became a soft, vicious taunt. "Your father agreed."

Sebastien pivoted unsteadily and grasped the bed rail. "Tell me what you mean."

"I mean that he *asked* me to visit you in Africa. That we talked about it many times before I actually went. That he wanted me to marry you and bring you home, where you belonged. And I, like a fool, listened to him."

"My father doesn't just talk. He bribes. What did he offer you?"

"Bribes? You hate him so, you always think the worst of his motives. He wanted to give everything to you—control of the family businesses, a world of opportunities that no mere *doctor* would have—but he knew that you would always throw them in his face. So he made plans to bestow everything on your eldest son. A family fortune, a small empire—all for our first son. Bribe? There was none, merely the understanding that I would never keep him from his grandchildren and that he would make your first son his heir."

The impact of his father's manipulation caught Sebastien like a staggering punch. All these years Sebastien had taken satisfaction in the belief that he was punishing his father for the sins of the past. Now he realized that his father had not been punished at all, or even outmaneuvered. Except now. There would be no more children. There would be no more marriage. No avenue for manipulation. A victory for Sebastien, but at a terrible price.

Swaying with rage and frustration, he stared at Marie. "You considered my father's promises worth this struggle we've endured for so many years? Was your ambition that obsessive?"

"Yes! We would have had a tolerable marriage—you must admit—if we'd had children. but now, now even I give up on you. Smile, Sebastien, you've disappointed your father magnificently this time!"

Sebastien flashed a hand forward and clasped her throat. He knew exactly how much pressure to use to frighten, but not to hurt. She made a choking sound and clung to his wrist. Her eyes met his in fury and fear as he leaned close to her. "Did you love our daughter?"

Tears slid down her face. "Yes."

"Then keep her memory. It's the only legacy your foolish ambition has gotten you."

He let go of her and she crumpled, burying her face in her arms and crying poignantly. He looked at her with disgust, at seven years of a marriage that should never have happened, and would not have happened if his ambition and pride had not made him blind to his emotions.

❦

He went to his father's office that afternoon and told him about the baby. There would not be an heir to the de Savin name. The news defeated Philippe de Savin as nothing else ever had; Sebastien watched the elegant old back slump and the blue eyes cloud with fatigue. Age seemed to capture him in only a few minutes' time.

"You still have Annette's children to manipulate," Sebastien reminded him. "Even if they don't bear the de Savin name, I'm sure you'll warm to the idea eventually."

"Get out," his father said, and sank down in his desk chair with his back to Sebastien. "I can't fight you anymore."

Sebastien laughed bitterly. He would never believe that.

❦

Christian d'Albret gave him an ultimatum—resign from the hospital or suffer severe censure for breaching protocols. He had known from the moment he had decided to end his daughter's feeble imitation of life that he was stranding himself in a jungle of rules designed to pacify the clergy and the politicians. Technically, he had taken the heart from a dying baby rather than a dead one.

Had not Christian been personally involved, the matter would have been forgotten. There was an understanding among physicians where medical dilemmas involving themselves or their families were concerned. But Christian had feared and disliked him for years, and Sebastien knew he'd supplied the perfect opportunity for revenge. His father-in-law, filled with rage, was determined to cut down Sebastien's pride, marriage, and career with one swift stroke.

"Do you think you'll be welcome at any other major hospital in the country?" he asked Sebastien. "No. I'll make sure of that. Take your career, Doctor—what's left of it— and see if anyone will even let you through their doors. Oh, and I'll use your father's influence to make doubly certain. He's as furious about this as I am."

"Not furious," Sebastien responded softly. "The baby was only a girl, you see. But he enjoys this chance to humble me."

Sebastien left the office. All he had to show for years of dedication was a bleak sense of failure when he contemplated the future. He knew that he was still a leader; that he would be a leader again, but the emptiness that had clung to the fringes of his life for so long threatened to overwhelm him.

Marie filed for divorce, then left for an extended stay with relatives in Lyons. Sebastien secluded himself at their home and sent the servants away. He let himself drift, sleeping at odds hours of the day and night, eating only as an afterthought, reading ponderous books of philosophy that no longer made sense.

One night he took the lacquered box out of his armoire and from it removed the old revolver. He took the gun apart and cleaned it carefully, put it back together, then left it on a table. For the next few hours he glanced at it each time he entered the room, not really thinking the thought, but aware of it, nonetheless. Finally he indulged the morbid fascination; he tempted his own fate. Was he doomed, or not?

Near dawn he took the lacquered box from the bottom drawer of the armoire again; this time he removed the box of cartridges. Snatching the gun and box of cartridges into his hands, he walked out onto the balcony. A white moon hung low in the autumn sky.

He touched the tip of the gun's barrel. Would it be a cowardly thing to do, or just the fulfillment of a fate that had been chasing him since childhood? The *Ankou* had been waiting almost thirty years to rectify a mistake, and Sebastien was tired of feeling its cold, unforgiving stare at his back.

No one will care. Do it. His breath short, his hands moving with sure, swift intent, he opened the cartridge box and dug his fingers inside. They touched the round, dimpled token and its gnarled chain.

Sebastien jerked the necklace from the box and held it in the moonlight, stunned and disbelieving. Logic told him that one of the maids, or perhaps even Marie, had found the necklace where he'd thrown it in the hedges and for some unknown reason had tucked it inside the cartridge box.

No. His hands shook. His legs gave way and he sat down on the balcony's cold stone floor. All the time he continued staring at the token. He knew a sign when he saw one. It gleamed in the light, reminding him that he had once had a chance to be more than the sum of bitterness and pride. Suddenly he realized the horror of what he had been considering only seconds earlier, and he knew that he had to change his life entirely if he was going to survive.

He had to start a new life where he could nurture emotions that had been shriveled through years of neglect. And when he felt strong again, he had to find Amy.

FOUR

NINETEEN

*B*ecause Amy still refused to be part of Elliot's private life, he paraded gorgeous women around the set to annoy her. She didn't have the heart to tell him that any jealousy she felt was minor compared to her wish that he'd stop harassing her and settle down with one of his playmates.

"Which one is that?" the show's makeup artist whispered, as they watched a leggy blonde in a black bodysuit stride into Elliot's dressing room and shut the door.

"Another model-actress." Amy turned resolutely and walked down the hall toward the office area.

"Oh, one of those hyphenated creatures." The makeup artist followed, anxious for more information, as was everyone else on the show's staff. They liked to stay one step ahead of Elliot's activities and quicksilver moods. "Has she ever acted in anything?"

Amy chuckled. "Sure. She's starred in several deodorant commercials. I suspect that most of her talent is in her armpits. I just hope she doesn't give Elliot some strange venereal disease. At her age, it might be diaper rash."

The makeup artist began giggling. Suddenly the door to Elliot's dressing room flew open. Amy pivoted warily as he lunged into the hall, bare-chested, his black dress slacks half-zipped and hanging low on his abdomen, a cordless phone clenched in one hand. He looked stunned. Spotting Amy, he yelled, "I want to talk to you *right now*!"

She steeled herself and walked slowly toward him. When

she reached him she smiled benignly. "You bellowed, magnificent one?"

He jabbed a finger toward the phone. "You're working the clubs at night! You traitor!"

Her stomach twisted. She had known this day would come, but she dreaded what might happen next. "I'm not a traitor. The material I use in the clubs wouldn't work for you. I'm not taking anything away from my writing for the show."

"I don't care! You're sneaking around behind my back, trying to compete with me, trying to make a fool out of me!"

"You're doing that without my help." She laid a hand on his arm. He pulled away. Inside the open door to the dressing room, the blond model-actress lounged on a white sofa, catlike, eyes wide and ears perked. Amy shut the door, then faced Elliot again. "What I do after I leave here every night is my own business."

"I ought to fire you."

"Go ahead. I need this job, but I won't quit working the clubs."

He paced the corridor. He threw the phone on the floor and shook his fists at her. "You're gonna push me too far one day, and you'll be out of here! Just wait until you have to beg for another bank loan to pay your old man's extra doctor bills. You won't be so cocky if *that* happens again. And I'll know when you're desperate. I'll know, and I'll make you squirm."

She felt as if she'd been punched. "How did you find out about that loan?"

"I hired a private investigator! That's how I find out anything I want to know about you these days. And believe me, baby, I'm gonna check up on you even more from now on. I'll know what clubs you work at night, and how much you get paid, and who you're with when you're not working."

Her sense of violation almost overwhelmed reason. She wanted to slap him; she wanted to sink to his level and hurl ugly accusations. It was the way she'd often felt around Pop when she was growing up. Back then she'd hated herself for being too afraid to fight back; now she realized that she'd misinterpreted some of the fear. She just hadn't wanted to fight on Pop's level. It was dignity, not fear, that had kept her quiet.

Calmly she reached out and touched the smear of bright pink lipstick on Elliot's stomach. "She's one of the hungry ones, Elliot. Don't let her eat you alive."

His mood changed at her touch, and his chin quivered. "I don't want her. I want you. I want you to love me again."

She felt white-hot inside. Between clenched teeth she said, "Spyin' on me is not my idea of romance."

"Okay. No more private investigators. I swear."

He leaned forward, and she feared that he'd try to kiss her. At that moment several staffers ambled into the hallway, and Elliot drew back. "Got to get ready for the show," he said gruffly. He hesitated. "You're never gonna get anywhere with a stand-up routine, baby. The competition is crazy—you know that. I don't want to see you get your heart broken."

Thanks for the encouragement, she thought bitterly. "I'll take my chances."

He clamped his mouth into a hard line and went back into the dressing room. Before he slammed the door she glimpsed the blonde hurriedly tucking something into a tiny black purse on the couch beside her. She brushed at her nose and smiled toward Elliot.

Amy stared at the closed door in grim recognition. Then she hurried to her office and began making phone calls to every friend and acquaintance she had. There was no doubt that Elliot would keep spying on her.

She alerted dozens of people, including Jeff Atwater, warning them that Elliot was on a rampage. They promised to sidetrack anyone who asked for information about her.

Even though Mary Beth was in the middle of negotiating the sale of her talk show to a national distributor, she took time to savor Elliot's paranoia. Amy could almost see her predatory, slit-eyed look of contemplation. "Sugar," Mary Beth drawled finally, "any private dick who tries to con me for information will get his dick ripped off."

"A 'no comment' will do."

After she hung up the phone she realized that she felt dirty, and when she examined the feeling she understood why. This must be like going through an ugly divorce, where you kept asking yourself how you ever could have loved the mean-spirited stranger wanting to hurt you. And what did it say about your judgment to have chosen such a man in the first place?

She put her head in her hands. The truth was that she'd never loved Elliot, that she'd always been drawn to his work more than to him, that she wouldn't have put up with his problems for so long if he hadn't been the key to the career she wanted. Her sacrifices on his behalf couldn't obscure the fact that she had used him as much as he'd used her.

❦

Sebastien leaned against one of the fieldstone columns that supported the veranda roof. Filling his lungs with night air, he absorbed the scents of freshly turned soil, forest, grape vines, and mild winter air. This small California valley had been poured full of everything that was good about the earth, and living here for the past two months had helped him find what was good about himself.

There were still dark moments when he felt shut away from his emotions, but he tried to have the same patience with himself that he allowed the neglected vineyards. He was much slower to flourish than they.

Tonight he felt restless and more than a little worried. He slid work-roughened hands into the pockets of khaki trousers stained with dirt. He'd dug holes for new trellis posts all day, and his body hummed with a comfortable fatigue that he had hoped would quiet his thoughts.

The wall phone in the kitchen rang with echoing urgency. Sebastien bolted indoors. "Yes?"

"Harry Brown, calling from Atlanta."

"Have you learned anything new?"

"Well, I found her old college roommate. Name's Liz Vandergard. Hosts a TV show in Atlanta. Sweetest little lady you'd ever want to talk to. We musta talked for thirty minutes. Just as open as you please."

"What did she tell you?"

"She says that Ms. Miracle moved to Alaska five years ago to do social work with the Eskimos. Hell, I didn't even know there were any Eskimos left in Alaska. Anyhow, that's where she is, somewhere north of Nome. Ms. Vandergard says that Ms. Miracle was married twice—once to a rodeo cowboy named Bill Hickok and once to a Greek olive farmer named Hercule Poirot. But as far as Ms. Vandergard knows, Ms. Miracle is single right now. But she's been dating an oil-rig worker in Nome for the past few months. Some Russian defector named Ivan Jackov."

Sebastien leaned against the kitchen wall and shut his eyes. *Bill Hickok? Hercules Poirot? Ivan Jackov?* Harry Brown's credentials hadn't mentioned his incredible stupidity. "That is the most preposterous fable I have ever heard."

"Huh?"

"Give me Liz Vandergard's phone number." When Harry complied, he memorized it distractedly, already thinking of new tactics. "Thank you, Mr. Brown. Your services won't be needed anymore. You may send me your bill."

"You don't want me to follow this Nome lead?"

Sebastien looked heavenward. "No."

As soon as Brown hung up Sebastian placed a call to Liz Vandergard's office in Atlanta. He glanced at the digital clock atop the refrigerator. Late, but undoubtedly that ambitious woman would be in her office. Biting back his impatience, he worked his way through a receptionist and a secretary at the television station where Liz Vandergard worked.

"You just don't give up, do you, Harry?" she said, by way of greeting. Her voice was butter-smooth and slightly amused.

"I beg your pardon. This is Dr. de Savin, as I explained to—"

"Right, sugar, right. Good accent. You sound like Charles Boyer with a stick up his ass."

"I am *not* Harry Brown—"

"Brown, huh? The last time, you were Harry Garfield. The only thing you haven't changed is your underwear, I suspect. So now you're Dr. de Savin, huh? And you want to grill me about Amy Miracle."

Sebastien gritted his teeth. "Didn't she ever mention my name?"

"Oh, sure, *Doctor,* she mentioned it to a lot of people. I'm sure she even discussed it with your boss, the guy who hired you to do this bullshit job. And he's so paranoid that he'd stoop to any kind of lie to get information on her. What's the point?"

She sighed coyly. "Oh, wait, I get it. You've been told to find out if she ever played around on Mr. Big. So you wanta know everything she's done over the past few years. Well, let's just say this. The only thing she ever did wrong was put up with a lot of bullshit from him. And if he thinks he's going to pester her, or hurt her, because she's left him, why, you tell him that I'll come out there and make him sing soprano. How would his fans like *that?*"

Sebastien gripped the phone. "Is she in danger? This singer, he wants to hurt her? How? You have to tell me. I assure you, I'm Sebastien de Savin—"

"Who dumped Amy ten years ago and never looked back. Yeah, right. You picked the wrong alias, Harry, if you wanted to get on my good side. Tell Mr. Big that he fucked up when he told you to con Liz Vandergard."

"I'll come to Atlanta and meet you in person. I'll *prove* to you that I'm who I say I am."

"Don't bother. I won't let you through the door. I won't buy your dog-and-pony show. I'm not meeting with anybody who wants information about Amy."

"At least send her a message for me."

"From *Doctor de Savin?* And upset her with your stupid hoax? Hell, no. Harry, stop taking your cues from those private-eye shows on TV. They suck for authenticity."

"I will do whatever it takes to win your confidence. You *cannot* assume I'm lying to you. If Amy needs help, I want to know about it. *I have to know about it.*"

"Right. Tell Mr. Big that he can help her by leaving her the fuck alone. And *you* leave *me* alone." She hung up.

Sebastien stared at the phone and cursed viciously. Amy was in some kind of trouble, and this maniacal friend of hers was contributing to it with her misguided secrecy. Cold chills crawled down his back. He grabbed a phone directory. This time he would hire a dozen investigators and follow-up their leads in person.

❦

"You *stink!*" a woman yelled from the back of the club, her voice slicing through the laughter around her. People gasped. Amy felt a momentary clutch of panic as the heat of embarrassment rose to her cheeks. Then she recovered and told the audience, "It's hell when the folks at the halfway house come here on a field trip."

The audience laughed with collective relief. Amy forced a nonchalant grin. One of the first rules of stand-up was to stay in control of the situation. You made the audience nervous when you let a heckler best you.

"You stink!" the woman yelled again. There was nothing worse than unimaginative hecklers. They bored the audience quickly, and it was hard to bounce comebacks off their one-note insults.

Amy glanced down to make certain her clench-hold on the mike stand wasn't obvious. *Keep the audience's respect. Don't let them feel sorry for you.* She sighed and shook her head at the audience, as if weary. "What do you say to somebody who probably got her brains at Toys 'R' Us?"

While everyone else hooted and cheered, the heckler, a young, athletic-looking brunette, stood up and fast-balled a beer bottle at Amy. Self-preservation overtook shock, and Amy ducked. Still, the bottle grazed her temple.

In the chaos that followed, with the club's bouncer wrestling both the brunette and her oversized boyfriend, Amy ignored the throbbing pain beside one brow and began emceeing the fight as if it were a wrestling match.

"I believe she's got him in a triple bovine lock, folks! Yes, yes, what a technique! She could squeeze a man to death with that attitude! And now the killer boyfriend is doing the famous hold called I-spent-twenty-bucks-on-this-date-and-I'm-not-leaving-without-a-grope-from-*someone.*"

After the cursing pair was hauled out, the thrilled audience remained in a hyper mood. No way were they ready to sit still and listen right now. Amy waved good night and left the stage to a scattering of distracted applause.

In the wings the club manager slapped a bar cloth wrapped around ice on her temple and asked fearfully, "Are you really hurt? Is this gonna go on my insurance record?"

"I'm fine. No big deal. I'll write about it in my memoirs. Is aspirin good for brain damage?" She trembled with humiliation and delayed nerves. Holding the ice pack in place with one hand, she made her way through a crowd of comics who commiserated fervently, though she knew that each was secretly thanking God the bimbo had gone crazy during *her* set, not his.

In the women's dressing room she slumped on a bench in front of a big makeup mirror and scrutinized the pink knot rising on her right temple. A woman wearing an African-print shirt and jeans breezed in through the rear door, a tote bag slung over one shoulder. "I'm late. What's going down?" she asked, throwing herself onto the bench.

"My career. Raneeta, there are nights when I think that this is no way for an adult to make a living."

"Since when are we making a living?"

"Good point."

"Listen, I gotta tell you something. A private dick called me about you the other day."

Amy's headache became a stab. "Oh, no."

"He heard that we worked together at WDIG. He said he's trying to find you for a client of his. What a load of crap. Elliot's really devious."

Amy felt sick. Why was Elliot checking so deeply into her past?

Raneeta chuckled. "The guy said he heard that you were involved with some singer."

Amy groaned. So that was it. Elliot's paranoid idea that she'd been seeing other men behind his back for years. "A *singer*?"

"I said I hadn't seen you since college." Raneeta punched her arm and chuckled again. "Then I got wild and made up this big story about you going to work for a TV station out in Oklahoma. As a weather girl. I said you were probably still there. I said you had changed your name. I gave him the name of this weather chick I know up there. She won't mind."

Amy stared at Raneeta in amazement. If all of her friends were making up stories like this one—and she *knew* that Mary Beth was doing it—then Elliot's private investigators must be pulling their hair out. Not to mention what Elliot must be pulling out. There was fierce satisfaction in the knowledge. She held her aching head and felt victorious.

❧

It was another dead end. After two months of ceaseless work, of chasing dozens of false stories all over the country, he had come to his last lead. Sebastian fought disappointment as the woman shook her ruffled gray head one more time.

"I don't know who told you that we had a librarian here by that name and description, but it isn't true." She waved a hand at the small, whitewashed room with its modest bookcases. On one wall was a handmade poster promoting the Dothan, Texas, Easter festivities, coming up in a month. "If I had an extra librarian around here, I wouldn't know what to do with her," the woman told him. She looked at him with sympathy. "You came a long way to see this gal in person. I could have told you over the phone that there's nobody named Amy Miracle workin' here."

Sebastian sank his fists into the pockets of the windbreaker he wore with brown slacks and the rumpled white shirt he'd had on since leaving San Francisco twelve hours earlier. Fatigue and frustration were gritty companions in his eyes. "I have a number of investigators looking for her, but I had hoped to find her myself, in person." After ten years, and with so much to be said between them, he wanted their first meeting to be special.

But it was growing less likely that there would be a meeting, special or otherwise. How could a person inspire so many bizarre stories from so many different people? Everyone the investigators had talked to gave wildly dissimilar accounts of her life and whereabouts.

"You look like you need some rest," the librarian said, and patted his arm. "This woman, you'll find her. Just don't give up."

The irony of those words rang in his head as he thanked her and walked outside to the waiting limousine. *Give up? How could one give up an obsession?*

❧

"You slayed 'em tonight, lady."

Amy swiveled toward the nasal male voice. A fortyish man with red spiked hair smiled at her. He was dressed in the kind of unstructured pastel suit that some California men considered de rigueur. He was vice president in charge of comedy programming for a major cable channel, and if he wanted to look like the emcee of a punk Easter bunny show, nobody was going to tell him different. "Hi there, Freddie. I didn't know you trekked out to clubs in the boonies."

"I don't, usually, but I wanted to catch your stand-up again. See how it was working. What kind of commitment have you got here?"

Her throat went dry. She took a large swallow of wine and said in a squeaky tone, "None. I show up at ten every night. I do my set. I get twenty-five bucks. I don't show up, nobody'd notice."

"I'm putting together a special. Gonna call it *Funny Women.* Cute, huh? I'll probably tape it at the Alexus Theater about six weeks from now. It'll be a showcase for the hottest new female comics. And you qualify. Interested?"

The crowd of comics at the bar stopped talking to stare. She began to shake even though she was smiling. "You want me, you got me," she said as calmly as she could.

Freddie beamed. "Great. Have your agent call me."

"Don't be surprised if my agent sounds a lot like me."

"That voice of yours is hard to imitate. Call me." He hesitated. "Are you sure this won't be a problem with Elliot?"

"No." *Not a problem. A disaster.* Elliot's erratic and sometimes violent behavior on the set had become com-

mon knowledge in the business. "No problem," she repeated. "I just work for Elliot now. We're just friends."

"The show's been sort of, uh, uh, *different* in the past
few months. It's not the writing—that's better than ever—I
can't quite put my finger on it."

"Don't be polite, Freddie. Elliot's losing control, and
everybody can see it. The ratings have slipped a lot."

"Don't let him hold you back. Right now the last thing
you need is a distracting man in your life."

"Like I said, Elliot and I are just friends."

"Great. Talk to you later. You're on your way, lady."

She remained riveted in place as he disappeared into the
crowd. Finally she realized that people were congratulating
her. She mumbled something polite and bolted for the
club's rear exit. Outside, by the dumpsters, under a balmy
spring night, she sat down on a trash can and cried. *I'm
gonna make it big, Doc, I really am. I wish you knew.*

❦

"Patience!" Sebastien begged from the night sky over the
vineyards, shaking a fist. In this isolated area he could
stare as far into the blackness as he wanted without seeing
the lights of any other house or farm. The hills seemed
endless. The world was empty except for himself and ten
years of mistakes that he couldn't undo.

Rain began to tap gently at the porch roof. *You have no
patience,* it taunted. He pivoted and walked inside, his
large shoulders hunched under a mud-stained work shirt,
his damp trousers clinging to legs that ached from carrying
sacks of fertilizer all day.

Sebastien went through the stone cottage, turning on
lights in the still-unfurnished rooms, anxious to push the
cool, damp darkness outdoors. He loved the cottage, with
its timbered hallway and tall ceilings. It reminded him of
the houses in French villages.

He loved the solid feel of the stone floor and the openness of the rooms; the way enormous windows made the
outdoors part of the cottage's soul. He liked listening to his
own footsteps echo through the halls and studying the
shadows cast by the bare light bulbs in the old iron sconces

that dotted every wall. Tonight, however, the sparseness of the cottage mocked him, making him think of his own emptiness.

Angry at his brooding, he went to the kitchen. It was a relic, but large and bright; he had built a wine rack from floor to ceiling on one wall, and the kitchen was crowded with pots, pans, bundles of herbs hanging from the ceiling, magazines stacked on a thick oak table and the heavyset chairs around it, and a portable television at one end of the scarred wooden counter beneath the cabinets.

Someday soon he would begin remodeling and furnishing, but for now he was content to let the cottage live comfortably with its imperfections, as he was trying to live with his own.

He started to make dinner, but decided he had no appetite. He went to the bedroom, where a few sparse pieces of furniture catered to a mattress and box springs set on a plain steel frame. Stretching out on his stomach, he forced himself to concentrate on reading a novel. Sometimes it amazed him to think that he had ever given up reading for pleasure.

Around midnight he put the novel aside and, rubbing his eyes, returned to the kitchen for a glass of water. Sleepless and raw-tempered, he flicked on the small television set and threw himself into a chair by the table. Propping his chin on one hand, he half-watched the program and listened to the murmur of rain on the windowsill above the sink.

American audiences liked the strangest things. He frowned at the program's smirking, hyperactive host, who was interviewing—or was that *intimidating*?—an elderly man whose hobby was to dip dead insects in polyurethane and stick them by the hundreds to canvases to form the silhouettes of famous people. The entertainer's questions were more cruel that funny.

The long day of physical labor caught up with him, and before he realized it he was dozing with his chin still braced on one hand. The loud blare of music at the program's end woke him up. He stood wearily, a little disgruntled at his fatigue. Even though his body had never been more fit, it reminded him some days that he was one year away from forty.

He went to the noisy television, squinting at the program's credits, which were scrolling down the screen. He was *not* becoming farsighted, he assured himself, idly testing his vision on the names and production titles. Perhaps a *little* farsighted, he admitted.

Dismayed at the thought, he reached for the set's off button. His hand stopped in midair as a list of the show's writers appeared on the screen. He grabbed the set and held it up, reading and rereading the name he could definitely see—but had trouble believing.

He had found her, right at the end of his fingertips.

❧

Amy didn't sleep much during the night. Exhilarated by Freddie's offer and worried about how Elliot would take the news, she left her apartment early and made the long rush-hour drive to Burbank in record time—one hour. *Thornton After Hours* was based in a five-story stucco building surrounded by palm trees. The writers shared a communal office on the top floor, in a ten-room suite next to the studio where the show was taped when it wasn't being shot on location.

"Is Elliot in yet?" she asked the show's receptionist.

She looked startled. "Oh, no. We thought he was with you last night. He disappeared right after we taped. We thought that he'd followed you, uhmmm, uh, that you two had a reconciliation, maybe."

Amy shifted uneasily. "No. Have you checked his office?"

"Are you kidding? I never go in there without a SWAT team."

Amy hurried down the hall to a door festooned with the covers of comic books. Pictures of Elliot's handsome, boyish face were taped over the heads of all the superheroes. Photos of Carson, Letterman, and Arsenio Hall also decorated the door. Each rival talk-show host wore a goatee, moustache, and devil horns. She knocked, listened, heard nothing, then slipped a key into the lock.

Inside, among the kind of garish kitsch an Andy Warhol fan might have coveted, a futon lay on the floor.

Elliott Thornton, comic genius, was sprawled on the futon wearing nothing but beard stubble. He was snoring loudly.

An empty bourbon bottle lay beside him, along with a mirror strewn with white dust, a box of straws, and a bottle of Valium. Amy ran to him and knelt down. After reassuring herself that he was no more stoned than usual, she sat back wearily and gazed at him with despair.

"You self-destructive jerk," she whispered, but took his hand. He was starting to go soft around the stomach, his all-American nose was swollen, premature gray showed among the wavy brown hair at his temples, and his once-unstoppable libido looked permanently flaccid. She wondered if it were even capable of chasing model-actresses anymore.

But she had spent years looking after him, needing to be needed by him, and old habits died hard. When he woke up she brought him a cup of coffee and sat on the futon while he drank it. He groaned. "I'm not doing so well by myself at night, baby."

"You didn't do much better when we were together."

"Comeon baby, how long are you going to turn the screws?"

"Like I always say, try some clean living. Then we'll talk."

"Oh, boy, more lectures." He stroked his limp penis and sighed with relief when it began to move. "Speak into the microphone."

"No, thanks, but I *do* have something to tell you."

"Yeah, it's about time you admitted the sonovabitch's name."

She exhaled wearily. "I wish this *were* about a man. You'd be less jealous."

He squinted at her and stopped stroking himself. "Huh?"

She told him about Freddie and his cable special.

Elliot's eyes narrowed to slits. His hand curled on his belly with ominous tension as she finished. "I've been Mr. Nice Guy, waiting for you to come back to me, giving you a job you didn't deserve just so you'd stick around! No more handouts, baby!"

"Handouts?" She tried to keep her voice light. One furious person in the room was enough. "I've been your comedy slave for years. I *earned* my way, and I'll put my yuks-per-joke ratio up against any writer's in the business. Good Lord, this is the first year your writing staff has been nominated for an Emmy. I contributed to that nomination, Elliot. There's no doubt about it."

"Egomaniac!"

"Calm down, Mr. Nice Guy. I don't want to quit writing for you because I got this break. I've still got a long way to go before I hit the big time—"

"Hit the big time!" He bolted upright and leaned toward her with a taunting and incredulous expression on his face. "Where do you get your fortune cookies, baby? They've been lying!"

"I know it's still a daydream, but I'm gonna try to be a name."

"Not while you're working for me, you're not!" He grabbed his coffee cup and threw it across the room. It splattered into a shelf filled with his awards. "You want to keep your old man in an expensive nursing home? Fine! But go pay for it some other way! You're history! Hit the street!"

She rose and went to the door, opened it, held onto it tightly. She was so disgusted that she almost didn't care that he'd fired her. Almost. This was it. Sink or swim. "Good-bye," she said softly.

"You'll be back! You'll never make it! You're nothing but a daydreamer. What is this, a midlife crisis? Hell, you're not even thirty!" He beat the futon with his fists. "You're a follower, not a leader! They'll eat you alive! You haven't got what it takes to compete in the big leagues!"

"Wipe your nose. It's bleeding." She would always take care of him. But she shut the door hard on her way out.

❧

She gathered her things in the office. The guys gathered around her desk looking morose at being left without her to run interference between them and Elliot. When one of the communal Mickey Mouse phones rang somebody slouched over reluctantly and answered it.

"Security guard says somebody's in the lobby to see you," he told Amy, tossing the mouse ears back on the receiver.

"Who?"

"You expect me to be efficient when I'm this depressed? I forgot to ask."

"Oh, nevermind, I know who it is. It's that guy we were reading about in that grocery-store tabloid the other day. The one who makes jewelry from pigeon skulls. I called him . . . told him to drop by this morning and see us. I thought we might build a piece around him." Struggling not to cry, she smoothed invisible wrinkles from the soft material of her dress. She had worn the flowing turquoise outfit with its neat little collar and double row of tiny buttons down the front because it had been one of Elliot's favorites . . . and because she'd read somewhere that turquoise was a soothing color.

Defeated, she tossed a turquoise-leather purse into the cardboard box that held her other possessions. "On my way out I'll send the bird man up to see you guys."

They groaned and looked more pitiful.

"A trooper to the end!"

"A trooper, you say? She's leaving us with Custer at the battle of the Little Big Horn. And Custer is nuts."

"Run, Amy. Save your own scalp."

She cried a little as she hugged each of them. Then she saluted. "It was nice knowing you while you still had hair."

"We'll go downstairs with you. See you off into the wicked world."

"No, I'm looking forward to blubbering in the elevator. Thanks, though."

Once she was hidden inside the elevator she clutched her box with one arm, allowed herself one loud wail, then wiped her eyes hurriedly. She didn't want to look deranged in front of the bird-skull man, who might be a sensitive artistic type. *He Makes Masterpieces From Bird Brains*, the tabloid headline had proclaimed with respect, if not anatomical accuracy.

The lobby downstairs was empty except for Jackson, the aging black security guard.

"Where's the guy you called about?"

Jackson pointed across the lobby to a sunny anteroom. "Stepped in there. Seemed kind of restless."

"It's a high-pressure job, looking for dead pigeons with artistic heads. Here, keep my going-away box while I talk to the guy."

She crossed the lobby, straightening her hair and brushing her fingertips over her face. Amy reached the anteroom's entrance and halted, startled. He stood with his back to her, silhouetted by the light of an arching, Spanish-style window. She hadn't seen a photo of the bird man. She had expected someone who looked as if he had nothing better to do than shellac pigeon skulls. This man looked like an extremely well built statue come to life. So maybe it was how he attracted the pigeons.

He was very still, his hands clasped behind him, his attention focused on some outside scene or inner distraction. Amy rebuked herself for standing there unannounced and ogling him, but she couldn't help it. An odd feeling of recognition bewildered her.

His solitude. His stillness and unmistakable elegance. His hair, the luxurious color of dark chocolate. His aura of wealth. Even from the back his suit appeared exquisitely cut. It was black, with a fine gray pinstripe. He was *not* a California native, not in that beautiful but solemn outfit. *Plus ça change, plus c'est la même chose.* The graceful window framed him in its old-world ambience.

When she finally stepped forward she was so clumsy that she almost stumbled. She stopped again and took a deep breath. A dreamlike quality came over her, and her peculiar sense of distraction increased.

He made a sound of exasperation, unclasped his hands, and flung them up in dismay. *"Ne t'en fais pas,"* he muttered, apparently speaking to himself. *"Sois patiente!"*

That voice. Ten years jumbled inside her, leaving her

stunned, uncomprehending, unable to fathom that the world could have brought him here, at this point in her life, when her life was falling apart and starting over. After all, he had set her on this course.

She took another step forward, reaching toward him with both hands. Joy and disbelief welled up in her throat. When she tried to speak, the best she could manage was a whisper. "You can stop tellin' yourself to be patient, Doc. I'm here."

TWENTY

$\mathcal{H}$e whipped around, his reaction so swift and intense that she felt the emotional power like a wave of heat. The large, dark eyes were deeply creased at the corners but had lost none of their breath-stealing effect. The face was even more brutal in its uncompromising strength, like granite that has been stripped of softer rock through the action of time and storms. But it was spellbinding. The scar still made a diagonal slash on his chin, and above it his mouth still held its tough appeal.

What was there to say? After her initial effort she went blank and simply stared up at him, her hands rising in shock to her face. She believed that she was smiling but couldn't think clearly enough to be certain. She *knew* that she was bewildered but also delirious with pleasure. And that she was afraid of the way he made her feel.

His eyes gleamed. They studied her with careful attention to detail before meeting her gaze again. "You remember me."

She almost choked at the irony. "Of course."

"But I can't tell if I've done the right thing by coming here today."

"Yes!" The emphatic word silenced them both again. He looked pleased, but she was alarmed. Control yourself, she thought desperately. This time, control yourself.

So she threw her arms around his neck and hugged him. Which, she reasoned, was a perfectly acceptable thing to do when greeting someone who had changed your life ten years ago.

Especially when he made a gruff sound of amazement and lifted her off the floor in an embrace that conveyed much more than a hello among old acquaintances. She cried out and pressed her face into the crook of his neck. After ten years he had remembered, and she had never forgotten.

"It is so good to hold you," he whispered. "So good."

His voice was an elixir that made her drunk. Self-preservation was a must. She stiffened and let go of him—not angry, just attempting to be dignified. He felt the change and set her down. His arms relaxed a little but still remained around her, his hands resting possessively on her back. The welcome in his expression made her weak.

"I don't believe this," she admitted. "Why are you here?"

"That, my dear Miracle, is a long story."

My dear Miracle. She clung to his shoulders. "You're visiting the States on business?"

"No. I bought a home north of San Francisco. An old vineyard, with a large stone cottage. I'm living there."

There is a Santa Claus. She tried to be nonchalant. The trance of excitement between them made it a ridiculous effort. She struggled for a diplomatic way to slap reality into the situation. "Where's Mrs. Doctor?"

He tilted his head and looked at her shrewdly. "How did you know that I had married?"

"Oh, somebody told me, years ago."

"I'm divorced."

"Oh?" Her voice squeaked.

"And you?"

"Just an old maid. Not a *maid,* but you know what I mean."

"Wonderful."

"I don't think I believe this," she said, swaying inside his arms. "I don't. What are you doing here—"

"Whatever it takes to explain the past ten years to you. More simply, I came here to see if you would be interested in hearing my explanation. Or in just having dinner with me . . . someone who wants to know everything that's happened to you, how you've fared in the world, how you're doing now."

"That could be a *long* dinner."

"I hope so."

The breath shuddered from her lungs. She was adrift in a fantasy come true, and right now she felt helpless, giddy, wild. If this was real then she was ripe for it. If it wasn't real, then she was going to throw herself into the jaws of the Venus-flytrap in the corner. Calming down, she cleared her throat and said, "I'd be glad to have dinner with you. I could meet you at a restaurant one night. How long will you be in L.A.?"

Her coolness brought a slight frown to his face. "Indefinitely."

"When did you get here?"

"I just drove down this morning."

"You drove all the way from somewhere above San Francisco and got here by this hour? You must have left in the middle of the night."

"Yes."

"A medical emergency? Do you have patients here?"

"No. Last night I saw your name on the credits for a television show. I made some phone calls to locate the show's offices. Then I packed a bag and left. I arrived in Los Angeles an hour ago, checked into a hotel, then changed into presentable clothes and came here."

She wondered what the maximum heart rate was for a woman her age. She thought she'd reached it. "When would you like to meet for dinner?"

"Right now, but I'll settle for tonight."

"Have you had breakfast?"

"No."

"Let's go, then."

His harsh features softened in a beautiful smile. "*Mon dieu.* Certainly. I'd love to."

She hesitated. "Doc, what's the deal here? Aren't you busy? What about your work? Haven't you set up a surgery practice?"

"No, I'm taking a sabbatical. I'll try to make sense of it to you. I've only just begun to make sense of it, myself."

"When anything makes sense, I plan to celebrate."

"It will. As long as you're glad to see me after ten years, anything is possible."

Anything? She wouldn't even think about it. In fact, she'd short-circuit it. "How long do you plan to stay in the United States?"

"Let's put it this way—I have no plans to leave."

"That's a diplomat's answer."

"Then here's a more specific one. My life is here now. I want to make California my permanent home."

She was dizzy from the verbal ricochets. There was so much to learn about the stranger who continued to hold her—and so much for him to learn about her. They weren't the same people as ten years ago. Yet they were falling together with reckless abandon as if nothing else mattered and no time had passed. He hadn't loved her before; he hadn't ever tried to contact her since; why would he care about her now?

"When did you move here from France?"

"In December."

"Why, you're still a newcomer."

"I could use a tour guide."

"At your service. We could start with breakfast, although I think that if I try to eat anything my stomach will just go, 'Honeychile, you couldn't get me interested in food even if it was grits.' "

"Your voice—your incredible voice. Thank God it hasn't changed."

"Lots of other things about me *have* changed, though."

He nodded. "I'm very different, too. For the better, in some ways. For the worse, in others." His arms tightened and he searched her expression in provocative detail. "But we still communicate very well with each other, don't you think?"

They were too close to avoid the touch of breath on parted lips, the scent of male and female, the maelstrom of unresolved questions and emotions and now, rising quickly to the surface, desire.

She flowed into his kiss and heard herself make small, frantic sounds at the overwhelming tenderness of it. There was no point in trying to analyze this situation. She wanted him more now than she had ten years ago, and if she weren't dreaming, he wanted her, too.

❦

It might take days for her to comprehend his presence and sort out her feelings. Right now she was caught in a tornado, and all she could do was hang on to anything that appeared solid.

She wasn't hanging on very well, either, because at the end of lunch when he said abruptly, "Would you like to see my new home?" she nodded without the slightest hesitation.

"Let's go right now," he said next, as if it weren't a nine-hour trip to the wine country.

And she replied, "I thought you'd *never* ask."

They left L.A. without even stopping at his hotel to get his suitcase or pick up any fresh clothes for her. They had only the clothes they wore—windblown and rumbled. Oh, she had her purse and the box with the things from her office, including a bola bouncer, which counted for something, she supposed.

Now she and Sebastien were more than halfway to their destination, a fact that both worried and excited her.

The sun was a piece of silver melting toward the Pacific. The Ferrari he had purchased recently—another Ferrari!—clung to the winding, cliffside road with the precision of a magnet on steel. Once again he was taking her someplace unknown at a speed she couldn't resist. She settled deeper in the seat. The wind washed away the need to talk. They had talked all morning, but these past few hours in the car they had been quiet by mutual agreement.

It was good to let the silence absorb the shock. Dancing on the edge of memories was tricky business; they had discussed a hundred things—mostly about her and her work, at his insistence—but avoided the real issues. Each time the unanswered questions overwhelmed her she felt as if she were trying to scoop the water from a deep well with nothing but her hands.

What had gone wrong with his marriage? Why were there

no children? Why had he searched for her after ten years?
What did he want from her?

And more important, what was she going to give him?

It seemed no more strange to spend the entire afternoon
in the car with him than it had seemed strange to spend
the entire morning at a cheap diner, where they had
ordered and mostly ignored breakfast, and then lunch.
Each time she had switched the conversation from her life
to his, all he would talk about were the vineyards and the
stone cottage he was restoring. The dark intensity still
seethed in him, in the private expression that came over
his face at times, in the commanding posture and impatient
hand gestures. But there was a lightness, too, that she
knew hadn't been there before. It showed when he talked
about his new home, and each time he stopped talking to
look admiringly at her.

"Do you know this area of the state very well?" he asked,
shifting gears as the road twisted above a panorama of
sandy inlets and granite jutting into the ocean among white
breakers.

"We're not far from Monterey."

"A fishing village?"

"Only for fishermen who have lots of clams. It's beautiful
and expensive. Why?"

"Would you like to spend the night there? We could
finish the trip tomorrow in only a few hours."

The thought made her dizzy. She was ready to walk off
the edge of the world if he asked, and it disturbed her. She
had no idea what to expect from him. He could vanish
tomorrow. Hadn't she learned anything in the past ten
years about self-defense?

She lifted her chin and stared straight ahead. "That'd be
fine. There are some terrific inns . . . old Victorian man-
sions. Would something like that suit you?"

"Certainly. Would it suit you?"

"Sure." She slumped under the weight of deciphering the
situation and asked bluntly, "Is this an indecent proposal?
If it isn't, I'm really embarrassed, but if it *is*, I'm not ready
for it."

"I didn't think so. I was going to suggest separate rooms."

Pleased, she laughed and patted his shoulder, loving the excuse to touch him. "I'm glad we got that settled. Miss Manners would be proud of me."

He took her hand and kissed it. "No need to be embarrassed. My indecent proposal will be waiting whenever you'd like it."

❦

The storybook inn overlooking Monterey Bay was a romantic place, which taunted her anxieties and made her angry that they were necessary. The strain of being with Sebastien reduced the breathless exhilaration of the early hours to a brooding confusion that made her head hurt.

She didn't regret being with him, whether it was foolish or not. But she was exhausted from the emotional shock, and when she looked into his weary face she knew that he felt the same way. They didn't talk much at dinner. The beautiful but formal Victorian dining room didn't encourage intimate conversation. A wall of windows framed an ocean burnished with the sunset, which she examined to avoid looking at Sebastien.

At twilight they took a walk along the narrow strip of rocky beach below the inn, still silent, side by side but not touching. She knew, though, that he was vividly aware of her, as she was of him, and when they returned to the inn she couldn't help but take his face between her hands and kiss him lightly. "Good night." It was absurdly inadequate, but she was too full of emotion to say more.

He pulled her to him and held her for a long time, one hand stroking her hair. "I never forgot you, Miracle. Please believe that."

She stepped back from him, her head up, dignity building a wall between them. "I'm glad you're here and we're together. I've never regretted what happened between us ten years ago. It changed my whole life, and it was wonderful, and I never met any other man who made me feel the way you did. But I'm not going to let you hurt me again, if I can help it. Hell, I probably *can't* help it, but I'll try."

He lifted a hand to her face, touched her with his fingertips, dissolved her dignity. "Go and rest, now. I'm just happy that I found you. I can take care of your problems, in time."

"I'm not used to being taken care of."

He smiled, but there was challenge in his eyes. "You'll learn."

❦

They walked through the cool, empty rooms, and she thought how the stone cottage suited him with its mixture of warmth and aloofness. A huge window in the main room captured the hills covered in trellises. Everything had the new green color of spring. Beginnings.

"I see why you love it," she said.

He stood beside her at the window, looking from the view to her. She liked the serenity she saw in his eyes. "It will never be a grand or self-important place," he told her. "Just comfortable."

He showed her a spacious room with nothing but a bed, a nightstand, and a dresser. The bed was simply a large mattress and springs on a metal frame, with a plain quilt and white-cased pillows. "My guest bedroom. For you." He glanced at the purse she carried, his expression droll. "Put your luggage wherever you like."

She studied the novels stacked on the nightstand and the bottle of cologne atop the dresser, plus the open closet door that revealed his suits. "I suspect, sir, that this is not only the guest bedroom, but the only bedroom." They hadn't discussed the arrangements before. They hadn't even discussed how long she was going to stay. It was something they both knew, that she would stay.

"I'll sleep upstairs," he said quickly. "There's an attic room with an old couch in it."

"My guilt level just skyrocketed, Doc. For heaven's sake, let me sleep on the musty, dirty, saggy old couch." She put her hands on her hips. "That's the polite thing to say, but I mean it, too. I insist."

"No. You sleep in my bed," he ordered mildly.

"Aw, Doc . . ."

"That way you'll think about me. If you sleep on the couch, you'll think about bats."

"There are bats up there?"

"Yes."

She tossed her purse on his bed. "My guilt just faded." Smiling at him, she asked, "Is there any place around here to shop for clothes? I'd like to buy a second pair of panties and a cheap sundress."

"There's a small town a few miles from here. I'll take you—but only if you let me buy."

"I don't want you to buy me a town."

He gave her a bewildered look, then caught the joke and smiled broadly. "It's marvelous to have you here. I see why you're making a good career as a comedienne."

"Oh, stop flattering me. You already paid for everything else on this jaunt, outfoxing me at the inn when we checked out this morning, grabbing restaurant checks. You're slick, Doc, and I don't approve. So thanks, but—"

"Amy, when you're with me, your money is no good. I know that you don't have much, not if you're paying for your father's nursing care. I know what it costs to live in California, too. So we'll go shopping for some clothes, something better than a cheap sundress. And I'll pay."

She shook her fists at him and started to protest, but he cut her off. "I have money. I was born with it, and I'll always have it. It's not meant to impress or manipulate, only to make life easier. If you want to use my money, good. Enjoy it. I approve of noble independence, but not pointless sacrifice."

"You gave me money ten years ago because it was easier than giving yourself! That's why I don't want your money now!"

He grasped her fists and pulled her off balance, then lifted her on tiptoe and kissed her until she was breathless. He set her back down and examined her confusion solemnly. "You can have me, but until you make up your mind about whether or not you like that prospect I think you'll be happier just taking my money. *Mon dieu*! If I wanted to *buy* a woman's affection I'd do it with a great deal more expense." He hesitated, arching a dark brow mischievously. "Would you like a diamond necklace?"

"A sundress. Panties. Read my lips."

"Hmmm. Later, when you're less argumentative."

They went shopping. Because he was impossible to thwart, they returned with bags full of clothes, plus toothbrushes, deodorant, and all the other items a woman might need to stay indefinitely with a man who, it seemed, intended to keep her.

❦

It was so easy to talk to him about the unimportant subjects. Barefooted, wearing a blue chambray sundress with tiny straps at the shoulders, she felt like a happy peasant in his one respectably furnished room, the kitchen. She followed him around the quaint old place, among dried herbs, pots, pans, piles of vegetables, and the scent of chicken roasting for dinner.

She made certain that it wasn't obvious that she was following him; she was careful to find little chores to do that happened to be next to whatever he was doing. But she noticed, when she crossed the room for some reason, that he found tasks that moved them close together again.

"Would you like a glass of wine?" he asked, going to a rack of bottles that covered one wall.

She had already perused the rack enough to know that it held a mixture of local wines and de Savin vintages. "Have you got the de Savin Pinot Noir, 1987?"

The look he gave her contained surprise, and then fascination. "You have studied the de Savin wines?"

It was the kind of opportunity she'd imagined in her daydreams years before. Speaking in slow but excellent French, she gave a list of the best wines from his family's label. Then she bowed.

He came to her and cupped her face between his hands. "Did you learn all of this because of me?"

She shivered with emotion; there was no point in playing games. "Yes. In school I studied French, and made good grades, and did everything else I could to make you proud of me."

"But why did you sell the Ferrari I gave you?" He looked at her somberly.

"Who told you about that?"

"Pio Beaucaire. You remember him, he managed the winery."

"But how would he know?"

"He was spying on you."

"You told him to spy on me?"

"No. He did it because . . . never mind why, right now." Her shoulders slumped. "My folks needed money. That's why I sold the car. I loved that car. I could feel you around me when I drove it."

"Miracle, I should have known. I apologize."

"You figured I wanted the money to play with, didn't you?"

"Pio made it sound like that, yes."

"And you believed him. You were angry at me."

"Yes, but you were young. And it was a gift without strings, I told myself."

"Young and backward, and who could expect a hick to appreciate such a gift, right?"

He shook her lightly. "Stop it! I never thought of you as a hick! I don't care what happened to the stupid car. One of the reasons I gave it to you was so you'd have it to sell if you needed the money."

"Okay, Doc, if you say so. Let's change the subject." She forced a smile. Hidden behind it was the dark realization that the past was catching up with the present, slowly but surely.

❦

She slept hard for a few hours, then woke in a sweat and bolted out of bed. Standing in the darkness of Sebastien's bedroom, she gulped for air and finally recalled where she was. She stared at the ceiling, thinking of Sebastien, upstairs.

Grabbing the bed's quilt, she wrapped it around her T-shirt and panties; she padded down the hall and out a back door that opened onto the veranda. She loved the back veranda with its rough stone floor and weathered roof supports. Going to one of the posts, she leaned against it and gazed up at a half-moon high above the vineyard. She hugged herself and tried to calm down.

"It won't do any good," Sebastien said behind her.

She whipped around. He stood at the veranda's far end. The moonlight showed that he was dressed in loose khaki trousers, and nothing else. "You have questions to ask. You can't sleep. Neither can I."

"There's so much we never knew about each other. And I don't understand why you looked for me again. As if I'd meant a lot to you."

"I hate the unhappiness in your voice."

"Not unhappiness: shock. I haven't had time to get my bearings."

"There's all the time in the world. But the important thing is that you *want* to know more about me, as I want to know about you, and you came away with me without looking back. Ten years might never have passed. We had a bond immediately."

"It makes me feel like I'm eighteen again, hanging on every word you say, doing whatever you want, but I'm *not* eighteen, and I'm not naive . . . reckless and impulsive, yes, but naive, no."

She told herself that she had no right to be upset, since he'd never promised her anything when he left ten years ago and had, in fact, been exceptionally wonderful to her, except, of course, for not loving her. But she was angry at him for not loving her then, and for acting now as though he *had* loved her.

"I've brought a lot of complications into your life," he said, looking troubled. "And there are questions we must ask each other, very honestly, about the past. They shouldn't be allowed to spoil the present."

"I don't want to talk tonight. I'm not sure I want to hear the answers yet."

"I'm not anxious to hear them myself. But it's necessary. Come. We'll take a walk and—"

"No. Please. I'm afraid I'd say the wrong thing."

"I remember when you would say exactly how you felt to me. I liked the openness."

"I had nothing to lose. I knew you didn't love me the way I loved you. I never thought I was worthy of being loved so much. But I *am*."

"I know. I've always known, even when you didn't."

She made a ragged sound. "It nearly killed me when you left for West Africa. I used to pray you'd write to me, or call me sometimes, even just to see if I was wasting the money you'd given me. But you never did. Why not, if you cared about me so much?"

"I was a fool. I wanted you to be strong and independent, and I feared that I'd hurt you if I let you depend on me at all, even in the small ways. I was so full of pride, and so certain I knew what was best for both of us." He stepped forward. The moonlight showed the restraint in his expression.

Sebastien took her in his arms, then held her with his head bent close to hers while his hands moved swiftly over her, stroking, soothing. She felt his chest moving in a harsh rhythm against her cheek. And when he whispered in her ear, his voice was filled with anguish. "Because of my pride, other people were able to come between us. I'm sorry, Miracle." His embrace became a fierce hold.

Did he learn about Jeff and me? she wondered suddenly. Oh, God, if that surfaced now to hurt her and Sebastien, she'd never forgive herself. She struggled to think calmly. Perhaps he meant Marie. "It wasn't your fault," she offered in a careful voice. "Maybe it was just too soon for us to be together. I made mistakes, too."

"It was so long ago. What I remember now are the joys, the way you made me laugh . . . and cry. It was good to cry."

Sorrow burst from her with a soft exclamation. "Oh, how much I've missed you over the years, and thought about you, and tried to be the kind of person you could love—"

"And you saved my life, more than once. Look. Look, Amy." He put a hand into his pants pocket and withdrew a necklace that caught the silver of the light.

She stared at the long silver chain he held up. From it dangled a battered silver coin of some kind. "What is it?"

"Remember the day I saw you perform magic tricks at a

festival in the mountains? And you used a video-game token to show me—"

"You kept it? This is it?"

"Yes."

"And you wore it?"

"Yes. I need to tell you about it."

She sank into a wooden chair. He settled by her feet on the veranda's edge and looked up at her steadily as he talked. She listened in stunned silence as he told her how the token had saved him from a knife wound in Africa, how he'd kept it in the years afterward, how he'd tried to throw it away, and how, finally, it had turned up at the moment that he needed the memory of her most. She was crying softly when he finished.

He stood up and pulled her up with him. "When I was in Africa I planned to come back to the States and see you. Except for wounded pride, I would have. It was very hard for me to appreciate the kind of emotions you made me feel. It was easier to repress them. I wasn't capable of showing or accepting love. Now I'm trying very hard to change that."

Tremors ran through her, through them both. "You were planning to come back for me?"

"Yes. I swear it. If I'd been open about my feelings for you, you would have known, then no one would have been able to take you away."

Jeff. He *had* found out about her and Jeff, that one terrible night they'd spent together. Had it angered him so much that he'd decided not to come back for her? The question tormented Amy, but she was afraid to ask it.

"Forgive me," he whispered.

Amy looked up at him in wonder. "For what?"

"I had trained myself to be callous, and I lost you because of it." He searched her face for answers. She saw the quiet desperation in his. "I hope that I didn't lose you forever, Amy. I know we have a lot to learn about each other, but being with you feels so right, so necessary."

She let her question about Jeff dissolve. Why dredge that up? A fierce sense of protectiveness surged through her. Nothing mattered except that Sebastien had wanted to find

her again, that he'd kept the old video token as if it were
sacred, and that he'd never forgotten her. She put her arms
around him and struggled to speak. Mended dreams were
filling her throat. "You didn't lose me, Doc. I was just
misplaced."

🍒

His slow caresses wound through her veins like a river of
silk, sinking her into the bed because her muscles had
become heavy with desire. He was patient as he conquered
each small kingdom of her body with his fingertips and the
languid exploration of his hands.

She tilted her head back on the pillow, strained gently
upward into each caress, felt her breasts aching, swollen,
waiting to receive his hands again, his mouth again, as
every other part of her had already been blessed. The
rhythmic throbbing between her legs became fiercer as he
returned there.

Reaching for him, she sang for him with her body, a fine
instrument responding to a virtuoso's care, now stretching
to its peak, the crescendo welling into his mouth as he
kissed her and drank her moans. Her welcome brought
hard words of devotion from him, tormented words straight
from whatever hell had trapped them until now. She took
him, held him with tears on her face, hugged him with her
legs both to comfort and invite.

Inside her he moved with convulsive energy, while his
hands knotted in her hair and he angled his face to catch
the touch of her fingertips. This first time was a struggle
between tenderness and greed, restraint and chaos, emotions so raw that they could only bleed before the healing
began. In the end she struggled with him, screamed against
his shoulder in contrast to the urging of her hands riding
his hips. Worlds of light were born in the frantic comple-
tion.

Afterward she stroked his back, trying to calm both him
and herself. Then he murmured *je t'aime, je t'aime* against

her mouth, and she fell apart again. "I talked to you in my mind for ten years," she told him, crying. "I wish you'd heard me sometimes."

"I did, love, I did," he said, thinking of the whispers he had been too distant from himself to understand, until now.

TWENTY-ONE

Outside the open bedroom window the spring afternoon was warm and peaceful, whispering with the winds and the birds, ripe, waiting. It was impossible to move without noticing everything about the man who lay under her, between her knees, his belly and chest a solid, thickly haired enticement that made her press herself down on him and wrap her arms under his neck. She moved— noticing, loving.

"I'm afraid to look at you," she whispered against his ear, her breath still fast, still recovering. "I'm afraid you're too good to be true."

Sebastien melted her over him with the stroking of his large hands, gentle but provocative as they journeyed down her back. "I thought it was beyond me to feel this way again," he whispered in return. He caught the tip of her ear lobe with his lips, then kissed her cheek and chin before nuzzling his face upward so that he could kiss her mouth. She looked down into his dark, gleaming eyes. Their happiness combined with the ruddy flush in his face to make her smile. "Doc, you were worth waiting ten years for."

She noted the hardening of his expression and the way his eyes began to see farther than her face. He protested gruffly when she lifted herself from his body and lay down beside him, but she shook her head. She curled a leg over his thighs and stroked his matted chest hair as she studied his change of mood, worried. "It doesn't matter," she said softly, sensing his thoughts.

"It does. We've lost so many years. I can't ignore a feeling of obsessive protectiveness toward what we have now, a feeling that it could disappear again too easily."

She touched a mildly rebuking finger to his lips. "Not if we admit the problems. Not if you want to solve them as much as I do."

"Problems?"

"I have a career and it takes a lot of my time. It's not the kind of work—or the kind of life-style—that's even remotely like anything you know."

"Oh, that." He dismissed the conflict with a bored sigh. "I don't mind being the power behind the throne. We de Savins have *always* played that role in French history. It's really the most important position."

She laughed. "I should have known your confidence wouldn't be threatened."

"I don't mind your devotion to your work, love. I respect it. When I return to medicine, you'll respect my devotion, I'm sure."

Amy cocked her head and eyed him warily. "There's a threat there, somewhere."

"Only the threat that we'll both have to compromise. I've never been good at compromising, I admit it. But I'll learn."

"I go to the other extreme. You're looking at an *expert* on compromising."

Her jaunty smile brought a soft chuckle from him. He tweaked one of her breasts. "Good. You can teach me."

"Oh, I will."

"Then perhaps our only significant problem is Elliot Thornton. Tell me about him." Frowning, she said nothing. Sebastien curled an arm around her shoulders and pulled her closer, taunting her a little with his possessiveness. "I've told you all that was important about my relationship with Marie. Now you tell me about this Thornton. *Compromise,* dear Miracle." He gave her a benign but commanding look. "Talk."

"I care about him. I'd like to help him. He used to be a pretty lovable person. But I think I loved being needed by him more than anything else. Eventually I realized that it wasn't the same as loving *him*. Does that make any sense?"

"Yes. But I want him out of your life. I'm not . . . hmmm, what would be the word?" Sebastien frowned, then found it and nodded. "I'm not *modern* enough to encourage you to remain friends with him. In fact, I would prefer that you never see him again."

"*Dear* doctor, there isn't a man on this planet you need to feel jealous of."

His free hand slid over her hip and dipped between her thighs. With his fingertips he spread the wetness that came from both their bodies. It was a loving caress, without domination. "I know. But indulge my fierce territorial instinct where you are concerned."

She could tell he was struggling not to let jealousy make him sound Neanderthal. It wasn't that he didn't trust her feelings for him—she knew *that*—it was that he wanted to drive away any other male who had ever coveted her. The attitude was surprisingly primitive for him, and it made her so happy that she was drunk with wanting to please him. But she knew that she had to be honest.

"I don't love Elliot, but I want to help him, if I can. I won't promise you that I'll turn my back on him if he wants to be friends again, if he's *capable* of being friends." She paused, girding herself for what she wanted to say next. "Elliot and I were finished a long time before you came back. You don't have to worry."

"I'm not accusing you of anything."

"Do you . . . want to talk about Jeff Atwater?"

Silence stretched between them. His expression became carefully shuttered as he held her gaze. "No, I think not," he said finally. His hand lay still on the top of her thigh, then began its slow caress again. But there was something hard and challenging in his eyes. "Do you want to remember him?"

He knew about that night. There was no doubt. "No, it ended ten years ago. It was a terrible mistake."

"You had given up waiting for me. I understand why. I never gave you reason to wait." He halted the line of conversation with an upraised hand. His eyes were colder than she would have liked. "Someday, when we're old and bored and have nothing better to discuss, we'll talk about Jeff. But not now."

She nodded but wondered how long they could let this painful part of their past remain unexplored.

"So you want to be friends with Elliot Thornton," he said abruptly, his tone grim. "And rehabilitate him."

"Yes, I do."

Sebastien lifted a hand and pointed at her in a slow and emphatic gesture of protest that held the future hostage. *You test my limits,* it said. She met his reproachful stare with an arch expression, while her fingers drummed a deceptively light-hearted rhythm on the center of his chest. "Compromise," she reminded him.

His eyes flickered. His attitude shifted to exasperation. He lowered his hand and engulfed her teasing fingers. "So be it. *Compromise.*" The word came hard, and she knew it. She kissed him in honor of it, and hoped that it would help her in the future.

❧

Sebastien went with her when she flew to New York to audition for *Late Night With David Letterman.* She was ecstatic when Letterman's producer offered her a stand-up spot on one of the following week's shows. She luxuriated in Sebastien's pride.

In their hotel suite the next morning she woke to find herself wearing a slender gold necklace from which hung a diamond pendant. "See what the tooth fairy brought me?" she said tearfully, looking up into Sebastien's solemn eyes. "And I didn't even trade a tooth for it."

"He must have known that yesterday was a momentous occasion and should be commemorated."

"I've been getting a lot of goodies lately."

"It's about time, I'd say."

"But I need to do something in return. For the tooth fairy, I mean."

"You could refer to him by some other title." He lay back and crooked a finger at her, a smug expression on his face.

Laughing, happier than she'd ever been in her life, she pounced on him.

❦

David Letterman liked her. He had always been nice to her anytime she and Elliot ran into him at the clubs. It was widely rumored that he considered Elliot a jerk, but she forgave him that insight.

After she finished her routine she sat down in the low-slung guest chair next to his desk and told him a lot of creative lies about growing up in the South. Judging by the sincerity in his gap-toothed grin, and the audience's enthusiastic laughter, she knew she'd done well. After he broke for a commercial he leaned over and congratulated her, asked her to stay for another couple of minutes, and said he hoped she'd come back.

"I'd chain myself to your desk and start polishin' your shoes if you wanted me to," she assured him.

He liked that idea.

But if he was nice he was also mischievous, and when the commercial ended the first thing he did was rear back in his chair and asked her about Elliot. "Come on, now, you used to hang around with this character," he said cheerfully. "What's a big night on the town like with Elliot Thornton? I bet he's the kind of guy who cheats at goofy golf."

She played awkward—it was easy under the circumstances—and told a couple of innocent anecdotes about Elliot's escapades on motorcycles.

The next morning, as she and Sebastien were crossing the hotel lobby on their way to take a limo to the airport, a photographer leapt out from behind one of the lobby's potted ficus trees and began taking pictures.

He was followed by a woman carrying a tape record. She thrust its mircrophone into Amy's face, barked her own name and the name of the tabloid newspaper that employed her, then asked, "Elliot Thornton's show has just been canceled. Is it true that your relationship with him contributed to his personal problems? Is it true that you

met Elliot Thornton when you were a college student and
that he seduced you during a drug orgy at his motel room?"

Which was as far as she got before Sebastien plucked
the microphone out of her hand, jerked it free of the tape
recorder, and dropped it into the potted ficus. He then
slapped the photographer's Nikon, which took a short flight
into a tiled wall. Amy watched in horror while marveling at
Sebastien's ability to silence both people with a look of
sheer menace. They gaped at him and stepped aside.

When she and he were safely ensconced in the limo, he
shut his eyes and leaned his head back on the seat. "I
suppose I overreacted."

"Yeah, I think you get the Sean Penn award today."

"What is that?"

She took one of his clenched hands and kissed it. "Never
mind, Doc. I love your intentions, even if your methods
need a little work."

"It's going to be like this often, isn't it, if you become
well known?"

She cringed. "I hope not. Nobody'd be interested in me
if it weren't for Elliot. They're after him right now, that's all
Sebastien?"

"Yes?"

"That reporter is probably goin' to write about you."

"Me?"

"Yeah. She'll call you something like 'the violent mystery
man who stole Elliot Thornton's girlfriend.' "

"I'll sue her for libel."

Amy shook her head, feeling miserable. "She'll just write
another article about you, and it'll be even uglier. Then I'll
have to go smack the fire out of her, because I won't let
anybody embarrass you, especially on my account."

"No. This is not your fault."

"This is not good publicity for a heart surgeon. I want
you to be able to work in this country without people
snickering at you because of me."

"Stop saying such nonsense. My reputation has survived
much worse than this." He settled back in the seat and
pulled her close. She hugged him and felt the anger in his

body. It alarmed her. She didn't want him to merely to survive here. She wanted him to flourish. What if he didn't?

❦

The *Funny Women* cable special was a grand new experience. It was taped at the Alexus, a small but prestigious theater in San Francisco. Her knees shook when she stepped up on the famous stage in front of a packed audience, with cameras recording her act and Sebastien seated somewhere in the darkness at the back of the club. She was one of ten female comics. Her agent, a plump powerhouse named Bev Jankowski, was from a small but respectable firm. Bev told her she blew the others away and was, indeed, moving up in a hurry.

Agents were supposed to say things like that, but Amy liked hearing them, anyway. More important was Sebastien's reaction. He'd never seen her work before. She met him in the crowded hall outside the dressing rooms, took one look at his smile, and knew that she hadn't made a fool out of herself in front of him. The tabloid story had been as garish as she'd feared, but he'd weathered it well. He held out his arms and told her gruffly, "I waited a long time to see you prove your talent to other people. But don't forget, I saw it first."

Laughing, she threw herself into his embrace. "My agent gets ten percent of me and you get the rest, I promise."

"Hmmm, I don't know. I doubt that she can appreciate that ten percent as much as I can."

"Well, she only gets the *public* ten percent."

"Fair enough."

They hugged, then stood there enjoying each other's presence and the moment. She suspected that she was giving him a goofy, tearful smile, but the look in his eyes said that he was loving it.

"Cut to the chase, baby, cut to the chase. This is the longest sap scene on record."

Elliot's voice was sardonic. She pivoted to face him. He was thin and his face gaunt. His nose looked raw, and purplish shadows tainted the skin beneath his eyes. Despite his sarcastic remark, he regarded her with a wistful, apologetic expression. "Hi ya, baby. Long time no abuse." His voice trembled.

"Hi." A flood of sympathy made her grasp one of his hands and pat it maternally. "I hope you're tired of not returning my phone calls. Where have you been?"

"Seeing the wild West." His gaze shifted to Sebastien. "You were busy, I heard."

Sebastien extended a hand and introduced himself. To her surprise, Elliot reciprocated. He looked beaten, lost. "Thank you, man. You've inspired me."

Sebastien regarded him without malice. "In what way?"

"To clean up my life." He sent Amy a hopeful look. "I'm off the bad stuff, baby. I swear."

She hugged him, held him, and he burrowed his head on her shoulder. She didn't know if he was telling the truth or not, but her heart broke for him. "I'm proud of you." She drew back and studied him sadly. She knew his melodramatic scenes too well, but still, he was pitiful. "If there's anything I can do for you—"

"You always said that you and I would have a chance again, if I went straight. Well, I'm going to hold you to your word, baby."

"Elliot, it isn't that simple." She glanced up at Sebastien. His jaw was clenched, but he seemed more annoyed with Elliot than angry. He knew Elliot was no threat. She grasped Elliot's shoulders and said as lightly as he could, "Why don't I meet you for lunch this week? And we'll talk. You know that I'm still your friend."

"Forget this guy, baby," he said, nodding toward Sebastien. "I've had him checked out. I bet you don't know him half as well as I do."

"Oh, Elliot, what a con artist you are. We'll have lunch, and—"

"Did you know that he killed his own kid?"

She blocked Sebastien's way as he took a step toward Elliot. Looking up into his face, she saw controlled fury but also acceptance. "Where did your investigator get that misinformation?"

But Elliot stared straight at Amy. She was hypnotized with horror. "His kid was born deformed," Elliot told her.

"So he didn't wait for it to die. He just did a little slice-and-dice job, a little salvage work, and tossed the rest. He got canned for it, too. Screwed his reputation big time. No wonder he came to the States looking for you. He's persona non grata among the French medical set. Did he tell you *that*?"

"Elliot, you'd better turn around and walk." Sebastien's silence made a terrible brand of dread form inside her.

"Ask the man, baby. Ask him. And call me, okay?" He turned and walked quickly away.

Slowly she looked up at Sebastien. She saw that what Elliot had said was true, at least in part. "Let's go somewhere quiet and talk," he said wearily. "Perhaps I understand the past well enough to explain it to you now."

❦

San Francisco Bay stretched below the knoll of the small park, an enormous, black mirror reflecting the pinpoint lights of boats and the city. But the night's fog edged up to it, threatening the clear view. Already the street lamp nearby was catching the mist in its glow. Amy leaned against the gnarled trunk of a small oak and wondered if yet another turning point in her and Sebastien's life together would be played out under a night sky. They had always seemed to find lonely, beautiful places by unspoken agreement.

He talked to her with his attention lost in the black distance, his head up, his hands knotted against his thighs. She listened to him describe the child he and his wife had wanted so much, and even though she knew that he hadn't loved his wife, she felt like an outcast, the same as when she'd stood in the rain outside his estate and watched the two of them. She had never told him about that day, and didn't think she ever would.

But she hurt for him when he talked about the baby daughter he'd loved, and about the way she had died, and his reasons for what he'd done to her. When he finished he turned toward her with a troubled expression. "What do you think of me now?"

"I think you have a deep capacity for love. I think you did

the right thing." She hesitated, struggling for composure, her emotions leaden. "But I wonder how you feel about children after all you've been through." A chill slid over her skin as she assessed his silence. "Please tell me, Sebastien."

"I don't ever want that kind of grief again." His voice had a desperate, bitter edge, but she realized it was part grief, part shame. "I have no idea why Marie and I couldn't have a healthy child . . . there was no obvious reason for it. If I were the cold-hearted bastard that so many people think I am, it would be easy to become a father again. But to take a chance that another child would be subjected to such torture would be obscene. I can't do it."

She lifted her hands through the mist and cupped his face. "You're afraid something's wrong with you? You'll bring another deformed child into the world? I don't believe it. Please, don't you believe it, either."

"I won't take the chance."

"Please don't say that. I love you for your reasons, but I can't let you be crippled by them."

"If you had gone through what I have—"

"But I haven't, and I've got faith." She caught her breath and stared at him, then added quietly, "What you're saying affects our future together. Do you really want to make this decision alone?"

He took her hands. "No. Your feelings are crucial. Is there any doubt in your mind that you and I will marry?"

All the years of waiting, of loving, fell into place. "None," she whispered. "But I want children."

He bowed his head to her hands. "I don't want you to suffer the way Marie did." His voice was hoarse, and she knew he was fighting for control. She made a soft sound of comfort and stepped closer to him.

"Everything I've ever wanted has been hard to get," she whispered. "I don't need guarantees things are going to work out perfectly. If I've learned anything from the way I grew up, it's that most of what I'm afraid of turns out to be what makes me feel strong, and confident, and happy—if I don't run from it."

He raised his head and gave her a troubled, tender frown.

"I've never run from my fears. I've confronted them head-on, like a bull too blind with anger to see the matador stabbing at him. And I assure you, the results never made me happy. But strong, yes. And confident? I hope so."

"But still blind."

"Blind, then, and nervous because of it." He gripped her hands harshly, and she couldn't look away from the intensity in his eyes. "Amy, I've decided to have a vasectomy."

Trembling, she pulled her hands away and stepped back. The thought of him putting an end to such an intimate part of their future was beyond her sympathy, but at the same time she forced herself to think about all the disappointment he'd been through and his fear that he'd never produce a healthy child. "I understand why you're afraid. But don't do it. Don't do that to us. To yourself."

"I wouldn't protest if you wanted to *adopt* a child."

"What about you? Don't *you* want one?"

He shook his head. "But I won't deny you the right to be a mother—"

"That's not good enough." She looked at him miserably. "I've never thought much about having children, but that was because I didn't picture Elliot as the father type. I couldn't depend on him. But I want a family. I've never had one—not like everybody else's, anyway—and there's this stubborn little dream of mine to have everything I missed when I was growing up. And that includes raising some happy, well-adjusted kids."

"You want a moral victory over your father. You want to rebuild your childhood by watching your own children grow up happy. Are those good enough reasons to bring them into an ugly world?"

"My world isn't as ugly as yours."

"You didn't have a pitiful, deformed daughter. You didn't watch her die and hold her heart in your hand, knowing it was all you could save of her . . . and all that was worth saving."

"But if we had a healthy baby, you'd feel different, don't you think?"

The mist was settling around them now, gray and cold. He raked a hand through his hair, his expression so distraught that she clasped his other hand in sympathy. "How would you feel?" she repeated.

"I'd worry about making the same mistakes my father made." He studied her reaction grimly. "You're certain you can triumph over your past. I'm not so certain I can defeat mine."

"You're a kind, thoughtful man. You're not your father. You're not *my* father, either. I won't let you turn into either one of them. You've always told me to believe in myself and go after what I want. Well, I want children, our children. And I believe in *you*. You can be a wonderful father. You will be. I know. He took her by the shoulders. "Miracle," he said gently, "your funny name has always suited you so well. You've changed so much about my life, about me. Now that I have you back, there's contentment, and pleasure, and a *quietness* inside me that I never had before. I want you with me for the rest of my life. I'll try to make you very happy." He hesitated, the softness fading from his expression. "I won't risk losing you in childbirth. I'm afraid of that too, you see."

She cried without sound, stroking his cheek with the back of her fingers. "Just be patient with yourself. You haven't had time to heal."

He pulled her inside his arms. "No, I have to be honest with you. What happened with my daughter nearly destroyed me. I'll never forget it. Call it a morbid idea, if you want, but I don't think I'll ever have children of my own. I don't think that I'm meant to. *Something will always go wrong.* I've always felt that I'm being chased by some awful fate that should have caught up with me long ago. Please try to understand. If anything terrible happened to you, I'd never forgive myself. If you died having my child, I'd die, too."

Her large, anguished tears slid under his fingertips as he cupped her chin. She believed she could teach him to trust their happiness; she knew she'd never love him more than at this moment. "Promise me this much, Doc. You won't have a vasectomy anytime soon. And you won't do it without telling me, first. Please." Her voice broke. "You know I'm not gonna surprise you with a baby you don't want. But you have to promise me you won't have a vasectomy."

"Love, I don't doubt your honor." He drew back, and they shared a tender gaze. He nodded. "I won't do anything unless we agree on it. I swear." He placed a light, slow kiss on her mouth. "Will you still marry me, after all I've just told you?"

Amy took his face between her hands. "Of course. I've intended to since I was eighteen years old."

"Thank God you believed in me. I never want to destroy that."

"You won't."

She kissed him. He frowned thoughtfully, as if looking into the past, while she saw only a future that held battles she would willingly fight.

TWENTY-TWO

"**Y**ou need to go on the road," her agent said. "With the Letterman spot and the cable special in your credits, you can headline at the better clubs all over the country. We're talking a couple thousand bucks a week, maybe more, not to mention more Letterman spots and the auditions I want you to start doing. This is no time to stay home and play footsies with your man."

Amy smiled at her. "Forget it. I'm still getting married in two weeks."

"Don't remind me. I'm sick about it."

"A small, intimate ceremony at a little chapel up in the wine country—"

"So why didn't you invite me? Because I'd drown my sorrows in cheap domestic chablis?"

"There won't be any guests. Only the minister and his wife."

"I'd hide the ceremony, too, if I were hamstringing my career."

"Sebastien and I have always been loners, see, but now it's me and him against the world—"

"Oh, God, *don't* start sounding like a bad song lyric."

"So we decided that we'd keep the ceremony between ourselves."

"This is so sweet that I may need a diabetes test."

Amy frowned past her at the smoggy L.A. skyline outside the office window. "I know you think that I'm getting myself in too deep and too fast. And I know that going on the road would be the best thing to do, careerwise. But there's more than one way to hatch this chicken, Bev. I can stay in L.A. and work the Comedy Store, and that's not a shabby way to get noticed, you have to admit. I'll go on auditions; I'll even audition for that voice work you told me about. Good Lord, this voice was *made* for cartoon characters."

Bev Jankowski sank her head in her heads and sighed. "But no road tour."

"Right."

"Tell me something, is this man worth it?"

"Yes."

"But you said that he's getting involved in his own career again. I thought heart surgeons led pretty high-powered lives, not much free time. He'd hardly notice if you were out of town—"

"I think he'd notice if I was gone for months at a time," Amy said dryly. "Besides, he's making sacrifices, too, so that he won't be working all the time. He'll probably go into research rather than private practice; he's had an offer to work at a research institute."

"All right, all right, true love wins out. Let's focus on the positive. Here." She handed Amy a file folder. "Hadley Rand is casting for a small part in a TV movie. He saw you on Letterman and took a fancy to you and your goofy southern voice. I want you to go up to his office in Burbank this week and read for him."

"Isn't he the guy who directed *Maid for Murder*?"

"Yeah. Won an Emmy for it last year, too. He's young, fresh, and really hot."

Amy opened the folder. "This movie he's casting . . . it's called *Bingo*? What's it about—game night at a VFW post?"

"Close. It's about a bunch of old people in a little Florida town who open an illegal bingo parlor so they can save the town from bankruptcy. There's a part for a geeky daughter. Not much to it, but you'd get a few good lines. Give it a shot."

"Okay. Hadley can only laugh."

"Let's hope so."

An audition. She was actually going to ask strangers to

believe she was an actress. All those years of devoted fandom, spent memorizing and mimicking the greats, might pay off.

Sebastien was waiting when she returned to their hotel room. She told him about the movie audition. "Even if I don't get the part, it's mind-boggling. Who would've thought I'd be auditioning for a part in a movie."

He applauded. "I'm not surprised. You have natural talent."

"Hmmm. More. More." She kissed him. "How did your meeting at the institute go?"

"Very well. They are eager to have me." He bowed.

"I know how they feel. Then negotiations are underway?"

"Yes." He studied the radiant smile she gave him. "You like the idea?"

"I just want you to feel at home here. And be happy."

"I already am, dear Miracle. But speaking of homes, we need a second one in California, something closer to Los Angeles. I think an apartment in New York should be a consideration also. Since television and film people always seem to be working here or there. Perhaps we should also buy a country estate in Georgia. You'd like that, wouldn't you?"

"You collect homes the way some men collect beer bottles."

"Don't look so stunned. Won't it be fun to pick them out and decorate them? Won't you enjoy that?"

She sagged against him, chuckling. "I have the interior-decorating skill of a rock. How do you feel about vinyl upholstery?"

"We'll hire professional help."

"I don't think there are any therapists who specialize in treating the decorating-impaired."

He laughed. "I meant professional *decorators*, of course."

"It's gonna take me a while to adjust to this, Doc."

"What?"

"Contentment."

He led her through the suite to its opulent bath. Water bubbled in the oversized, sunken tub. He'd set candles around the marble ledge, along with a silver ice bucket containing a bottle of champagne. "A celebration," he said, beginning to undress her. "Of contentment."

❦

The ringing of a phone in the middle of the night was always a frightening sound to Amy. But Sebastien, who had spent most of his adult life answering emergency calls concerning his patients, didn't even fumble in the hotel room's inky darkness. His voice was coherent and calm. He listened for a few seconds, began to converse in French, then sat up and swung his legs off the side of the bed.

Her heart pounding, Amy wrestled with a tangle of sheet and covers while listening in bewilderment. She couldn't tell much from his brief questions. Finally she wiggled free and turned on a bedside lamp.

Squinting at his bare back, she watched it stiffen as the conversation continued. A hard timbre crept into his voice. A small muscle along his spine quivered with tension. Amy sat up and put a hand on his shoulder; he pulled it down and tucked her arm around him, holding her hand next to his chest. She felt the accelerated thumping of his heart under her fingertips. Worried, she slid close to his back and put her other arm around him, then rested her cheek between his shoulder blades.

When he hung up the phone he sat motionless, staring at the floor. "What's wrong?" she whispered.

"There's been an airplane crash."

"Oh, no, no, not your family—"

"My brother-in-law was flying to Monaco in a small private plane of his. He crashed in a storm not far from Paris. My sister and father were with him."

She cried out and moved around in front of him, kneeling on the floor and taking his hands in hers. His expression held sorrow, but also the kind of black anger she thought he'd lost forever. "My brother-in-law was killed," he told her. "My sister is badly injured, but is expected to live. The doctors think it will be months before she recovers fully." He was silent, his face shuttered, his control absolute.

"What about your father?"

"His back was broken. He's paralyzed. And there are other injuries, as well. He's in a coma. The doctors doubt he'll survive."

"I'm so sorry, sweetheart."

"I'm sorry for my sister."

She shivered. "Be sorry for your father, too. He can't hurt you anymore."

Sebastien's brutal laugh frightened her, and she drew back quickly to look at him. His eyes glittered. "That, dear Miracle, remains to be seen."

❦

She just wanted to get this over with. Sebastien had left for Paris two days before. He had insisted that she stay behind for this audition. Also, he didn't want to inflict his brother-in-law's funeral on her. Or so he said. Nagging self-doubt made her wonder if he was reluctant to have her meet his family's friends and business acquaintances.

Oh, don't be oversensitive. You've outgrown your inse-curity, remember? He loves you. He's proud of you. He's going to marry you in two weeks. Right? Right.

Hadley Rand looked friendly and bookish, like a hamster wearing glasses. He squinted at her across a desk that was more battered than stylish. "Amy?" Hadley said. "It's a simple part. No need to meditate about it."

She smiled quickly. "Sorry."

"No problem. I'm Shirley's grandmother; you're Shirley. We're in the laundromat. You're confused. Shirley is perpetually confused. Start with the line, 'Is that a piece of lint, or did Frankie leave his mouse in the clothes hamper again?' "

She dutifully went through the scene with him, but her attention was in France, worrying about Sebastien. She didn't expect to get this movie role, even though it was a minor part that didn't require great skill. Good Lord, she wasn't even an actress.

When she and Hadley finished, he stared at her open mouthed. Everyone else in the room had strange expressions, half-smiling, half-stunned. Her heart sank. So she had been *that* bad. She was reminded of the terrible night during college, at the dinner theater auditions in Athens.

Oh, well, at least this time she hadn't failed because of an anxiety attack.

"Guess that's it," she said awkwardly. "Thanks for givin' me a chance."

"We'll call you."

Don't call us. She shook Hadley's paw and left the office.

At the hotel she began to pack. She had a dawn flight to New York, where she'd connect with a flight to Paris. Restless, she wandered around the suite, thinking about Sebastien.

His brother-in-law's funeral would be held tomorrow, in the early morning hours by L.A. time, late afternoon by Paris time. Sebastien would be with his sister's two small children. What kind of emotional support could he offer them in his dark, cold mood? His change of attitude made her distraught. He had been reserved and brusque since the phone call, and it was more than concern for his family. She sank her hands into the pockets of her slacks and paced, thinking about Sebastien and children, Sebastien and his family problems, Sebastien and her career.

The phone rang. It was her agent. "I didn't do real well," Amy said immediately.

Bev hooted. "That must be why Hadley Rand has just offered you the part."

"You're kidding! After I read for him he stared at me like I was a wart on a frog's butt."

"A talented wart. You intrigued everybody in the office, he said. They think you're terrific."

"I'm leaving for Paris tomorrow. I'll give you my phone number there, so call me if Hadley was only kidding."

"Try not to sound so excited," Bev muttered. "It's only ten thousand dollars for two weeks' work and a part in a very respectable made-for-TV movie."

"My man needs me in Paris."

"This is no time to focus on your personal life. Come back soon. You've got to be on location in Florida in three weeks."

"Oh, we'll be back by then. No problem."

"Make your agent happy. Become celibate until we're both rich."

❦

She had expected Sebastien to meet her at the airport in Paris. Instead she found a very dignified chauffeur waiting for her. He was holding up a sign with her name written on it. "Doctor de Savin regrets that he cannot meet you himself," the chauffeur said in heavily accented English. "He is spending the evening in meetings with officers of the family corporation."

Amy was dismayed. It was past midnight. His brother-in-law's funeral had been held in the afternoon. Did the family businesses require attention tonight, while Sebastien's sister and father lay in the hospital and his sister's children stayed with servants? She tried not to frown and forced a gentle shrug. "Okey dokey. Let's hit the trail, then."

"Pardon, mademoiselle?"

She felt herself blushing. "I mean, uhmmm . . . I'm ready to go whenever you are."

The chauffeur arched a brow at the tattooed wrist showing below the cuff of her blue-cloth coat. She had thought she looked very chic in the flowing, shawl-collared garment, with the white collar of her dress turned up so that it peeked out a bit. Very Katharine Hepburn. Now she tried not to fidget.

"Very good," the man said finally. "I'm to drive you to the home of the doctor's sister. The doctor is staying there."

She cleared her throat and said with great elegance, *"Bien. Merci."*

He gave a wall-eyed glance to her canvas tote bag stuffed with paperback novels, the latest issues of *Rolling Stone* and *Variety,* and her bola bouncer. Then he bowed and held out a hand. She hung the tote's handle over his palm. His nails, she noticed, had a much nicer manicure than her own.

She felt woefully out of place.

❦

While the chauffeur carried her luggage up a wide staircase of silver marble, a matronly housekeeper in a crisp black dress stared at her politely. "The doctor called to say

he'll be here soon. He has requested that a late supper be
served in his suite. But in the meantime, can I have the
cook bring you coffee, wine?"

Amy tried not to stare at the villa's furnishings and said
she'd wait for the doctor to arrive, first. Even her life among
California's wealthy glitterati had not prepared her to deal
with this setting. From the chandelier-draped entrance hall
she could see into a drawing room where luxury seeped
from every wall. It was old-world luxury—eighteenth-century, ornate giltwork, rich tapestries and rugs, exquisite
porcelain and terracotta—more appropriate to a museum
of prerevolutionary France than to a private home.

"I will show you to the doctor's suite, then, if you
please," the housekeeper said. The woman was gracious
and unassuming, though formal, and as they ascended the
long staircase she exclaimed gently as she looked up at
the landing. "*Au dodo!*"

Two pajama-clad children looked distraught but curious,
and took several hesitant steps back when the housekeeper
ordered them to bed. Amy returned their scrutiny, searching her memory. Sebastien had said that his nephew was
six years old; his niece, only four. They were handsome
blond-haired children who stood silent, holding hands.
The boy looked haggard, but his sister, too young to
comprehend much about her father's death, smiled at Amy
immediately.

The housekeeper sighed. "May I present Jacques and
Louise? They were sent to bed hours ago. Their nanny has
the night off, and well, tonight my discipline is . . . oh, it's
not important, tonight." She stroked a hand over Jacques's
disheveled hair; he pulled away, looking angry at the world.

Amy knelt in front of them. Her throat ached at the boy's
obvious grief and his sister's innocence. "*Allô. Je m'appelle
Amy.*"

"We speak English," Jacques told her somberly. "Are
you Uncle's girlfriend?"

"Yes. Hmmm. Oh, my!" She flicked a hand out and
brushed Louise's ear. "A centime was hiding in your hair!"
Slipping her hand across the pocket of Jacques's pajama
top, she found another one. "There must be magic here."

Louise laughed merrily, but Jacques shook his head. "Not today. Our papa died. We went to his funeral today. Our *maman* is in the hospital, and she won't be coming home for a long time. And *grand-père* is in the hospital too. He may not wake up."

"I know," Amy said in a small voice. "Why don't both of you come to my room and sit with me while I unpack my clothes? Who knows? I might find more magic."

"Oh, yes," Louise said.

The housekeeper intervened quickly, shaking her head at the children. "Your Uncle Sebastien will be very tired when he gets home. He needs to rest. And so do you."

"He doesn't want us around," Jacques informed Amy, looking mad. "He doesn't like us."

Amy bit her lip. "That's not true. He loves you very much."

"No. He has never liked us. Good night." He had the dignity of a stern little man. Tugging Louise's hand, he led her away. She wandered along sadly, looking back over her shoulder at Amy and the housekeeper.

"Poor things," the housekeeper said.

Amy stood up slowly, feeling exhausted and depressed. "The doctor has trouble dealing with children, I know."

"Yes. I suppose he's told you about his . . . his past marriage—"

"Yes."

They walked down a hall hung with enormous gilt-framed mirrors and paintings, then turned down another hall equally impressive. The housekeeper exhaled wearily. "The doctor lost his own mother when he was only a few years older than Jacques. I worked for the family even then. I was around when the accident happened. The doctor was never the same little boy after it. He was not a little boy at all. Years passed before anyone saw him smile or heard him laugh."

"Is there any more news about his sister or his father?"

"No, nothing." The housekeeper opened massive double doors to a suite filled with a mixture of antiques and heavy modern pieces. The walls and windows were done in muted gray-and-gold brocades; soft light spilled from gold sconces. It was an elegantly masculine place, sensuous but also forbidding in its grandeur.

"Is this used as a guest room ordinarily?" Amy asked.

"In a sense. Madame had it decorated for her father. His home is not far from here, but madame wanted him to have his own suite."

Amy looked at the oversized bed with its bronze silk coverlets and imposing frame. It didn't appear to be antique, but the design was more grand than that of most modern furniture. It was heavily ornamented and made of some exotic black wood. Thick posts carved with vines and grapes rose almost to the ceiling. She didn't want to sleep where Sebastien's father had slept; she kept her bitterness toward *le comte* de Savin to herself, not wanting to encourage Sebastien's hatred of him. But the stories Sebastien had told about his unrelenting manipulation both disgusted and frightened her.

"Has the *comte* stayed here often?" she asked.

The housekeeper sighed. "Never. Madame was so disappointed. I put the doctor in this suite because it seems appropriate . . . and because the bed was designed for a man with long legs. The doctor has his father's height."

Amy exhaled in relief. The housekeeper sighed again as she pointed Amy to the dressing alcove where her luggage had been placed. "The *comte* has not regained consciousness. No one expects him to. Poor madame, she is conscious, but so badly hurt! Her legs and pelvis were crushed. It will be months before she recovers. Ah, well, we will do the best we can. The doctor will be a dutiful brother and son. He won't let the family down. There's so little family left."

Crying softly, the housekeeper fled to the doors. "He will not desert his poor, cursed family. Forgive me for upsetting you with my sorrows. Please don't tell the doctor."

"Sssh. I understand. Good night."

"Good night."

Amy stood in the center of the magnificent room, a hollow spot growing inside her. Sebastien hated returning to a world that haunted him, but he had too much honor to desert his sister. She shivered. He would put his family first. She would be second. Ten years ago he had chosen his career and his pride over her. Now she might lose him to his family.

She took a shower and changed into red-silk pajamas, then sat among the cushions of a recessed seat before the room's enormous widow, staring blankly into a night mist that shrouded the villa's formal garden. The light from the window caught splashes of color from a kaleidoscope of flowers. Spring in Paris was as moody and as beautiful as she'd always heard.

Her nerves jumped as footsteps halted outside the suite's doors. Sebastien knocked once, loudly, then stepped inside. His black suit looked as if it had had a long day, but it had not lost its handsomeness. He tossed his trench coat at a chair and crossed the room to her as she stood, holding out her hands, her throat too tight for words. *I won't put up with being second choice anymore.*

Inside his desperate embrace she absorbed his anger, his sense of futility, his grief. When he looked down at her, caressing her cheek with the backs of his fingers as he did, his eyes were dark and tired. "Forgive me for not meeting you at the airport."

"It's all right."

"No. I can tell from your face, it's not."

"Forget about the airport. Tell me what's going on with your family."

She drew him to the window seat, and they sat down. He pulled her against him so that her back rested on his chest; wrapping his arms around her and pressing his face against her hair, he cursed wearily.

"There are problems among my father's executives— there have been for some time, I learned tonight—power struggles, charges of mismanagement, perhaps even embezzlement."

"Did your father know?"

"No, I'm sure he didn't. He would never have tolerated it. I've always thought of him as young and commanding. Tonight I realized just how old and careless he had become."

"Did your sister know?"

"Probably. She has never discussed the businesses with me—a point of pride and jealousy to her. I imagine that she has been struggling to control matters from the weak position my father gave her." He hesitated, and for a moment Amy heard only the harsh sound of his breath, the anger and defeat flowing in and out of him like a tide. "When he dies, my sister gets nothing, even though he has known for years that I will only turn the businesses over to her. He mocks me with his demands, even now."

Amy gripped his hands. "What are you going to do?"

"Save what I can, for Annette's sake." He bent his head against her shoulder; they both knew what his words implied. Amy could feel the anger in his body; his arms tightened around her fiercely.

"You have to stay," she whispered, her voice strained.

"Yes. Until my sister is capable of taking over."

"Months."

"Yes."

The word sank into her with chilling finality. She turned inside his arms, pulled her knees under her, and scrutinized his eyes, finding so much apology and unhappiness there that she made a guttural sound of pain, in response. "I'm trying real hard to understand," she told him.

"My God, do you think I'm choosing sides here? Do you think I'm forgetting about you?"

"I'm not jealous of your family. I'm just afraid that you'll decide that you belong here, in France. That you'll forget why you wanted to change your life when you came to California."

"And you're telling me that you can't live here, if I ask you to?"

She nodded woodenly. "I can't give up everything I've worked for. I wouldn't fit in here. That's the real issue, and we both know it."

"There's a part of you that will never accept your own worth. Nothing I can say will make any difference. I can't conquer your insecurities right now. I can only say that I love you, that I will always love you and be proud to have you with me."

"In the States. Not here." She bent her head to his chest.

The fight left her. "I'm pretty good at waitin' around for you to come back—I had ten years of practice. But I'm not so good at enjoying it. After I get through with the movie—"

"The movie?"

"Lord, I didn't even tell you that I'd gotten the part. I guess I have jet lag. It seems like it happened in another century." She glanced around the room. "And a different world."

He cupped her face in his hands and looked at her with tears in his eyes. "I'm so very proud of you."

"It's a little piss-ant part, but—"

"You'll be a star someday, and I'll be unbearably pompous about telling people that I always expected it."

Her defense broke apart, and she scrambled into his arms, tangling her legs between his. He lifted her onto his lap and held her tightly. "I spent a long time tryin' to figure out what I ought to have, and what I *deserve* to have," she told him. "I won't let go of that. I won't let go of you or my career. When I finish with the movie I'm goin' on the road with my act."

"You mean you'll tour the clubs across the country?"

"Yes." She drew back and looked at him sadly. "I'll be working or traveling every day of the week."

He regarded her with a resigned expression no happier than her own. "It will be difficult for us to see each other."

"It'll be just about impossible."

"I want you to marry me before you leave to go back. I'll make the arrangements tomorrow."

"No."

There was a long stretch of silence. Finally he said, "Is this some form of punishment?"

"No more for you than for me. I can't believe I'm turning you down. But I *am*, until everything is settled here and you come back to California. I'm not gonna start our marriage with a separation. There's been too much of that in our lives already."

"These are not the same kind of circumstances! What are you trying to do—prove to yourself that I *will* come back?"

"That's part of it."

"Goddamn." He looked at her as if she were a stranger, then stood and jerked her to her knees, dragging her against his torso. "You know how to push me . . . you know what I respond to best."

"Do you think it's easy for me to leave you? To think about waking up in the night reaching for you, and you not being there? To know I'll only be able to hear your voice over a telephone? To know I won't be able to look into your eyes, or see you smile? It makes a physical pain inside me. I'll miss you every second."

"Then you'll know what kind of hell you're putting *me* through as well." He stepped back and pulled her off balance then bent and scooped an arm under her legs. Lifting her, he walked to the bed that had been designed for his father and laid her down on the darkly patterned cover. His hands were rough on the pajamas, tearing buttons, ripping the material, but when they touched her skin they turned from violent to persuasive. She watched him with hypnotized silence, her hands on either side of her head, digging into the pillows.

He held her gaze with unfaltering challenge while his other hand tore at the fastenings on his own clothes. "You're mine, and you will always be mine, and you will wait *forever* if I tell you."

"On my terms, but . . . yes." She admitted it with anger rather than surrender, and pulled him to her.

🍃

"Tell me where we're going," she said between gritted teeth. "I mean it."

The hilly countryside flashed by, green-on-green with spring's flowers splashed among the emerald. They passed a village and an abbey, and the road continued to rise toward the jagged, snow-capped Alps in the distance.

"Isn't it obvious?" Sebastien asked, hands knotted on the steering wheel of yet another Ferrari. "We're going to the mountains. I thought you liked to be whisked away like this. It's become an intriguing game with us, don't you think?"

She hugged her arms over her coat and studied his face

in profile. Roman gladiators must have had faces such as his—noble but scarred, and too harsh for prettiness. And the battle-ready tension in it . . . they must have had *that,* too. He should be dressed in armor, not a sweater and slacks.

"This is not like the other times," she said. "You weren't angry at me then."

"I'm not angry at you now. Keep quiet, Miracle. You'll understand sooner than you'd like."

Her apprehension increased. This had started at dawn, when the strained emotions from the night before had broken through their light sleep. Waking with the fresh pain of separation filling the unguarded moment, they had made love again in a savage, heartbroken way that hurt more than it helped. Afterward he had cursed bitterly at the world in general then told her to get dressed, that he had something to show her.

So now, hours later, they were here, without having eaten much of anything or said much to each other since leaving his sister's home in Paris. She was furious with him for being mysterious and afraid that something terrible waited at their destination.

The mountains towered over them with a grandeur that threatened her; she stared resolutely at the road and continued to worry. The road burst into a wide, flat valley that cupped a dark blue lake at its center. The valley overflowed with houses, shops, and hotels that seemed to be of relatively modern vintage, through they were country French in a deliberately quaint manner.

"Garonne," Sebastien said with obvious disgust. "A resort town. Thirty years ago it was charming. Now it is merely profitable."

"Thirty years ago?"

"I came here often as a child. With the family." His mouth flattened into a harsh line, and she knew that he had said all that he intended to say, at the moment.

She traced the paths of ski lifts up the green mountain side. The lifts were in use even now, filled with people who just wanted to enjoy the scenery, she assumed. Apparently the town was popular even in the warmer months.

Sebastien left it behind and sought a narrow road that began snaking up the mountain side. Her eardrums throbbed and popped; she clung to the sides of her seat and flinched as the Ferrari's wheels squealed around sharp curves. She looked out at a dizzying panorama of the valley that was falling away beneath them. "Please slow down."

"You don't trust me? Believe me, I know where this road is dangerous, and we haven't reached that point, yet."

She stared at him in fear and bewilderment. She had never seen him like this before. Something ancient and ugly seemed to be at war inside him, maybe the thing that he had always fought. It was coming to the surface. It threatened everything between them.

In a low, careful voice, she said, "If you're going to kill us both, at least tell me why."

Abruptly he slid the Ferrari into the road's inner shoulder. It halted inches from the sheer rock face of the mountain. The color had drained from his face. His hands shook. "Forgive me. I was tormenting myself, and I didn't realize how it must look to you."

This caring man was someone she knew. She shuddered with relief and bent her head to his shoulder. "For God's sake, tell me what we're doing here."

"Wait. It's just a little farther. I swear."

He lifted her hands to his mouth and kissed them, then guided the car back onto the pavement and drove at a reasonable speed. Amy vaguely noticed the road bending around another hairpin curve. Then she saw a jutting lip of mountain spread into a grassy apron beside the road, a small sweep of green between the road and the plunging mountainside dotted with clumps of trees. At the edge of the grassy area was a thick barricade of steel posts and rails.

Sebastien turned the Ferrari onto the grass and stopped well back from the barrier. He cut the engine and sat in silence, looking at the gray steel wall, his breathing noticeably shallow, his eyes slitted with thought.

Suddenly she understood, at least in part. "Is this where your mother had the accident?"

He inclined his head in an almost indiscernible nod. His

attention never left the steel wall. "It was made of timbers, then. Not nearly so strong as now. Now, no matter how much one tried to break through, the barricade would probably hold."

No matter how much one tried. Trembling, she got out of the car and went to the driver's side. Opening his door before he could reach for the handle, she knelt on the door ledge and put her arms around him.

His control faltered inside her embrace. Bending his forehead against hers, he sighed raggedly. "You need to understand why I feel so pulled apart by my family. How I came by this ridiculous mixture of loathing and dedication. Perhaps you'll see why I can't leave them when they need me—"

"Sebastien, I didn't say that I *want* you to desert them—"

"You'll see why I can't leave them," he repeated. "But also why I never want to share—why I can't share—in any true sense of family with them. Come. Let's walk over to the railing."

He got out of the car and took her hand. Her knees were weak with dread as they walked to the chest-high barrier and stood looking down the steep, forested slope.

"It's changed a great deal. The trees . . . are all different."

"This is the first time you've come back?"

"Yes."

"Sebastien, you always let me think that this accident didn't affect you very much. You made it sound like something you'd forgotten years ago." She squeezed his hand as tight as he was squeezing hers. Something was more horrible about this place than she could imagine. She wanted to scream with the anticipation of it. "What really happened here?"

He turned his proud, agonized face toward her. The wind raked his hair roughly. "It was no accident."

"*What*?" She glanced down the slope, feeling sick to her stomach, then looked back at him for answers. He couldn't mean what he'd said. "How could it not have been an accident?"

"My mother drove through the barricade deliberately.

She wanted to kill herself as well as my brother and sister and me."

Amy swayed against him. "Why?"

"Because she blamed herself for my father's unfaithfulness. He had mistresses. My mother decided that the shame and the fault were all hers. She wanted to punish herself, but she didn't want to die alone."

Amy's knees buckled. He caught her by the elbows and they sat down together. She looked between the steel rails at the pretty spring slope, trying to picture it covered in snow, a van twisted among the trees, blood and bodies on the snow . . . and Sebastien, hurt, terrified, and all alone with so much death.

She held his hands in her lap. "How did you know that she meant to kill you all?"

"She told me before she died. She was convinced that she was talking to my father. She thought I was dead, like Antoine and Bridgette." He swallowed harshly. "I always felt doomed after what happened here. As if I'd cheated on an exam and would be caught for it, sooner or later." A bitter smile crossed his mouth. "A self-destructive attitude, wouldn't you say?"

"Tell me exactly what happened. Everything. *Please.*"

He began. She leaned her head against the barricade and listened dry-eyed while a large, broken ache settled in her chest. When he finished she put her arms around him again. This time he returned the embrace, holding her hard, with his face buried in her hair. "You're one of only three people who know the truth," he whispered eventually. "My father and I are the other two. How does it feel to be part of an unholy triumvirate?"

She stroked his shoulders. "It's much better than being an outsider."

"Do you feel reassured about my intentions, or just convinced that I'm too much trouble?"

"Reassured. I'll go back to America and wait."

"All right. Good. I don't want you to be drawn into the ugliness that surrounds my family. The . . . curse. There, I'll risk sounding ridiculous and call it what it seems to be. No one in the family escapes it."

Cursed. She'd never expected Sebastien to be so melodramatic. "You don't believe that."

"I believe in this curse, yes, whether it's simply coincidence or not. Perhaps it's only the ugly results that have come from my father's manipulations. Whatever the cause, I don't want you caught up in my family problems."

She struggled to speak without breaking down. "After ten years of bein' apart, I thought that *now*—"

"We are together, and nothing has changed."

"*You've* changed, just in the past few days. All the bitterness has come back; I look at you and see something so cold it scares me." She covered her face with her hands. "Jacques and Louise need you so much. How can you treat them so bad?"

"I try very hard not to. I try to avoid them." His voice was soft, anguished.

"But that's exactly *how* you hurt them!"

"No. I fear that I might harm them some other way— spiritually, I mean." He faltered, stopped, swallowed thickly. "I'm afraid to care too much about them. Children are so fragile—"

"Like that little boy who saw his family die? And he was never the same. It colored his whole life. Like him?"

"Perhaps I see myself, yes. I only know that it's very hard for me to encourage their affection."

"How are you going to live in your sister's house with them for the next few months? They need affection, not the cold-blooded supervision of some stranger who calls himself their uncle."

"The house staff will take care of them. They have a nanny. They spend their days at school. Annette will be brought home from the hospital in a few weeks. They'll be fine."

"Look, Doc, I can help you with Jacques and Louise. I'll work on your attitude like a dog with a bone." She tried to coax him with a teasing tone, but he shook his head.

As the impact of the upcoming months settled, they shared a look of quiet misery. "Stay with me until you have to return for your movie work," he said, his voice hollow.

"And I will visit you afterward, before you begin working on the club tour."

Nodding, crying, she kissed him. "Can you keep that ol' curse off of us for the next couple of weeks?"

"I'm sure I can." He stroked her, kissed her in return, then bowed his head against hers and shut his eyes. "It's the months afterward that I dread."

❦

He went to the de Savin offices every morning at six and came back at six in the evening, his face haggard with frustration and fatigue. Each night after dinner they went upstairs to their suite, where she massaged his shoulders and listened to him describe the maddening tangle that his father's businesses had become. They made love during those hours, sometimes in bawdy and quick couplings, sometimes with such unhurried tenderness that her throat ached with emotion. Afterward, his eyes more peaceful, he would shower, dress, and leave to spend the rest of the evening at the hospital.

Amy saw how much her support meant to him, and it magnified her feeling that she alone could make his problems insignificant. That sense of her value in life had been firmly instilled during the years when she'd struggled for and craved Pop's approval, and now it drove her relentlessly.

Late each night when he returned from the hospital, worn down and depressed, she greeted him with a sympathetic ear, a stiff brandy, and pampering hands. She refused to let herself fall asleep until she made certain he was content and sleeping soundly, and she rose ahead of him every morning to hurry downstairs, where the cook would arrange his breakfast on a bed tray. When he woke up in the cool predawn light, Amy had the morning paper, his breakfast, and her devoted attentions ready.

After he left for the office she worked doggedly on new comedy routines, worrying about her upcoming tour. When she wasn't working she spent the hours with Jacques and Louise, trying with all her energy to bridge the gap Sebastien's indifference had created, so that when she went back to the States his niece and nephew might approach him more openly, and draw him into their lives.

She ran on adrenaline and felt so tired she was weak, but she never slowed down. Sebastien wanted to pamper her, but she disliked being dependent and preferred to be the caretaker, as usual, in her life. With Elliot it had been a maternal job, but with Sebastien it was a satisfying partnership. She ignored its dark side: the obsession always to be supportive, to read Sebastien's mind and anticipate his every need, the sense of inadequacy whenever she failed.

It took a toll. When he came home a little early one night he found her curled up on the blue-carpeted floor of Jacques and Louise's playroom, asleep. She woke to his hand squeezing her shoulder lightly and his voice speaking her name with awkward command. Amy blinked groggily and sat up. Sebastien had dropped to his heels beside her. He presented his usual elegant, forbidding image in a tailored black suit, and he frowned at the floppy cloth doll she'd been using as a pillow, then pushed it aside.

Amy fussed with her disheveled hair and wondered if her face was imprinted with the doll's dress buttons. "Oh, Lord, I was goin' downstairs to wait for you, but Jacques started showing me one of his picture books, and—where are he and Louise?"

"Having supper with their nanny. They said you were here." He pulled her up with him as he stood, kissed her brusquely, and glanced around as if the playroom were a strange, discomforting world. "Why do you spend so much time with them? What were you doing in here?"

She wrapped her arms around his neck and eyed him with wicked melodrama. "I'm having an affair with one of Jacques's toy soldiers. I admit it. I have a fetish for tiny, plastic men." His frown lightened into a hint of a smile, but lines of exhaustion fanned from the corners of his eyes. She touched them with a fingertip. "Not to worry, Doc. I'm only kidding about my toy boy. I'm sorry I wasn't waiting downstairs when you got home."

"The children adore you. Are you trying to make me feel guilty for avoiding them?"

"Yep."

"It won't work."

"Well, on to Plan B, then." She kissed him, hiding her chagrin beneath a determination to be patient and cheerful. "Come along. The table in our suite is set for supper, and I bought a new bottle of massage oil today. Edible. Herb-flavored. We can put it on the salad and play cute with the lettuce."

"You look pale." He held her chin and studied her face. "You have dark circles under very bloodshot eyes, dear Miracle. This is not the face of a woman who claims to lounge about the boudoir all day."

"I'm fine. Stop diagnosing me, Doc. You're the one who needs rest and pampering, not me." She kissed him again and danced away, pulling at his hands. "I'm making myself indispensable, see? So that when I leave a week from now you won't forget me. Now come on. I want to be alone with you and our lettuce."

"Hmmm. I think I'll put you to bed and give you a mild sedative. I'm beginning to see that I've taken advantage of your compulsion."

"What compulsion?"

"The one that drives you like a maniac when you want to please someone you love."

"I'm not driven."

"You blame yourself because I'm depressed, even though it has nothing to do with you. That's an attitude I hope to break you of, but I can see that I have a long way to go."

"I simply want to take care of you. Now be quiet and come to supper."

"This won't do, Miracle. I don't intend to spend the next week worrying about you. You *will* stop running after me with your hands held out. If I want a slave, I'll hire one."

Her facade crumpled, and anger took its place. Didn't he understand that she only knew how to be a caretaker? That the constant attention to other people's pleasure—making them laugh when she was on stage, making *him* her absolute focus during this troubled time in his life—was a habit that made her feel secure, and without it she wouldn't recognize herself?

"I'll have to go home early if you won't let me take care of you," she told him.

"What nonsense."

"I'm not kidding. I don't know how to act any other way. I'd feel lost. I'd brood about you all the time. I have to feel like I'm helping you. Like I can control all your problems for you, if I just try hard enough. Don't be mad at me for that."

Swiftly he scooped his arms under her and picked her up. "Love, I'm not mad at you. But I'm not going to let you exhaust yourself. To bed, now. I'll feed you and keep you still until you fall asleep."

"You and what army?" She tried to joke, but her voice trembled. "I've got a hundred little plastic soldiers on my side."

"Not any longer." Leaving the playroom with her still cradled in his arms, he shoved the heavy wooden door shut with one foot. It closed with a solid, authoritative thump. "It's just you and me, now. No one to rescue you from my orders. Surrender."

She ate supper in dull silence, anxious because he had rebuked her for the one thing she did best. Her skin felt clammy and tight. The meal's roast lamb and delicately flavored vegetables weren't welcome in her stomach, and she stopped eating halfway through the meal. Finally it occurred to her that she was suffering more than an emotional slump.

"Are you all right?" Sebastien asked, reaching over to touch her damp face. "No! You're sick. I knew it. You've made yourself ill!"

"Excuse me." She left hurriedly and went to the suite's black marble bath, locking the door behind her. He stood outside listening to her throw up, scolding her for locking the door, his voice worried. "I'm *fine*," she yelled, clutching the commode stubbornly while her stomach told her that its problems were far from solved.

"There's a stomach flu going around," Sebastien called. "You've probably caught it."

"Nope."

She cleaned herself up, shivering and feeling weak but

determined not to spend the night in a marble palace of plumbing. Opening the door, she straightened her shoulders and frowned up at Sebastien. "See? I feel better. I don't need you to fuss over me."

"Perhaps I'd enjoy taking care of you. Or is that an honor your dignity refuses to grant me?"

"You're a sweetie, but I'm *not* sick. Now you go to the hospital to see Annette and your father, like usual, and I'll be perked up again by the time you get back."

"No. You look like hell. Stop being stubborn."

"*You're* making me sick by arguing with me. All Frenchmen like to argue. It's a national sport." She sucked in a sharp breath as her lower stomach cramped. Without thinking she rubbed a hand over the front of her wraparound blue dress.

He saw her reaction and shook his head. "Are you getting diarrhea?"

"What a romantic question. Yes!"

"Don't blush, for God's sake. I spent years studying, smelling, and cleaning up every unlovely by-product the human body can make. Nothing offends me. Or embarrasses me. And after all the intimacies you and I have shared, I'm surprised that you're embarrassed."

"We only have a week left! I don't want to be sick!" She sagged against the door frame, shook her head angrily when he stepped inside, then groaned with exasperation when he picked her up. "Shall I take you back to the toilet, my lady?" he asked in a gentle, if somewhat droll, tone.

She clutched her stomach and gave up with a weary nod.

Sebastien sent one of the house servants to a pharmacy with a prescription, but the medicine barely eased Amy's stomach. All that night and the next day she struggled with what she began to call Napoleon's revenge. Sebastien waited on her hand and foot, forcing her to accept a new role in their relationship. She loved him for it but was miserably uncomfortable with her helplessness. He refused to leave her for the office or the hospital. His father, still unconscious, wouldn't know if he visited or not, he told her, and Annette would hardly notice his absence among her nightly parade of friends.

The next afternoon Jacques and Louise peeked in at her once when the suite's door was open. She waved at them wanly from under the bed covers, and they waved back. Louise looked tearful, and Jacques frowned with anxiety. She knew that the adult world must seem unpredictable and dangerous to them right now.

"I've only got a stomach ache," she called, with all the cheerfulness she could muster. "And boy, do I stink."

They clasped their mouths and giggled. Sebastien watched from a desk across the room, where he was reading business documents. "Let Amy rest, now. Go and play."

They dragged their heels when their nanny herded them away. Amy shut her eyes as her stomach made gurgles of queasy protest. "If you want to make me feel better, go visit with them."

"Sssh. I'm going downstairs in a minute and fix you another cup of tea."

"I don't want a cup of tea. I want—" Her stomach revolted unexpectedly, and she flung herself to the edge of the bed. When she threw up on an antique tapestry rug beside it she burrowed her head on her arms and began to cry, thumping the mattress with one fist as frustration overwhelmed her.

Sebastien came to her with soothing murmurs, then cleaned both her and the rug. She pulled a pillow against her face to muffle weak, indignant sobs. "This flu usually disappears as quickly as it comes," he whispered, sitting down beside her to caress her hair. "Try to sleep, love."

"I want to take care of you. I wanted everything to be perfect. We don't have very much time left. It's all ruined."

His patience deserted him. He grasped her chin, turning her face toward him. "Goddammit, you're ruining it by being too hard on yourself. Do you think I'm going to desert you if you're not always strong? Why is it fine for me to have faults, but you have to be some kind of Joan of Arc, always riding to my rescue?"

"It's why you loved me in the first place. You wanted me because I tried to save you from yourself."

"And you did. You do." He gently wiped her face with a

damp washcloth as she stared up at him in puzzlement. "Dear Miracle, do you think I would be capable of putting aside everything else to take care of you this way if you hadn't already accomplished your rescue mission? If I'm able to be human, to give and deserve love, it's because of you. God knows what I would have become if we'd never met. God knows what I *did* become before I found you again."

"Oh, Sebastien."

"You've done your duty, Joan of Arc. You continue to do it, just by loving me and wanting me to love you in return. Now please, let me take care of you. It's what I'm best at myself, believe it or not."

"I believe it," she said tenderly. "It's why you became a doctor, isn't it?"

"It was the earliest motivation, yes. Somehow . . . it became lost as the years passed." His expression hardened, and he looked sad.

"You miss your work, don't you? It was your whole life. I'm beginning to understand how much it hurts you to be away from it."

"I thought I'd die when I was forced to leave my career. But then I realized that I'd been dying *because* of it. I've needed this time to get my perspective straight." His eyes filled with tenderness as he studied her. "When I return to medicine, it won't be my life's only focus. I'll be a better doctor, because I'll be a complete person. Because of you."

He held her hand while she fell asleep. By the next morning she was recuperating, eating dry toast and watching him thoughtfully over cups of honeyed tea. "Since you're a great doctor, I'm trying to be a great patient. You see?"

He winked. "Your attitude certainly smells better."

That night, in honor of her recuperation, he offered her brandy with her tea. Soon she was smiling at him impishly and beckoning with a crooked finger. When he took her in his arms she felt a greater gentleness and confidence than she'd ever known before. They made love slowly, simply, but every sensation seemed full of portentous meaning. She tried to decipher it but lost track in the flood of emotion. Afterward she lay with her head on his shoulder, his warmth spreading through her, great changes whispering just beyond the edges of her control.

TWENTY-THREE

*H*e met her three weeks later, in Illinois, after she finished her work in the movie. They had three days before her first club date, in Chicago. She was booked in an unending grind of shows for the next four weeks. Her agent was thrilled.

She and Sebastien drove to the state's rugged northwestern corner and rented a cabin overlooking a steep ravine filled with wildflowers, a waterfall, and majestic granite boulders. Even in June the nights were crisp; they built a fire in the cabin's fieldstone fireplace and put the mattress by the hearth. Wrapped in quilts, they made love there with the slow, thorough attention of connoisseurs sampling the last bottle of a vintage wine.

She slipped away during the night and went to the bathroom. Behind a closed and locked door she washed herself and scrubbed between her legs with a white towel until she burned. Desperation fed her frantic examination of the towel. There wasn't even a tiny red trace of reassurance. She had begged her body to show some evidence of it by today. There was no reason for the delay. She always took her pills. She hadn't been careless.

The pristine towel mocked her. She threw it on the floor and sat down beside it, hugging her knees. Over the past two days she had searched her memories through the years with Elliot, trying to recall whether her pill-regulated cycle had ever been late before. It hadn't. She hoped, for both her and Sebastien's sakes, that there wasn't a baby. She had agreed to honor Sebastien's wishes. What now?

Compromise. But there might be no way to compromise on this.

Shivering, she got up and tiptoed through the cabin. Beside the mattress she paused, looking down at him as he slept. He lay on his back, the quilts twisted around him like a patchwork landscape that had been wrenched by earthquakes, his turbulence and powerful spirit evident even when he was at rest.

In her own way she was as strong as he, but if what she feared came true, she didn't know if strength would help. Wrapping herself in a blanket, she went to the cabin's front deck and sat on the edge, grateful that the darkness hid her and that the rush of the waterfall a few yards away muffled her crying.

He woke up and came searching for her, a long quilt bound around his waist and trailing the wooden floor in a graceful train that was suitably, and disturbingly, majestic. Unaware of his effect on her anxieties, he knelt down beside her and touched her damp face, then crooned a word of sorrow and took her in his arms.

"Nothing to cry over, dear Miracle," he whispered, rocking her. "We'll only be apart a little while longer. It's only a temporary setback. Only a temporary parting. You know that. Now convince me that the time will pass quickly, or I'll kidnap you."

She thought she'd die from missing him, even before he left.

There was something he felt he had to do, Sebastien told her on the last day of his visit. He conceded that it was impulsive and impractical, but he'd already chartered a private jet for the trip.

He wanted the two of them to fly down to Atlanta for the day. He wanted to see her father, at the nursing home. "Why?" she asked, bewildered.

"Perhaps the visit will help me deal with my own father."

"You met Pop ten years ago, and that was enough for me. I don't want you to see him again. He's pitiful. I'm ashamed of him in a different way, now."

"Be fair, love. I'm ashamed of my father, also, but I took you to see him."

While in Paris she had talked Sebastien into taking her to the hospital one night. She had needed to put Philippe de Savin in perspective for her own peace of mind. When she had seen him—thin, frail, paralyzed, unconscious—she could hardly imagine the commanding patriarch Sebastien described, the man who had alienated or destroyed most of his family because he had refused to live by anyone's traditions but his own. She felt that she understood him, to Sebastien's shock. No one understood his father, he told her.

She had touched one of the blue-veined hands, examined it with her fingertips, noted the strength and grace still evident in it. Her father's hands were like it; so were Sebastien's. She kept that observation private and told Sebastien that his father and hers were more alike than not, products of their own disappointments, their own inability to see the world outside their grand expectations.

So now Sebastien insisted on seeing Pop. She dreaded the visit. On the chartered jet she paced and fidgeted, not soothed by Sebastien's reassurances.

At the nursing home they located Pop by a sunny window, dressed in one of the jogging suits Amy had bought for him during an earlier visit. He was strapped into his wheelchair because he couldn't sit up without help. His face was slack and tranquil. He'd had several small strokes over the past year; his few coherent thoughts were expressed with garbled sounds and weak movements of one hand. One side of his mouth hung downward, and the skin around it sagged like wax that had been warmed and allowed to melt a little.

She kissed his pale, mottled forehead and watched his hand flutter; she felt sure that he recognized her, but whether he was pleased, she couldn't tell. All her life she'd had that problem with him, so it didn't depress her now.

"They cut his hair," she said, frowning as she touched the short, red-gray strands. She called a nurse's assistant over and asked about it. From the first she'd told the staff to leave his hair alone. "We hired a couple of new attendants," the woman explained. "One of them took Mr. Zack down to the barbershop by mistake. Just didn't know he wasn't supposed to."

"I want it left alone. He likes it long."

"We'll let it grow."

After the assistant walked away Amy promised, "It'll grow back, Pop."

He made a noise. It might have been an oath or a laugh. She glanced at Sebastien, who was watching them both closely. "It was his sign of rebellion," she said with a choked voice. "He ought to be able to keep it, even in this place." She patted Pop's shoulder then pointed to Sebastien. "This is Dr. de Savin, Pop. You met him once a long time ago. At a medieval fair up in the mountains. Remember?"

He blinked sluggishly and said nothing. Sebastien took Pop's hand and introduced himself, squeezing gently. Poignant hope rose in Amy's chest, but Pop looked at him with vague, curious eyes that soon moved away absently, then rested on her. "Ellen?"

He said the name with startling clarity. Amy felt goose bumps on her arms. To Sebastien she whispered, "My mother's name was Ellen." To Pop she said in a patient voice, "I'm Amy."

"Ellen." His hand wavered, crept forward, prodded her stomach with a bony knuckle. "Baaaah-be. Don't dah."

Amy felt the blood drain from her face. *Baby. Don't die.* She cleared her throat and told Sebastien, "My mother died when I was born. He's just gettin' confused."

Her hands trembled as she took his and held it on her knees. He repeated the warning, his crooked mouth having trouble with it but still managing to say it louder than before. Amy stroked his hand fervently. *I'll let Sebastien worry about curses. I refuse. Stop it, Pop.*

He said the words again, then shifted in his chair with growing agitation. Sebastien put a hand on Amy's shoulder, and she jumped. "I don't know what's gotten into him!"

"Calm down, love. Just talk to him." Sebastien leaned forward and placed his other hand on Pop's knee. "She is not Ellen," he said in his deep, attention-holding voice.

Pop stared at him. "She is not Ellen," Sebastien repeated. "She doesn't have a baby. She's not going to die."

Pop was mollified. His eyelids drooped, and after a few seconds he returned to staring benignly out the window. "I think he loves you more than you know," Sebastien told her, stroking her shoulder. "He obviously loved your mother very much."

"Maybe so, but I think he's always resented me because I was the reason she died. I was a big mistake, right from the beginning."

"*Look at me.*" The fierceness in his voice startled her. He grasped her face between his hands and frowned harshly into her eyes. "We are more than we were expected to be. So to hell with how we got here. I love you."

"Oh, Doc, I love you, too." Amy hugged him and concentrated on thinking positive thoughts. She would not let their future be affected by anyone's morbid memories—not Pop's, not Sebastien's, and especially not her own.

❦

She had sold Pop's place more than a year ago to cover his nursing-home bills. She'd given most of the furnishings to the Salvation Army and put the personal items—his circus memorabilia and the paintings—into storage at a warehouse. Sebastien wanted to see them, and she took him reluctantly.

"It makes me feel bad to look at them," she explained. "Just reminds me of too much, I guess. I spent so many years watching him paint and drink and smoke dope." Inside the small storage room she opened a wooden crate and gestured toward the canvases. "Flip through 'em and see what you think."

When he came to the ones of her, he stopped. "Of course he loved you. It shows here."

"You have a kinder eye than mine."

"When we furnish our homes, I'd like to have some of these framed. They should be displayed."

She kissed him gratefully, but shook her head. "I can't imagine putting these paintings out where they can see me."

"*See you?*"

"I feel like Pop's watchin' me when I look at these. And I'm not sure whether it's good watchin', if you know what I mean."

"I think it is."

She gently laid a hand along his cheek but looked at him with reproach. "You can be awful magnanimous about *my* father's sentiments."

"While still being utterly cynical about my own father's? Yes, but you see, dear Miracle, that's why you and I are so wonderful together. We want the best for each other. Without deception or dishonesty."

Guilt made her look away quickly. "I do want the best for you," she whispered, resting her head on his shoulder. She couldn't bring herself to tell him, not yet.

❦

In the back of her mind she considered the B-movie quality of the scene. All she needed was a white handkerchief to wave as she watched the big jet taxi away from the gate. A gold-and-pink sunset streamed across the horizon; standing by the concourse's windows, she rested her forehead on the glass and thought that the sunset would break her apart with its beauty.

She didn't cry, though she knew she would later. She tried to think in terms of beginnings, not endings. That was how Sebastien had wanted it too. That was why he'd waited until they reached the gate to give her the ring—a large sapphire surrounded by diamonds, with their initials and the date engraved inside the band. And he'd given her a sterling-silver cross that had belong to his mother. It was a Celtic design, delicately ornamented with a circle surrounding the crucifix. He told her that to the ancient Celts the circle had represented both the sun, and as a symbol of endlessness, eternity.

He had placed it around her neck on a woven sterling chain, and now, as she watched the jet leave, she clasped it in her fingertips. It was warm in the sunlight, a promise of faith and, knowing Sebastien, of protection.

This doctor knew how to deliver news with style. "You guessed right. The bunny has gone toes up."

Amy stared dully at a painting of frolicking lambs on the obstetrician's office wall. "Could we try CPR on it?"

"Welcome to the world of improbable odds. You're part of the two percent failure rate for the pill."

"A few weeks ago I was sick. I throw up everything but the kitchen sink for two days. I took my pills, but maybe they never hit home."

"It's possible. How do you feel about being pregnant?"

"Worried."

"I'm sure that you know what your options are."

"Yeah." She looked down at the flat abdomen covered by her sundress. She had tried to disassociate herself from the life that might be inside her. At the same time a deep, loving conviction had been growing along with that life. Bittersweet certainty made goose bumps rise on her skin. She put a hand on her stomach and said softly, "Hello, there. Your daddy wants you as much as I do. He just doesn't know it, yet. But don't get upset. Everything'll be fine."

"I guess I know which option you picked." The doctor sat back in her chair and began scribbling notes on a pad. "You're healthy, and everything seems okay with the pregnancy. Go see your regular ob/gyn when you get back to Los Angeles."

"I'll be traveling a lot in the next few months. That's bad, isn't it?"

"Not if you take care of yourself and arrange to have regular checkups."

"Can do."

"Will the baby's father be around?"

"Nope."

"He's not interested?"

"Oh, he'd be very interested, if I told him. But I can't do that to him right now. It's complicated."

Her hand became a fist. She *would* tell him when she was further along, when he had his family's situation under control, when he might let himself see shades of light instead of shadows. Until then, she could only take care of her health and think good thoughts for the baby inside her. *This* baby would not be born under a father's curse.

TWENTY-FOUR

*T*he cool autumn day turned rainy before noon; it was not a good day to be working the docks at a warehouse and shipping company, especially one that was poorly managed, losing money, and should never have been purchased by his father's officers in the first place. But Sebastien liked the release of pent-up energy that came from lifting heavy boxes of automobile parts onto the wooden pallets that lined the docks.

Here he confronted forces he understood. In a peculiar way they reminded him of performing heart surgery: His hands were guided by instinct, his energy could burst through obstacles, he made decisions and watched them spring immediately into action. Stacking boxes made him ache to be in an operating room again. He smiled to himself at the strangeness of the comparison.

He was no businessman, and he didn't pretend to be. Statistics bored him when they were attached to profit margins rather than blood pressures. There was nothing human about them, nothing touchable, nothing he could use to fix a damaged body and observe its owner's recuperation with a sense of the most primal victory, life over death.

When called upon to make a business decision he had to sort through advice from a dozen executives, weighing each one's points with painstaking skill but no talent; he was forced to hide his uncertainty behind a facade of confidence, lest they suspect his vulnerability and take advantage of it. How different from surgery, where he had known every answer before the question!

Today his frustration was at a peak. He took fiendish pride in the way the managers crept around him in their white shirts and dress slacks, trying to look useful and hide their dismay. None of his father's executives had ever donned canvas overalls and labored alongside the dock-workers. The dockworkers grinned at him now that their initial shock had worn off. They were enormous, brawny men of bawdy good humor. Sebastien remembered his mother's people in the fishing villages of Brittany, and felt at home.

He watched sinews strain in his hands and wondered how much longer it would be before those hands could return to the work they did best. He wanted his surgical career back; he wanted his life with Amy back.

She called every night at twelve o'clock Paris time, and he was always waiting. Depending on what city she was in, it would be late afternoon or early evening there, and she would be getting ready to go to work, two shows a night, three on the weekends. Often she and he talked until the minute she had to leave her hotel room. A month had passed since they parted. He would see her again next week. It seemed years away.

Anticipating her nightly calls kept him going. His days were filled with meetings, travel, and paperwork. His father still clung to life in the hospital, though each day he remained in a coma made it less likely he would survive. Annette had been released from the hospital a few weeks ago, but only because Sebastien had arranged nursing care and daily visits from physical therapists at home.

What he could not arrange, no matter how hard he tried, was her contentment. Her jealousy over his new power had riddled the core of their relationship. Annette's injuries and her grief over losing Giancarlo were no less potent than her suspicions about Sebastien's authority. He had lost his sister, the one member of the family who had been close to him.

He threw boxes atop the highest stacks and felt neglected muscles stretch taut in his torso. The company's general manager came over for the fourth time in a half hour, wringing his hands. "Please, sir, there's no need for this. I really don't understand the point."

"Stop bothering me, or I'll put you to work at a job that requires more than a talent for making excuses."

The manager turned red when the dockworkers failed to hide their smiles. "Sir, I'm tired of this humiliation! You complain about my organization of the warehouse, you say that my accounting procedures are unsatisfactory, and now you try to show me that my dockworkers are overburdened and underpaid. I won't accept this! I'll resign if you push me too far!"

Sebastien paused long enough to glower at him. "Your resignation is accepted. Good-bye."

So much for diplomacy in management.

❦

Annette's anger was waiting for him, as usual, when he returned home that evening. From the hospital bed in her suite, she glared at him, though her eyes were glazed from pain medication. "You made quite a show today, I hear. Demonstrating your affinity for the downtrodden employees. Firing a reasonably efficient general manager. How melodramatic."

Sebastien smiled and gritted his teeth. "I wanted to see if the docks were being managed as badly as I thought. They were. I don't have your diplomatic knack for getting the best from mediocre managers; I have to solve problems in other ways."

"You humiliated the lower managers as well."

"They deserved it. Calm down, sister. You're not well enough to dabble in business gossip, yet. It's a strenuous hobby." He tolerated his sister's irrational jealousy because of her condition; he hoped it would pass as she recuperated. But it was one more reason that he counted every day, sometimes every hour, until Amy finished her club tour next month. At least he could visit her then.

Sebastien sank into a thickly stuffed chair near the foot of Annette's hospital bed. He crossed his legs and pretended to be absorbed in brushing a bit of dust from the perfect crease in his trouser leg. He had showered and changed into a fresh suit at the office; he had other duties to perform, and had only stopped at home to soothe Annette's daily need for business news.

"I'm attending the opera league dinner tonight in your place," he told her.

"You loathe the opera. The only music you've ever considered worthy of serious attention is that squawking American jazz."

"That's beside the point. Is there any message you'd like for me to convey? They've asked me to say a few words on behalf of your volunteer work."

She jerked the bedcovers. "Oh, just tell them you've taken over everything. That by the time I'm able to return you'll have grown so accustomed to being in control that you'll ignore me just as Papa always has. Tell them that Papa would be very pleased if he woke up and found that the prodigal son has finally assumed command."

"If you waste your energy on paranoia, your recovery will take even longer."

"Why should I care?" Tears slid down her thin cheeks. "I've lost Giancarlo, I'm an invalid, and you're just waiting for Papa to die so that you can inherit everything that you already control!"

Sebastien leaned his head back on the chair and shut his eyes. Annette would always distrust him, even though he didn't doubt that she loved him. Their father's stubborn favoritism toward him had scarred her, as it had scarred their brother Jacques.

"I only want my freedom," he told Annette, as he had countless times before. "As soon as you're well, I'm going back to America."

"Oh, I know, I know, and you'll live there and return to medical practice and marry your strange American woman."

Sebastien straightened and watched her closely. His tolerance sank to a low point. "Who has been discussing her with you?"

"Oh, the servants told me about her. That she's some

kind of actress who has an odd voice and performs magic tricks. That she has a tattoo on one wrist and a scar on her face. I will never believe you'd marry someone like *that*."

He stood, went to the side of her bed, and took her hand. He looked down at her until color rose under her tears and she turned her head to stare at the far wall. "Don't glare at me like that, Sebastien. I apologize." Her face crumpled. "I don't like being hateful to you. I'm so confused. I'm so— so furious with Papa for putting you in this predicament and leaving us to fight over it."

"He hasn't left yet."

"He'll never come out of the coma."

Sebastien subdued a grim smile. "There is the sun, the moon, and our father. I'd bet against the first two rising, if I were you."

He was right. A week later, their father opened his eyes and, in a firm whisper, demanded attention.

❧

He was paralyzed from the neck down, a fact not even his indomitable willpower could change. "Does this please you?" he whispered.

Sebastien turned from studying the catheter bag tied to the foot of the bed. He kept his expression neutral and his bearing rigid, while inside he struggled with sympathy he did not want to feel. "No. I don't enjoy running your affairs for you."

"Why did you come back?"

"For Annette's sake."

"Ah. You will never admit any sense of duty to me."

"I have none."

"Why did you come here today, then?"

"Because Annette requested a firsthand report on your condition. She loves you. It's amazing, considering how little you deserve her love."

"Oh, my son, my son. You think that I don't love her? and you?"

"Please, no confessions now. They don't ring true."

"Why should I tell less than the truth at this point?"

"So it has been your secret all these years? How interesting."

"I've always wanted the best for my children."

"That must be why three of them are dead."

"Hear me out. I wanted the best for all, but a wise man knows that he must concentrate his hopes on the strongest child. After Antoine . . . that child was you."

"Antoine wanted to be your favorite. I never did. Why force your goals on me?"

"*Force my goals*? I wanted to give you my *dreams*."

"The only thing I wanted from you was Antoine, and Bridgette, and Mother. Which you couldn't give back to me."

"I know. I thought the rest would make up for it . . . eventually."

Sebastien sank into a hard metal chair near the hospital bed. He stared at his father in shock. "You ask me to believe that you have badgered and manipulated me all these years out of guilt?"

His father's gaze moved weakly around the room, as if searching for answers. "Guilt and pride make terrible companions. One fights the other. But yes, *yes*, I felt that you had suffered nobly and should be rewarded nobly."

"Even if the reward was nothing I wanted."

"You didn't *know* what you wanted, except to punish me. I reasoned that your attitude would change, in time." He managed a thin smile. "Well, look at me now. Have I been punished enough?"

Sebastien refused to answer. To say yes would end thirty years of bitterness. "Didn't Jacques and Annette deserve rewards?"

"No. They were raised in luxury; they had all the advantages."

"So did I."

"But their strength was never tested, the way yours was."

"Mother, Antoine, Bridgette—their deaths were no test of my strength. If I'd been strong, I would have killed you. For a long time, I thought about it. I was ashamed of my weakness for not doing it."

"A child considering murder. That *is* strength. Come

here. I can't turn my head to look at you over there. Come. Look straight into my eyes."

Sebastien felt vulnerable, threatened, then angry. The emotions shook loose deep memories of the confusion that had racked him in the years after the tragedy. He leapt to his feet and bent over his father's bed, clasping the handrails on either side, staring down into his father's eyes with fury.

"You can take your revenge now," his father whispered, holding his gaze with unblinking command. Understanding numbed Sebastien's fury. He heard the blood roaring in his ears. With horror he continued looking into his father's eyes. They taunted him. "Kill me," the soft, determined voice ordered.

Sebastien leaned on the handrails for support. He realized that his legs had gone weak. "You want salvation, not death."

"Isn't that your specialty, Doctor?"

"To ruin myself for your benefit? No. Not any longer."

"Then have mercy. You think I want to live like this? I know I can't last long, but this is . . . torture."

"I know that."

"Ah. You approve."

"No." Trembling, he put a hand alongside his father's cheek. The older man's eyes flickered with surprise at the tender touch. "I wish I could help you."

"Why?"

"Because of my medical training."

"No. Love."

Sebastien stepped back. The word hung in the air between them, unparried, unreturned, but not denied. "Rest now. I'll be back tomorrow."

"I'll be waiting." His father's eyes were warmer than Sebastien had ever seen them before.

Sebastien came back every day after that. He and his father sometimes didn't talk; the effort was too much for Philippe physically and too much for Sebastien emotionally. When they did talk, it was about the businesses. The mood was wary. Sebastien wouldn't admit that he wanted to comfort his father, and his father would never admit the need for it.

🌿

"Hi," she said in her most sultry voice.

Sebastien cradled the phone closer to his ear and, shutting his eyes as he conjured her image, lay back on the bed. "Hello, love."

"How was your father today?"

"Growing weaker. He has fluid in his lungs." Sebastien hesitated, then added gruffly, "I realize something today. I can stand to be around him now because I know that he no longer has the power to keep you and me apart. I have that satisfaction. And also, after seeing how you reconciled your feelings for your father—how you have become stronger *because* of him—I feel that I should be able to do the same with mine."

"I'm glad, Doc. I'm so glad you don't despise your father anymore."

"Don't credit me with too much generosity, Miracle."

She sighed and changed the subject. "How is your sister?"

"She took her first walk outdoors. The therapist wrapped her in a heavy coat and they walked across the garden and back."

"Terrific! And how are Jacques and Louise?"

"Angry with me. I wouldn't let them go to a movie. *Bambi.*"

"Why not? Have you ever seen it? It's a classic!"

"I heard that the fawn's mother is killed. That, I decided, is not good for them to see right now." He frowned, feeling foolish. "I don't know much about children. Do you think I was wrong?"

After a second her voice came back soft and gentle. "No, Doc, I think you're a sweetie."

"Ah. Hmmm." Her sentiment pleased him but ignited his loneliness even more. He couldn't think of a dignified response.

"Doc? Those kids want to love you. If you'd only give them a chance, they'd climb inside you and never leave."

"It's not good for children to be too dependent."

"You want them to be little grown-ups? Don't do that to 'em. Let 'em be carefree and have fun and . . . help 'em learn from their mistakes. Don't expect little folks to be perfect."

"Miracle, you know the value of self-reliance as much as I do."

"Yeah, we both had to grow up too fast. I *understand* your point, Doc, I really do. But just because *we* had it rough, why should Jacques and Louise? I wouldn't wish my childhood on those kids. Would you wish *yours* on 'em?"

"Are you saying that I want them to suffer the way I did? That I'm being cruel?"

"Not *cruel*. Just forgetful. Can't you remember what you were like before your mother died?"

"No."

"You have to, Doc. If you want to be good with kids, you *have* to remember what it was like to be a kid."

He masked his discomfort in exasperation. "Why are we talking about children? I don't need to be good with children."

"Yes, you do." Her voice didn't rise, but the light-hearted melody had a new, urgent pitch to it. "I want you to try. Be fair to me. To us. Try to change your attitude toward having a family."

"And if I can't?" Her tense silence made him regret his bluntness immediately. "Don't answer that. It was a foolish question. There's no point in speculating about the distant future. I'm sure we'll reach an understanding."

She said softly, "If you don't ever want children, it'll hurt me worse than I can tell you."

The anguish in her voice shocked him. He'd thought there was nothing that could drive her away from him, but suddenly he realized this problem might. "I'm sure we'll reach an understanding," he repeated, shaken.

"We'll have to."

Strained silence filled the phone line between them. "So . . . how was your day?" she asked. The question drove a wedge between the awkward mood and more comfortable conversation.

"I'm fine," he lied.

"You sound tired. Was it another long day at the office?"

"Yes. Chaos. I suppose it's always like this when a corporation cleans house."

"I bet you wield a mean broom."

"Of course. I'm a dictator. All surgeons are, by their nature. I belong in the operating room. And will be returning there within the next few months. Ah! I have so much remedial study to do to catch up!"

"Doc, you'll be fine. Most heart surgeons would give their right aortas to know as much as you've *forgotten*."

"Such wonderful faith. Now I know why I love talking to you." He paused, then added gruffly, "Why I love you."

She made a soft, broken sound. "Love you, too. Miss you. Wait." She took a moment to get herself under control. He heard her clearing her throat and sniffing. Her loneliness merged with his and made him rub the ache in his eyes.

"Only a few more days," he reminded her.

"I woke up kissing my pillow this morning. I was on a plane at the time. The flight attendants were staring at me. It was embarrassing."

He smiled. "You're in Kansas City tonight?"

"Yep. I'll be at a club called Happy's tonight through Sunday." She paused. "And then I'll be on a plane to Paris."

He shut his eyes, anticipating her arrival. "I have a surprise for you. I've arranged for you to take another flight when you arrive there. To Rennes."

"Rennes?"

"I'll meet you there, and we'll drive through the countryside. I've reserved a cottage in Beg-Meil. It's one of the prettiest seaport towns in Brittany."

"Brittany—the province your mother was from?"

"Yes."

"I'd love to go there! But . . . one favor. Instead of meeting me at the airport in Rennes, could you meet me at a hotel there?"

"You sound so mysterious."

"No, I just want everything to be *perfect* when I see you. I want to meet you in private." Her tone became teasing.

"I've got a list of lewd things I want to do the second I get my paws on you, and I can't do 'em at an airport. Not without drawing a crowd, anyway."

"I like your impatience, love. All right. I'll make the arrangements. Lewd, hmmm? I can't wait."

"Oh, I'm gonna shock you." Her voice went on one of its whimsical flights upward, as it did whenever she was tense. "You can *count* on it."

Sebastien worried about the nervousness in her voice. "Yesterday you said that your movie was in the editing process. Any more news?"

"Oh, yes! I nearly forgot! My part didn't get cut! I have a good ten minutes of screen time."

"Marvelous!"

She sighed. "Careers are not made on ten minutes of goofy lines like, 'Hon, your duck just ate the laces out of my tennis shoes.' This *ain't* art."

"I'm sure I'll enjoy it. I've always preferred Jerry Lewis over François Truffaut."

"Yeah," she said drolly, "but that's because your idea of entertainment is playing Simon Says with cadavers."

"What is Simon Says?"

"It's a game. I'll show you how to play it when we meet in Rennes."

"I'm counting the days."

"Four. Plus six hours and forty-seven minutes that are left in today."

"Amy?"

"Hmmm?"

"After you arrive, let's discuss wedding plans." The silence that settled over the phone bewildered him. "Amy?"

"Yes. Yeah. It'd be a very good idea. Very good."

"Is something wrong?"

"Of course not. I was just thinking."

"About what?"

"Oh, that I hope you like the way I look. I've gained a little weight."

He exhaled in relief. Women and their vanity. "Is that all? Miracle, I hold nothing against a woman who likes to eat."

"That's what I'm afraid of. That you might not want to hold anything against me."

Smiling, he shook his head. "Never fear. Whatever you've added, I'll love it."

She made a garbled sound and changed the subject. Later, after he hung the phone up and lay in bed frowning into space, Sebastien realized that he was the one who felt afraid.

❦

One night when he returned from the office he found Marie visiting Annette. They were in the enormous drawing room in the villa's lower level. Annette lay on a couch bundled in pale yellow blankets; Marie sat on the edge of a Louis XVI chair upholstered in tapestry as colorful as she was dark. She looked crisp and formal in a black sheath dress. Gone was all sign of her earth-mother phase. She even wore her trademark pearls.

She stiffened as Sebastien walked into the room and scowled when he kissed her hand. "I hear that you plan to marry again. An American actress."

"She's first and foremost a comedienne, then an actress. And yes, I do plan to marry her."

"We've been divorced less than a year. I never expected that you would miss married life enough to take it up again so soon."

"I amaze myself, sometimes. And how are you?"

"Busy, very busy. I'm starting a chain of bookstores."

"I wish you very good luck."

She dismissed luck with an elegant wave of one hand. "When has luck meant more than serious work and the ability to put aside sentiment while one achieves a goal?"

Sebastien laughed softly and went to a marbled fireplace, where he leaned against the mantel and lost his thoughts in the crackling orange flames. Marie had just given a neat summation of her attitude toward life. It was certainly the attitude she had applied to their marriage. He didn't resent her for it—in fact, he had shared her view of life for many years—but he was damned glad that Amy had saved him from it.

". . . please pardon Sebastien," Annette was saying. Sebastien lifted his head and saw that both she and Marie were watching him, Annette with amusement, Marie with cool puzzlement. "His mind wanders these days. He's not suited for business. Too much pressure."

He smiled. "Yes. I'll give it all to you, willingly. A few months and I'm sure you'll be taking my place."

"I'll hold you to your word."

Sebastien was still distracted by pleasant thoughts of the future. It occurred to him that he had no emotional investment in Marie anymore, and he regarded her as if she were a stranger rather than the woman who had shared so much tragedy with him. He went to her quickly, bent down, and kissed her forehead. "I'm glad to see you again," he said sincerely. "Please excuse me for not visiting longer, but I have some paperwork to do. Good night."

She gaped at him. "What has come over you? You've changed. I hardly know you."

"A blessing, wouldn't you say?" He kissed her forehead again and left the room, feeling contented and free. Tomorrow he would meet Amy in Rennes. Nothing mattered except spending a few precious days with her. More than ever she was the center of his self-discovery and the reason that he liked what he was learning about himself.

❦

Rennes was as old and imposing as the granite that composed nearly all of its eighteenth-century buildings. It was a handsome though somewhat pompous neoclassical city, with a few large boulevards and the distinguished Palais de Justice, where once the regional parliament had met. The newer areas bustled with modern industries and crowded suburbs.

Sebastien drove through the city without noticing it. His mouth was dry with excitement. He pulled a sterling pocket watch from the trousers of his pinstriped black suit and checked the time. He had not wanted to be dressed so formally for her arrival, but business had kept him an hour late. He hadn't wanted to waste minutes changing clothes. It was a long drive from Paris.

When he reached the hotel he pressed his suitcase and several francs into a porter's hands and called the suite number to him as he strode through a plush lobby. He had no patience for the ancient elevator with its heavily ornamented cage; instead he went to the wide staircase at the lobby's back and ran the four flights to the top. The porter, panting for breath, scrambled after him. By the time he caught up, Sebastien was halfway down the hall on the fourth floor, searching for the suite's door.

"Four-fifteen. There, sir." the porter said, pointing. "The lady arrived an hour ago." To Sebastien's dismay, the overzealous man leapt ahead of him and knocked on the heavy door. "Porter, madame!"

Exasperated, Sebastien put a restraining hand on the man's arm. "No need to carry on, thank you. You may go."

"Come in!" Amy called from somewhere inside the suite. The porter pushed the door open and Sebastien forgot everything except the desire to see her. He stepped inside and halted, his gaze going immediately to where she sat, smiling at him over the back of a brocaded couch, one arm artfully draped along the top. Her auburn hair was a mass of soft waves pulled back on one side with a gold comb. What little he could see of her was covered in a silky black jacket over a matching blouse that scooped low on her breasts. Her green eyes crinkled with amusement.

Her pose and her appearance were so purposefully dramatic—and so effective—that he felt frantic with a mixture of pride, arousal, and love. She had gone to some trouble to please him.

"This is the one you told me to look out for, isn't he, madame?" the porter asked.

She nodded. "He is, indeed. Thank you." Her French was charming with its eccentric American drawl. Sebastien craved the sound of her voice.

He pushed more money into the porter's hand, then led him to the door. The porter grinned and waved as he shut it behind him. Sebastien pivoted and walked toward her, his hands held out, but she didn't leap up and run to him, as he'd expected. Instead she stood with elegant slowness, swirling the long silk jacket around her and holding it closed in front of her stomach. He saw that she wore a slender black skirt and delicate black pumps. Around her neck was the Celtic cross, and on her left hand was the ring he had given her.

The girl he had fallen in love with more than ten years before had become a woman of style and beauty, and he had never been more aware of the fact than now. But there was something new about her, too—a reserve, a mystery. Sebastien frowned a little as he circled the couch and reached for her. "No," she said, stepping back and grasping both of his hands. "Just let me look at you for a minute."

Bewildered, he stood still and gazed down at her, noting now that he was close that her face had a pallor but her cheeks were flushed, and the makeup on her eyes failed to disguise their fatigue or anxiety.

"I love you," she said, staring at him with an anguish he couldn't fathom.

Sebastien squeezed her hands. "What is it? What's wrong?" He glanced down and saw the slight thickening around her abdomen, revealed now that she'd let the jacket fall open. He stared at it, not wanting to believe what it might mean.

"I didn't want to tell you before now," she said, her voice troubled. "You were overcome with your family's problems. I wanted you to have time to get them under control a little."

The sharp kick of truth made his breath short. She was pregnant. He stepped back from her and dropped her hands. "When did this happen?"

"In Paris. When I was staying with you at your sister's home." He listened through the roar in his ears as she reminded him of her flu and explained how it might have affected her birth control pills. "You know I wouldn't have done this deliberately," she told him. "I wasn't careless. Please believe that."

He knew before he raised his eyes to her wretched expression that he believed her. "How it happened is not the problem. Why didn't you tell me as soon as you suspected?"

Tears glistened on her lashes. "I wanted the baby, and was certain that you didn't." She hesitated, her eyes searching his. "That you don't." Her shoulders slumped.

He struggled not to shout at her. "Of course I don't! I have every reason to believe that you and I have no better chance of producing a healthy baby than Marie and I had!' He swallowed convulsively and forced a calmer voice. "I told you I couldn't go through that again. You betrayed my trust by not telling me about this pregnancy immediately."

"I was trying to make it easier for us both. So many first pregnancies miscarry during the first three months . . . I was afraid I'd lose the baby. If I had, you never would have known."

"Goddamn your secrets! I don't want you to be a martyr. I want you to include me in *every* decision that might hurt you, that might hurt us both."

"I've been walking a fine line between what's best for us and what's best for our baby. It hurt not to tell you."

What's best for our baby. He felt a strangling combination of love for her and fury at what she wanted. *The baby will miscarry. Or be born deformed. Or cause Amy to die from complications.* He was certain of it, more than just from a rational judgment based on his past attempts at fatherhood, but from a deep, mocking fear that hollowed his insides. "My wishes don't matter," he said curtly. "That's obvious."

There was only silence between them, a frozen silence as she stared straight into his eyes. He saw the anger and disappointment in hers. But she gave him one chance to save himself. "Tell me what you'd prefer that I do," she whispered.

He sank back into the old darkness. "Have an abortion."

Slowly she lowered herself to the couch and, folding her hands in her lap, stared straight ahead. "No. I have enough faith for both of us—for all three of us. I even have enough faith to think that you don't really mean what you just said, and all it would take to change your mind is for me to have a healthy baby."

"You won't have a healthy baby." He clapped his hands in brusque dismissal. "So be it! If you have no respect for my wishes, at least don't make this more difficult." Out of fear grew a need to bully her, to take charge of the remnants of his shaky control. He would fight his superstitions any way he could. He snapped his fingers at her. "We'll be married as soon as I can arrange the ceremony. You will *not* return to America. We'll take an apartment in Paris. I'll select several doctors for you to see on a regular basis, and you will—"

"Go back to Paris tonight and take the first flight home."

He looked down at her livid face. She sat on the edge of the sofa, chin up, hands clenched so hard the bones of her knuckles looked as if they might break through the skin. "I won't have your confusion and your anger around this baby for the next five or six months. And I won't marry you like some embarrassed teenager who's afraid of what people will think. Our child is not going to see our marriage license some day and wonder if we really wanted to get married. I'll marry you after this baby is born, *if* I'm sure you love it as much as you love me."

"You're not going back to America and live alone, much less travel and work. I forbid it. Don't you understand? No matter how I feel about this pregnancy, I want to take care of you."

Her stiffness faded. Tears crept down her face and she looked up at him with yearning. "You wouldn't be *taking care* of me if I knew that you hated our child."

"I don't hate what I can't believe in!" He slashed the air with his hands. *"Don't you understand?* There's too much pain involved in waiting and hoping. I don't want to drive you away, but don't ask me to play the happy, expectant father!"

She wiped roughly at her face. "All right. But you'll love the baby when it gets here. So why not pretend it's going to be fine?"

"Listen to me." He bent over her, his hands out in fierce supplication. "I don't even know anymore what kind of father I'd make. I wonder if I'm even capable of showing the kind of warmth and patience that children need."

"You are."

"Damm it! You live inside some kind of hopeful little cocoon that's no more protection than a coat of thin air! You think if you want something badly enough, you'll have it."

"I wanted you. I have you. I wanted to be in show business. I am. So don't make fun of my cocoon."

"You can't always win." He sent a scathing look at her abdomen, and she pulled the jacket over it. "This time I think you're being a fool."

She stood, wobbling a little. "Maybe. At least your reaction is no worse than I expected. Excuse me." She kicked her high-heel shoes off and disappeared quickly through a doorway to the suite's bedroom. He followed her to the pink-marble bath and found her in the confines of the toilet closet, retching into the commode. When he knelt beside her and pressed a wet washcloth to her forehead she began to sob.

He cleaned her face, ignoring her when she tried to push his hands away. Finally, looking exhausted, she leaned against him. He helped her up and poured a glass of water so that she could rinse her mouth. They were both silent and avoided looking at each other. He led her to the suite's damask-draped bed and they lay down. She turned away from him but didn't protest when he curved himself to her back and hips. He put his arm over her but avoided touching her abdomen. If she noticed, she didn't comment, but clasped his hand tightly inside both of hers.

His throat was raw, so he didn't say anything, either. Nothing was needed. He felt bitter and frightened, and he didn't want this baby. She knew. He loved her. She knew that, too. As for the rest, she'd have to accept that they were going to deal with this situation *his* way, which meant she would come back to Paris and live under his strict supervision.

Eventually she fell asleep. He considered it a sign of surrender, and kissed her tangled hair before allowing his own emotional exhaustion to take him under. His dreams were vivid and troubling; in them she died or disappeared, and he saw faceless babies.

When he woke up the room was dark and he was alone in bed. He ran through the suite, looking for her, but she and her luggage were gone. He found a note tucked under the handle of his own suitcase. *You work on loving our baby, and I'll take care of myself.*

TWENTY-FIVE

$\mathcal{A}$ week later, when she finished her set and walked off stage at a club in Minneapolis, Sebastien was waiting for her. She wavered between welcome and dread when she saw him, his thin black windbreaker pushed back along the side of his powerful torso, his expression above a pale golf shirt as cool as the Minnesota summer, his hands shoved aggressively into the front pockets of tailored slacks. He was an elegant anomaly posed against a background of neon liquor signs and autographed publicity photos from road comics no one knew.

Leaving him in the Rennes hotel suite had been one of the hardest decisions of her life, but she didn't regret it. She had to force him to choose between his past and their future.

She walked to him slowly, her knees weak. She wanted so badly to hold out her arms and beg him to say that everything was all right, that he had come here to say that he wanted the baby. Then she noticed the stoic little woman in a stern brown raincoat standing beside him with an enormous leather suitcase by her feet.

Amy glanced from his matronly, graying companion to his frown. Nothing she could say would sum up her dilemma better than the truth. "I haven't changed my mind, but I'm glad that you found me," she said, halting close to him and looking directly into his eyes.

They betrayed his turmoil for a moment before he

cleared his throat and gestured brusquely toward the woman. "Meet Magda Diebler. Frau Diebler, this is Amy Miracle."

"Hello, Frau Miracle," Frau Diebler said with an accent as heavy as bratwurst.

"Hello." Amy shot Sebastien an astonished look. He jerked his head toward the open area behind him, which included the lobby, bar, and club offices. "Is there someplace where you and I can talk in private?"

"I'm the headliner. I've got my own dressing closet. I think we can both squeeze in there."

"Good. Frau Diebler, excuse us a moment."

Frau Diebler straightened and gave a little snap with her head. Her braided coil and salt-and-pepper hair shifted forward with the subtle salute. "*Ja*, Herr Doctor."

Amy led him down a side hall to a narrow door that bore a sign hand-lettered with her name. Occupying the tiny space inside was a vanity, a bathroom, a clothes rack, and one folding chair for guests. She lowered herself onto the vanity bench as he took the chair. She could feel the pulse ticking swiftly in her throat.

"You mock our love and respect for each other," he said stiffly.

"I refuse to live with you unless you try to love our baby." She leaned forward and grasped his hands. "No baby of mine is gonna be born unwanted . . . or at least, it's never gonna *know* that its father didn't want it. You saw what I went through because of my father. Dear Lord, Sebastien, *look what you went through because of yours*. Don't do that to your own child."

He imprisoned her hands inside his and gripped them harshly. A muscle worked in his cheek. "That's *exactly* what I'm trying to avoid. Another mistake."

"Or a chance to make things right!"

"You and I have our lives in order now. Every happiness we want is within our grasp, because we're together. I've waited so long for this. I don't want to feel cursed anymore. I don't want anything to jeopardize our relationship."

"I know, Doc. Don't you think I want to protect what we have between us? But now that includes a baby. I didn't plan it, and I certainly wouldn't have deliberately gone against your wishes. It happened. If you believe in signs and omens, take this as a *good* one."

He released her hands with an exclamation of angry defeat. "It's pointless to discuss this. I have a plane to catch."

"You just got here!"

"I came here for one purpose. It won't take long. I have a dozen meetings with my father's executives this week. Annette is having skin grafts on her legs, Jacques has been suspended from school for fighting, and yesterday he even blackened his sister's eye. I punish him and he hates me. I don't know what to say to him. My father has developed a kidney infection." He rammed a hand through his hair. "I want to be here, but I *have* to be there."

With a sympathetic murmur she slid forward and reached for him. He let her put her arms around his neck and hold him, and after a second he gave in and embraced her desperately, pulling her between his legs so that her torso pressed tight against his.

She held him so hard her arms quivered. "Don't you know I'd do almost anything to make you happy? I didn't want to upset you this way. At first I even hoped that I'd miscarry, to make it easy for both of us. But this baby wants so badly to be born—it's healthy, and it's growing, even though it was conceived against all odds. We're *supposed* to have this baby."

"Miracle, your pregnancy was only an accident."

"You believe so strongly in fate bringing bad things into our lives. Why can't you believe that fate brings *good* things, too?"

"We're talking about your *life*! I don't want to lose you, Miracle! I don't want you hurt or disappointed."

"Then don't hate me for wanting this baby."

"You know that's not it. I'm afraid for you, scared out of my mind. Nothing you can say will change that."

"Go home," she whispered, her voice broken. "And stop worrying about me. That's one reason I waited to tell you about the baby. You have too much to worry about, already.

I don't need for you to take care of me. I need for you to be ready to accept this baby when it's born."

He set her back on the bench, his expression shuttered and hard. "As I said, I have a plane to catch. There's no more time for arguing."

"Doc, did you come all the way to Minnesota just to— who is that woman?"

"Your nurse. She's a specialist in obstetrics. Here." He whipped one side of his coat back and pulled a thick envelope from an inner pocket. He tossed the envelope on her lap. "Her credentials. I've made all the arrangements for her work visa. She goes where you go. When you have medical problems—"

"I *won't* have problems."

"She'll take care of you. Please." He looked away, his jaw clenched. Amy watched his struggle for control and knew that his anger hid a great deal of fear and sadness. When he looked at her again he had regained his composure. "You owe me this much."

"I don't want a stranger hovering over me, Sebastien." *I want you, you arrogant, stubborn bastard.*

He tapped the envelope. "There's a set of credit cards for you. And checks for a New York bank account in your name. Buy whatever you'd like. See that you and Frau Diebler travel in comfort. You don't have to share your hotel rooms with her. I suggest that you book suites for the two of you."

"Damn, I was plannin' to let her sleep at the foot of my bed, like a German shepherd."

"Then you won't argue about this? You accept her?"

"A spy? A warden? Is that what you want me to accept? Don't you *ever* trust me? You left me with a *guardian* when you went off to Africa, remember? I didn't like it then, and I don't like it now!"

"You liked it well enough, as I recall." His voice was low and brutal. "Perhaps I should locate Jeff Atwater again."

Her hands rose to her mouth, and she looked at him in shock. His cruelty had the effect of a hand twisting inside her chest. She already saw the painful backlash in his eyes. "I can't believe you said that to me. I don't deserve it."

His control exploded. "I want you to be safe!" He stood, kicking his chair aside. "I want to know you won't suffer during this insane pregnancy! I can't stay in America with you, and I can't force you to come back to France with me! The least you can do is keep the damned nurse with you for my peace of mind!"

She threw the envelope at a wall and went to him, winding her hands into his shirt and trying to shake him. "Hiring a nurse to traipse after me is not going to solve your problem! Please, Doc, try to want this baby. Try to love it. I don't want to go the next five months without seeing you."

"The choice is yours. Anytime you decide to come to me, you'll be welcome."

She grabbed one of his hands and pressed it to the thickness at her waist. "Say that to both of us."

His hand trembled on her abdomen. He looked at her with bitter resignation. "Will you accept the nurse?" he asked between gritted teeth.

Slowly she moved his hand away. She leaned against him, her anger fading. There was no winner on either side of this battle. She rested her head on his shoulder but turned it away from him. "She's a poor substitute for what I need from you, but I guess she's the best you can do. All right. I accept."

He stepped back, hesitated, then raised a hand to stroke her hair. She continued to keep her head twisted away from him, but a soft cry escaped her. She listened to the room's door open and close, then slumped onto the vanity's bench and covered her face.

When she got herself under control she went back to the lobby and found Magda Diebler gaping at a comic who was preparing to go onstage with a bouquet of white mums tucked into his unzipped fly. Amy touched her arm, and even through the raincoat it felt plump and hard. *I bet she'll want to watch wrestling on TV.*

The nurse turned wide blue eyes on her. "Hello, again, Frau Miracle. This is interesting, your work." She went back to watching the comic wiggle his mums.

Amy looked toward the club's front doors, her throat

hurting with trapped sorrow. Sebastien was alone with his disappointment and anger, heading back to the airport, only a few minutes separating him from her. Even her anger couldn't stop the ache of missing him or the defeat clotting her veins like cold syrup. She dreaded the next six months of lonely waiting, but more than that she dreaded what would happen if she had to choose their child over him, afterward.

❦

Her first confrontation with Magda Diebler came the next morning, when the nurse stormed her hotel room at six A.M. Amy drew a robe around her floppy T-shirt and sat on the edge of the bed in a stupor, while Frau Diebler, who *did not* want to indulge in first-name familiarity, sat stiffly in a chair, a starched brown dress emphasizing a middle-aged physique that was fueled by high-fat foods and discipline. Frau Diebler opened a black-leather notebook.

"Let's begin by discussing your daily schedule, Frau Miracle."

"I finish work at two A.M., most nights. I go to bed around three. My daily schedule begins at noon. And if you ever wake me up at this time again, I'll call hotel security and tell them that a foreign terrorist has broken into my room."

"Your schedule is not healthy," Frau Diebler made a note. "I will be reporting your condition to Dr. de Savin twice weekly. You may refuse to cooperate with me if you wish, but every infraction *will* be included in those reports."

"I follow every instruction my obstetrician gives me. I eat right, I exercise right, I get plenty of rest, I do *everything* possible to take care of myself and this baby. Not to mention all the other stuff I do." She jabbed a finger at her abdomen for emphasis. "I read children's books to this baby. I put headphones on my belly and play Sesame Street music for this baby. I *talk* to this baby all the time. We're a team. We don't need a watchdog."

Frau Diebler was oblivious. "Now I am part of your team, also. We begin." She opened a black medical bag by her feet. "Every morning I will check your blood pressure and your temperature. Please lie on your side and lift your robe."

Amy stared at the thickest thermometer she'd ever seen. It had an industrial look. She recalled the most humiliating moment of her stomach virus, in France, and Sebastien's gentle amusement at her reaction. *Love, only Americans put thermometers in their mouths. Now turn over, please.*

"Never again," she told Frau Diebler. "I had my experience with European thermometers already, thank you. I'll buy you a nice American thermometer."

"Don't tell me you're one of those Americans who are embarrassed to admit that they have rectums."

The absurdity of the situation burst from Amy in a strangled laugh. *Good Lord, it's six A.M. and I'm discussing rectums with this woman.* "I know how to find mine and how to use it. That's all that matters, I'm aware that Europeans have their own ways of doing things, but don't try to hornswoggle me. And if you've got any herbal suppositories in that little bag of yours, you can forget about them, too."

"This will go in my report!"

"Frau Diebler, you could find yourself bound and gagged in the hold of a cargo plane to Frankfurt, if you're not careful."

"No, you will honor your agreement with Dr. de Savin. *Compromise.* He told me so as he left last night. He said you will keep your word to him."

That was true. Amy grimly considered honorable alternatives. She scrubbed her hair out of her face and gave Frau Diebler a smile of reconciliation. "All right, let's start over. Let's be pleasant to each other. Tell me a little bit about yourself. What do you like to do in your spare time?"

Frau Diebler brightened a little. "Well, I love to shop. That's one reason I knew I would enjoy this assignment. You Americans have such wonderful stores. Of course, the clothes I admire most are beyond my means, but—"

"Not if you're willing to negotiate."

Silence pervaded the room. Frau Diebler's sharp eyes bored holes into Amy's. "I don't take bribes. I do my job."

"This isn't a bribe. It's a compromise. A little business

deal between two women who want the same thing. We do have common goals, don't we—a peaceful partnership, a healthy baby, and an unworried Dr. de Savin?"

"*Ja,*" Frau Diebler admitted, but she sounded wary.

"So . . . maybe I could help you with your shopping if you're willing to overlook insignificant disagreements in our prenatal plan. By that I mean that you'll be, hmmm, *careful* about what you report to the doctor."

"I can't ignore my professional responsibilities, Frau Miracle."

"Oh, of course not! But you could forget about rectal thermometers and suppositories, and six A.M. wake-up calls, couldn't you? And in return I could make certain that my nurse is dressed fashionably." Amy gave her a solemn look. "In my business, I have to insist that my . . . my entourage is chic."

"Ah, yes, I see. I wouldn't want to embarrass you."

"I *insist* that you let me buy you some new clothes."

Frau Diebler put her thermometer away, took her medical bag, and stood formally. "Good morning, Frau Miracle. I will see you at noon."

After she left Amy crawled back under the covers and, chuckling darkly, pulled them over her head.

❦

Her agent wanted her to audition for some television shows, and there were offers to do Letterman again, and another cable show. Bev Jankowski discussed these projects with enormous sighs and listed them with a code beside each one: B.M. and A.M. Before Mommy and After Mommy.

At least being pregnant was funny. Amy grew accustomed to people telling her how *huge* she was to be only five and a half months. All she had to do was amble out on stage with a coy expression on her face and the audience started to chuckle. Thank goodness *something* about backaches, stretch marks, and swollen ankles was enjoyable.

Tonight she was more tired than usual, and she felt as if someone had hung a watermelon around her middle. A rambunctious watermelon. The baby seemed to love being on stage. Maybe it was some internal bond that alerted it to Mom's change in mood. As soon as she stepped to the microphone every night there was a tumult of movement inside her uterus. Tonight it felt like a game of water polo between elephants.

By the time the second show ended she was desperate to sit down. Laughing wearily, she grabbed her stomach with both hands the instant she stepped into the wings. "Game's over, sweetie." Frau Diebler, her stout little body housed in an Armani dress suit, was waiting with a paper cup of orange juice and a pill. "Time for another vitamin, Frau Miracle."

"Danke." Amy swallowed the juice and palmed the vitamin, then tucked it into the sand of an ashtray cannister when Frau Diebler wasn't looking. She and the nurse headed toward the dressing rooms through a crowd of people doing various forms of nothing. Dimly she heard running feet behind her.

"Comic mama, don't waddle so fast."

She halted and swung around. "Elliot!"

He looked better than the last time she'd seen him, but not good. He smelled like a scotch distillery. His eyes were bloodshot. They should have been plaid. *"Amy,"* he said with sincere, if slurred, greeting. "Nobody tol' me that you got knocked up."

He hiccupped and swayed in place. He seemed cheerfully benign, more like the old Elliot, before the cocaine. She put an arm around his waist, and he patted her stomach through the candy-cane striped maternity blouse she wore with red slacks. "Did the French Dr. Kildare do this?"

"Where have you been?" She held his hand. "The last I heard, you were negotiating for a cable special."

"Aw, kids are runnin' things now. I'm too old."

Since he was only thirty-four, she suspected other reasons. It was no secret that he was still an alcoholic, if not a cocaine addict. He seemed to have compensated for giving up cocaine by drinking even harder. "So what are you doing with yourself these days?" she asked.

"Writing, writing, writing. A screenplay."

"Great. What's it about?"

He thought for a minute. "I can't remember."

"Comeon. I'll call you a taxi."

"Won't do any good. Can't remember what hotel I'm at."

"What happened to your place at Malibu?"

"Something about the mortgage payments. Bank expected 'em."

"How rude. So you moved into a hotel?"

"Hmmm-huh."

"Think, now. What's the name of it?" She ignored his incoherent answer as a strange little cramp hit her low in the abdomen. She sagged and bit her lip. The pain passed quickly, but left her cold with fear. She decided to go back to the hotel suite immediately and rest. She shot a glance at Frau Diebler, who was distracted by frowning at Elliot. Elliot continued to smile at her and hiccup. "What hotel are you living at?" she repeated.

He shook his head. "I'll find it . . . eventually."

She sighed in defeat. "If you behave, you can come to my hotel. Magda and I have an extra bed in our suite. You can pass out on it."

"I will have to call Dr. de Savin about this," Frau Diebler said, eyeing Elliot for her report.

"Frau Diebler, did I tell you about the Gucci purse I saw in *Vogue*? I think you'd like it."

She pursed her mouth and thought for a moment. "*Ja*, I'm sure that I would." Her silence was bought. Elliot pointed at her. "Whozit?"

"My personal bodyguard. Frau Diebler, meet Elliot Thornton. I'll explain later."

Frau Diebler arched a brow. "You can trust this man?"

"Yeah. He might look and act disgusting, but he's not a masher."

Elliot patted Army's stomach. "I'd never mash a pregnant woman."

"I know. Let's go."

He draped an arm around her shoulders and hiccupped louder as she led him away.

🐛

"Breathe slowly," the emergency-room doctor said. "Calm down."

Amy lay back on the gurney and nodded. "I'm just scared. When I woke up and found blood—"

"It's not uncommon in a pregnancy. It doesn't mean that you're having a miscarriage."

Amy shook her head. "You don't understand. I can't let anything go wrong with this pregnancy."

"We'll keep you in the hospital overnight, and tomorrow you can see your obstetrician."

"I don't have one in Los Angeles. I've been traveling for the past few months. I've carried my records around with me and gone to doctors in whatever city I was in. I've been fine, just fine! Until now—"

"We can arrange for you to see one of the staff obstetricians and have some tests."

"Good."

"I'll have someone tell your husband that you're being admitted."

"My husband?"

"The man who's asleep in one corner of the waiting room. He's under a potted tree."

"Appropriate." She held her head and tried to think. What could she do about Elliot? She couldn't desert him. "He's not my husband. He's a friend." Elliot had helped her sneak out of the hotel suite without alerting Frau Diebler to the problem. Amy smiled grimly when she thought of the diligent nurse unsuspecting and asleep in the midst of a major-league crisis that would be worth another Armani with a Chanel scarf as a bonus.

The doctor shifted with embarrassment. "Excuse me, but is your friend drunk?"

"You noticed." She rubbed her stomach protectively. "He helped me get here. I don't think he can make his way back to the hotel alone. Can he sleep in my room tonight?"

"I'm sure we can arrange something. I'll be right back."

The doctor squeezed her arm and walked away. She stroked her stomach and talked urgently to the baby, trying to give reassurance with hands that shook.

❦

"Twins." The obstetrician grinned at her and pointed to the video screen where the movie of the week—her sonogram—was playing. "Fraternal twins. A boy and a girl."

Amy stared in shock. "A boy and a girl."

Frau Diebler, her expression like a thunderstorm over the Rhine, sat in a chair beside the examining table, taking copious notes and asking clinical questions. She was in a very bad mood over last night's deception. This time Amy wondered if there was any way to bribe her silence.

No wonder the kicking was rough. They had a coed chorus line. The obstetrician continued talking, telling her that bleeding wasn't uncommon with twins, that although there were many more complications and risks to consider, everything looked fine.

"Risks?" She froze on the word. "What risks?"

He described the list of potential problems, pausing occasionally to remind her that she could relax, that everything looked fine, except that she needed more rest. By the time he finished talking she was in emotional agony.

"*Ja,* I'll have to call the doctor about this," Frau Diebler said darkly.

Amy twisted toward her. "Don't overreact. There's nothing wrong."

"Twins! Bleeding! Frau Miracle, this time I cannot—"

"I don't want Dr. de Savin to worry about me. He's not going to find out about these twins until I decide to tell him. You can shop all you want, and I'll pay, as long as you keep my secrets. You talk, and you'll be out of a job so fast your sauerkraut won't have time to sour. I'll make sure of it. *Do we have an understanding?*"

"I'm flexible, yes. But . . . I'm not *too* flexible. I have my professional pride to think of."

"Which means?"

"You have to stop working. No compromise on that."

"I agree. I'm not going to take foolish chances. But you won't tell Dr. de Savin that I'm having twins. There's no point. It will only upset him. Are we clear on that? *He's not going to find out that I'm having twins.* I'll tell him myself, when the time is right."

Frau Diebler sighed. "I like you, Frau Miracle, I really do. I don't want to complicate your personal problems with Herr Doctor. All right, I won't say anything to him about the twins. But you *must* cooperate with me in every way possible."

Amy grasped her hand and shook it vigorously. "It's a deal."

"Would you like for me to go get your husband?" the obstetrician asked, staring from her to Frau Diebler in puzzlement. "I used to watch Mr. Thornton's show all the time—"

"He's not my husband. I'm not married. Would you ask him to come in, please?"

After the doctor left, she listened distractedly as Frau Diebler muttered about more vitamins and more rest. Keeping this news from Sebastien made her feel disloyal and deceptive. She argued with herself. *He's so afraid that this pregnancy will hurt you. Do you want to put him through more hell by telling him about the twins? All he can do is worry.* On the screen, the two babies looked perfect. Amy found herself crying and smiling at them.

"My God, two for the price of one!" Elliot said, when he was slumped in a chair by her stomach. "They're incredible! This looks like a *National Geographic* special on satellite photography! Look, there's Texas! I see the Alamo! What are you gonna name 'em? Let me name 'em!"

"Calm down." She patted his head.

"You've *got* to call Le Doctor Kildare about this."

"No." Wearily she conceded that she'd made up her mind. She prayed that Sebastien would understand her reasons, after the twins were born safe, healthy, and beautiful. She explained to Elliot.

He loved being part of a secret, especially one that involved Sebastien. "You can trust me," he assured her with a solemn nod.

"I'm gonna quit working and find a quiet place to hole up for the next few months."

"Wait a second!" He grabbed her hands. "I know what

we can do! We'll get an apartment! I'll play male nurse! I'll take care of you!"

"Not while I'm still breathing," Frau Diebler interjected.

"Elliot, sweetie, right now you have mustard on your neck from lunch. You can't even take care of yourself."

His crestfallen response was no joke. All the defeat of the past year sank into him. He looked at her with troubled, pleading eyes. "I'll sign up for an outpatient rehab program. If you and I stick together, maybe I can accomplish something. I swear I'll try, baby. I'll go to booze school every day, and then I'll play nurse for you and the bambinos."

"Elliot, I can't let you do that—"

"Please. If you need me, instead of me needing you, it gives me inspiration to go straight. Crazy, huh?"

"Crazy enough to make sense, I guess." But she wasn't going to take chances with Elliot and his erratic moods. She didn't know when he might go off the deep end again, and what might happen if he did. She took his hand and squeezed it. "I can't take you up on the offer. I need my privacy, Elliot."

"*Ja,*" Frau Diebler added, glaring at him.

"But, baby—"

"No. I'm sorry."

"What if I move into an apartment nearby? Like maybe we find two places in the same complex. Please. *Please.*"

His desperation tore at her. She wanted to help him. Despite every demeaning, selfish thing he'd done to her over the years there had also been times when he was thoughtful and giving. He had always been loyal, in his insecure way, and she owed him for the help he'd given her career, even if he hadn't always been magnanimous about it. "All right. Being neighbors might work. *If* you go into an outpatient program and stay sober."

"Let's do it." He looked happier than she'd seen him in months. "Who knows, baby, when I get respectable again you might decide to give me another chance."

Frau Diebler snorted in dismay. Amy said something lighthearted, trying to keep the peace, but felt a wave of claustrophobia. The next three months would be a crucible, and she had a panicky need to keep her escape routes open.

❦

"How are you feeling?" Even when hampered by poor phone connections, Sebastien's voice was compelling. Loneliness and doubt washed over her. She glanced around her hotel room, feeling isolated. "I miss you," she answered.

"I miss you, too. That's an understatement. Believe me."

"But I'm glad that you can't get away to visit me. I look like I swallowed a beach ball."

"Frau Diebler says you're healthy. That's all that matters. Is it true?"

"Yeah, sure. No problems out of the ordinary."

"What do you mean?" he asked quickly.

She laughed. "My feet hurt, my ankles swell, and I have giant hooters that are gonna smother me if they get any bigger."

"Ah. Send me a picture of *those*." Relief and amusement were evident in his voice. "But otherwise, you feel good?"

"Yes." It saddened her that he never asked about the baby, as if by ignoring it, it didn't exist. But now that there were *two* babies—her secret—she was almost grateful for his attitude.

She wound the phone cord around her fingers so tightly that they began to go numb. "I feel good, but I'm a bloated cow, and audiences are beginning to *moo* at me when I'm onstage, and I stay tired all the time, so . . . so I'm gonna stop working and sit out the next three months in an apartment. With Frau Diebler, of course. We're looking at some places in the suburbs. With nice San Fernando Valley views of highways and other overpriced apartment buildings."

"If you're not working anymore, you should come here."

"I can't, not unless I take a boat. My obstetrician just grounded me. No flying. Standard rule, he said."

"I'll charter you a special flight. With a private doctor. You'll be fine."

"No, I can't do that. It'd probably be safe, but . . . I think it's better for me to be here."

"Better for you not to be around me, you mean." He said it without rebuke, sounding tired. "I wouldn't try to upset you, love. I'd keep my opinions to myself."

"Doc, you and I are two strings on the same violin. Even if you vibrate without making a sound, I feel it. I always have."

After a moment of silent thought, he said grimly, "For once, I wish you and I weren't so close. It would make this easier."

She forced a chuckle. "You know that I'm not very good at being helpless around you. I'd just waddle around in a dither, trying to take care of *you*, and you'd worry about *me*, and we'd drive each other crazy."

"That's not a good reason."

"Please, Doc, try to understand. I'll let you know the second I decide on an apartment. This'll only be until February, you know. I'm due then."

"I'll be there during your last two weeks. I don't care what I have to arrange here in order to get away."

"I'm glad. I want you to be with me. Would you like to go into the delivery room and coach me? I know some men don't get a kick out of—"

"Dear Miracle. I'll not only be in the delivery room, I'll be supervising every hand that touches you. You might as well warn your obstetrician about me now. I want to be with you at every moment."

He's going to be all right, she thought happily. *He's excited about this. I can hear it in his voice.* "I'll tell him," she promised.

"I might not be able to change one mistake, but I'll certainly prevent any others."

Her pleasure faded. Softly, trying to hold back her anger and disappointment, she told him good night and hung up the phone.

❦

She had never seen Elliot sober at Christmas before. He was waiting at her door at nine A.M. with a bottle of apple cider, a smoked ham, and a present. Behind him warm sunshine filled the breezeway along the top floor of the two-story apartment complex, heating the fake adobe and pseudo-hacienda trim. He wore plastic reindeer antlers.

"Rudolph?" she asked.

"Bruce, the gay reindeer. Nobody mentions him much."

She kissed his cheek. "Come in, Bruce."

"Where's Frau Hitler?"

"She took an early bus to Beverly Hills. To window-shop."

"Means she probably has more blackmail in mind."

"As long as she keeps quiet, I don't care."

He helped her lower herself onto a couch near the Christmas tree, then sat down beside her. Elliot grimaced. "What would Sebastien do if he knew that I'd been living downstairs and hanging around for the past six weeks?"

She rubbed her forehead wearily. "He wouldn't like it."

"Well, a little deception keeps the french fries hot." Elliot looked smug, then grew disgruntled as he studied her face. "Don't get mad."

"I'm trying to be your friend and help you get straightened out. I'm trying to have two healthy babies. I'm trying not to go crazy wondering if Sebastien really wants children, but can't admit it, even to himself. I am *not* going to complicate all this by telling him that you're back in the picture. But don't get the idea that I like deceiving him. I hate it."

"Okay, okay, calm down." He patted her stomach. "Just remember, I want these bambinos, even if he doesn't."

"Elliot, don't—"

"Merry Christmas, comic mama." He lunged forward and kissed her gently on the mouth. She caught his antlers and drew back, determined to be firm but diplomatic. "Merry Christmas, Bruce. Remember, you're gay."

"Amy, I love—"

"Don't say it. Please, don't say it."

He lounged backward on the couch, removed the reindeer antlers, and handed her the gift box beside him. "Open your present."

It was a sterling-silver hand mirror with her monogram engraved on the back. The expense of it troubled her, but she thanked him. "Here, open yours." He tore into a box filled with a half-dozen new Nintendo games. "Oh, God, this is great! Thank you, baby!" His enthusiasm was sincere. Immediately he went downstairs and got his Nintendo controls, which he then attached to her television set and, like a distracted kid, forgot all about her as he played the new games. She was glad.

Later he wandered around her apartment with a puzzled expression on his face, as if he'd never been sober enough to notice Christmas decorations and rented furniture in combination before. She had to admit, the place looked like a Howard Johnson's that had been decorated by a rogue elf.

Amy stayed in the rambling, Spanish-style kitchen and kept busy by making a huge Christmas lunch—turkey, cornbread dressing, vegetables, and pumpkin pie. She worked slowly, her thoughts on Sebastien, missing him, loneliness causing a dry burn in her throat.

She envied him the enormous workload that kept his mind off of their separation. To maintain her sanity she spent the days reading novels, writing new comedy routines, and sometimes venturing into the living room to watch one of the half-dozen movies Elliot brought by every morning. He made himself indispensable by running errands, driving her to the doctor, and hosting dinners for their old friends, who viewed his rehabilitation with polite disbelief.

Mostly she kept Elliot on track, making certain that he went to his therapy sessions each afternoon, listening to him when he was depressed, which was often, and cooking huge meals for him. Overeating was an addiction he could afford, and his doctors encouraged it, for now.

Frau Diebler dogged her steps with vitamins and protein drinks, recorded her blood pressure, temperature, and weight every morning, and reported every innocent detail to Sebastien. Everything was fine. At seven months Amy felt gargantuan but healthy, and there hadn't been any other medical problems.

The doorbell rang. Amy watched Elliot spring up and lope over to the door, then peer through the security peephole. "Looks like a delivery guy, but on Christmas *day*? I better hide." He hurried to the back bathroom and shut the door. He had heard that some of the tabloid reporters were going to start pestering him. As much as he craved attention, he didn't want to go public with his problems right now.

Amy rolled her eyes and went to the door. A very officious-looking courier handed her two-dozen red roses and a small gold-wrapped box. "From Dr. de Savin," he said, then departed.

Elliot came out of the bathroom as she sat down on the couch and opened a jewelry case. She gasped at the emerald earrings inside. A piece of fine writing paper was carefully folded underneath them. Its note was written in Sebastien's bold, flowing script:

Missing you, love. Next Christmas you and I will celebrate together, just us, and this year's sadness will be forgotten.

It was a tender message, but his casual exclusion of her pregnancy hurt worse than if he'd ignored her today. If he couldn't deal with one baby, how could he possibly deal with *two*?

Elliot was reading over her shoulder before she realized it. "He doesn't want to play daddy," Elliot muttered. "Wise up, doll."

"Go downstairs and give me a little while alone."

"I *want* the kids, okay? I love you *and* them—"

"Stop it!" Her tension and sadness darkened into an overwhelming sense of desperation wrapped in the irony of Christmas sentiments that were just ashes hidden in glitter. "Elliot, I'm sorry. I don't want to hurt you. You're a sweetheart for carin'. But don't say anything else." Feeling huge and ugly and alone, she dragged her unwieldy body to her bedroom and locked the door behind her. She lay down and hugged her stomach. *Both of you have to be perfect. You have to be. You have to be.*

❦

Early in January Elliot felt strong enough to start working at the clubs around town. Amy had mixed feelings about it. There were too many temptations in the clubs—too many comics living in the fast lane and looking for trouble. Her obstetrician had given her strict orders to rest more; she couldn't be Elliot's bodyguard every night. She wanted to send Frau Diebler with him, but she refused, even for bribes. She loathed Elliot.

Some club owners, such as Mitzi Shore at the Comedy Store, were eager to help comics who wanted to kick drug and alcohol problems. Amy didn't worry about him when he was at the Store. He couldn't take much pressure right now, but Mitzi gave him late-night spots so that he could slip in unannounced and work smaller, less demanding crowds.

And Mitzi watched over him with ferocious maternal care. She wouldn't let Elliot get into trouble while she was around. But there were too many other club owners who didn't baby-sit their comics, and some who encouraged a macho party attitude. Elliot had always been a sucker for a challenge, especially the self-destructive ones.

Amy tracked him closely but saw no signs that he was meandering from the straight and narrow. He admitted that it wasn't easy, but his determination was set. He was a Perrier-and-vitamin man, now.

Then he didn't come home one night. He was supposed to stop by her apartment when he finished at the clubs, no matter how late, and he always had before. She made some calls and traced him to the Hollywood condominium of a well-known comic with a well-known coke habit.

"I'm testing myself," he assured her over the phone. "I swear to God, baby, I'm just sitting here watching everyone else get high."

"I'm sending a taxi. Come home."

He hung up on her. But he did take the taxi. When he arrived at the apartment she took one look at him and knew that he was flying. He knew that she knew. "One time. No big deal. I'll confess tomorrow at the shrink session, and it'll be okay." He was so wired that he spent the rest of the night playing Nintendo.

His doctors told him to stop working the clubs until he fortified his willpower again. He dropped out of the rehab program and began spending more time at the clubs.

Amy watched helplessly. There was no doubt that he was dabbling in drugs and alcohol. He insisted that he was in control, but she knew that he was headed downhill again. And she was terrified that he'd hit bottom this time.

TWENTY-SIX

A hospital seemed so peaceful in the middle of the night. The solitude and quiet made the world feel secure, as if death would have to wait until morning, when more people were awake. It was an illusion.

Sebastien sat by his father's side, watching his labored breathing. With each inhalation he made a gurgling sound deep in his lungs. A tank stood at the head of the bed. Sebastien adjusted the clear tube that fed oxygen into his father's nostrils. His eyes opened halfway, their bold blue power still evident. "You came," he said, his voice airy, filled with fluid.

Sebastien smoothed a strand of silver hair back from his father's forehead. Like Amy's father, Philippe had always been particular about his hair. It was not a sign of rebellion, as with Zack, but of control. But maybe they were the same things.

Amy. He needed her tonight, more than ever. His anxiety and frustration over her decision to continue her pregnancy had never made him love her any less, even though he still resented the hopeless clump of cells growing inside her. She was almost eight months along now. Whether she was uncomfortable in his presence or not, he had to be with her in the last two weeks of the pregnancy. No matter what kind of arrangements he had to make here, he would be with her at the end.

At the beginning, he corrected bitterly. The beginning of

the real torture. How he loved that woman . . . and how terrified he was for her. He flailed himself imagining the delivery. God help him, he knew it was foolish to recall how her mother had died, but he couldn't stop thinking about it. And when he did, his dislike for the obstinate accident living inside her turned to black hatred. But then he felt sick for despising their child.

She could bear the same kind of pitiful, deformed thing that Marie had borne, a baby that would break Amy's heart and convince even her that he wasn't meant to be a father, and that nothing in his upbringing had prepared him to be a good one.

He rubbed a trembling hand over his forehead and looked down at his own father, who had seen him only as a substitute for Antoine, the first son, the one who had been groomed to take charge, who was eager to learn empire building and business maneuvers. The rest of the family, including their mother, had been unimportant to Philippe de Savin. "You came," his father repeated.

"I'm here, yes," Sebastien said to him, feeling empty and confused.

His father struggled for enough air to speak. "I told the doctors long ago—no extraordinary measures. Will you make certain?"

"Yes." Sebastien leaned over him, where they could look at each other more easily. "Annette will be here soon. Her private nurse is bringing her."

"Good. I was afraid I wouldn't be able to talk, if I waited much longer." For a moment his father gasped for breath. His eyes burned into Sebastien's. "I have something to tell her."

A few minutes later the nurse arrived with Annette, who was seated in a wheelchair. She guided the chair close to the bed. Annette looked at her father with stark grief and grasped one of his limp hands. "This is just another of your bad nights, Papa. Don't be morbid. You'll be better in the morning."

"No. This is different. I can feel it." Pleasure, hard and proud, glittered in his eyes. "I still . . . control my own destiny."

Annette moaned softly. "I love you, papa."

"I know."

Sebastien looked away, old anger renewing itself. *I know.* Annette, at least, deserved better than that.

"Sebastien." His father's voice drew him back. He looked into the pale blue eyes, which searched his for a moment than shifted to Annette. "I have already told Sebastien, and now I tell you. I want you to take over the businesses. Sebastien has agreed to relinquish his claims to you."

Annette clutched his hand and said tearfully. "Oh, Papa!"

"I do this because you deserve them more than he. He knows this, too. You have earned them. He will only wait until I'm dead and go back to his career as a surgeon. What would become of all I've worked for, then? From what I've heard in the past few months, he doesn't have half your talent for business."

She bowed her head against his side and cried. He turned his gaze to Sebastien. Sebastien stood rigid for a moment, fighting for control, knowing that even now his father expected it. A truce, an apology, respect—his father had given all three to him. He had given Annette's affection back to him, as well, because now she would forget her jealousy.

"My decision is final. I demand your cooperation, Sebastien," his father ordered, staring at him, tears threatening his eyes. *Tears.*

Sebastien smoothed a hand over his father's hair. Gratitude and victory closed his throat so tightly that he had to whisper to get the words past them. "I will honor your wishes."

"For once," his father said, his voice raspy with disdain. But there was no anger in the covert look he gave Sebastien. He knew that secrets were what they shared best.

❦

"Amy called while you were at the office," Annette told him. Their father's funeral was only a few hours away. Sebastien dropped his briefcase on a table in the entrance hall and shoved both hands into the pockets of his overcoat. He looked up at Annette, who was propped with the aid of her crutches against the balustrade at the landing above the massive staircase. Her dressing gown floated around her, giving her an even more queenly air than usual. She was pale with grief, but her eyes had a teasing glint.

"You were polite to her, I hope."

"Yes. Actually, I like her, Sebastien. She seems very sensible. And it's obvious that she adores you. Nothing sensible about *that*, I suppose, but those of us who adore you must stick together. There are so few of us."

"An elite group."

"No need to call her back until . . . afterward. She simply wanted to check up on you. She has a notion that underneath that stern exterior beats a vulnerable heart. I told her that I think she may be right."

"Obviously, you two didn't discuss anything remotely practical."

"She spoke with Jacques and Louise and made them feel a little better. They were clamoring to talk with her. They became very fond of her when she was here, you know, and she has a lovely camaraderie with children. She told them that their Uncle Sebastien loved Grandfather de Savin and was sorry that he died. And that they could turn to you for help today. Jacques reported this to me with disbelief, afterward. Whatever are you going to do with this charming, misguided woman who's convinced that you'll be an affectionate father to the child you've given her?"

"Let's bury one bad father before we mourn another, please." Feeling that his past had come full circle today and was about to confront him, he went to a liquor cabinet and poured himself a stiff drink. *Here's to you, Papa. Goddamn your soul.*

🍂

He had hoped that his father's funeral would be easy to endure, a farewell to bitterness, an open door through which he could see the rest of his own life with new clarity, even if his and Amy's child was everything he feared it would be.

But his gloom deepened at the graveside. He despised the way such things were designed to provoke the most morbid thoughts. The crowd was enormous, elite, power-ful, all dressed in black, all faithfully respectful but dis-creetly bored. The bleak, ancient cemetery was filled with the hulking statuary of medieval angels who seemed to hover and threaten, their stone faces streaked as if melting like the slate palate of the January sky above them. The rain held off, but a chilling mist crept over the cemetery and into Sebastien's blood.

He scanned the dozens of people who crowded closest around the low granite vault carved with *de Savin* in scrolling letters. Only Annette, seated next to him in her wheelchair, was crying. It struck him like the classic scene from Dickens's *A Christmas Carol.* Scrooge watching his own funeral, where hardly anyone mourns him at the end of his cold, lonely life. *As will be the case with me.* Sebastien shivered inside a black cashmere overcoat. *Don't be absurd and maudlin.*

But his mouth went dry. Would he drive Amy and their child away? Assuming foolishly, he reminded himself, that he and Amy could have a healthy child who lived. As the priest droned on beside the vault Sebastien fought nausea. His distracted gaze fell on Jacques and Louise, standing beside their mother. Recognition tore into him. Their young faces held the same kind of horror that he felt, the same fear of the unknown, but also, on Jacques's six-year-old countenance, the most terrible grief.

He had loved his grandfather, Sebastien realized, amazed.

When the priest finished, a crowd began to cluster around Annette. Sebastien, his heart racing, kissed her tear-stained cheek and said, "I'll take the children home. Don't hurry. Talk with your friends, if you'd like."

"You want to take the children? Are you sure?" She stared at him in surprise. Over the months his avoidance of them had become an unswerving routine.

"Don't look at me as if I might be planning to sell them to trolls, Annette. I'm only offering to escort them home."

"Well . . . oh, go ahead. Stranger things have happened. Thank you."

"I don't want to go with Uncle Sebastien," Jacques said.

He was dressed in long pants for the first time. His black suit and tailored overcoat gave him a maturity that made his swollen, grief-ravaged little face affecting in its attempts at anger and control. Beneath the blond hair his large dark eyes glared at Sebastien. *He has de Savin blood. He will learn to hide his emotions soon enough,* Sebastien thought wearily. Louise huddled close to her brother.

"Come with me, both of you," Sebastien ordered, then held out his hand. At four years old it was even difficult for Louise to comprehend that people died, much less that this morbid ceremony was just something to be endured and forgotten as quickly as possible. She eyed Sebastien under tangles of blond curls, then wound one hand into the black wool cape over her dress and stuck the other up to be swallowed by his. From her wide-eyed inspection of his large sinewy hand, it was obvious that she expected it to crush her fingers at any second. "Amy told us to love you today," she noted. "We promised."

"I don't want to go with him," Jacques repeated to his mother.

Annette glanced at the people around her, who included many of her business associates. She didn't want a scene, Sebastian knew. No tantrums. She drew herself up tightly in the wheelchair. "Go with Uncle Sebastien. Not another word."

Jacques was too well-disciplined to do more than clamp his mouth shut and look at Sebastien in silent dislike. Sebastien nodded to him. "Come."

When the three of them were insulated in the plush backseat of one of the limousines that lined the cemetery streets, Sebastien let go of Louise's hand and reached over her to touch the intercom button. Louise sat on one side of him, and Jacques on the other. As he told the driver to take a long route home he noticed her dark curious eyes—his mother's eyes—watching him with increasing bravado. But Jacques stared at the limousine's carpeted floorboard, his demeanor polite but resentful.

After the car began moving Sebastien settled back and looked at him. Sensing the scrutiny, Jacques turned his gaze up to Sebastien's. "You didn't love grandfather. You don't love us, either. Well, we don't love *you.*"

Sebastien had wanted to say something comforting, but the boy's words made him feel foolish and ugly. "I don't expect you to love me," he told Jacques. "But you should show me respect." *Spoken just as my father would have said it.* Sebastien grimaced.

Louise tugged at the sleeve of his overcoat. He turned warily to look at her. Her delicate face was contorted with anger. Her mouth trembled and tears gathered in her eyes. "Why don't you love us? We haven't done anything bad."

He opened his mouth, shut it, and frowned at her. "I—I *do* love you."

"You *do*?"

"No," Jacques interjected sharply. "You think we're too much trouble." His chin came up. "If my papa were here I wouldn't even have to talk to you."

"Our papa went away in a plane crash," Louise explained, as if Sebastien might not remember.

Jacques added loudly, "And I wouldn't have to talk to you if Grandfather de Savin was still—"

"He's dead." Sebastien didn't soften his tone; he wanted a brutal effect. "He's never coming back. And neither is your father. Wishing and making childish threats won't change the truth." *How well I remember.*

Jacques's shoulders sagged. He twisted away and pressed his forehead to the limousine's window. Louise began to cry with little mewling sounds. Sebastien felt remorse pulling up harsh, vivid memories. He had been like Jacques and Louise thirty years ago, so easily hurt, but for him there hadn't been anyone who might understand, no one who could be trusted with the bitter reasons for his grief and fury.

And now he was sentencing Jacques and Lousie to suffer as he had.

Louise's crying broke off with a startled gulp as Sebastien lifted her into his lap and wrapped an arm around her. He snaked the other arm around Jacques's shoulders.

The boy pivoted in the seat and gaped at him. Sebastien pulled him close to his side. He was stunned at his own actions, but remorse was tearing him apart inside, and he was overwhelmed with so many conflicting emotions that logic couldn't take command. He expected Jacques to shove him away. But the boy, though obviously shocked, sat still.

"I do love you, both of you," Sebastien repeated gruffly, the words rushing from him as he looked from Jacques to Louise. "And I know how hard it is to understand what happened to your papa, and to Grandfather de Savin. It's hard for me to understand, too."

"No, you used to be a doctor," Jacques answered. "You've seen a lot of dead people. That's why you don't cry. Maman said so."

"I'm still a doctor. And doctors cry, just as everyone else does."

"Not you. Not for Grandfather de Savin."

"That doesn't mean that I don't love him." Amazed that he had said those words aloud, he watched Jacques's eyes scrutinize his face for the truth.

Sebastien's troubled thoughts were distracted by Louise, who curled herself around him and planted her face in his line of vision. Shyly she whispered, "I'd cry if you died, Uncle Sebastien."

Only a heart of stone could resist such a wistful appeal. He stared at her, his chest filling with wonder. *What a maudlin fool I could become, if I had children such as these.*

"I wouldn't cry," Jacques announced. He nudged his sister aside and looked up into Sebastien's eyes. "What did we ever do to make you so mad at us?"

"I have never been mad at either of you. You haven't done anything wrong."

"Then why don't you like us?"

"I like you very much, but, you see, adults and children don't have a great deal to talk about with each other."

"We talked to Grandfather all the time. He told stories about the war."

"Did he ever tell you about your grandmother de Savin? Or about your uncle Antoine and your aunt Bridgette?"

"No."

"Who are Antoine and Bridgette?" Louise asked.

"Our uncle and aunt. Like Uncle Jacques," Jacques told her. "Maman's brothers and sister. Maman said they died a long time ago. Uncle Jacques's the one I'm named for."

"Oh." Louise looked dubious. Her questioning eyes rose to Sebastien's. She was obviously confused. "You are Maman's brother too?"

"That's right. Your Maman and I had a sister," he explained patiently. "Bridgette. And two brothers. Antoine and Jacques."

"Jacques is *my* brother," she countered.

Her brother snorted. "He and I have the same name, you dumb turtle!"

"Enough," Sebastien interjected, feeling strangely light-headed and hopeful. "Would you like to hear about them? And about your grandmother de Savin? She came from a place filled with legends and fairy tales."

"Where?" Louise demanded.

Sebastien took a deep breath and began to tell them about Brittany and a fanciful fisherman's daughter who fell in love with a gallant young soldier on holiday. They listened without blinking, hypnotized.

He finally knew what he could share with them, and it was a gift that no one else could give.

🦢

He woke to find Annette bending over him, smiling with tears on her face, her arms braced on her crutches. After a bleary moment he remembered where he was—sitting upright with his back against the headboard of Jacques's bed—and with whom. Louise was asleep in his lap, slumped sideways with her head on his chest. Jacques lay beside him, one arm flung across Sebastien's legs, his face pillowed on the folds of Sebastien's overcoat, which Sebastien had never gotten around to removing.

"What magical thing has happened to you?" Annette whispered, studying the three of them.

He shook his head, not certain yet, feeling awkward but also pleased. "We have more in common than I thought."

"Go back to America. Immediately."

"What?"

"Hurry before you forget this moment. Tell Amy about it. Tell her that you are a better candidate for fatherhood than you ever suspected."

"You read too much into a simple—"

"*Go.* I want you on a plane tomorrow. I can take care of everything here by myself, now. You've done more than your share. Now go and live your own life, and don't disappoint that amazing American woman who understands you better than any of the rest of us do, and who sees a great deal worth waiting for."

Freedom. He relished it like a fine wine that had been aging just for this moment. He didn't know if Amy would welcome him, neither did he know how he could hide his fear when he saw her eight months pregnant. But looking down at the children who had won him over and been won in return—all because of Amy's patient coaching—he had hope for himself.

TWENTY-SEVEN

*A*my sat on the living-room couch with a bland white lamp on the rented end table making a pool of light on the script she held. She shivered inside her pink tent of a nightgown, tried to pull her feet under her, then gave up when her stomach made the effort too great.

Again she tried to study the script. Again her thoughts fled to Sebastien at the funeral. She looked at the phone on the end table, wishing that he would call.

When the phone rang she grabbed for it, groaning under her breath because her stomach got in the way of even the simplest task. "Hello."

"I'm still shopping," Frau Diebler announced. "There is a sale on shoes at Neiman-Marcus. I'll be back in an hour. Did you drink your milk?"

"A quart of it. And all I've been doing since you left is sitting on the couch like a huge potato. I'm resting, I promise. *Whales* don't rest this well when they beach themselves."

"Very good. I'll be there soon."

"Would you rub my back when you get here?"

"Of course. Frau Miracle, you always ask me these things so politely. It isn't necessary. I'm your employee. You may simply *tell* me what you want."

"Nah, we're partners."

"Partners? Frau Miracle, thank you. I respect you and am

glad you've come to respect me." Frau Diebler cleared her throat. "Well, enough chatter. You rest!"

"Don't worry. I can't get off the couch without a tow truck."

After she hung up the phone she tossed the script aside and rubbed her tense forehead. Why hadn't Sebastien called? *Maybe he doesn't want to share his feelings with you. Maybe he doesn't need to, anymore.* "Oh, stop," she muttered to herself. "Crazy pregnant woman. Hormones running amok." Chocolate milk would settle her nerves. Chocolate milk over fruit cocktail. It was a nasty craving, but a healthy one. Even Frau Diebler approved. Amy braced her hands on the couch and, huffing, started the rocking motion that she hoped would propel her off the couch's deep cushions.

Just as she staggered to her feet she heard running steps on the concrete walk outside. Footsteps resonated loudly on the second-floor breezeway, making a hollow, *pinging* echo that alerted her anytime a visitor was headed toward her door. The footsteps ended abruptly and their owner ignored the bell, pounding instead on the veneered metal security door. "It's Elliot. Lemme in, baby."

A warning instinct held her still. Even though he was using cocaine lately, he'd remained calm and reasonable, not like before. Tonight's urgency was new, and she didn't know what it meant. She moved slowly to the door but didn't open it. "Are you all right?"

"I need to talk, baby. It's only nine o'clock. Gimme a break. It's sort of important. Please."

She relaxed at the *please.* In the old days Elliot had never been polite when the coke was talking. "Okay. Just a second." She flipped the door lock and unhooked the chain.

He shoved the door open with a force that shook the walls. Its edge caught her on the right shoulder and she stumbled back, almost falling, dull pain shooting down her arm. She stared at him in astonishment and then fear as she noted his disheveled hair and furious eyes. He stepped into the apartment and halted, his legs spread, his hands clenched into fists by his sides. Though he stood still, he was so tightly wound that she could see a quiver in the short sleeves of his Raiders football jersey. His snug jeans revealed the faint, rhythmic popping of the muscle of one knee; his weight was balanced on the balls of his custom-made jogging shoes.

"You bitch," he said in a low, deadly voice.

As casually as she could, she stepped backward. Her heart raced. He looked capable of anything. He had never called her that kind of name before, no matter how crazy he'd been. She reached the couch and moved behind it, using it as a barrier. One hand rose protectively to her stomach. Behind him the door remained open, the January night mild and damp outside. She wondered if any of their neighbors were outdoors and would hear her if she screamed for help.

"Get out," she told him. "Get out before you say something else that you'll regret later."

He advanced on her with measured steps, crouching a little, stalking her. "You got the lead in that television pilot Hadley Rand is gonna make. That fucking *big-deal* pilot that everybody has been talking about. Why didn't you tell *me* that you were up for the part? Why did I have to hear that you got it from some piss-head flunky of Hadley's who was stoned and couldn't keep his mouth shut?"

She sidled along the couch, gripping the back. Again she glanced at the open door. Her stomach twisted with the almost-forgotten sensation of being trapped and panicky. In her condition she wouldn't be able to move fast enough to reach the door before Elliot did. She halted, looking at him with as much composure as she could fake. "It's only a pilot for a sitcom. It may sink like a rock. I didn't want you to know that I was up for the lead, because you're vulnerable right now. I didn't want you to feel competitive toward me again. I only found out this afternoon that I got the part. I was going to tell you tonight when you came in from the clubs."

"Liar." He reached the couch and halted a few feet away from her. He trembled visibly. "All this time I thought you wanted to help me go straight, but you don't care if I survive or not. You've been working on your career, and now that you've hit the big time, you won't give a rat's ass if I pull myself back up or not."

"Listen to yourself, Elliot! How much coke did you do tonight? You *know* that I care about you. You *know* that you don't mean what you say when you're messed up."

Veins stood out in his neck. *"I know that you love me!"* he shrieked, and leapt forward. He grabbed her by one wrist, twisting so hard and fast that she felt a muscle tear before the pain exploded into fragments of light before her vision. Her knees buckled, but she balled her free hand into a fist and hit him in the center of his stomach as she sank to the floor.

He doubled over, coughing. Then he slapped her. Her teeth snapped together and she bit her tongue. "I know that you love me," he repeated, yelling, spit flecking her face because he was so close. "Goddamn, I want you to prove it."

She drew back her first again, but even in her terror she realized that hitting him was the most dangerous thing she could do. *The babies. Don't make him hit you back. Do whatever you have to do to protect the babies.* She tried to curl forward over her stomach, but he grabbed her under both arms and hauled her to her feet. "Show me. Show me that you care, you self-serving bitch." He wound a hand around the nape of her neck and, bracing himself behind her, pushed her to the hallway that went to the bedrooms. "Don't scream. Don't make a noise, or goddamm it, I swear I'll knock you down."

Her mind raced with horror. She dug her bare feet into the carpet, but he shoved her step by step down the hall and into her bedroom. "You're not going to do this, you don't want to do this, Elliot. Elliot, this isn't you, this isn't something you're capable of doing, Elliot—"

"Shut up!" he pushed her to the foot of the bed and shoved her hard. She twisted and fell on her back, groaning as her weight and awkward size trapped her on the mattress, trying to turn over and crawl off the bed.

But as she managed to roll over Elliot threw himself down behind her and pinned her with a forearm on the side of her neck. "Show me that you care!" He slid his free

arm around her and mauled one of her heavy, sensitiv
breasts through the nightgown, while she choked an
struggled. Amy clawed at his hand wildly as it left he
breast and skimmed over the huge mound of her stomach
He was sweating, shaking, making guttural noises tha
became sobs.

"Stop, Elliot, please stop," she begged between gasps.

"Do it! Show me! Love me!"

He grabbed her between the legs and tried to shove hi
fingers inside her, but the barrier of the gown and he
furious kicking delayed him. When he jerked the gown u
she knew that he wasn't going to stop until he raped her o
hurt her badly in the attempt. She slammed her head bac
as hard as she could and caught him in the nose. He jerke
in pain, and it loosened his grip for a second. Amy elbowe
him and in the same move dragged herself off the edge o
the bed.

She landed on her hands and knees as he flung himsel
toward her, snatching at the back of her gown. She lunge
toward the short dresser several feet away and caught th
handle of the top drawer. It slid out of its berth and crashe
to the floor, spilling scarves, hosiery, and her handgun.

Elliot was crying hysterically, now. "I'll fuck you on th
floor if that's the way you want it!" She heard the bed crea
as he careened off of it.

Oh, God, I don't have any choices. Half-kneeling, half
braced against the dresser, she twisted with the gun in he
hand, cocking it, her thumb jabbing at the safety catch, ar
objective part of her mind praying. "Don't! *Don't!*" she
screamed as Elliot grabbed for her again.

"Love me!"

He had a look of disbelief when she pulled the trigger.

❧

She was dimly aware, through the sorrow, humiliation
and physical pain, that Frau Diebler had arrived at th
police station. Amy heard the brusque German accen
coming down a hall outside the detective's office, ordering
officers aside as if they were her lackeys. Amy looked up a
her with a grim smile as she marched into the office, where

Amy waited, alone. The nurse's face lost its sternness. She threw herself into the chair beside Amy's and clucked like a distraught hen. Amy was glad to see her. "The neighbors gave you my message?"

"*Ja*. And they said that Elliot will recover. It's just his shoulder?"

"Yes. When the paramedics came they told me it was serious, but not life threatening."

Frau Diebler pulled back and muttered darkly at Amy's swollen wrist. "I'm taking you straight to the hospital. Right now!"

"I have to answer a few more questions for the detective. It's routine, and I have to do it."

"That Elliot, he didn't say that you—"

"No. He told the officers who came to the apartment exactly what happened. The truth." She bent her head into her hand. "The truth. He *apologized* to me." She hugged herself and shut her eyes.

The detective, a portly, pragmatic veteran with kind eyes, came back into his office. "I need to talk to Ms. Miracle," he said pointedly to Frau Diebler.

Amy patted her hand. "This is Detective Rodriguez. Wait outside."

When Amy and Rodriguez were alone behind his closed door he sat on the edge of his desk, facing her, and studied her closely. "It will work the way you and I discussed it."

"Meaning that a judge will probably reduce the criminal charges if Elliot agrees to be hospitalized for drug rehab?"

"Yeah."

"Good. But what happens to him right now?"

"He stays under guard at the hospital for a couple of days. When he's discharged, either his lawyer gets him set free on bond or we transfer him to jail." Rodriguez touched her shoulder. "Go home. The worst is over." But it wasn't, not when she left the detective's office and found Frau Diebler hanging up the phone on a clerk's desk. "Thank you," she told the man. "I charged the overseas call to my employer's phone, just as I promised."

Amy pulled her into a quiet corner. She hurt all over and

felt sick at her stomach. Wavering in place, she stared at Frau Diebler with dread. *"Did you call Dr. de Savin?"*

"Yes. I'm sorry. But yes." Frau Diebler looked distraught. "I can't keep this from him. I told him everything. He's leaving to come here immediately. I'm sorry to do this to you, but he is, after all, the one I must answer to, the one who pays my salary. I am ashamed for deceiving him. If I had told him about Elliot Thornton a long time ago, maybe tonight wouldn't have happened."

Amy leaned against a wall and cursed. "What else did you tell him in your little frenzy of guilt?"

"That you are carrying twins, and that one time you had a problem with bleeding, and . . . that you've been trying to help Elliot Thornton. That he has been our neighbor for almost three months."

Amy went to a chair and sank down. What did Sebastien think of her for concealing her medical problem, hiding the fact that there were two babies instead of only one for him to accept, and letting Elliot back into her life, making it possible for tonight's confrontation to jeopardize her own safety as well as the babies'?

The chance of him softening toward the babies was now ruined. She even wondered if he still wanted *her.* Not that it would matter as long as he rejected their children. Would he understand that she had been trying to keep him from worrying, that she had wanted to present a perfect facade, the perfect pregnancy, so that he'd approve? Not now. He wasn't coming here to tell her that he'd had a change of heart, of that she felt certain.

"There's no point in your staying with me anymore," she told Frau Diebler. "What happens next will be between me and the doctor. I doubt that he believes that I've kept my word about *anything,* so it doesn't matter if I send you away."

"But Frau Miracle—"

"You called him. I respect your reasons. But I don't have to bargain with you, anymore. Go back to the apartment and pack your things. I want you gone by tomorrow. That's all I have to say to you. I won't be going back there with you tonight. Good-bye."

"But—but Frau Miracle, you can't . . . where are you going tonight?"

"A hotel. I don't want to stay where Elliot almost . . . I just don't want to stay in the apartment. And I don't want to see you again. You've done your duty, but you've hurt me and the doctor more than you know."

"Frau Miracle . . . I apologize, but I don't understand."

"Good-bye." Amy lumbered into Detective Rodriguez's office. He looked up from his desk. "I need a ride to a good hotel. Can someone take me, or should I call a taxi?"

"You need a sympathetic listener, from the look on your face."

"I'll settle for a lift to a hotel."

"I think I can provide both." He stood up and grabbed his car keys from the desk, while smiling at her in a fatherly way that made her want to cry.

❦

She hardly slept that night. Rodriguez called the next morning. "I checked your apartment. The nurse is gone. But I have to warn you about something. A half-dozen reporters and photographers are camped on your doorstep, waiting for you. Word got out about last night."

Amy's sense of isolation and despair increased. With it came the anger that had been growing steadily. "I'm sitting here with nothing but my purse, my coat, and the maternity dress I put on last night when I called the police. And those vultures are waiting to eat me alive when I go home."

"I can send someone with you to plow a path to your door."

"I'm not going back there. I won't be treated like some kind of ripe fruit they can peel to check for rotten spots."

"Look, you might as well get used to it. They're not going away. And sooner or later they're going to find you."

"I'll go up to San Francisco. I'm not supposed to fly, so I'll hire a car and driver."

"Good. When you get to a hotel there, call me. Let me know where you are, in case I have any more questions." She thanked him and hung up, then called Mary Beth, who had been waiting for more news all morning. "I need your help," Amy told her. "At eight months, with twins, I shouldn't be traipsing around by myself."

"I'll meet you at the airport in San Francisco. Give me five minutes and I'll call you back with my flight number."

While she waited by the phone, Amy held her stomach and rocked slowly, trying to soothe herself as well as the babies. The hotel room made her shiver with its impersonal charm. She wondered when Sebastien would arrive in Los Angeles. More than ever she felt desperate for peace, rest, dignity. Sebastien would be too angry to give her that. The media's greed for scandal wouldn't give her that. And she had to deal with her own shame for getting herself into such an ugly situation with Elliot.

She had to take care of herself and the babies. She knew more than ever that she, and they, were survivors.

❦

She bought a change of clothes and a few toiletries, then climbed into a small gray limousine for the all-day trip to San Francisco. The driver, a balding, stocky man as dapper as his car, gave her curious looks but said little. Amy napped fitfully during the hours that followed, between frequent pit stops for her overburdened bladder. Her stomach became queasy and she couldn't eat. But the driver was patient and helpful, stopping to buy sodas for her and coaxing her to nibble crackers. By the time they arrived at the airport in San Francisco she was exhausted but felt strong enough to carry on alone.

Lugging a new tote bag filled with her meager possessions, she found a ticket agent and checked on Mary Beth's flight. "Mechanical trouble," the agent told her. "The flight made a stop in Dallas and just got back in the air thirty minutes ago. You've got a long wait."

Amy dragged herself to a coffeeshop. Her ears buzzed with fatigue. She drank a glass of milk and, feeling restless, decided to make rental car arrangements, then find a place to lie down.

As she entered the queue at a car-rental booth, she staggered and clutched her stomach, prompting an airport customer service manager to rush over and radio for a wheelchair. Though she protested, he hustled about, loudly calling to the car-rental people to hurry her paperwork through. She cringed at the curious stares from other travelers.

And then a strobe flash went off right beside her. She pivoted clumsily, throwing up one hand to cover her blinded eyes.

"What are you doing in San Francisco, Ms. Miracle?" The photographer was a small, fast-moving ferret with an abundance of gold chains and cameras around his neck. He continued to snap her picture, his shutter clicking repeatedly, an automatic weapon loaded with film.

"Who are you?" She turned her head and covered her face, feeling defenseless and trapped.

"Ron Falcone. Free-lance."

She gritted her teeth. He was one of the paparazzi who hung out at the airport, hoping to catch celebrities on their way in or out. She'd watched Elliot preen for this brand of photojournalist often, when she was traveling with him. "I don't have anything to say, Ron. Please—"

"How is Elliot Thornton?"

"I have nothing to say."

"Leave her alone," the customer service manager ordered, planting himself between them. To the car-rental clerk he yelled, "Get Ms. Miracle's car ready! *Now!*"

"Did Elliot try to rape you?" the photographer asked loudly.

"No. No." She snatched at the forms that were pressed toward her by a clerk, signed them shakily, and took her keys.

"Who's the father of your baby? Is it Elliot? Why did you shoot him?"

"Get this lady to her car!" the airport man ordered. A security guard arrived and took her arm. "Need some help, ma'am?"

"Yes. Thank you—"

"Do you think this publicity will promote your career?" Falcone called, shoving at the customer service manager, holding his camera above the man's head and continuing to photograph her.

She leaned against the security guard as he propelled her out of the crowd toward a side exit. "I hate that sonovabitch Falcone," the guard muttered. "You shoulda seen how he dogged Pat Boone last week."

"Pat Boone?" She chortled, heard herself making frantic little hiccupping sounds, and clamped her mouth shut. Her insides had turned to water. She decided that if she reached the car, she would drive until she felt safe. It might be a long trip.

❦

The entrance to the hospital's police ward was blocked by thick double doors with heavily reinforced glass. A young, harried-looking officer intent on adhering to rules staffed the desk outside. He seemed even less likely to compromise each time he scanned Sebastien's rumpled trousers and shirt, the beard stubble darkening his jaws, and his generally frazzled appearance. Sebastien realized that to the officer he looked desperate. He *was* desperate, because he hadn't been able to locate Amy thus far.

Frau Diebler's words kept coming back to him with remnants of shock. *Twins.* Amy hadn't wanted him to know. Nor had she wanted him to know that she was trying to help Elliot Thornton. She had feared and distrusted his reaction; he had made it impossible for her to confide in him, or ask for his help.

"I left Paris late last night," he explained again, his voice raw with fatigue. "I just arrived in Los Angeles an hour ago. When I called your superiors, they told me that the detective would be here this afternoon, and I might be able to talk to him."

"There he is. Good luck."

A heavyset man had just stepped out of one of the rooms that lined the hallway beyond the security doors. He negotiated an obstacle course of nurses, orderlies, and gurneys as he walked toward Sebastien, studying him with a neutral expression. When he arrived at the doors, Sebastien saw from the badge on the lapel of his brown suit that he was Rodriguez, the detective in charge of Elliot's case.

Rodriguez opened a door and stuck his head into the anteroom. "Yeah?"

"This guy's looking for Amy Miracle."

"Yeah, him and every other sleazeball reporter in town."

Sebastien gritted his teeth. "My name is de Savin. I'm not a reporter. I'm her—" he searched for words, feeling foolish and impatient, "I'm her husband-to-be." *If she still wants me.*

"I can't release any information on her without her permission. She's safe, I'll tell you that much."

"Let me see Elliot Thornton."

Rodriguez laughed. "This isn't a country club, hombre."

"Amy is eight months pregnant with twins," Sebastien said with barely controlled anger, emphasizing every word. "*My* children. She was beaten, terrorized, and almost raped last night. Is it so hard for you to understand why I want to talk to the man who did that to her, and why I want to find her?"

"Pal, from the look on your face you might strangle Thornton, and that would put a nasty cloud over my day."

"Would you at least send a message to Amy—tell her the name of my hotel, so that she can call me?"

"Write it down and leave it with this officer. I'll think about it."

"Maybe I can help," a voice said behind Sebastien. He pivoted and found himself facing Jeff Atwater, who looked as if he'd just stepped from the pages of a men's magazine but whose eyes held haggard sympathy.

After a second of stunned appraisal, Sebastien's anger rushed to his last memory of Jeff, sprawled on the floor of a San Francisco hotel with his mouth bleeding.

"Get out of my sight," Sebastien said softly, his voice as stark and unyielding as the ugly concrete wall that framed Jeff's humble attitude.

Jeff turned paler than he already was. "I heard months ago that you and Amy had found each other again. I've always kept track of her, asked about her discreetly, that kind of thing. She came to me once for help, about Elliot Thornton."

"Whatever she felt for you died a long time ago. You can't

ingratiate yourself with her because she's no longer with Thornton. I won't let you come between us again."

"You make it sound as if I ever had a chance."

"Damn you, she hasn't needed you for ten years; why would she need you today? Was it that good between the two of you? Don't expect it to mean anything to her now."

"My God, didn't you ever ask her what really happened? We had one night together, Sebastien. One lousy night. I charmed her into doing something she didn't really want. She hated me for it. I hated myself. Is that what you're talking about? There was no affair. I only let you think that to keep you away from her. Hell, I *wanted* there to be more, but I couldn't compete with your sainted memory. The poor kid was sure you'd come back for her any day. If old Pio Beaucaire hadn't convinced her otherwise, she wouldn't have been easy prey for me."

Sebastien took a step toward him, restraint losing its hold. "You did that to me—and to her? You lied. *Why, goddamn you?*"

"I was a fool. I was confused. I was greedy. Your father didn't want you involved with Amy. He paid me to make sure the two of you went separate ways. I'd put up with enough middle-class bullshit in my life. I wanted money."

"My father paid you?" Sebastien grasped Jeff's crisp white shirt and shoved him against the wall. "You betrayed us for *money*?"

Rodriguez stepped into the hall. "I don't want to deal with this. Back off, both of you."

"It's all right," Jeff assured the detective, his eyes never leaving Sebastien's. "He only hits me at medical conventions."

"Why?" Sebastien demanded. "Why did you betray us?"

"For the money, yeah. But also . . . because of Amy. You're not the only one who fell in love with her."

Sebastien kept him against the wall and stared into his eyes, searching for the truth, hating him no less but understanding him a little more. He thought of Amy, of what she must have gone through blaming herself, as he knew she must have. All this time he'd kept a small, hurt, unforgiving place hidden inside him because he thought that she'd traded him for Jeff. Once again, she made him ashamed of his cynicism. He had to find her and make things right, everything.

"You hopeless piece of trash," he whispered to Jeff finally, his hands winding tighter into Jeff's shirt. "You don't know what it means to love anyone besides yourself."

"Then why do you think I showed up here, today? Out of some charitable instinct for Thornton? Hell, no. I'm trying to help him for Amy's sake. And for yours. Look, believe what you want to believe about me. But this is my way of apologizing. I've talked to Elliot's attorney on the phone. He asked Thornton if he'd meet with me." Jeff looked toward Rodriguez. "I'm Dr. Atwater. The psychiatrist. I'm authorized to see Thornton."

"All right."

Jeff nodded toward Sebastien. "Can this deceptively murderous-looking person come with me?"

Rodriguez grunted. "Is he really Dr. de Savin?"

"The one and only," Jeff replied.

"If you say so, then. Five minutes."

Sebastien scrutinized Jeff, who was beginning to flush deeply above his shirt's twisted collar. "If there's any truth to your apology, this is all I want from it."

"Fair enough," Jeff answered, and gestured for Sebastien to follow him.

The pale, gaunt man who lay in the hospital bed with one shoulder bandaged and his arm in a sling filled Sebastien with both loathing and pity. Elliot looked at his two visitors with sunken, dull eyes. "Where is she? Is she okay?"

Sebastien stepped to the foot of the bed. Regardless of pity, he could find it very easy to forget that a uniformed police officer stood in one corner of the room. He could find it easy to put his hands around Elliot Thornton's throat. "You tell me," he replied.

Tears slid down Elliot's face. "I don't know."

Jeff stepped forward. "Your attorney says that she won't press charges if you hospitalize yourself for a full rehab program. I want you to enter the program at my center. It's the best. If you really want to get well, you will. I'll oversee your treatment personally."

"Right now I'd like to die. Everytime I think about what I did to Amy, what I tried to do . . . I know that I was crazy. She hasn't loved me for a long time." He glanced at Sebastien while he raised a trembling hand to wipe his face. "You were always there. Right from the beginning. A freaking shadow from before I met her. But it's not your fault that things went wrong. It's mine. This is the first time I've admitted it."

"How noble, you son of a bitch, now that you've hurt her and shamed her so badly."

"I'll give interviews. I'm gonna do it—tell everything— how she tried to keep me sober, how she wrote for me when nobody knew it, how much shit I gave her for wanting to leave me. And . . . what happened last night. Everything. I'll make it up to her. I want her to be happy." Elliot turned his face to one side, his throat working, the white pillow framing his ravaged features and swollen profile. "I know it's over. Tell her that I love her, but I know."

"I have to find her, first." Sebastien went to the door, paused, and met Elliot's distraught, beaten gaze. Sebastien despised him, and always would, but the man was broken, not an enemy any longer. "I'll tell her what you said," he promised. *But God, where is she?*

Jeff came to him and held out a hand in farewell. "I envy what you and Amy have together. I'll never let my guard down enough to have that kind of relationship with anyone. She saved you from yourself. I wish she could have done the same for me. Tell her I said . . . just tell her that . . . it wasn't only the money I wanted."

Sebastien would never offer this man any consolation, not even a nod of acceptance. When he looked at him in killing silence, Jeff's shoulders slumped. He returned to Elliot.

"Let's make this easy. We'll talk about *your* future," he said to him, sitting down in a chair near the bed. "I have every reason to think that you have one, now."

❦

Amy's mind was a dungeon of exhaustion. Her back ached. Her sore neck and breasts combined with her throbbing wrist to make a circuit of pain. She held the ledge of the pay phone and tried not to gag over the acrid fumes rising from the pavement of the convenience store's gas station.

"Detective Rodriguez, please."

After what seemed like an eternity he came on the line. "Where are you?"

"Headed toward Mendocino. I'm in the wine country."

"My God, are you alone?"

"Yes. I had to make a fast getaway." She explained briefly.

"You shouldn't be driving!"

"You're tellin' *me*. If my stomach were any larger, I couldn't reach the steering wheel."

"Listen, I had a visit from your Dr. de Savin."

She sagged with relief. "Did he say where he was staying?"

"Yes. He left the name and phone number of his hotel."

"Can you get a message to him? I'm going to his place at the vineyard. The house has been closed up for almost a year. The phone's not connected. I don't want to be alone there. He needs to come up as soon as he can."

"I'll try to find him."

"And can you try to find my friend Mary Beth? Page her at the airport, find her once she gets there, somehow? Tell her why I left."

"I'll do my best. Are you sure you're all right? It'll take five or six hours, or longer, for Dr. de Savin to get there, even if I reach him at his hotel right now. I have a feeling that he's not the type who'll just be sitting around in the room waiting for a call. He's probably out interrogating every person in L.A. who might know where you are."

"I'm fine. Just tired. I know I shouldn't be alone like this, but everything's okay. Really. I'll rest and wait for him to get here." Nothing mattered now except doing what was best for the babies, even if it meant exposing herself to Sebastien's anger.

"You get yourself to his house and take it easy," Rodriguez urged. "Soon as he gets there everything'll be better."

Amy thanked him and slipped the phone back on its hook. She shut her eyes. *No, the worst hasn't even begun yet.*

❦

She shuddered with relief when she finally guided the rental car down the long, forest-shrouded driveway to Sebastien's cottage and vineyard. She had a house key he'd given her almost a year ago, during the heady, promising days right after they'd met again. As she hobbled through the cottage's cool stone rooms, holding her back with one hand and her stomach with the other, Amy was surprised at how comforted she felt.

There *had* been that time, that wonderful time before he had to return to France, and before she became pregnant. It had really existed. So much had happened in a year. Her head swam with the memories and the fear that nothing would ever be as wonderful between them again.

She went to his bedroom and lay down on the bare mattress, wrapping herself in musty blankets, immediately grateful for rest above all else. The late-afternoon sun didn't warm the room. Later she would light the gas heater in the corner. The electricity was turned off, along with the phone and water, but on the way up she'd stopped at a little grocery and camping supply store, where she'd purchased a lantern, bottled water, and food that wasn't perishable. She'd fix herself something wonderful to eat.

Just as soon as I feel better, she thought now, sinking into a bare, stale-smelling pillow with a soft moan of appreciation. Her thoughts faded before a tidal wave of exhaustion. *Comfort.* She was as close to Sebastien as she could get, wrapped in the dreams they had shared here.

❦

The house was dark inside, now. She found her way to the lantern, lit it then carried it gingerly down the hall to the kitchen. She'd lost her appetite, but she forced herself to take bread from a grocery bag and eat a slice. She checked her watch. It would still be a few hours before Sebastien could possibly get here.

She dragged herself back to the bedroom, set the lamp on the nightstand, and burrowed under the covers again. Dozing, she had a dream about elves dancing on her stomach. It hurt. She made herself wake up to dispell it. Then, going breathless with disbelief, she knew why she'd been dreaming about a pain in her stomach. She felt the blood drain from her face as the slow, deep contraction built inside her until it had the severity of a bad menstrual cramp.

The silent shout of protest ricocheted inside her head. *Not now. Not yet. Not here.*

The contraction faded. Sweating, she checked her watch and waited. It could mean nothing, just a reaction to all the stress. Of course. She was going to have a perfect labor and delivery. Not a month early. Not up here in the middle of nowhere, without a hospital. Without a doctor. without Sebastien. Sebastien. Was every circumstance conspiring to make his fears come true?

Cursed. The babies are cursed. He was right.

Stop thinking that way!

The next contraction, another relatively mild one, came twenty minutes later. Staring at her watch in the flickering lantern light, she told herself that twenty minutes was great. If she was going into labor, it would probably take a long time.

She listened to cool winter wind rattle the oaks outside the cottage. The bedroom was a dark cavern with a small, desperately bright center where she huddled, counting the minutes, refusing to let her imagination find ghosts in the shadows.

❧

She yelled as she woke up from the brief, pain-soaked nap. Dawn light made a sieve of the loose-weave curtains on the room's windows. Another contraction hit her. Then she felt a rush of fluid between her legs. She threw the covers back. During the night she'd rummaged through Sebastien's dresser and found a flannel workshirt of his, which was now all that she wore. She pulled the front of it up and felt between her legs. When she couldn't deny that her water had broken she cried out. *Where was Sebastien?*

All right, stay calm. Put on some clothes and go get in the car.

Yesterday she'd bought a blue-wool maternity jumper and a blouse. She pulled the jumper over Sebastien's work shirt and shoved her feet into tennis shoes. With her overcoat around her shoulders, her purse clutched under one arm, and a washcloth stuffed inside her panties, she went out into the crisp morning.

When the next contraction came she said, "Yow, oh yow," because that made it sound a lot funnier than it was. Then she staggered to the wooden fence that flanked both sides of the drive and hung onto it until her knees buckled. She sat down on the damp, cold grass beside the driveway and tried to breathe the way she'd been taught in birthing classes.

After the pain passed she pulled herself to her feet and walked back to the cottage. The contractions were now only five minutes apart.

She gathered towels and put them beside the bed, then found a bottle of rubbing alcohol and poured it into a glass. She lit the heater and opened the curtains to increase the light.

She put a kitchen knife into the glass and set it on the nightstand, so that she'd have something with which to cut the umbilical cords. She took the laces out of her tennis shoes and washed them, then laid them on a towel to dry. They were the only things she could think of that could be used to tie off the cords.

Finally she set a glass of orange juice and a hunk of cheese on the nightstand so that she'd have food to keep up her strength. Then she stripped off everything but Sebastien's shirt and got into bed.

It was time to face the truth. She was going to have the babies before Sebastien got here. They might be too small and too weak. They could easily die from complications, and she might die as well. She was terrified that she was going to fulfill the de Savin curse.

"Sebastien, I need you," she whispered. "I'll fight as hard as I can. I won't give up." She bit into a folded towel as the next contraction came.

🥢

The rental car hurtled under the oaks of the cottage's front yard and slid to a stop. The yard was bright with morning sun. Sebastien cut the motor and leapt out. Climbing the stone steps to the small veranda, he reached for the cottage door while pulling a key from the pocket of wrinkled, blue-gray trousers. When Rodriguez called he'd just stepped from the shower at two A.M. after spending half the night in L.A.'s comedy clubs, tracking down various friends of Amy's, none of whom had known where she'd gone.

You didn't get my message. I had a hunch, the detective had muttered.

Sebastien had dressed and left in five minutes. Now as he glanced down he noted that he'd misaligned the buttons of the short ivory cardigan he'd thrown on over his bare chest. He wore his dress loafers with no socks.

She'll get a grand laugh from the way I look. He needed to hear her laugh, even though he was angry and frightened. Why had she run away without him? He knew, deep within his conscience, that it was because he'd lost her trust. Now he was intent on regaining it. Frowning, he stepped into the cottage and shoved the door shut. The slamming of it echoed through the cool stone rooms.

His hands shook. "*Dear* Miracle," he called sternly, looking down the central hallway. "You had better come here right now and see what a state you've put me in." From the open doorway to the master bedroom came a muffled cry. The pain in it galvanized him. He ran to the room and halted, staring in disbelief at the scene on his bed.

She stared back with glazed eyes, her hands twisting the pillow casing beneath her head, her face haggard, her hair drenched in sweat. Her updrawn legs made a tent of the sheet, but her swollen belly heaved against the fabric. A low, keening sound came from her throat.

Sebastien was beside her in two long strides, jerking the

sheet back, looking in despair at the straining body covered only in an old shirt he recognized as his. It was bunched under her breasts. He heard himself groan with frustration and fear. Quickly he knelt beside her and, cupping her face in his hand, kissed her. She cried out and raised her mouth to his with desperate welcome.

He frantically smoothed damp hair from her forehead. Her head moved from side to side. Her eyes scanned him with misery. "I wanted to wait until the babies were born, so that you'd see that they were fine, just fine, and then you could love them. But . . . everything's gone wrong! I went into labor last night, and I'm only eight months, and I thought I could hold out until you got here, and . . ." Her voice trailed off as she searched his eyes. "And I don't want you to hate me if I die."

"Listen to me! Listen! All I could think about was finding you! You're going to get through this and then we'll forget it ever happened!"

Sinews strained in her neck. Fighting pain, she said between clenched teeth, "You don't want . . . the babies."

He stroked her flushed skin and struggled to keep his voice calm. "I'm going to carry you out to the car—"

"It's too late." She gasped for breath.

"Sssh. Here. I'm going to lift you. We'll find a hospital—"

"It's too late!" Even as she spoke her head tilted back. She bit her lip and moaned in a deep, primal expression of pain. "I'm having contractions . . . every minute . . . have to push. Ah. Push."

Sebastien pulled her upright and sat down behind her, bracing her against his chest. She grasped his hands hard. He wrapped his arms around her. "Breathe, love. Breathe through the pain."

She panted and nodded. "Through it . . . under it . . . inside it . . . it's *everywhere.*"

Sebastien cursed helplessly. His life had been devoted to winning battles such as this. Now twenty years of medical training mocked him. Once again he could only watch in agony as someone he loved suffered. The old fury grew inside him, laughing at him for thinking that he could correct the mistakes that had begun before his own birth. And had now led to this.

When the contraction passed she sobbed and pushed weakly at his arms. "You don't want the babies. There's nothing you can do to help if you still don't love 'em."

"I love *you*. Do you think I want you to suffer?" He leapt to his feet. "Now we get to work," he told Amy. "Together."

He ran to the kitchen and scrubbed his hands. Slinging water from then, he returned to the bedroom and knelt between her feet on the bed. "I'm going to examine you."

She clung to the sheet beneath her, twisting it into wads. "Something's wrong. The first baby should have been born by now. I'm too tired to go on much longer."

"Easy, love, easy. I'm putting my hand inside you. All right? Does that hurt?"

"Everything hurts."

He slipped his hand upwards and probed with careful fingertips. "Nothing wrong here, or here. Very good dilation, love. You're doing very well."

"Save the babies. Please, save them. Even if you don't love 'em. Please. For me."

He bent his head to one of her knees and made a hoarse sound of grief. "Do you think I won't try to save all three of you?"

Her answer was unintelligible as new pain cut through it. She screamed. Sebastien explored inside her frantically, praying that his fingers would touch the smooth, curving surface of a baby's head. Shivers went through him when they found tiny feet instead.

"What's wrong?" she begged, panting. "I can tell by the look . . . on your face . . . something terrible—"

"The first baby is turned the wrong way."

She cried out. "I'm so sorry, Doc! Please . . . don't hate . . . our babies for this."

"Hate them? Hate them? Goddammit, they're innocent victims. The same as you. I only wish that I had prevented this."

"Don't say that! You make it sound like you did something wrong! You didn't! And the only way you can hurt me, or the babies, is by not loving us now! What . . . what are you doing?"

He rotated his hand palm up and latched his fingers around the baby's ankles. "Concentrate on breathing. I'm going to pull very slowly."

"Can the baby . . . come out this way?"

"Yes."

She made guttural sounds of pain. "Y-yes, I g-guess it can. I feel it!"

"You're doing beautifully. Just another few seconds." He was dizzy with fear.

"Will it be alive?"

"I don't . . . of course. Of *course*. I wouldn't let it be any other way."

"Arrogance. I like that. Good."

Shaking his head, he watched delicate feet and legs emerge, covered with the waxy coating typical of newborns. He pulled steadily and felt the baby begin to slip free. He thought his heart would burst with agony when Amy screamed again.

She sank back on the pillows, groaning. "It's here. It's here."

"Almost." Suddenly the hips and torso appeared. Sebastien cupped the body in his hand. "A boy," he said numbly.

"A *son*," she whispered.

Sebastien worked the baby's arms free, thinking frantically, *The color is good. The cord isn't choking him. Please, please, let him be alive.* "Push, love," he urged. "Push his head free."

She pushed and he pulled, and a second later their son lay in his hands.

"Is he all right?" Amy asked, trying to sit up. "He's so little!"

Sebastien felt dazed. He laid the tiny form on Amy's thigh and desperately began checking him. "His pulse is strong. His reflexes are good."

"He moved! He tried to lift his head!"

Crying, she stretched a hand around her bulging abdomen, trying to reach the baby. "Is he all right? Please tell me that he's all right!"

Sebastien cut the cord and quickly tied the stump with a shoe lace. Then he placed the baby on her stomach so that she could stroke his head. Sebastien probed and cleaned and tested. "I can't tell, I can't tell," he said raggedly. "So much could be wrong! I'm sure there must be something!"

"Don't say that! There isn't any curse here! Just love us, Doc, love us! I want these babies to feel wanted. Not like when you and I were born. *Wanted.* Don't repeat the only mistake that matters."

"I'm trying to make everything right! I swear to you, I'm trying."

"The only mistake . . . that matters! Don't do it to us!"

He kissed their son's head with quick, desperate apology. "I love you. I love your sister. I love your mother. I'll never let any of you suffer." He looked at Amy. "Believe me. Give me a chance to prove it."

She searched his face for a moment, and a look of wonder lit her eyes. Their son made a strong mewling sound. His arms and legs moved, testing the freedom of his new world. Amy's weak hands fluttered over him, stroking the waxy, wrinkled skin. "I guess he was just waitin' to hear you say that," she whispered. "Now he's glad to be alive."

Now she and Sebastien shared the wonder. Her pain-glazed eyes had an empyreal glow. "He really is all right, Doc. And his sister will be, too. We're safe because you came to help us. You saved us. *You saved our lives.* That's powerful magic. Trust me. You and me together, Doc. We've got a future, and so do our babies. Because of you."

She met his outstretched hand with her own.

Their daughter was born a few minutes later, ruddy and active and bearing a cap of auburn hair very much like Amy's. Sebastien put her alongside her brother on Amy's stomach. He bowed his head between them. Amy stroked the side of his face tenderly as he cried. He was finally complete, and the burden was gone. She understood. There were no mistakes here, none at all.

EPILOGUE

*A*my stood quietly for a moment, lifting her face to the spring breeze, gathering her thoughts as she studied the unfurling white blossoms on a dogwood. There was so much to say, and so much that she couldn't even put into words. *I wish you had been at the wedding. I wish you could see your grandchildren. I wish I knew what you thought of me now. And what you'll think of me in the future.*

She decided to talk about the easy things. "I got a part in a television show. It films close to home, my home out in California, you know. So I won't have to be away from the babies or Doc. That's the way I wanted it. The part—it's the lead. I'm the star. How about that? Guess I surprised you. Surprised myself."

She looked down at the orange day lily in her hands, idly turning it while she swallowed bitterness. The lily had come from the old home place. It was both ordinary and beautiful. "I guess I had to work twice as hard as anybody else to get ahead. But maybe I've gone twice as far."

Kneeling, she put the lily beside the grave's granite headstone. "I'll never forgive you, but I don't need to hate you anymore. I can survive *anything* because I know I survived *you.*"

She allowed herself to cry for him, for the anger and pain that had twisted him into such an unhappy human being. Then she stood and shook the fresh earth of the grave from the hem of her dress. "I've got a long way to go, Pop. I won't be coming back here. I don't owe you anything."

Her head bent in thought, she turned from the grave and descended the grassy hill toward a paved drive below. The sound of a car door made her look up. Sebastien stepped from the backseat of their limousine and stood beside the open door, waiting for her, his expression grim as he glanced around the cemetery.

There are no ghosts here, she told him silently. *And no curses.* He tilted his head and arched a brow at her as if questioning such confidence. She brought her chin up and swung her arms, sashaying down the hill in gentle defiance. *Trust me. See? Ghosts know better than to mess with the two of us as long as we're together.*

She felt lighter. There would always be bad memories, but those would never be as powerful as the good ones she and he were creating every day. He had become a loving father to his children, the kind of father that neither he nor she had ever had. The love he gave to her and received full in return had made the kind of marriage that would nurture itself more with each year. She had the confidence to walk toward him now with absolute freedom from the memories she had finally buried, buried without reconciliation but also without regret.

She smiled at him as she crossed the remaining few yards, the moment merging the years behind with the years ahead. The wind pushed a cloud in front of the sun. A shadow moved over him, clung to him, and made her catch her breath. There would always be shadows. But then he held out his hands to her, and the darkness slipped away.